The Beekeeper's Daughter

Also by Santa Montefiore

Secrets of the Lighthouse

The Summer House

The House by the Sea

The Affair

The Italian Matchmaker

The French Gardener

Sea of Lost Love

The Gypsy Madonna

Last Voyage of the Valentina

The Swallow and the Hummingbird

The Forget-Me-Not Sonata

The Butterfly Box

Meet Me Under the Ombu Tree

Santa Montefiore

The Beekeeper's Daughter

SIMON & SCHUSTER

London · New York · Sydney · Toronto · New Delhi

A CBS COMPANY

First published in Great Britain by Simon & Schuster UK Ltd, 2014
A CBS COMPANY

3 5 7 9 10 8 6 4

Simon & Schuster UK Ltd
1st Floor
222 Gray's Inn Road
London WC1X 8HB

www.simonandschuster.co.uk

Simon & Schuster Australia, Sydney
Simon & Schuster India, New Delhi

A CIP catalogue record for this book is available from the British Library

HB ISBN: 978-1-47110-099-4
TPB ISBN: 978-1-47110-100-7
EBOOK ISBN: 978-1-47110-102-1

Typeset by Hewer Text UK Ltd, Edinburgh
Printed and bound in Great Britain by CPI Group (UK) Ltd, Croydon CR0 4YY

Dedicated to:

My darling Uncle Jeremy
One of life's great characters,
with love and gratitude

The Bee-Boy's Song

Bees! Bees! Hark to your bees!
'Hide from your neighbours as much as you please,
But all that has happened, to us you must tell,
Or else we will give you no honey to sell!'

A maiden in her glory,
Upon her wedding-day,
Must tell her Bees the story,
Or else they'll fly away.
Fly away – die away –
Dwindle down and leave you!
But if you don't deceive your Bees,
Your Bees will not deceive you.

Marriage, birth or buryin',
News across the seas,
All you're sad or merry in,
You must tell the Bees.
Tell 'em coming in an' out,
Where the Fanners fan,
'Cause the Bees are just about
As curious as a man!

Don't you wait where the trees are,
When the lightnings play,
Nor don't you hate where Bees are,
Or else they'll pine away.
Pine away – dwine away –
Anything to leave you!
But if you never grieve your Bees,
Your Bees'll never grieve you.

Rudyard Kipling

PART ONE

Chapter 1

Tekanasset Island, Massachusetts, 1973

Of all the weathered grey-shingled buildings on Tekanasset Island, Crab Cove golf club is one of the prettiest. Built in the late nineteenth century by a couple of friends from Boston who shared the sentiment that an island without a golf course is an island deficient in the only thing that truly matters, it dominates the western coastline with an uninterrupted view of the ocean. To the right, a candy-cane red-and-white lighthouse stands on a grassy hill, used more for birdwatchers nowadays than sailors lost at sea; and to the left, yellow beaches and grassy sand dunes undulate like waves, carrying on their crests thick clusters of wild rose. A softer variety of climbing rose adorns the walls of the clubhouse, and dusty pink hydrangeas are planted in a border that runs all the way around the periphery, blossoming into a profusion of fat, flowery balls. The effect is so charming that it is impossible not to be touched by it. And rising above it all, on the grey slate roof, the American flag flutters in the salty wind that sweeps in off the sea.

Reachable only by small plane or boat, the island of Tekanasset is cut off from the rest of the country, so that while the Industrial Revolution changed the face of America, it missed Tekanasset altogether, leaving the quaint, Quaker-inspired buildings and cobbled streets as they had always been, and allowing the island to settle into a sleepy, wistful rhythm where old-fashioned values blended harmoniously with the traditional architecture.

There are no unsightly road signs or traffic lights on Tekanasset, and the shops that thrive in the town are charming boutiques selling linen, gifts, pretty toiletries and locally crafted lightship baskets and scrimshaw. It is a nostalgic, romantic place, but not unsophisticated. Famous writers, actors and musicians from all over America escape the frenetic, polluted cities to breathe the fresh sea air and find inspiration in the beauty of the landscape, while wealthy businessmen leave the financial centres of the world to summer there with their families.

Crab Cove golf club is still the heart of the island, as it was always intended to be, but now it is no longer the hub of gossip that it was in the Sixties and Seventies, when society struggled to keep up with the changing times, and the old ways clashed with the new like waves against rock. Nowadays the young people who had fought so hard for change are old and less judgemental than their parents were, and conversation around the tables at teatime is more benign. But on this particular evening in July 1973, an incident which would not even merit comment today had whipped the ladies of Crab Cove golf club into a fever of excitement. They had barely glanced at their bridge cards before the subject which had been teetering on the end of their tongues toppled off into an outburst of indignation.

'Well, my dear, I think it's immoral and I'm ashamed on her behalf,' said Evelyn Durlacher in her low Boston drawl, pursing her scarlet lips in disapproval. Evelyn was the weathervane of polite society. Everything in her environs reflected her conservative values and high moral standards. From her immaculate cashmere twinsets and auburn coiffure to her beautifully decorated home and well-mannered children, nothing escaped her attention. And with the same scrupulous application, and a habitual lack of generosity, she passed judgement on those around her. 'In our day, if you wanted to be alone with a man you had to lose your chaperone. Now the young are out of control and no one seems to be keeping an eye.' She tapped her red talons on the table and glanced at her cards distractedly. 'Terrible hand. Sorry, Belle, I fear I'm going to let you down.'

Belle Bartlett studied her cards, which were no better. She took a long drag on her cigarette and shook her blonde curls dolefully. 'The youth of today,' she lamented. 'I wouldn't want to be young now. It was better back in the Forties and Fifties when everyone knew where they stood. Now the lines are all blurred and we have no choice but to adapt. I think they are simply lost and we mustn't judge them too harshly.'

'Belle, you always try to see the good in everybody. Surely even *you* must concede that Trixie Valentine has let herself down,' Evelyn insisted. 'The fact is, she has not behaved like a lady. Ladies don't go chasing boys around the country. They allow themselves to be chased. Really, it's very distasteful.'

'It's not only distasteful, Evelyn, it's imprudent,' Sally Pearson agreed, giving her lustrous waves of long brown hair a self-conscious toss. 'By throwing themselves at men they tarnish their reputations, which can never be restored.' She waved her cigarette between two manicured fingers and smiled smugly, remembering the exemplary young woman *she* had been. 'A man needs the chase and the woman needs to be a prize worth fighting for. Girls are far too easily won these days. In our day we saved ourselves for our wedding night.' She giggled and gave a little snort. 'And if we didn't, we sure as hell didn't let anyone know about it.'

'Poor Grace, to have a daughter shame her in this way is very unfortunate,' Belle added sympathetically. 'Horrible to think we're all picking at the pieces like vultures.'

'Well, what do you expect, girls?' interjected Blythe Westrup, patting her ebony up-do. 'She's British. They won the war but they lost their morals in the process. Goodness, the stories that came out of that time are shocking. Girls lost their heads . . .'

'And everything else,' Evelyn added dryly, arching an eyebrow.

'Oh, Evelyn!' Sally gasped and placed her cigarette holder between her lips to disguise her smile. She didn't want her friends to see her taking pleasure in the scandal.

'But do we really know she ran off with him?' Belle asked. 'I mean, it might just be malicious gossip. Trixie's a character but she's not bad. Everyone's much too quick to criticize her. If she wasn't so beautiful no one would even notice her.'

Evelyn glared at her fiercely, the rivalry in her eyes suddenly exposed. 'My dear, I heard it all from Lucy this morning,' she said firmly. 'Believe me, my daughter knows what she's talking about. She saw them all coming off a private boat at dawn, looking the worse for wear and very shifty. The boy is English, too, and he's . . .' She paused and drew her lips into a line so thin they almost disappeared. 'He's in a rock 'n' roll band.' She articulated the words with disdain as if they gave off a stench.

Belle laughed. 'Evelyn, rock 'n' roll is over. I believe he's more Bob Dylan than Elvis Presley.'

'Oh, so you know, do you?' Evelyn asked, put out. 'Why didn't you say?'

'The whole town is talking about them, Evelyn. They're handsome young British boys, and polite, too, I believe.' She smiled at the sour look on Evelyn's face. 'They're spending the summer here at Joe Hornby's place.'

'Old Joe Hornby? Really, you know how eccentric *he* is,' said Sally. 'He claims to be a great friend of Mick Jagger's, but have you ever seen *him* on the island?'

'Or anyone of any importance at all? He claims to know everybody. He's an old boaster, that's all,' said Blythe.

'Those boys are writing an album, apparently, and Joe's helping them,' Belle continued. 'He has a recording studio in his basement.'

'Joe hasn't produced anything in fifty years!' said Sally. 'He was a very mediocre musician in his day. Now he's simply past it. Anyway, who's bankrolling the project? Joe hasn't got the money, for sure.'

Belle shrugged. 'I don't know. But the word is, he's taking them on tour around the country in the fall.' She raised her eyebrows. 'That'll cost a small fortune, don't you think?'

Evelyn was determined to bring the subject back to the scandal. She glanced around the room cautiously and lowered her voice. 'Well, according to Lucy, Trixie Valentine and her friend Suzie Redford disappeared in a boat with the band on Friday evening and didn't come back until early this morning. Suzie told Lucy not to breathe a word to anybody. They clearly went behind their parents' backs. I can't say what they all got up to, but I don't think we have to stretch our imaginations too far to get close to the truth. You know how those sort of people live. It's disgusting!'

'Maybe Grace thought Trixie was at Suzie's!' Belle suggested. 'There must be an explanation.'

Sally cut in. 'I dare say, but that Suzie Redford can do whatever she likes. There are no boundaries in *that* family.'

'Well, I'm surprised,' said Belle quietly. 'Though I know Grace has a difficult time with Trixie. But I really don't believe Trixie would have disappeared for three days without telling her mother. Besides, Freddie would never have allowed it.'

'Freddie's been away on business,' said Sally gleefully. 'While the cat's away . . .'

'It's all in the nurturing,' said Blythe. '*Cherchez la mère*,' she added darkly.

Belle stubbed out her cigarette. 'Isn't the saying *cherchez la femme*?'

'It amounts to the same thing, Belle,' Blythe retorted. 'You need look no further than the mother. Grace might be a paragon of virtue and I am the first to say she is the sweetest person alive. But she's much too lenient. Trixie needs a firm hand and Grace is weak.'

'Grace is indulgent because it took her years of heartache and miscarriage to conceive,' Belle reminded them. 'Trixie is the longed-for only child. It's no wonder she's a bit spoiled.'

'Grace buries her head in her gardens and tries not to think about it, I imagine,' said Sally. 'With a daughter like Trixie, wouldn't you?'

'Oh, she's a wonderful gardener,' Belle added emphatically. 'The gardens of Tekanasset were all very ordinary before she arrived from England and transformed them with her wonderful taste and expertise.'

Evelyn scowled irritably. 'No one is questioning her talent, Belle. It's her mothering which is open to debate. Now, come on, who dealt?'

'I did,' said Blythe. 'And I'm bidding one no trump.'

At that moment the four women were struck dumb by the appearance of Grace herself, followed by a large soufflé of a woman known to everyone as Big. Evelyn closed her mouth sharply. Big was the most respected and formidable woman on the island. Not only did she own the largest and oldest home, which had once belonged to the first settler back in 1668, but she was the only daughter of the wealthy oil baron Randall Wilson Jr., who died at the age of ninety-five leaving his entire fortune to her. It was said that she had never married because she could find no man qualified to match her in either wealth or spirit. Now that she was in her seventies, marriage was never mentioned or alluded to and Big showed no sign of regret. She treated her closest friends like family and took great pleasure, as her father had done before her, in sharing her wealth through the highly esteemed Randall Wilson Charitable Trust, or simply by writing cheques when she felt so inclined.

Grace Valentine looked as out of place in the clubhouse as a shire horse in a field of thoroughbreds. Her long mouse-brown hair was streaked with grey and pinned roughly onto the back of her head with a pencil, and her taupe cotton trousers and loose-fitting shirt were in sharp contrast to the starched perfection of the four bridge players. The only thing she seemed to have in common with them was the sparkle of diamonds in the form of a surprisingly exquisite bumblebee brooch pinned to her chest. Her nails were bitten down and the skin on her hands was rough from years of gardening. She wore no make-up and her fine English skin had suffered in the Tekanasset sun and sea winds. And yet her hazel eyes were full of softness and compassion and her face retained traces of her former beauty. When Grace Valentine smiled, few could resist the sweetness of it.

'Hello, Grace,' said Belle as the two women passed their table. 'Hello, Big.'

Grace smiled. 'Good game?' she asked.

'It's not looking good for me,' Belle replied. 'But I'm not very good at bridge.'

'Oh, really, Belle Bartlett, you're just fine,' chided Evelyn, tossing Grace a smile and scrutinizing her for signs of shame. 'She's just being modest.'

'Where would you like to sit, Grace?' Big asked, striding past the four women without so much as a nod. They shrank into their chairs guiltily. Big seemed to have an almost psychic sense when it came to unpleasantness, and she narrowed her eyes knowingly and struck the shiny wooden floorboards with her walking stick without any concern for the noise it made.

'Let's sit outside, if it's not too windy for you, Big,' Grace replied.

Big chuckled. 'Not at all. If there was a hurricane I'd be the last person standing.'

They walked through the double doors onto a wide veranda which overlooked the ocean. Small boats cut through the waves like swans and a pair of black dogs frolicked about the dunes while their master strolled slowly up the beach. The evening sun was low in the sky, turning the sand a pinkish hue, and an oystercatcher pecked at the remains of a fish with his bright-orange beak. Grace chose a table nearest the edge of the veranda, against the balustrade, and pulled out a wicker chair for Big. The old woman handed Grace her stick, then fell onto the cushion with a loud whoosh. A few wisps of grey hair fell away from her bun and flapped against the back of her neck like feathers. 'There, the hen is on her nest,' said Big with a satisfied sigh. She clicked her fingers and before Grace had even sat down she had ordered them both a cocktail. 'You need fortification, Grace,' she told her firmly. 'Never mind those hyenas. They're all so jealous of you, as well they might be: they have not an ounce of talent between them.'

'They're all right,' Grace replied. 'Believe me, I've encountered far worse.'

'I'm sure you have. British women make those four look positively tame.'

Grace laughed. 'Oh, I don't care what people say behind my back, as long as they're friendly to my face. The trouble with British women is they're much too outspoken, and I do hate confrontation.'

'I prefer the British way, if that's the case. If people have something to say, they should say it to your face and not behind your back. They should have the courage of their convictions or not speak out at all. Evelyn Durlacher is a terrible old wooden spoon and I'm quite prepared to tell her so. She should be ashamed of some of the trouble she's caused on this island with her stirring. It's as if she goes around looking for things to gossip about. The smugness of the woman is intolerable. She has placed herself so high on her pedestal, the fall will be devastating.'

The waiter placed their cocktails on the table with a china bowl of nuts. Big thrust her fat, bejewelled fingers into the bowl and grabbed a fistful of pistachios. Her face was deceptively gentle, with a wide forehead, full, smiling lips and spongy chins that gave her the look of a gentle grandmother, but her eyes were the colour of steel and could harden in a moment, turning the unlucky recipient of her displeasure into a pillar of salt. When she looked at Grace, however, she did so with surprising tenderness. 'So, what's Trixie up to, then? I imagine Evelyn has exaggerated the story for her own ends – anything to make her Lucy look good.' Big inhaled through her nostrils and the steel in her eyes briefly glinted. 'If she knew half of what her Lucy gets up to, she'd keep her mouth shut.'

Grace sighed. 'I'm afraid Evelyn's probably right. Trixie has fallen for a young man who plays in a band. I don't mind that, he's perfectly nice, I'm sure, but . . .'

'You haven't met him?'

'No.'

'Go on.'

'She told me she was going to stay the weekend in Cape Cod with her friend Suzie . . .'

Big raised her eyebrows cynically. 'Suzie Redford! That girl's trouble, and wherever there's trouble, *she's* in the middle of it.'

'I would honestly say they're as bad as each other.' Grace smiled indulgently. 'But they're having fun, Big, and Trixie's in love for the first time.'

Big looked at Grace's gentle face, her soft hazel eyes and soft windblown hair, and shook her head at the sheer *softness* of the woman. 'What am I going to do with you, Grace? You're much too kind-hearted. So, tell me, where did they *really* go?'

'With the band.'

'Where, with the band?'

'To a private concert they were giving in Cape Cod for a friend of Joe Hornby, who's in the industry.'

Big sipped her cocktail thoughtfully. 'But she was found out.'

'Yes, Lucy saw them all returning on a boat this morning and told her mother. Now, I imagine the whole island is talking about it. Trixie came clean before she went off to work. You know she's got a summer job at Captain Jack's. Anyway, I didn't have time to talk to her. In spite of her rebelliousness, Big, she's a good girl at heart. She confessed, at least.'

'Only because she was spotted by Lucy. I'm sure she wouldn't have told you if she thought she had got away with it. I'm afraid she's a disgrace, my dear, and you should ground her for the rest of the holidays. In my day I would have been beaten for less.'

'But it's not your day, Big, and it's not my day, either. Times are changing. Young people are freer than we ever were and perhaps it's a good thing. We can disapprove of the music they listen to and the inappropriate clothes they wear, but they're young and full of passion. They demonstrate against inequality and war – goodness, you only have to look at my poor Freddie with his one eye and that terrible scar down his face to know that there are no winners in war. They're brave and outspoken and I rather admire them for that.' She pressed her rough fingers against the bee brooch on her shirt. 'They're idealistic and foolish, perhaps, but they realize that love is the only thing that really matters.' She turned her hazel eyes to the sea and smiled pensively. 'I think I'd like to be young now with my whole life ahead of me.'

Big sipped her cocktail. 'Heavens, Grace, you baffle me sometimes. When everyone else is pulling in the reins, you're letting them out. Is that a British trait, I wonder? Or are you just contrary? Tell me, does Freddie know about Trixie's little adventure?'

The mention of her husband cast a shadow over Grace's face. 'I haven't told him yet,' she replied quietly.

'But you will?'

'I don't want to. He'll be furious. But I'll have to. Otherwise he'll hear it from someone else. Bill Durlacher teeing off at the fifth hole, most likely!' She laughed out of anxiety rather than merriment.

Big's large bosom expanded over the table at the thought of Bill Durlacher gossiping on the golf course. 'Bill's as bad as his wife,' she retorted. 'But you're right to tell Freddie. He won't want to be the last person on the island to know.'

'He'll be horrified, Big. He'll give her a lecture on discipline and probably put her under house arrest for the remainder of the summer. Then she'll spend all her time finding ways to see this boy behind our backs.' She chuckled. 'I know Trixie. She's got more of *me* in her than she knows.'

Big looked surprised. 'I can't imagine *you* breaking any rules, Grace.'

'Oh, I wasn't always so well-behaved.' She smiled wistfully at the memory of the girl she used to be. 'Once I was even quite rebellious. But that was a long time ago.' She turned her gaze to the sea again.

'What whipped you into shape?' Big asked.

'My conscience,' Grace replied with a frown.

'Then you would have done the right thing, for certain.'

'Yes, I suppose so.' Grace sighed heavily and there was a hint of defeat in it as well as regret.

'Do you want the advice of an old matron who's seen it all?' Big asked.

Grace drew her mind back to the present. 'Yes, please.'

Big wriggled in her chair like the nesting hen of her own description. 'You go home now and have stern words with

Trixie. Tell her she's not to deceive you like that again. It's important that you know where she is and who she's with, for her safety as well as your peace of mind. You also tell her that she's not to leave the island again for the rest of the summer and it's non-negotiable. You have to make it very clear, Grace. Can you do that?'

'Yes, I can,' Grace replied half-heartedly.

'It's a matter of respect, Grace,' Big stated firmly. 'Really, my dear, you need to toughen up if you wish to assert any control over your child, before it's too late.' She took a moment to sip her cocktail, then resumed. 'When her father arrives, you tell him what happened but inform him that you've reprimanded her and that the business is done and dusted. Period. You think he'll drop it?'

'I don't know. He'll be very cross. You know how he likes everything to be in order.' She shrugged. 'I could play it down . . .'

'You mustn't lie to him, Grace. That's important. You two have to stick together. You're a soft-hearted woman and I know you want to support Trixie, but you chose your husband first and it's your duty as a wife to stand by his side on all matters.'

Grace looked beaten. 'Duty,' she muttered and Big detected a bitter edge to her voice. 'I do hate that word.'

'Duty is what makes us civilized, Grace. Doing the right thing and not always thinking of ourselves is vital if we don't want society to fall apart at the seams. The young have no sense of duty, and by the sound of things they don't have much respect, either. I fear the future is a place with no morals and a distorted sense of what's important. But I'm not here to preach to you. I'm here to support you.'

'Thank you, Big. Your support means a lot to me.'

'We've been friends for almost thirty years, Grace. That's a long time. Ever since you came to Tekanasset and turned my backyard into a beautiful paradise. Perhaps we bonded because you never knew your mother and I never had any children.' She smiled and took another handful of nuts. 'And everyone sucks up to me but you,' she said with a chuckle. 'You're a gentle creature but an honest one. I don't believe you'd ever agree with me just because I'm as rich as Croesus, as old as the Ark and as big as a whale.'

'Oh, really, Big!' Grace laughed incredulously. 'You might be as rich as Croesus but you're not as old as the Ark and you're certainly *not* a whale!'

'Bless you for lying. My dear, when it's a matter of age and size I give you my full permission to lie through your teeth.'

When Grace returned to her home on Sunset Slip the sun had turned the sea to gold. She wandered onto the veranda with her two retrievers and gazed out across the wild grasses to the beach and glittering water beyond. She soaked up the tranquil scene thirstily. The sound that soothed her more than anything else, however, was the low murmur of bees. It filled her heart with melancholy, and yet that wasn't an unpleasant feeling. In a strange way it gave her pleasure to remember the past, as if through the pain she remained in touch with the woman she had once been and left behind when she had set out for America all those years ago.

She went round to the three hives she kept along the side of the house, sheltered from the winds and sun by hemlock planted for the purpose, and lifted one of the lids for a routine check. She didn't mind getting stung occasionally. She wasn't afraid, either, but it caused her distress to think that, on stinging, the bee was sacrificing her own life to protect the hive.

Arthur Hamblin had taught his daughter everything he knew about bees, from their daily care to the tinctures of propolis he made to cure sore throats and other complaints. Beekeeping had been their shared love and tending the hives and extracting the honey had brought them close, compounded by the fact that they only had each other in the world. Grace remembered her father fondly every time she saw a bee. His kind face would surface in her mind with the gentle humming of the creatures he had so loved, and sometimes she could even hear his voice as if he were whispering into her ear: 'Don't forget to check that the bees are capping off honey in the lower supers.' Or: 'Can you see the bees guarding the entrance? There must be a threat. Wasps or robber bees perhaps. I wonder which it is.' Arthur Hamblin could talk about bees for hours and barely draw breath. Often he would talk *to* them, reciting his favourite poem, which Grace had heard so often she knew it by heart: *Marriage, birth or buryin', News across the seas, All you're sad or merry in, You must tell the bees.*

Now as Grace looked inside the hive, the bees were settling in for the night. The temperature had dropped and they were sleepy. She smiled fondly and allowed her memories to ebb and flow like a vast sea of images and emotions. Time with her bees was time to be herself again, and time to remember.

As she replaced the lid she sensed the familiar presence of someone standing close. She knew not to turn around, because the many times she had glanced behind her had revealed nothing but the wind and her own bewilderment. She knew to sense it and not to analyse it; after all, hers was an old house and Tekanasset was an island well known for ghosts. Even Big had stories to tell. The presence didn't frighten her; in fact, she felt strangely reassured, as if she had a secret friend no one else knew about. When she was younger she had confided in her mother, who she hoped was able to listen to her from Heaven. Nowadays, when she felt low or lonely, she'd come and talk to the bees and feel comforted by this ghost who gave out a loving energy and was perhaps as lonely as she was.

Recently she had begun to sink more often into her former life. It was as if with the passing of the years her regrets grew stronger and her attachment to her memories more desperate. For the last twenty-odd years she had thrown herself into motherhood, but Trixie was growing up and soon she would move away, and Grace would be left alone with Freddie and the fragile remains of their marriage.

'Hello, old friend,' she said and smiled at the absurdity of talking to someone she couldn't see.

Chapter 2

Trixie Valentine stood in nothing but a diaphanous floral sarong outside old Joe Hornby's boathouse. Inside, her lover reclined in the fishing boat with his guitar across his knee, strumming the tune he had composed that morning. He trained his eyes on the entrance. First, a slender white arm appeared around the wall and long fingers splayed against the wood. Next, a shapely leg followed suit. It bent at the knee and positioned itself diagonally, pointing its shell-pink toes to the ground. Trixie paused like that for dramatic effect before changing position and appearing slowly to lean back against the door frame, one leg up, arms extended behind her, palms flat against the wall. She looked at him from beneath a thick, sun-bleached fringe, cut into a severe line just above her eyes, and held his stare for a tantalizing moment. Then she parted her lips, revealing two slightly crooked eye teeth, and her smile was full of promise. Jasper watched her pull at the knot behind her neck and let the sarong float to the ground, where it formed a puddle at her feet. She stood naked, silhouetted against the ocean background, the curve of her waist catching the last golden light that bounced off the water.

Jasper Duncliffe gazed at her admiringly. Everything about Trixie fascinated him. She was unpredictable, spontaneous, fun-loving and wild. She was also beautiful, with wide indigo eyes and curves in all the right places. She approached him, without taking her gaze off him, and he put his guitar aside and felt himself straining his jeans with desire.

She stepped into the boat. It rocked gently but not enough to unbalance her. Both knew there was a danger of being discovered, but for two people flouting the rules at every turn, the thought of being caught only heightened their excitement. She sat astride him and put her hands on the sides of the boat to steady herself. Then she lowered her face and placed her lips on his, her long hair forming a curtain around them that smelt of the sea. 'You're all mine,' she breathed and he felt her smile against his face. It was true; he couldn't move much, pinned to the boat. He slid his hands around her neck and caressed her jaw with his thumbs.

'You can have me body and soul, Trixie,' he whispered. 'As often as you like.'

'I love the way you speak, Jasper.'

'Why? You said your parents are English.' He moved his hands down to her breasts and lightly brushed her nipples.

Catching her breath, she arched her back like a cat. 'But they don't talk like you do. I like the way *you* talk.'

He pulled her head down and kissed her passionately. Impatient to feel him inside her, she fumbled with his belt and released him. He let out a deep groan as he was swallowed into her warm body. She moved on top of him without inhibition, tossing her head and flicking her hair as the desire built and she lost herself. He held her hips but was unable to control her. At last he grabbed a fistful of hair and pulled her face down to his. 'Not so fast,' he said. 'If you're going to be on top you must do as I say.'

'I like your assertiveness, Mr Duncliffe.'

He laughed. 'I like the sound of that.'

'What? Mr Duncliffe. Sounds very ordinary to me.'

'That's why I like it.' He pressed his mouth to hers before she could distract him further, and kissed her deeply.

Some time later they sat in the boat sharing a joint of marijuana. It was now twilight. The sun had sunk behind the horizon and the sea was calm. Trixie was feeling pleasantly lightheaded and relaxed. 'I like this time of day, don't you?'

'Sure, it's beautiful,' Jasper replied. She fed him the joint and he took a long drag. 'Shouldn't you be getting home?'

'Not yet. I'm already in trouble, a little more won't hurt.'

'What'll you tell her?'

'Mom?' She shrugged. 'She's a romantic. I'll tell her all about you and that will distract her from the fact that I lied about the weekend with Suzie and spent it with you.'

'You're nineteen, Trixie. You have a job. You're earning your own money. You're independent. I'd say you can do as you please.'

'Sure, but she's very conservative. She grew up in a little town in England, fell in love with Dad when they were in their teens and married just as war broke out. She's never been with anyone else. She expects me to do the same, but look at me, having sex before marriage with a rock star – and a rock star is not what most mothers want for their daughters.'

'A rock star,' he chuckled sceptically. 'You flatter me.'

Her eyes blazed with confidence. 'You're going to be a big star, Jasper. I can tell. You're fine-looking, talented and everyone loves your music. I have a nose for success and I can smell it all over you.' She took another drag and grinned at him through the smoke. 'And I'll be there, clapping in the wings, having known you before you became a millionaire, with thousands of fans shouting your name and singing your songs, selling records all over the world.'

'I love your enthusiasm, Trixie. We're doing our best.'

'What do they think of you in England?'

'Not enough.'

'So that's why you came here?'

'Of course. Everyone wants to make it in America.'

She laughed. 'Not everyone wants to make it in Tekanasset!'

'I have a connection to this place. My grandparents had a house here. A long time ago. It seemed a good place to start.'

'Why not make it in England first, like the Beatles did? Don't you want to be big in your own country?'

He sighed and looked pained. 'Because my mother would murder me for the shame.'

Trixie screwed up her nose. 'You're kidding, right?' He shook his head. 'Your mother disapproves?'

'Of course she does.'

'And your father?'

'Dead.'

'Oh, sorry.'

'Don't be. We didn't have the best relationship. He was a military man, as was his father before him. He didn't understand music: at least, not *my* sort of music.'

'How narrow-minded! He should have been proud of your talent.'

'He saw no talent in me, Trixie. But that's OK. I'm the second son. All the responsibility sits on my brother's shoulders, and fortunately he's big enough and conventional enough to carry it.'

Trixie laughed. 'So you're free to be whatever you want to be.'

'That's right.' He grinned. 'With whomever I want to be with.'

'That's me.' She looked at him coquettishly from under her fringe.

'That's you, sweetheart,' he replied.

'You know what? One day I'm going to be successful, too,' she told him. 'But in a different field.'

'What are you going to be?'

She drew her knees up to her chest and hugged them. 'Editor of a well-known magazine.'

'Like Diana Vreeland?'

'People will say, "Who's Diana Vreeland?" because my name will be so much more famous.'

'Infamous, I think is more likely,' he teased.

'Well, I'm going to work in fashion. I love clothes and I have a good sense of style, I think. I'm not going to stay here in Tekanasset, waiting on tables for the rest of my life. There's a big world out there and I'm going to see it.'

'I'm sure you will. I think you can achieve whatever you set your heart on, Trixie Valentine.'

'I think so, too. I'm going to travel to all the fashion shows. I'm going to explore the world. I'm going to hang out with all the greats like Andy Warhol and Cecil Beaton and party at Studio 54 in New York with Bianca Jagger and Ossie Clark.' She laughed and the light of the joint danced in her eyes. 'I'm going to be a career girl.'

'Most girls want to marry and have children. I know my sisters do.'

'But I'm not most girls. I thought you'd have figured that out by now. I want to be free, like you, and be whoever I want to be.'

'Then do it. There's nothing stopping you.'

'Only my father.' She sighed heavily. 'He'd like me to go to college and finish my education, but I doubt he could afford it anyway. He says there's nothing more unattractive than a stupid woman.' She laughed. 'I'm a lot smarter than he realizes, but I'm certainly *not* going to college. I want to get out there and start living. This place is stifling and before you arrived it was deadly dull!'

'Will he support you?'

'Look, he came over from England with nothing but a good brain and made a success in business. If he'd stayed in England, ruined by war with no jobs anywhere, he'd still be a farmhand. I think he'd admire me for wanting to make something of my life – isn't that the American Dream everyone talks about?'

'And your mother?'

'Mom would support me in whatever I decide to do. She just wants me to be happy. She didn't have a good education, but her father was an intellectual and read everything under the sun. He educated her and I tell you, there's nothing she hasn't read. Anyway, she works. She's a landscape gardener and a very good one. She's not one of those women who does nothing but lunch and gossip all day, like some I know.'

'Your mother sounds terrific.'

'She is. She's gentle and sweet, but I know if Dad and I came to blows, she'd support *me*. When it comes to her child, she's fiercely protective. Most mothers would be crushed by some of the things I get up to, but I feel mine is secretly fascinated by them, as if she wishes she could have lived like me. I sense there's a secretly wild side to Mom. I don't know . . .' Her voice trailed off and she turned to gaze out into the night, where bright stars gave a tantalizing glimpse of a world beyond the familiar. 'It's just a hunch. Perhaps I'm wrong.'

Jasper stopped playing and drew her into his arms. 'You're cold,' he said.

'A little.'

He kissed her head. 'Let me walk you home.'

'Would you?'

'Of course. I might be a future rock star, but I'm a gentleman, too, and I'm mindful of my manners.'

'Your mother wouldn't disapprove of that,' she said, standing up.

'No, but she'd disapprove of pretty much everything else.'

'Would she disapprove of me?' Trixie was surprised by the question, which had popped out of her mouth without any prior thought. It was really irrelevant what Mrs Duncliffe thought of her, as Trixie was unlikely ever to meet her. But, oddly, his answer was suddenly important.

'Yes,' he replied, taking her hand and helping her out of the boat. 'She'd disapprove of you.'

'Why?' She couldn't help but feel a little affronted.

'What does it matter?'

'I don't know. It doesn't, I suppose. I'm just curious.'

'Curiosity killed the cat, and you're a very pretty cat,' he said, taking her chin in his hand and kissing her.

'Well then, let's not kill the cat.' But she desperately wanted to know why she wasn't good enough. Was it because she was a waitress at Captain Jack's beachfront restaurant or because she wasn't presentable? She could dress up if she had to and wear a twinset and pearls like Grace Kelly, and she certainly wasn't going to spend the rest of her life waiting on tables.

Jasper escorted her to her front door on Sunset Slip. The scent of the roses that swarmed over the facade of the house was heady, and for a moment it reminded him of the garden back home in England. He picked a flower and threaded it behind her ear. 'Be good to your mother,' he said, kissing her softly.

Trixie grinned. 'You don't even know her,' she laughed huskily.

'I like the sound of her.'

'*She* wouldn't disapprove of *you*,' she whispered. 'I think she'd like you in spite of you being a rock star.'

'I'll see you tomorrow, Delixie Trixie.'

She giggled at the silly name. 'You know where to find me,' she replied, opening the door. He watched her close it behind her before wandering off into the empty street.

Jasper smiled to himself as he took the plank path that cut through the wild grasses to the beach. The shore was lit by an incandescent moon. It seemed as if the stars had fallen from the sky onto the water, where they glittered even more brightly. The thought of Trixie made his heart swell. He had never been in love before. Sure, there had been girls. *Lots* of girls. But he'd never felt about them the way he felt about Trixie. He loved her crooked eye teeth; they made her look raffish and jaunty. He loved her wild spirit and her exuberance, and her steadfast belief in *him*. He knew she'd travel across America with him if he asked her to. The more he thought about it, the more appealing that thought became. He knew for sure he wasn't going to leave her on these beaches in the autumn.

Mr Duncliffe. He liked the admiration in her voice when she said that. He liked who he was when he was with her. She made him feel good. Her devotion was like the sun's rays burning through the shadows of his self-doubt. He began to hum a tune. As he walked, the sound of the waves gave him a gentle sense of rhythm and little by little the tune evolved into words. Inspired by the warm feeling that thoughts of Trixie evoked, he sat cross-legged on the sand with his guitar and set the lyrics to chords, which he played over and over until the song was composed and committed to memory. *I held you in my arms for one last second, and then I watched you slowly walk away. I felt a sudden yearning to run after you, and hold you once again and never let you go.*

From her bedroom window Trixie was sure she could hear the distant sound of a guitar, but it could just be the murmur of the sea. She stood there a moment, letting the cool breeze brush her face. She gazed out at the night's sky. It was dark now, but for the moonlight and the mysterious twinkling of stars. Below, the garden was silent. The birds were sleeping. The bees had returned to their sticky cells. The rabbits were deep in their burrows. In the eerie silver light the shrubs and flowers looked other-worldly. Her heart expanded with the beauty of it all, and the knowledge that Jasper was out there only enhanced the splendour. His arrival on Tekanasset had changed the way she saw everything. The world looked more beautiful because he was in it.

A moment later her mother knocked softly on the door. 'Trixie, can I come in?'

'Hi, Mom,' she said, stepping away from the window and slipping her arms into a long Aran cardigan.

'We need to talk,' Grace began, remembering Big's advice to be firm.

Trixie was quick to apologize. 'Look, I know I let you down and I'm really sorry.' She folded her arms defensively.

Grace noticed the flower in her daughter's hair and her solemn expression melted into a smile. 'Did you have a nice time?'

'I was just hanging out with the band. It was all very innocent, I promise. Suzie and I had our own bedroom and we were guests of Joe Hornby's friend, Mr Lipmann, who's a powerful man in the music industry. He predicts they've got a good chance of making it really big.'

Grace sat on the bed and folded her hands in her lap. 'You like Jasper very much, don't you?'

Trixie grinned as her enthusiasm broke through her hostility. 'You'd like him too, you know. He's a real gentleman. He walked me home. It's not what you think.'

'And what do I think?'

'Well, he's going to be a rock star.' She said it as if being a rock star was a crime.

'There's nothing wrong with being a musician, Trixie.'

'Even his own mom disapproves.'

'*I* don't disapprove. You can love whoever you like, darling. I certainly don't care what anyone else thinks about it.'

'Then what is there to talk about?'

Grace hesitated a moment, unsure of her conviction. 'I want you to remain on the island for the rest of the summer,' she said evenly.

Trixie looked horrified. 'You can't be serious!'

'I am, darling. You can't expect me to condone what you did.'

'I'm nineteen. I have a job, for goodness' sake. I'm earning my own money. I'm an adult. I should be allowed to do whatever I want. You were married at my age!'

'That's irrelevant. You're my daughter and as long as you're under my roof and unmarried I have a right to know where you are. Your father and I are responsible for you. What you did was inexcusable, Trixie. What if something had happened?'

'I was perfectly safe with Jasper. He's twenty-four. We were guests of Mr Lipmann, it wasn't like I ran off with him.'

'You should have asked my permission. You should have been honest about where you were going.'

'You would have stopped me.'

'Yes, I probably would have,' Grace conceded.

'Well, that's why I didn't ask.' Trixie perched on the edge of her dressing-table stool and brought one knee up to hug. 'Have you told Dad?'

'Not yet. I wanted to talk it through with you first. I'd rather like to tell him that it's over and needs no further discussion.'

Trixie looked relieved. 'OK, I promise to remain on the island. I think the boys are staying until September anyway. They're making an album at Joe's.'

Grace was relieved, too. 'So, that's a deal. Good. Now tell me, what's he like?'

Trixie let go of her leg and began to brush her hair. It was thick and lustrous like her mother's used to be before it aged. 'He's very handsome.' Her face softened into a smile.

'I bet he is.'

'He has the most beautiful eyes. They're grey-green, like sage, and he's funny. We laugh all the time. But he's gentle, too, and he's kind.'

'He's English, isn't he?'

'Yes, he sounds like a prince.' She remembered the rose behind her ear and pulled it out. 'Of course, he's not a prince. But he's going to be famous one day. You should hear him sing. He has the sexiest voice on the planet.'

'I'd like to hear him sing,' said Grace.

Trixie sighed happily. 'Well, maybe you will. Maybe he'll sing one of his songs for you. I think you'll be impressed. He loves me, he loves me not . . .' She began to pull petals off the rose.

Grace laughed. 'I think he loves you, by the sound of things,' she said.

Trixie grinned at her knowingly. 'I think he does, too,' she replied.

Chapter 3

Freddie Valentine had once been a handsome man. That was before one half of his face had been disfigured in the war. A bullet had taken his eye, shattering his cheekbone and ripping his flesh apart. The wound had healed, as wounds do, but an unsightly scar remained to remind him of the day that changed everything. The day the world turned on its head and robbed him of all he held dear. The eyepatch he had worn ever since was symbolic of the way he had picked himself up and got on with his life. Beneath, the hurting never stopped.

He arrived on Tekanasset by boat the following morning with a warm sense of satisfaction after a weekend on his boss's farm in Bristol County. For the last ten years he had managed the Cranberry farm on Tekanasset, which cultivated over two hundred acres of bog, and had made such a success of it that Mr Stanley was keen for him to lend his expertise to his other farm on the mainland, which grew blueberries, raspberries and strawberries as well as raising livestock. Freddie had spent three days doing what he loved best and Mr Stanley had raised his salary to reflect his gratitude. He had left with a heightened sense of self-worth and the conviction that the disappointments he faced at home were more than compensated for by the pleasure he derived from his work. It was only unfortunate that he happened to bump into Bill Durlacher at the newsagent's as he stopped to buy cigarettes on his way home, extinguishing as surely as peat on fire the remnants of his enthusiasm.

'I hear your Trixie's in a bit of hot water,' said Bill, slipping his newspaper under his arm and patting Freddie with his free hand.

'What kind of hot water?' asked Freddie impassively. His reserve was considered characteristically British by Tekanasset society, but Bill usually managed to bring out a jollier side on the golf course or over a beer at the clubhouse.

'I don't want to be the bearer of bad news,' Bill continued, delighted to be the bearer of bad news.

'You might as well tell me, since I'm going to hear it soon enough from Grace.'

'She ran off with one of the boys from that English band staying up at Joe Hornby's. Guess he thinks he can turn them into the Rolling Stones.' Bill gave an incredulous laugh. 'Grace must be beside herself. Evelyn says Trixie didn't come back for three days.'

Freddie paled. He rubbed the bristles on his chin as he deliberated how to deal with Bill Durlacher. His response would determine how long this scandal would run. He made a hasty decision. 'Oh, *that*,' he said dismissively. 'I know all about *that*.' He chuckled convincingly. 'I wish I could say she takes after her mother.' Bill was caught off guard. Keen not to look foolish, he laughed, too. 'They're good boys,' Freddie continued. 'If I'd wanted a safe chaperone for my daughter, I'd have chosen him myself. What's the young man's name again . . . ?' He feigned vagueness.

'Jasper, I believe,' Bill responded, visibly disappointed.

'That's right. Jasper. Nice fellow, Jasper.' He patted Bill in the same over-familiar way that Bill had patted him. 'Good to see you, Bill. Give my best to Evelyn.'

When he arrived home he could hear Grace humming in the shed at the bottom of the garden. 'Grace!' he shouted, and the tone of his voice brought her hurrying up the garden path, heart thumping against her ribcage. She thought of Trixie, and the anxiety felt like a clamp around her throat. Her husband stood on the veranda, hands on hips. Beneath his hat his face was dark with fury. 'Why do I have to hear about Trixie and this Jasper boy from Bill Durlacher?' he demanded. 'You've made a fool out of me.'

She swept the wisps of hair off her sweating brow with the back of her hand. 'I'm sorry, Freddie. I should have telephoned you.'

'I'm away for one weekend and *this* happens!' He began to pace the veranda.

'It's all right. I've spoken to her and she's grounded.'

'Grounded! She should be smacked from here to Timbuktu. What the hell's going on?'

Grace tried to play it down. 'She went to Cape Cod with some friends to watch the band play in a private concert. She told me she was going to stay with Suzie and I believed her. I mean, she stays with Suzie most weekends, so I thought . . .'

'But she spent the weekend with this Jasper no-good.' He swiped irritably at an intrepid bee that buzzed a little too close for comfort.

'She was with Suzie. They went together. It sounds worse than it was.'

'She lied to you, Grace. How much worse could it get? She's nineteen and she spent the weekend getting up to all sorts of trouble with a young man she's only just met. It's a disgrace. Who is this Jasper, anyway?'

'He's English.'

'As if that makes it any better. He's in a band, for God's sake?'

'Yes, but he's a nice boy.'

Freddie sank onto the swing chair and took the cigarette packet out of his breast pocket. 'Have you met him?'

'No.'

'So, how do you know he's a nice man?'

'I trust Trixie.'

He popped a cigarette between his lips and lit it. 'Do you have any idea of the lifestyle of these people? Do you?'

'They're not all Mick Jagger and Marianne Faithfull.'

'Drugs, alcohol, sex. Do you really want our daughter hanging around with boys like that? Grace, don't be naïve.'

'What else did Bill tell you?' She tried to control the tremor in her voice.

'He didn't have to tell me anything else. I can imagine what everyone's saying.'

She sat beside him and placed her muddy hands in her lap. 'Is that what's worrying you? What everyone else thinks?'

Freddie looked at her through a veil of smoke. The nicotine seemed to calm him down a little. 'Grace, we arrived here twenty-seven years ago and made a new life for ourselves. These good people welcomed us onto their island and made us feel at home. But we've worked hard to belong. You've built up a reputation as the best landscape gardener for miles around and I've gained the respect of the people I work with at the farm. It's not easy, looking the way I do, but they've accepted us and we've got some good friends. I don't want all that destroyed in one summer by Trixie behaving like a slut.'

Grace felt the word as keenly as a slap. 'How can you say that about our daughter, Freddie? She's not *that*.'

'She's compromising her reputation, Grace.'

'But she's in love, Freddie,' she protested passionately.

'She's nineteen. What does she know of love?'

'Might I remind you of another young woman of nineteen, who married her childhood sweetheart all those years ago?' She smiled tentatively, but Freddie was unmoved.

He took another drag. 'We had known each other all our lives. We came from the same place. I know nothing about this boy Jasper, and I bet you she doesn't, either. Do you really think a boy who travels around in a band is a good match for our daughter?'

'Trixie's not conventional.'

'She likes to think she isn't, but she is. It's fun to flout the rules, and bad boys will always be attractive to girls like Trixie. But he'll break her heart, and she's conventional enough to be hurt by it.'

Grace blanched. 'Don't say that,' she said quietly. Of all the things that might afflict her daughter, a broken heart was surely the worst.

'I'm saying it now, for the record. You know I'm right.'

'Let's meet him. Let's at least find out what he's like before we forbid her to see him.'

He stood up and tossed his stub into the garden. 'I've got to get to work. I'll think about it.'

Grace stood up, too. 'Be kind, Freddie,' she said, and her voice sounded harder than it was meant to. 'I don't want her to resent you for preventing her from being with the man she loves.'

He stared at her. His eye, usually so aloof, looked suddenly wounded. 'Is that what you think?'

'I only want her to be happy,' she replied, aware that her face had reddened.

'So do I. As her father, it's my job to stand in the way of the potholes and direct her to safe ground. What's for dinner?'

'Chicken pie,' she replied.

He nodded his satisfaction. In spite of having left England twenty-seven years before, Freddie still preferred quintessential English cooking. He disappeared inside to pick up his jacket, then left through the front door without another word.

Grace was left trembling on the veranda. She took a deep breath to calm her nerves, but her insides felt like jelly. She was ready to defend Trixie like a lioness, but if Freddie really forbade her to see Jasper, she'd be terribly torn. But what if he was right and Jasper was simply enjoying a summer romance with a local girl to whom he had no intention of committing? She didn't want marriage for Trixie: not now, she was much too young – if *she* hadn't married so young she might never have got into the trouble she had – but she didn't want her daughter's first love to break her heart, either. Anything but that.

Grace sat on the steps and watched the bees buzzing about the lavender. Their low humming assuaged her anxiety. It lifted her spirits to watch them gathering pollen for the hive. Back in England her father had looked after twenty hives; here she kept only three. She didn't have the time to keep more, and besides, it was a hobby; she was what they called a backyard beekeeper. She didn't make any money from her crop, to Freddie's chagrin, because anything she made from selling her honey in the local shops went straight into repairs, replacements and equipment. Freddie had tried to persuade her to give them up, but as soft as Grace was about most things, when it came to bees, nothing and no one would convince her to dispense with them. She would sooner have ripped out her heart.

She wandered over to the lavender and snapped off one of the heads upon which a little bee was feasting. She smiled as it crawled busily over the tiny flowers, extracting nectar. It didn't notice her, so intent was it on its mission. A moment later the bee was making its way up her arm, tickling her skin. She watched it for a while, forgetting all about Trixie and Jasper, feeling the pull of the past in the cracks in her broken heart that had never fully closed. Twenty-seven years sounded like a long time, and yet to the heart time means nothing. Love wasn't something that wore out or disintegrated with the passing of the years, but something that glowed like an eternal sun. Grace was in her fifties now, and had certainly done her fair share of disintegrating, but only on the outside. The love she carried in her heart was as shiny as new and would remain so for as long as her memory clung onto its radiance. And remember she did, all the time, with every little bee that graced her garden.

Trixie finished her shift in Captain Jack's at three and wandered over to Joe Hornby's. It was just a short walk along the beach and a steep climb up a plank path to the grey-shingled house that sat regally on top of the bluff. She made her way to where the boys were lying by the pool, smoking spliffs and chatting in the sunshine. Old Joe was asleep in a wicker armchair, his hat placed over his eyes, his large belly rising and falling beneath his pink polo shirt as he slept off a large lunch. Jasper was in a pair of red swimming shorts, his lean body tanning easily in the afternoon sun. 'Well, look who's here,' he said, grinning at her. 'Fancy a swim, beautiful?'

'It's really hot today,' Trixie replied, putting her bag down on the grass. 'I might have to cool off.'

'If you put on a swimsuit we'll *all* have to cool off,' said Ben, who played the drums in the band. He swept his unruly mop of hair off his forehead and took a swig of beer from the bottle.

'I see you're working hard,' she retorted sarcastically.

'We were just praying for inspiration,' Jasper replied. 'And here you are!'

'Where's *my* inspiration, then?' asked George, stretching languidly on his lounger.

'Her mother won't let her out, I imagine,' said Ben with a chuckle.

'She can bring her mother,' George replied. 'I like a woman with experience.'

'Who's this?' Trixie asked.

'Some bird George was chatting up in the diner this morning,' Ben informed her.

'*Lucy in the sky with diamonds*,' sang Jasper.

'Not Lucy Durlacher!' Trixie exclaimed in astonishment. 'Believe me, you really wouldn't want to meet *her* mother! Anyway, you'll be lucky if she lets Lucy anywhere near you. I suspect she'd rather her daughter caught the plague!'

George grinned and put his hand on his heart. 'Forbidden fruit! Now she's even more appealing than she was before. I'm dying of love for Lucy Durlacher.'

'Trust me, she's not the one playing hard to get. Any fool can win *her*.'

'Miaow, claws like a cat!' Ben teased.

Jasper took Trixie's hand and pulled her down so that he could kiss her. 'I know all about your claws,' he whispered. 'I wear the scratches down my back like badges of honour.'

Trixie laughed throatily. 'I'll see *you* in the pool, Mr Duncliffe!'

She took her bikini into the house to change. The place was beautifully decorated and very tidy. She found the lavatory across the hall and slipped out of her clothes. As she stepped into her bikini she swept her eyes over black and white photographs of a younger, slimmer Joe with various musicians she didn't recognize, hanging in a collage over the walls. He was smiling out from party scenes with dashing young men in tuxedos and glamorous women with the Fifties up-dos her mother had managed to resist. Then she spotted a photo of Joe with Elvis Presley. She took a closer look. It was most definitely Elvis. She was immediately impressed. Perhaps Joe was going to turn Jasper and his band into a global success like Elvis. A shiver of excitement rippled through her body. It was all desperately thrilling. She thought of Marianne Faithfull, and the idea of being the girlfriend of a rock star was very appealing. Trixie skipped back through the house to the pool with an extra bounce in her step.

They spent the afternoon swimming and sunbathing. Joe woke up and Trixie discovered that he was a jovial old man with a fruity Boston drawl and a wealth of entertaining stories about his past in the music business. He sat like a lazy toad in his chair, smoking a cigar and holding forth, clearly enjoying his young and admiring audience. 'I haven't been so excited about a band since I first heard John and Paul,' he told them importantly, as if it had been he who had discovered the Beatles. 'These boys are going to go far. You heard it here first. The music world is looking to England. The timing couldn't be better.' He flicked ash onto the grass. 'We're going to hit the road in the fall and I'm going to open my address book, which is one of the finest in the business, and we're not stopping until we've reached the top.'

Trixie grinned at Jasper and he smiled back. At that moment the future looked as bright as a gold coin.

Later, when Trixie returned home, her excitement was duly dampened by her father, who was waiting to speak to her in his study. Immediately irritated that she was made to feel like a schoolgirl again, she dropped her beach bag onto the hall floor and marched in. Sometimes it felt as if he had never left the army. He still wore his trousers high, sat with his back straight, had a mania for orderliness and a habit of speaking to her in formal tones more suitable for an officer with his men than a father with his daughter, and he was so terribly serious. Freddie Valentine was a man to whom laughter did not come easily. Trixie wanted to laugh all the time, except now, of course. Right now she wanted to shout at him in fury.

'You wanted to see me?' she asked, standing in the doorway.

'Come in, Beatrix,' he said. Her father only ever used her real name when he was cross with her. 'Sit down,' he commanded. Trixie was baffled. She was sure her mother had said the episode was over. She did as she was told and sat on the sofa, silently wishing she was old enough to be free of her father's control. She stared at the coffee table, which was neatly piled with big, shiny books on history and war, and braced herself for a severe telling-off. 'I'm very disappointed in you,' he said quietly.

That was a bad start. Her heart sank. 'I've said I'm sorry,' she muttered.

'I've spoken to your mother.'

'She's grounded me,' she added, hoping that being grounded would be enough.

'I'm aware of that. But I'm not happy that you lied, Beatrix.'

'I won't do it again, I promise.'

He sighed. 'I don't know why you feel the need to break the rules all the time. Rules are there for a reason. To keep you safe. To prevent you from getting hurt. If rules are broken in the field, men die.' He sighed again, irritably. 'If you want to make a success of your life, Beatrix, you have to be disciplined. Everything requires discipline. I don't think you understand that.'

'Oh, I do,' she replied quickly. She had learned from the past that trying to fight her father was only a waste of energy and always unproductive.

'I've been thinking of this young man you've been seeing. What are his plans?'

'Plans?'

'Yes, what's he going to do when the summer comes to an end?'

She shrugged. 'I don't know. Joe says he's going to make them into superstars, like the Beatles.'

Freddie rolled his eyes. 'Joe Hornby's a big talker. I wouldn't put my money on him.'

Trixie felt deflated. 'He knew Elvis Presley,' she said defensively.

'I'm sure he did. I met Marlon Brando once, but that doesn't make me a film producer.'

Trixie huffed crossly. 'Are you going to tell me I can't see Jasper?'

'I'm trying to warn you, you foolish girl.' Freddie stood up and began to pace the room. 'Do you think he's going to remain faithful to you while he forges his career as a musician? No, he's going to leave at the end of the summer and you're going to be left here, broken-hearted. What sort of father would I be if I didn't warn you?'

'How many times have you told me that my life is a learning curve? Surely it's my choice if I want to run the risk of being broken-hearted?'

He looked at her thoughtfully. 'You don't even know him,' she mumbled.

'I know his sort.'

'I don't think you do, Daddy. You just know the stereotype.'

He took a swig of gin and tonic from the crystal glass on his desk. 'I don't want you seeing him,' he said, but there was a weakness in his voice that Trixie seized upon hopefully.

'But you're not going to stop me.'

'You're a young woman. Your mother was married at your age.'

'Why don't you meet him?'

'Yes, I think that would be a sensible idea.'

'I know you'll like him.'

'Let me be the judge of that, Trixie.'

She smiled, encouraged by the fact that he was now calling her Trixie. 'He's a nice man, I promise you, and he's gallant.'

'I suppose there's every chance he'll ditch his plans and go into business.'

'That would be a terrible waste of talent, Daddy.'

'But a better prospect for you.'

Trixie hurried upstairs to change. There was a party at Captain Jack's beach club that evening and she was going to meet Jasper there with the boys. Perhaps they would even play, then everyone would see how talented they were. Barely able to contain her excitement, she showered then slipped into a miniskirt and white camisole top embroidered with flowers. She left her hair loose but picked a rose from the front of the house and clipped it behind her ear. She found her mother in the kitchen in a cooking apron. 'I'm off to the party,' she said.

'Don't be too late back,' Grace replied, glancing at the short skirt and biting her tongue. Trixie's legs were too long for a skirt so tiny. She imagined Evelyn Durlacher would have a lot to say about *that*. 'Have a good time,' she said instead.

'I will, Mom. Are you sure you don't want to come? It's a party for everyone.'

'I know, darling. But your father's tired. He's worked all weekend. I'm going to stay here and give him a good dinner.'

Trixie shrugged. 'All right, but it's going to be fun.'

'You enjoy yourself, and be *good*.' Grace attempted to inject a little firmness into her voice, but if she'd succeeded, Trixie hadn't heard her.

'How do I look?' She swivelled round like a dancer. 'Like it?'

Grace couldn't help but smile at her daughter's exuberance. 'You look lovely, darling, though you'd look just as pretty in a longer skirt.'

'Oh, Mother, you are so old-fashioned! Don't worry about me,' she laughed. 'I'll be exemplary!' She grinned mischievously and skipped out of the house, leaving the screen door to bang behind her.

Grace put the chicken pie in the oven then took off her apron and hung it on the back of the door. She poured a glass of wine and went out onto the veranda to watch the sunset.

It was a golden evening and the light was soft and dusty, except when it caught the waves and gleamed a brilliant white. She took a deep breath and savoured the fresh sea air that never ceased to give her pleasure, even after all these years living by a beach.

She sipped her wine and felt herself relax. Freddie was in his study and likely to remain there until supper. She had time to sit on the swing chair and enjoy the solitude. She watched the bees humming about the pots of hydrangeas beside her, and slowly, but with the greatest pleasure, she allowed their gentle buzzing to transport her back to the past.

Chapter 4

Walbridge, England, 1933

A fat bumblebee crawled up Grace's arm. She lay on the grass in the churchyard, dressed in her best Sunday frock, white ankle socks and freshly polished brown shoes, and watched the bee in fascination. It had a large bottom and its stripes were bright and furry. She wanted to run her finger down its abdomen but thought it might take exception and fly off, so she remained perfectly still as the summer sunshine warmed her back and bare legs, waiting for her father to finish chatting to the other parishioners who gathered outside the church.

'I hope that bee doesn't sting you,' came a deep voice from behind her. She could tell from the clipped upper-class accent that he wasn't one of her father's friends, and she felt herself stiffen with self-consciousness.

'Bees only sting to protect the hive,' she replied, without daring to look at the stranger. 'This bee won't sting me. I'm no threat, you see.'

He laughed. 'You must be Mr Hamblin's daughter.'

'Yes, I am.'

'Thought so.' He crouched down to take a closer look at the bee. 'You're a brave girl. Most children are afraid of bees.'

'That's because they don't know them like I do. Dad says people are always afraid of what they don't know. Fear is the root of all prejudice, he says.'

'Your father is very wise. Do you think the bee might be encouraged to crawl up *my* arm?'

'We can give it a try, if you like,' she said, forgetting her embarrassment and sitting up slowly. The young man had taken off his jacket and was rolling up his sleeve. Grace took the opportunity to glance at his face. She recognized him at once, for he had sat in the front pew in church beside her father's employers, the Marquess and Marchioness of Penselwood. She concluded that he must be their eldest son, Rufus, Lord Melville, and her hands began to tremble, not because he was handsome but because he was an earl and she had never spoken to one of his sort before.

'The trick is not to let it know you're afraid,' she told him, searching for confidence in the subject she knew better than any other.

'I'll do my best,' he said with a smile. Grace sensed he was teasing her, for a man of his age was surely not afraid of a little bee. He took her thin arm in his hand and rested it on top of his. Against his brown one hers looked very white and fragile. She strained every muscle to stop herself from shaking. They remained with their arms touching for what seemed like a very long time, during which Grace tried to remember to breathe. At last the bee wandered down her arm and onto his. As it stepped lightly onto his skin, he flinched.

Grace forgot her nervousness and took his wrist in her hand to steady him. 'Don't move,' she whispered. 'It won't sting you, I promise. Bumblebees rarely sting, only the worker bees and queens. I'm not sure which this one is – a worker bee, I think. Certainly not a queen; you can tell those immediately as they're bigger. Anyway, if it does sting you, it's no bad thing. Dad lets his bees sting him on purpose.'

'Why would he do a silly thing like that?'

'He says bee stings cure his arthritis.'

'Really? Is that true?'

'I think it is. He swears by it.'

'My grandmother has terrible arthritis. Perhaps I should bring her down to your cottage for a sting or two.'

Grace chuckled. 'I'm not sure she'd thank you. A bee sting really hurts.' They watched the insect crawl up his arm. Grace let go of his hand.

'What's your name, Miss Hamblin?'

Furious with herself for blushing, she lowered her eyes. 'Grace.'

'I'm Rufus. I'd forgotten how boring Reverend Dibben is. He does go on.' Grace giggled timidly. She was quite happy talking about bees, but she didn't know what to say about Reverend Dibben, except to agree stupidly – he *was* an exceedingly dull man. 'You know, I've been up at Oxford for a year and it's been a pleasure not having to listen to the old bore every Sunday. Sadly, he's coming to lunch so I'm going to have to suffer him through three courses.' He sighed. She glanced at him again and he beamed a wide, mischievous smile. 'Well, Grace, you've been a fine teacher. Tell me, do you help your father with the hives?'

'Yes, I do, I love everything about bees.'

He looked at her steadily and frowned. 'So, you'll be a beekeeper when you grow up?'

'I hope so.' She smiled back shyly.

'And you'll invent a cure for arthritis that will make you rich.'

'I don't think anyone would pay to be stung by a bee.'

'Then you'll have to find a way to bottle it.'

'That could prove difficult.'

'Not for a clever girl like you.' His dark chocolate eyes twinkled warmly. 'You'd better take back your bee or I'll be late for lunch.' He looked across the churchyard to where his parents were graciously extracting themselves from the crowd of townspeople. The Marchioness was wearing the most magnificent fox stole, even though it was summer. It was so intact the creature could easily have been asleep and not dead. Her husband's face was hidden behind a thick grey beard. He resembled the King. Rufus watched them a moment, as if reluctant to join them any sooner than necessary. 'Can't be late for the vicar!' he sighed.

Grace gently lifted the bee with her fingers and placed it back on her arm. Rufus stood up and unrolled his sleeve. 'I'll tell my grandmother about your father's remedy for arthritis,' he said, threading the cufflink through the hole in his cuff. 'I think the idea is a capital one.'

'Oh, you mustn't!' she protested.

'Oh, but I must. She's an eccentric old bat. I wouldn't be at all surprised if she doesn't come knocking on your door.' He shrugged on his jacket. 'Don't worry, if it doesn't work we won't burn you at the stake for witchcraft. Bye now.'

Grace watched him saunter off. He was tall and athletic with the bearing of a young man for whom life had been generous and kind. He walked with his shoulders back and his head high, and everyone who saw him smiled with admiration, for he was indeed attractive and charismatic. Grace's heart began to beat at a regular pace again but her hands were still damp with sweat. She felt very hot. She was flattered that he had bothered to talk to a fourteen-year-old.

Before she could dwell on it any further she was startled by Freddie, springing upon her from behind. The bee took fright and flew into the air. She rounded on him crossly. 'Really, Freddie! You've scared her away!'

'You and your silly bees,' he retorted, sitting on the grass beside her. 'What did *he* want?' He nodded in the direction of the grown-ups, who were now beginning to disperse like homing pigeons. Rufus walked with his mother down the gravel path towards the waiting motor cars. Grace didn't think she'd ever seen a more glamorous woman, even at the flicks.

'He wanted the bee to walk up his arm,' she replied.

Freddie swept his auburn hair off his forehead. His skin was damp with sweat. 'Strange man.'

'He was nice.'

'You're a soft touch for anyone who shows an interest in your bees.' He grinned at her mischievously. 'Fancy a swim in the river after lunch? It's boiling!'

'Maybe,' she replied. 'Depends.'

'On what?'

'On whether you are man enough to let a bee walk up your arm like Rufus.'

'So he's Rufus now, is he?' He elbowed her playfully – and a little jealously.

'He said his name is Rufus.'

'He's the Earl of Melville. Lord Melville to you and don't you forget it.'

'Then I'm Miss Hamblin to you, Mr Valentine, and don't *you* forget it.'

Freddie laughed and stood up. 'Find me a bee,' he demanded, keen to show that he was as brave as Lord Melville.

'All right. Let's see.' She ran her eyes over the daisies and buttercups that grew among the grass and spotted what could easily be the same fat bee which had only a moment ago walked up her arm. She bent down and picked it up as if it were as innocuous as a bird's egg.

'Come on, Freddie, don't be a big girl!' she teased. Gently, she placed the bee on Freddie's arm. He trembled. She held his wrist as she had held Rufus's but it didn't excite her as Rufus's had, for Freddie's skin was almost as familiar as her own. Ever since her mother died and *his* mother May, a distant cousin and her mother's best friend, had stepped in to help her father raise her, Freddie had been like a brother to her. In the beginning, her grandmother had come up from Cornwall to live with them, but mother and son had soon clashed and Mrs Hamblin had been unceremoniously sent home on the train. After that her aunt had attempted to fill her mother's shoes but she had only lasted six months before *she* was packed off back to Cornwall, too. That was years ago. Grace couldn't remember her grandmother or her aunt; only May and Michael Valentine and her father had been constants in her life. She couldn't remember a moment when Freddie hadn't been around, either.

'How does that feel? Not scared, are you, Freddie?' she asked.

'No!' he exclaimed through gritted teeth. His face had gone very red, enhancing the indigo colour of his eyes.

'You know, without bees to pollinate our world, humans would die out in four years.'

'Fascinating,' he replied sarcastically.

'And bees have been around for thirty million years. Just imagine that!'

'Can you take it off now? It's going to crawl into my shirt.' Freddie began to pant in panic.

'Am I boring you?' She laughed. 'Well, I suppose you've earned a swim in the river now.'

Just as she was about to lift it off his arm, the little bee must have sensed his fear for it lowered its abdomen and stung him. Grace paled. Not because Freddie gave out a yelp of pain, but because the sting had lodged itself in Freddie's skin and as the bee pulled away, half of its insides were left behind. She stared at it in anguish. The insect tried to fly away, but it was too weak. It fell onto the grass where it made a pathetic attempt to crawl. Grace's eyes filled with tears. She bent down and picked the creature up and placed it in the palm of her hand where she stared at it helplessly.

Freddie was appalled. 'You don't care about me! You only care about your silly bees!' he accused, his voice rising as the pain throbbed and his skin turned pink.

'You're not going to die, Freddie,' she retorted crossly. 'You shouldn't have let her know that you were afraid!'

'I wasn't afraid. Bees sting and that's all there is to it.' He nursed his arm and tried to hold back the tears. 'You and your silly game!'

She glanced at his glistening eyes and softened. 'I'm sorry, Freddie. I didn't think it would sting you.'

'That's the last time I go anywhere near a bee, do you understand?' He grimaced. 'It bloody hurts, Grace. I hope you're satisfied. I heard of a man who died of a bee sting!'

Grace took a look at his arm. He had wiped the sting away, but the venom was making his arm swell. 'Come, I'll get you home and Auntie May can put some garlic on it.'

'Garlic?'

'Or baking soda.'

He looked horrified. 'You really are a witch!'

'They both work a treat. Come on.'

They hurried down the path into the lane. Freddie bore the pain bravely. He was determined not to cry in front of Grace. He didn't imagine Lord Melville would have cried had he been stung.

Freddie's house wasn't far from the church. It was down a narrow lane near the river and the Fox and Goose Inn, where his father went every evening after work to drink beer with his friends. They found his mother, whom Grace had always called Auntie May, in the kitchen, peeling potatoes at the sink. 'Oh dear, what have you done to yourself, Freddie?' she asked, taking his arm and looking at it closely.

'A bee stung him, Auntie May,' Grace told her. 'Do you have any garlic?'

'Garlic?'

'To put on the sting. It'll make it better quicker than any fancy ointment from the chemist.'

May smiled. 'You're just like your father, Grace,' she said, going to the cupboard to find some. 'I bet it's sore, Freddie. You're being very brave.' May squashed the clove on her chopping board and pressed it onto the sting. 'Does that hurt?' she asked softly.

'A little,' said Freddie.

Grace rolled her eyes. 'I've never known so much fuss!' she chided. 'Boys are big babies.'

'Boys fight wars, Grace. They're courageous when it matters,' said May quietly.

'Not Freddie,' Grace laughed. 'Freddie's a big girl!'

'He's only fifteen. One day he'll be a man and think nothing of a bee sting.' May kissed his forehead affectionately. 'All done now.'

'You have to come swimming with me this afternoon, Grace. You made a promise,' said Freddie.

'I did, and I will honour my word.'

'Will you come by after lunch, then?'

'As soon as Dad lets me go.'

'I'll make you sandwiches for tea if you like,' May suggested, picking up a potato to peel.

'Thank you, we'd love that, wouldn't we, Freddie? We can eat them on the river bank. It'll be fun.'

'Don't tell your sister, Freddie. I won't be making sandwiches for her.' May shook her ginger curls. 'If your father knew how much I spoil you, he'd have words to say. Now off you both go. I've got to cook lunch. We've got company.'

Freddie walked Grace back to the church where she had left her bicycle. It was a short ride home if she took the shortcut along the farm tracks through the wood. 'How's your sting?' she asked.

'Better,' he replied. 'I suppose you were right about the garlic.'

'I'm a witch, after all,' she laughed.

'But I stink.'

'You can wash it off in the river.'

'The fish will love that!'

'I'm sorry, Freddie,' she said. 'I didn't mean for the bee to hurt you.'

'I know. It's OK. It's feeling better now.'

'Still, I feel sorrier for the bee.' She picked up her bicycle, which she had leaned against the church wall. 'I'll see you later,' she said, climbing on.

Grace pedalled through the village until she came to the farm entrance of Walbridge Hall. She cycled in, past a cluster of pretty farm cottages where chickens wandered freely, pecking at the earth, and where barns were swept clean in preparation for the harvest. It was quiet, being a Sunday. She pedalled hard up the track towards the wood. The grass had grown long and was thick with clover. On her left the hedges were high and bushy with cow parsley and blackthorn. Small birds darted in and out and hares lolloped up ahead, disappearing into the undergrowth when she got too close for comfort. As she was about to cut through the wood, she felt the desire to take a look at the big house. She'd seen it lots of times before with her father, but now she had met Rufus, it took on a whole new meaning. It was no longer just very fine bricks but Rufus's home.

She changed direction and walked her bike along the field at the foot of the wood. From there she could see Walbridge Hall nestled in the valley, protected by sturdy plane trees and surrounded by acres of gardens, lovingly managed by her father who had held the position of head gardener for over twenty years. His knowledge and skill were said to be unmatched by anyone else in Dorset. She remembered with a smile how he'd stop and admire the house and say: 'That's a mighty fine building, that is.' And being a man who loved history and read a great deal, he'd tell her about it without caring that she'd heard it a dozen times already.

Arthur Hamblin was right. It was a magnificent seventeenth-century stately home built in the soft, pale-yellow stone of Dorset. With three floors, tall gables, large imposing-looking windows and chimneys set in pairs, it was undeniably grand yet not at all formidable. Perhaps it was due to the gentle colour of the stone, or the prettiness of the bay windows and gables, or the general harmony of the design, but Walbridge Hall seemed to welcome the onlooker with a silent salutation.

Grace thought of Rufus at lunch with the vicar and smiled to herself, thrilled to have been taken into his confidence.

She could see a number of motor cars on the gravel in front of the house. There was a sleek black Bentley which belonged to the Marquess, with its long bonnet and exquisite leather interior. She had seen that vehicle many times, parked outside the church and motoring through the village carrying the Marchioness off to London. A little red Austin was parked beside it, which belonged to the vicar, but outshining both was a sleek racing-green Alfa Romeo. She imagined that one belonged to Rufus. It seemed to be a motor car worthy of a dashing young man like the Earl of Melville.

She remained there a long while, watching. Before, she had barely noticed the house. Her father's fascination with the place had rather baffled her. How was it possible for someone to be so fixated on a pile of bricks and mortar, however well constructed? Gardens she could understand, because flora and fauna had always held her in wonder, but houses had never held such appeal. Walbridge Hall certainly hadn't warranted more than a glance. But now it seemed to breathe with life. She imagined the people inside it and wondered what they were all doing. She fantasized about knocking on that great door. She couldn't imagine what it looked like inside because she had no experience to draw on. But she knew it would be superb.

After a while her stomach began to rumble and she turned her thoughts to dinner. Her father would expect his meal on time. Reluctantly, she tore herself away from her vigil and cut through the middle of the wood, along a track where the grass was kept short because the Penselwoods liked to ride there. She loved this part of the forest with its ancient oak trees, whose gnarled and twisted branches reminded her of fairy tales she had read as a child. In spring the ground was a sea of bluebells, but now, being July, bracken and ferns had grown dense and strong – perfect cover for pheasants and rabbits.

She reached the other side of the wood and pushed her bike out into the field. From there she could see the thatched roof of the cottage she had lived in all her life. It didn't belong to her father; it was part of the estate, but it was his for as long as he was head gardener and beekeeper. Its official name was Cottage Number 3, but because of the hives it had become known as Beekeeper's Cottage, and Grace thought the name suited it well.

Perfect in symmetry, with white walls and a grey thatched roof, it was a harmonious little house with a great deal of charm. Two windows peeped out from beneath a fringe of thatch and seemed to survey the surrounding countryside with a constant look of wonder, as if the magic of those green fields and ancient woods never lost its power to enchant. A trio of chimneys made perfect perches for pigeons grown fat on the bounty of wheat and barley from the surrounding fields. They settled in up there and cooed softly until the winter fires sent them into the trees, where they cooed grudgingly instead.

Grace found her father on his knees in the garden, pulling out weeds. He never stopped. When he wasn't working at the Hall he was toiling in his own garden or at the hives. The only thing that brought him inside was the dark, and then he'd sink into his favourite armchair with his loyal spaniel, Pepper, at his feet, light a pipe and read. For an ill-educated man Arthur Hamblin was extremely well read, with a natural intelligence and an enquiring mind. He devoured history books and biographies and reread his favourite classics in fiction so that the pages were dog-eared and the hard covers shabby. Recognizing the same curiosity in his daughter, he had set about teaching her with love and patience everything he had learned. They shared books and discussed the great mysteries of the world, but the knowledge Grace most treasured was the wisdom of bees. Father and daughter were never closer than when they were looking after the hives and pouring honey into jars to take up to the Hall.

'Ah, Gracey,' he said, looking up from the border. 'Where have you been?'

'Freddie got stung by a bee.'

Arthur chuckled, pulling out a handful of bindweed. His greying hair curled beneath his cap like old man's beard. 'Bet he made a fuss.'

'Of course he did.'

'Did you put garlic on it?'

'Yes, although Auntie May thought I was mad to suggest it.'

'What's she up to, then?'

'Cooking dinner. They have company.'

'Oh, they do, do they? Well, what shall we have for dinner then, you and I?' he asked, always eager for the next meal.

'I don't know. What do you feel like?'

He stood up and walked across the grass towards her. 'Let's go and see what's in the icebox,' he said jovially. 'I'm sure we can cook up a feast as good as any at May's!'

Chapter 5

That afternoon, after a simple meal of cold lamb and mashed potatoes, Grace cycled to Freddie's house, where they both continued on foot to the river to bathe. It was hot. Dragonflies hovered over the water with mayflies and pond skaters. Swallows dived gracefully to drink and, below, fish swam in and out of the shadows. They changed into their bathing suits beneath their towels and left the sandwiches May had made them against a tree with their clothes. The water was cold and they squealed in delight as they slowly waded in.

'This is lovely!' Grace sighed, relishing the feeling of the slimy riverbed beneath her feet.

Freddie plunged under the water then shot up like a torpedo. 'Cold!' he exclaimed, throwing himself in again up to his neck. He swam further out to where the limpid water gleamed in the sunlight.

'How's your arm?' she asked.

'Better.' He didn't seem to want to dwell on that embarrassing episode. Instead, he showed off his front crawl, cutting smoothly through the water. Freddie might have been afraid of a bee sting, but he was brave and adept at swimming. Grace preferred to loll about near the edge and watch him. She'd find a frog or toad to inspect, or forage about for snails.

'Why don't you dive off the bridge?' she shouted across the water.

'All right,' he replied. Delighted to be given the opportunity to impress her, he swam over to the bank and climbed out. He was strongly built and athletic, on the brink of manhood. She watched him run around to the bridge. It was a pretty stone bridge, built of the same pale-yellow Dorset stone as the houses in the town. Freddie climbed up onto the edge and stood tall. His father had told him on many occasions not to dive, in case his head hit the bottom. But Freddie was a good diver and knew how to keep it shallow. He put his hands in the air, checked that Grace was watching, then bent his legs and sprang off. His dive was straight, his body stiff, his head between his arms. Grace caught her breath as he sliced through the water, just below the surface. A moment later his head appeared like a duck and she clapped wildly.

'No one dives better than you, Freddie!' she cried.

He swam over to join her. 'No one applauds louder than you, Grace!' He waded out and went to sit on the bank in the sun to dry. She followed and laid her towel on the grass beside him.

'You're brave in the water,' she said, sitting down.

Her comment pleased him and he grinned at her broadly. The sun had made his freckles come up and he was a little red across the bridge of his nose. 'So, not a big girl then, after all!' he joked.

She nudged him playfully. 'Of course not. I was only teasing. You *did* make a fuss about the sting, though.'

He laughed and held her eyes for an extended moment. A sudden shyness crept over them and they both felt strangely awkward. He turned to look out over the river.

'Hungry?' she asked.

'Not really. I've just had my dinner.'

'Me too.' She lay on her back and closed her eyes. 'Ah, this is nice.'

He lay back as well. The heat spread over his body and dried the water that had collected in drops in the dip of his belly. 'Nothing nicer than a lazy afternoon,' he said. They lay a while in silence. Grace found her mind wandering back to the morning at the church and the thought of Rufus made her feel warm inside.

'Freddie, what are you going to be when you're a grown-up?' she asked after a while.

'Work on the land. As long as I'm not inside doing a boring desk job like Dad, I don't really mind. Why?'

'Rufus asked me this morning. He asked me whether I was going to be a beekeeper.'

Freddie's mood deflated at the mention of Rufus Melville. 'What did you say?'

'I said yes. I think it's a nice life looking after bees.'

'It doesn't really matter what you do, because you're a girl. With any luck you'll marry a rich man to keep you,' he said grudgingly.

Grace rolled onto her stomach. 'Chance would be a fine thing! Girls like me don't marry rich men, Freddie!' She laughed carelessly and plucked a daisy.

Freddie sat up. 'I'll look after you, Grace,' he said in a rush of enthusiasm. Grace looked surprised. 'I know I'm only fifteen. But one day, when we're older, I'll look after you.' She frowned; she had never thought she'd need looking after. At fourteen she hadn't ever contemplated life beyond the present where she lived very contentedly with her father, and as for being looked after, she would say she cared for her father as much as he cared for her.

She smiled softly and twirled the daisy between her finger and thumb. 'You're adorable, Freddie.'

'I'll work hard, make lots of money, and buy you anything you like,' he said, warming to his subject.

Although Grace was younger than Freddie, she sometimes felt older. Being motherless, she had had to grow up faster than other girls in order to look after her father. She now smiled at Freddie in the indulgent way adults do when children share impossible dreams. 'That's nice,' she replied. 'I'd like a red dress, then.'

'A red dress? Why red?'

'Because there's something wild about red, don't you think? It's a wicked colour. Nice girls like me don't wear red.'

He grinned. 'Then I'll buy you a red dress.'

'Good.' She rested her head on her arms and closed her eyes. 'You'd better think of doing something other than working on the land, then, because Dad works on the land and he doesn't earn much.'

'Your father doesn't care to be rich. Mum says he's content just to be. But I'm ambitious. I'll run the entire estate one day, you'll see.'

'That *is* ambitious.'

'If you don't aim high in life you won't get anywhere.'

She giggled. 'Who told you that?'

'Dad.'

'Well, he's right, I suppose. Anyway, by the time you're old enough to get a job, Mr Garner might be dead so there'll be space for you.'

'Old Peg Leg.' He closed his eyes and thought of Mr Garner who had lost his leg at Ypres. 'I suspect an old walrus like him will go on for ever.'

'Do you think you'd be brave in war, Freddie?' she asked, thinking of the war her father had fought in but never spoke of.

'I don't know.'

She laughed, remembering his bee sting. She didn't imagine he'd be brave at all. 'I suppose it's hard to tell until you're there,' she said tactfully.

'I hope I'd be brave,' he said.

'God willing, we'll never know,' said Grace, and she pushed the talk of Hitler's menacing manoeuvres that she heard on the wireless and read about in the papers to the back of her mind.

They ate their sandwiches as the early evening light grew mellow. Grace suggested she'd better be getting home to help her father in the garden. She felt guilty lying about all day like a lady of leisure, even though it was Sunday. They slowly made their way back through the village with their wet bathing suits rolled up in their towels. Grace's hair had dried into thick curls that tumbled down her back and the sun had bronzed her arms and chest to a warm honey colour and turned her cheeks pink. When they reached Freddie's house she put her towel in her bicycle basket and made to leave. 'Will I see you tomorrow?' she asked.

'I'm going to help out with the harvest,' Freddie said. 'Mum says I'm old enough now and they'll pay me.'

'So you'll be busy?'

'Yes, I meant to tell you.'

Grace was a little disappointed she was going to lose her playmate. 'Well, they always need more hands,' she reasoned.

'I'm going to see Mr Garner tomorrow and put myself forward.'

'Careful he doesn't see you have your eye on his job!'

He laughed. 'I don't imagine he'll see *me* as a threat.'

'Not if he sees you getting stung by a bee!' With that, she began to pedal off.

'You're never going to let me forget that, are you?' he shouted after her.

'No!' she shouted back, laughing. 'Buzz buzz buzz!'

On the way back to the cottage, Grace stopped to look at the big house again. This time there was only the Alfa Romeo parked outside. It gave her a frisson of pleasure to think that Rufus was still at home and she wondered what he was doing in that enormous house. With all those rooms to choose from, how did he decide which one to sit in?

When she reached the cottage she was surprised to see the Marquess's grand black Bentley parked on the grass in front. It looked incongruous there, all gleaming metal and glass, beside the rustic simplicity of the thatched house. She wondered what Lord Penselwood wanted with her father and where the chauffeur had gone. He usually sat in the motor car in his hat and gloves, looking important.

She pushed open the door to find the little stone hall crowded with people. When she saw that one of them was Rufus, her heart stalled before hastily spluttering to life again. She was immediately self-conscious in her crumpled dress with her unbrushed hair hanging in damp tendrils down her back. 'Ah, there you are,' said Rufus happily, as if he'd been looking for her. He took off his hat.

'Grace?' enquired her father, shooting her a bewildered look.

Grace glanced at the frail woman who was holding onto Rufus's arm and realized with a sinking feeling why they had come. 'Good afternoon, Lady Penselwood,' she said shyly, not sure whether or not to curtsy. The Dowager Marchioness didn't respond. Grace turned to Rufus.

'Grandmama doesn't hear very well so you have to shout like this: She said good afternoon, Grandmama.' He raised his voice in his grandmother's ear.

The old lady looked Grace up and down with large, hooded eyes and gave a little sniff. 'So you're Mr Hamblin's daughter, are you?'

'Yes, m'lady.'

'Do you have green fingers as well?'

'I'm learning,' Grace replied.

'From the very best, my dear. Ah, the wonders I created with your father's guidance and expertise, and now I'm reduced to a sedentary life and can only look from afar and imagine what more could be done in those borders. At least I have my greenhouses. Yes, I'm not too crippled to enjoy *those.*'

'Shall we go through? I think my grandmother should sit down,' Rufus suggested.

'Please,' said Arthur, leading them into the sitting room. He raised his eyebrows enquiringly but Grace didn't have time to explain.

Rufus was so tall that he had to bend his head to pass beneath the door frame. 'What a nice place you have,' he commented jovially, sweeping his eyes over the room. 'Very cosy in winter I suspect, with the fire lit. Goodness, look at all your books. You must be an avid reader, Mr Hamblin.'

'Where are the bees?' asked the Dowager Marchioness, scanning the room impatiently. Her voice was unexpectedly shrill for her small, birdlike frame.

'Hopefully not in here,' Rufus replied dryly.

'They're outside,' Grace interjected. She watched Rufus settle his grandmother into an armchair, then take a seat on the sofa and cross his legs with a satisfied sigh. He was much too big for that small room. Beside him her father looked like a dwarf. Grace perched at the other end of the sofa as her father sank uneasily into his favourite chair opposite Lady Penselwood.

'So, you'd like to look at the bees, Lord Melville?' Arthur asked, trying to understand why he suddenly had the honour of their company.

'Not exactly,' Rufus replied slowly. He glanced at Grace and smiled apologetically. 'Your daughter told me that bee stings cure arthritis and I happened to mention it at lunch. Grandmama suffers terribly, so I thought . . .' He looked at his grandmother. 'Well, *she* thought, to be more accurate, that she'd like to give it a go.'

'But bee stings are very painful,' Arthur explained anxiously. 'Not to mention dangerous. I've known people bedridden for a week with swellings.' Grace remembered Freddie and the fuss he had made, and felt a twinge of guilt.

'It's a trifle,' said the Dowager Marchioness stoically. Grace and her father caught each other's eye.

Arthur kneaded his hands. 'I'd hate to be responsible for your discomfort, Lady Penselwood,' he began. 'I'm really not sure it's wise. You might have an allergy, for example.'

She stared at her gardener imperiously. 'What did you say?' she demanded. Arthur raised his voice and repeated his sentence. 'Nonsense!' she trilled. 'I've never heard anything so silly. I won't hold you responsible, young man.' Grace stifled a giggle. Her father was in his forties. 'So, where are they, these bees?'

Grace looked at the old woman's hands and realized that her arthritis was nothing like the mild stiffness her father suffered. Her fingers resembled the claws of an old crow. They looked very painful, too. She felt a stab of compassion and hoped that the bees would cure her. If they did, Rufus would think very highly of her – but if they didn't? She felt the sweat collecting in beads on her forehead. Rufus smiled at her encouragingly. 'Well, let's go and set the bees on Grandmama!'

Arthur led them into the sunshine and round to the hives, which were shaded by plane trees and placed in a row along the side of a border thick with bee-loving sedum, angelica and potentilla. Rufus put his hat on and walked slowly with his grandmother leaning heavily on his arm. 'What a charming little cottage. I've never been here before,' he said. 'You've done wonderful things to your garden.'

'Your father knows every inch of the estate,' interjected Lady Penselwood stridently. 'And so should you. It's your duty, Rufus.' She said the word *duty* with emphasis, as if little else mattered in life but that.

'Yes, yes, Grandmama,' he replied, dismissing her effectively with his weary tone.

'I'd be very surprised if Arthur Hamblin's garden was anything less than marvellous,' she continued. 'He's the best gardener Walbridge has ever had, and we've had a few.'

'Thank you, m'lady,' said Arthur humbly. 'You're much too kind.'

Rufus grinned. 'I assure you, Grandmama is not at all kind. If she says you're a genius, you must be nothing less,' he said, his voice low enough for his grandmother to miss it. 'Ah, the hives. Good.'

Lady Penselwood looked them up and down with an imperious gaze. 'So, what do I do? Put my hand in?' she asked.

'No, no, m'lady. I place a bee on your hand and let it sting you,' Arthur explained. 'If you're . . .'

'Good God, young man, it's only a sting. It's not going to blow my hand off, is it?' She gave an impatient snort and held out her claw. 'Go on, then. Let the bee do its worst.'

Grace winced as her father placed a bee on the bony joints and made it sting her by covering it with his hand. The old lady didn't even flinch. Arthur wasn't sure she had been stung until he looked at the red mark and the ensuing swelling. The bee flew off, but Grace knew it would die and suffered a moment of anguish. Rufus looked at her and arched an eyebrow. 'Well, that was painless,' he said. Then raising his voice he turned to his grandmother. 'How does that feel, Grandmama?'

'I hope it's doing some good. Are you sure I don't need another one?'

'Absolutely sure,' Arthur replied. 'One should do the trick.'

'Well then, I'll pray for a miracle.'

'So will I,' Rufus agreed. Grace wanted to offer garlic to stop the pain, but she sensed that Lady Penselwood would refuse. She was certainly made of tougher stuff than Freddie. She couldn't wait to tell him.

Rufus walked his grandmother round to the Bentley and helped her into her seat. Grace was impressed by the soft leather and shiny wood interior. She had never been so close to such a motor car in all her life. It was like a rare and beautiful beast. 'Thank you, Grace, for your advice. If it works you'll have the whole of the county queuing up to be stung.' Grace felt a stab of panic and blanched. If the whole county came to be stung, how many bees would die? Rufus laughed. 'Don't worry, I'm only teasing,' he said, his face suddenly creasing into a frown. 'Few are made of steel like Grandmama!'

'She is very brave,' Grace agreed.

'They should have sent women like Grandmama to the front line. We might have won the war sooner.' He chuckled at the thought. 'Well, I'll let you know if it works. Now I'll need a miracle to get her back into the house without my parents finding out. I'm not sure they'd wholly approve of this rather unorthodox treatment.'

Grace and Arthur watched him drive off. He waved cheerfully while his grandmother sat stony-faced, staring ahead. 'What was that all about?' Arthur asked his daughter once they had disappeared into the lane.

'I simply mentioned that you allowed yourself to be stung on purpose to cure your arthritis,' she explained. 'I never thought anything would come of it.'

'When did you talk to Lord Melville?'

'Outside church, this morning. I was lying on the grass, playing with a bee, and he came up and said hello.' She paused. 'Do you think it'll work?'

'It might do. It certainly helps me.' He walked back into the cottage. 'Old Lady Penselwood is a cold fish.'

'Perhaps because she's in pain. Those hands look really bad.'

'Or perhaps because she's just sour.'

'Sour people are unhappy people. You told me that, Dad.'

'I also told you that there are exceptions to every rule,' he replied with a grin.

* * *

Darkness crept up slowly. The twittering of roosting birds grew silent and the flute-like calling of a cuckoo was replaced by the eerie hooting of an owl. Arthur sat in his chair, smoking his pipe, reading glasses on the bridge of his nose, a history book on his knee. His spaniel snoozed at his feet. Grace stared at the pages of her novel, but although her eyes scanned the words, her thoughts were elsewhere. It had been a shock to find Rufus in her hall, but now he had gone, she found herself going over every moment of their encounter and wishing she had behaved differently.

She was only fourteen, so there was no reason why a young man like Rufus Melville should even notice her. But since he had spoken to her, and not as a man speaks to a child, but as equals, she wished she had been somehow wittier. There was a light tone to his voice that suggested he found most things amusing. She wondered what sort of repartee he was used to with his friends at Oxford. She imagined they were all very clever, like him, and witty, too. She could be funny with Freddie. He thought everything she said was clever, but with Rufus she had felt gauche, immature and self-conscious. And her hair – oh, how she wished he hadn't seen her with her hair wet and tangled.

She closed her book with a sigh. Her father raised his eyes over his glasses. 'You all right, Gracey?'

'Yes, Dad. I think I'll go upstairs now. I'm rather sleepy.'

'Too much sun. That's what it does to you, dries up all your energy.'

She bent over him and kissed his cheek. 'Night, Dad.'

'God bless,' he replied, patting her gently. 'Sweet dreams.'

A little later she knelt by her bed and prayed. She prayed for her father and for her mother who was in God's keeping. She prayed for Freddie, Auntie May and Uncle Michael; for Freddie's sister, Josephine, even though she didn't like her very much, and she prayed for Rufus. Her prayer for Rufus went on and on. It was more like a confession than a prayer.

When she climbed into bed she lay on her side, staring into the black-and-white photograph of her parents that she kept in a frame on her bedside table. Her mother had a long face, like hers, and deep-set hazel eyes, although one couldn't tell the colour from the photograph. They just looked dark. She had a kind face. The sort of face one could trust to keep secrets. Grace was sure that, were she alive, she would listen to her daughter with understanding and indulgence, and Grace would tell her everything. She would sit on Grace's bed and stroke her cheek and gaze at her lovingly. She might laugh at the absurdity of Grace's infatuation, but she wouldn't make her feel ashamed. She wouldn't belittle it. Of course, nothing would ever come of a crush such as this. But there was no harm in admiring him. It made Grace happy to think that he was in the world. Happier still that he knew *she* was in it, too.

So Grace whispered the contents of her heart to the one person she could trust to understand.

Chapter 6

The following morning Grace was in the garden picking vegetables for lunch when the black Bentley rumbled onto the grass in front of the cottage. She stood up and wiped her hands on her apron. Her heart began to thump hard against her ribcage. Like a fist, it was, and her stomach felt as if it were full of bees. She put her hand up to shield her eyes from the sun. To her surprise she saw the chauffeur climb out and walk towards her. 'Miss Grace,' he said. His tone was officious.

'That's me,' she replied.

'I've been sent by the Dowager Lady Penselwood. She requests your presence most urgently.'

Grace felt sick. She envisaged all sorts of terrible things that might have happened as a consequence of the bee sting. Perhaps the old lady's hand had swollen so badly that she was now in greater pain. She wished her father could come with her, but he was working in the gardens up at the Hall and there wasn't time to find him. Why couldn't someone have summoned him instead? After all, he was already there?

'Does she want me to come now?' It was a silly question, for clearly the lady demanded her presence immediately.

'Most urgently, were her words, Miss Grace.'

Grace hurried into the house to change out of her slacks into a frock, wash her hands and pin up her hair. As hard as she scrubbed she couldn't shift the mud from beneath her nails. She wished she had a mother or a grandmother to go in her place. More than ever in her life she wished she wasn't the woman of the house. When she emerged the chauffeur was holding the back door open for her. He looked solemn under his cap. For a fleeting moment she felt uplifted by the thought of Rufus and what he'd have to say about the chauffeur. She was sure he'd find his seriousness amusing.

The motor car purred like a big cat. Grace watched the countryside whizz past, but she was much too nervous to take pleasure in the birds diving in and out of the hedgerows. At last they turned into the entrance of Walbridge Hall and passed smoothly through the grand iron gates. On either side, set high upon stone pedestals, were two statues of a lion and dragon, their faces frozen into mighty roars. Her fear mounted as the car swept up the gentle curve of the drive and the magnificent house came into view. It was even more splendid close up, with its many glass windows twinkling in the sunshine, and tall gables rising into imposing chimneys. Her throat went dry at the thought of having to walk inside on her own and she wished more than ever that she was up on the hill, at the foot of the woods, watching from afar.

The motor car drew up and the chauffeur switched off the engine. Without a word he climbed out onto the gravel and opened her door. She stepped out unsteadily and waited to be told what to do, fidgeting nervously with her bitten-down fingernails. She glanced at a couple of gardeners in brown overalls clipping the yew hedge. One of them paused his cutting to watch her. She hoped she might see her father, but he didn't appear.

She didn't need to wait long. They were obviously expecting her. The great door of the house opened slowly like a terrifying mouth about to swallow her in one gulp. She stifled her fear, expecting a butler, as formidable as the chauffeur, to summon her inside. To her great relief Rufus appeared, grinning in his usual cheerful way, and ran down the steps two at a time towards her. 'Hello, Grace. I hope we haven't taken you away from something important,' he said, his dark eyes sparkling at her.

She wanted to cry with happiness, for surely if something dreadful had happened Rufus wouldn't be smiling at her so joyfully. 'I was picking vegetables,' she replied, then wished she had lied and said something more interesting.

'Then you must be thirsty. Johnson,' he shouted up to the waiting butler. 'Please bring Miss Grace some juice. We'll be in the garden room.'

Rufus looked casual in a sleeveless Fair Isle pullover of pale rusts and browns, his blue shirt rolled up at the sleeves to reveal muscular forearms and an elegant gold watch with a leather strap. A gold signet ring glinted on his little finger as he put his hand on her back to lead her up the steps into the hall. It was a vast room with a fireplace so large that Grace's entire bed would have fitted inside it. The hall table was ablaze with the most stunning arrangement of lilies, and Persian rugs covered the flagstone floor, threadbare from centuries of footsteps. A dark wooden staircase swept up to an arresting portrait of an ancestor in a suit of armour before dividing into two and joining a gallery on opposite sides of the hall. 'That's great-great-great grandfather Aldrich,' said Rufus, nodding towards the portrait. 'And a fine figure of a man he was, too. Aldrich means "king", but still, I'd rather be named after a pauper than be called Aldrich. Poor Papa: of all the family names to choose, his parents chose the most ridiculous!'

Grace laughed, but she couldn't think of anything clever to say. 'I like his armour,' she replied, feeling foolish.

'So do I. It's hanging in the games room. I used to dress up in it as a boy, but I'm much too tall for it now. Funny how small people were in those days. Much smaller than one imagines.'

'He doesn't look small at all.'

'Not there. Perhaps the painter was keen to curry favour and painted him looking bigger than he actually was.'

Grace was now feeling much more comfortable. In fact, she was almost dizzy with happiness, being shown around the house by Rufus. It was as impressive inside as it was outside. He showed her the other portraits hanging around the hall. They all had funny names like Winthrop and Morven, except the one that was called Rufus. 'I'm named after him,' said Rufus, screwing up his nose. 'I'm not sure why, considering he's the least handsome of the lot.'

'I think Rufus is a nice name. You could have been called Broderick.'

He chuckled. 'That would have been a terrible fate. Come on, I don't suppose we can keep Grandmama waiting much longer.'

Grace felt afraid again. She took a sharp intake of breath and must have paled, for Rufus grinned at her kindly. He leaned down and whispered in her ear. 'Don't worry, Grace, deep down she's as soft as a pussycat. She's in a good mood this morning, so she's positively purring.' He directed her down a long corridor. They passed a room on the right which immediately caught Grace's attention. It was a square room with bookshelves either side of a marble fireplace, but instead of books, row upon row of model boats were placed beneath glass covers. There were hundreds. 'My father's study,' said Rufus, pausing a moment at the open door. 'Papa is mad about boats. It must have been a bore to inherit a house in the middle of the countryside when all he wants to do is sail. Have you ever sailed, Grace?'

'No, I think I'd be a little nervous of the sea,' she replied.

'Rubbish, you'd love it. Papa taught me how to sail as a little boy. There's something magical about the ocean.' She swept her eyes over the paintings which adorned the other walls. They were all of seaside scenes: sailing boats on blue seas, azure skies with soaring white seagulls, busy harbours, sand dunes and swathes of pink roses.

Reluctantly, she pulled herself away and followed Rufus further down the corridor into a large conservatory at the end, which looked over the glorious gardens of Walbridge Hall. There, seated in regal splendour on a wicker garden chair, with a small fluffy dog on her lap, was the Dowager Marchioness. When she saw Grace her wizened old face was transformed by an unexpectedly warm smile.

'Ah, come over here, my dear, and let me thank you.' She held out her hand. Grace stepped forward and took it shyly, bobbing into a curtsy, because she felt the Dowager Marchioness demanded more than a polite nod of the head. 'Look!' The old lady waved her hand. It was no longer bent into a claw. 'Barely any pain this morning. The swelling is down. You're a good little doctor, aren't you?'

'I'm happy it's better, m'lady,' Grace replied, surprised that the bee venom had worked so effectively.

'Speak up, child. I can't hear if you whisper.'

'I'm happy it's better,' she repeated, louder this time.

'So am I,' said the Dowager Marchioness.

'Thank you, Johnson,' said Rufus, taking a glass of juice off the tray. The butler departed with a little bow. 'For you, Grace. Strawberry and raspberry juice. It's rather good. I had some for breakfast.'

'The fruit is from the garden,' said Lady Penselwood. 'We have a splendid vegetable garden, but you know that of course, being Arthur Hamblin's daughter. Gardening used to be my hobby before arthritis set in and stopped me enjoying myself. Perhaps those bees will save my hands and I can be useful again.' She raised her eyebrows at Grace. Grace swallowed her juice. It was the most delicious thing she had ever tasted. She felt she should say something, but wasn't sure what.

Rufus cut in, defusing any awkwardness. 'Grandmama so enjoyed being stung, she'd like to do it again.'

'Oh, really, Rufus. You *are* a ridiculous boy. A person doesn't enjoy being stung, ever. One simply endures the pain for the rewards to come. It's like life, Rufus. One endures it for the promise of paradise and the joys of Heaven.'

'I wouldn't say life is to be endured, Grandmama,' he retorted, sitting down opposite her. 'I'd argue that it offers a lot of pleasure.'

'I dare say, for a young, pleasure-seeking boy such as yourself. When you are old, Rufus, and look back over your life, you will see a bumpy road of pleasure and pain. The past will be strewn with misfortune and mishaps, not to mention the terrible losses of people dear to you. You will have to endure their loss . . .'

'Like yours, Grandmama,' he interrupted, his mouth curling mischievously. 'I shall be very sorry when it's your time to go.' Grace feared he had gone one step too far, but his grandmother smiled, clearly finding amusement in his bluntness.

'I dare say you will. I hope you enjoy a long life, dear boy, but to outlive the people you love is not necessarily something to be celebrated. One endures but one never recovers. Miss Hamblin, I remember when your dear mama died. You were too young to know her, which is a great shame. She was a sweet girl.' Grace's cheeks flushed as pink as her juice. The Dowager Marchioness acknowledged Grace's tragedy with a grunt. 'Who brought you up?'

'My father.'

'On his own?' Lady Penselwood narrowed her eyes and gave a disapproving sniff.

'Yes, m'lady.'

'Good gracious. I commend him. Not an easy task, bringing up a child on one's own, especially for a man. Men are useless in the nursery.'

'He was helped. Auntie May helped,' Grace interjected, hoping Lady Penselwood might approve of that.

She did. 'Family. You see, one simply can't exist without family.' Grace didn't feel like telling her that Auntie May was a distant relative and not really family at all. She called her Auntie because she had been as close to her mother as a sister. 'Grandparents?'

'Yes, m'lady. My grandmother helped when I was little.'

This pleased Lady Penselwood enormously. 'Grandmothers, there's no substituting them. Now Rufus here has always taken great trouble with me.'

'Trouble being the operative word, Grandmama. You've always been trouble.'

She chuckled. 'When one is a grandmother, one is entitled to say exactly what one thinks. I endured years of keeping my thoughts to myself. Now that I am old and there is no one in the family above me, I have the right to speak my mind.'

'And you most certainly do,' he added wryly.

'Now, I would like to endure another sting. On the other hand. What do you say, Miss Hamblin?'

Grace was too young and unimportant to speak *her* mind, so she had no choice but to agree to the unfortunate killing of yet another precious bee. 'Would you like me to find one in your garden?' she volunteered dutifully.

'That's a splendid idea. Rufus, show her the lavender. There are always plenty of bees on that.'

'As I'm a pleasure-seeking man, Grandmama, it will give me nothing but pleasure to show Grace the garden.' He stood up. 'Come on then, Grace. Let's go outside and enjoy the sunshine.'

'Take Amber, here,' said his grandmother, gently pushing the dog off her knee. 'She's been inside all morning. It's about time she did her business.' Reluctantly, the white Maltese followed Rufus and Grace into the garden, where it soon disappeared into a bush.

'So you see, two miracles in one day,' said Rufus, putting on a pair of sunglasses.

'What's the other one?' Grace asked.

'Mama and Papa have gone up to London. They're going to the theatre tonight.' When Grace didn't reply he added, 'I didn't want them to know about Grandmama's sting, you see. They'd think I was brutal.'

'Your grandmother doesn't think you brutal at all.'

'*She* doesn't, no. But Mama is a different kettle of fish. She'd think it was all a lot of hocus-pocus and there'd be a great deal of tutting and rolling her eyes and "Really, Rufus, can't you think of something better to do with your time?" She finds her mother-in-law tiresome and demanding, which of course she is. Even though she thinks the old girl is about to pop off at any moment, and is rather wishing she'd exit sooner rather than later, she'd find the idea of a bee sting on purpose barbaric and do her best to stop her. There'd be the most almighty row and I'd be in the middle of it, as usual, trying to keep them apart. It's bad enough that they live in the same house. Two devilishly strong women standing their ground; it's hopeless. That's why Mama disappears to London as much as possible. Grandmama likes to stay here, rattling around in this big old house all on her own.'

'And you? Do you like rattling around in it, too?'

'I don't rattle much. I fill it with friends. Much less rattling that way.' Grace laughed at his turn of phrase. 'Now, this is the vegetable garden.'

He pushed a wooden gate cut into an old, weathered stone wall. It opened into a vast garden in the middle of which was an orchard of various fruit trees, planted equidistantly. The borders were immaculate. From the air, Grace thought, it would look like a kaleidoscope of harmonious shapes, one side the mirror image of the other. She counted three gardeners working away among the vegetables, weeding and picking, but none was her father. She wondered what he'd make of her being shown around by Rufus Melville. At the far end there stood two enormous palaces made out of glass. Grace longed to go in and have a look, but was too shy to ask. She'd have to ask her father about them later.

'Now, where is the lavender?' Rufus asked.

'Over there.' Grace pointed to the wall. One entire side was taken up by a thick strip of it.

'Gracious! What does she do with all this lavender?'

'Maybe she makes lavender bags,' Grace suggested.

'What are they?'

Pleased she knew something he didn't, she enlightened him. 'Then you put them with your clothes to make them smell nice, or hang them from the bedpost to help you sleep.'

'Just what I need. I have terrible trouble sleeping. I'm too excitable, that's the trouble. Counting sheep doesn't work because they all start bickering about who's going to jump over the fence first. I don't think it works for anybody. It's a silly myth.'

'Lavender works.'

He shook his head. 'I don't think it would work for me, sweet Grace. I'm a lost cause.'

They walked over to the bushes. 'Look at all those bees,' he exclaimed. 'Big, fat, clumsy ones and small, lean, agile ones. They're very busy, aren't they?'

'It's the honey bee we need for your grandmother.'

'How are we going to get it to her?'

'That's easy. I'm sure one of your gardeners has a flower-pot we could use. I don't want to frighten the bee by carrying it in my hands.'

Rufus called to one of the gardeners. While the man hurried off to get a pot, he crouched down to watch the bees. 'Extraordinary, aren't they?'

'They're the most brilliant creatures,' Grace agreed, and before she could stop herself she began to share her knowledge with great enthusiasm. By the time the gardener returned, Grace had told Rufus the differences between the honey bee and the bumblebee and how the honey bee dances to communicate the location of food sources to other bees. Rufus listened with interest. He seemed impressed by how much she knew.

'You really are a little bee, aren't you?'

She laughed. 'I love them, that's all.'

'I can't think of a nicer thing to love,' he said, grinning at her as a brother might smile on a cherished younger sister.

Grace set about preparing the pot. She put some lavender inside, then picked an ear with a bee on it and put that in, too. Finally, she covered the entrance with her hand. She heard the bee buzzing inside, much too busy with the lavender to notice it had been imprisoned. They returned across the lawn to the house to find Lady Penselwood's dog waiting by the conservatory door to be let in.

'Silly animal. It's more like a toy than a dog,' said Rufus. 'Most dogs like going for walks, but not this one. She's been very spoiled. Haven't you, Amber?' He opened the door and let her in.

'Did she do her business?' the Dowager Marchioness asked.

'She did everything,' Rufus lied.

'Good girl!' Lady Penselwood exclaimed. 'Off you go now! Johnson, take her to the kitchen. I don't want her to jump on me with muddy paws.'

Grace brought over the pot. Lady Penselwood put out her hand. Grace hoped the bee wouldn't fly away. Carefully, she lifted it out, still clinging to its piece of lavender. It pained her to place it on the old lady's hand, even more so to squash it onto her skin as her father had done, giving it no choice but to sting and thus end its own life. Once again the Dowager Marchioness didn't react. It was only when Grace saw the sting, and half the creature's abdomen sticking into her flesh, that she realized the deed had been done. She felt her eyes well with tears. In spite of her efforts a fat tear plopped onto the old lady's hand.

'My dear child, don't shed a tear for me,' said Lady Penselwood gently. The old lady seemed surprised by Grace's compassion. 'How old are you, Miss Hamblin?'

'Fourteen,' Grace replied with a sniff.

'You're very grown-up for fourteen. I suppose that comes of having to look after your father. Most girls your age are still playing with their dolls, I should imagine.' Grace put the bee back in the pot and watched it crawl about at the bottom in bewilderment. Another tear fell into the lavender. 'You're a very kind girl. Your bees are making me better and I'm very grateful to you. Now, Cummings will drive you home.' Rufus took the flowerpot and handed it to the butler, who had returned with a silver coffee pot on a tray. 'Good, my mid-morning coffee. Don't be alarmed, Johnson, it's a little bee sting. A mere trifle. I can't feel a thing.'

Rufus escorted Grace into the hall. Before opening the door he turned to her, a troubled expression clouding his face. 'You're upset because of the bee, aren't you?' He looked down at her sympathetically. 'So it's true that bees die when they sting?'

She nodded. 'Not all bees, but the female honey bee, yes.'

'Silly Grandmama thought you were crying because it had hurt *her*, but I knew better. You love those bees, don't you?'

'Yes, I do.' She took a deep breath.

'I'm sorry we had to kill another one. I tell you what, we'll make a deal. We'll keep this secret so you don't have all the ladies in the county killing bees to cure their arthritis. I'll make sure Grandmama doesn't tell any of her friends. If they notice her hands, we'll make something up. She whacked me for being insolent, for example. What do you think?'

'That's a good deal,' she replied gratefully.

'Now, no more tears. Those bees are in heaven now, where they can sting to their heart's content, to no consequence.' She nodded. 'Come, I'll drive you back. It doesn't feel right leaving you to the mercy of Cummings' ill humour.

In all the years I've known him I haven't seen him smile once, and that's not for want of trying. I've often wondered whether he has some terrible affliction that prevents his mouth from widening. But I doubt it. I think he's just sour, like a lemon. In fact, from now on I'm going to call him Lemon.' Grace laughed and wiped her eyes. 'That's better. Now I'll give you a ride in my Alfa Romeo. It's much more exciting than Papa's boring old Bentley.'

Rufus was right. His open-topped motor car was much more exciting than the Bentley. With the wind raking through her hair and Rufus by her side, Grace didn't think she'd ever been so happy. She wanted to laugh out loud. Rufus turned and grinned at her and those dark, kind eyes twinkled with affection. In that moment time seemed to stand still and allow her to commit his face to memory. She blinked and he turned his gaze back to the lane, but Grace would treasure that look for years to come, like a picture postcard imprinted on her memory and secretly cherished.

'Look after those bees, now,' he said as she climbed out of the car.

'I will,' she replied and thanked him for driving her home. He smiled and motored into the lane. She remained there long after the car had disappeared, trying to make sense of the strange longing that pulled on the tender strings of her heart.

Chapter 7

Tekanasset Island, Massachusetts, 1973

'Grace?' It was Freddie. He walked out onto the veranda with his habitual glass of gin and tonic, followed by the dogs. 'What are you doing sitting here all on your own?' he asked.

'Watching the sunset,' she replied, sighing for the past that now slipped away with the sun.

'May I join you?'

'Sure.'

He sat down beside her on the swing chair and swirled the ice around his glass. 'Where's Trixie?'

'She's gone to a beach party.'

'With that boy, I suppose.'

'Yes, Jasper.'

'I don't like it,' he said, taking a swig. 'I don't like it at all.'

'But you didn't stop her seeing him.'

'Because I knew how upset *you* would be.'

'That's very considerate.' She smiled, silently forgiving him for interrupting her reverie.

'And I don't want a fight on my hands. You rein a horse in and it will only want to bolt. Give it a loose rein and most likely it'll put its head to the ground and graze.'

'I hope you're right.'

She dropped her gaze into her empty wine glass. 'I was remembering the first time you got stung by a bee.'

Freddie's jaw stiffened. 'I've never liked bees, as you know,' he said, taking another swig. He didn't relish talking about the past. It was as if he had wilfully left it behind when he moved to America all those years ago.

Grace sighed and stared out over the ocean. 'Sunsets make me sad, but in a nice way,' she said, suddenly feeling very alone, for Freddie wouldn't understand the bittersweet blend of pleasure and pain.

'What's nice about being sad?' he asked.

She smiled wistfully. 'It gives me pleasure to think of my father, but it hurts too, because I miss him.'

'He was a good man, your father,' Freddie acknowledged, nodding thoughtfully.

'He was all I had,' she said softly. In the old days Freddie would have replied, 'You have me, too.' But that Freddie had gone, like her father.

'Then nothing good comes from thinking about him,' he said.

Grace felt the need to take Freddie's hand. When they'd been young, she would have held it and he would have squeezed hers affectionately. But the war had changed him. It was as if he had left his love on the battlefield with his eye. Gone was the tenderness. Buried deep were his recollections of happier times. Fierce was his determination never to look back. He was no longer playful, but serious and troubled. In the early days of his homecoming it was as if he resented her for not understanding what he'd been through, even though he never gave her a chance to understand by sharing his experiences. He had shut her out and she had felt shunned.

But they had remained together. Duty was the bond that tied them to each other, bitterness the impediment that kept them apart.

But he had mellowed a little over the years. His resentment had eased into a less aggressive form of detachment. A politeness of sorts, which, although desperately inadequate for a passionate woman like Grace, was something she could live with, not unhappily. Moments of unexpected ardour had brought him to her bed, only for her to find herself deliberately disregarded in the morning as he buried his face in the newspaper and sipped his coffee, settling back into the security of routine. As long as he didn't deviate from the mechanical rituals of that routine, Grace knew he felt safe from intimacy. She often wondered whether things would have been different if Freddie had come back from the war with open arms and an open heart. If she had felt loved by him she wouldn't have pined so.

'But I had you,' she said, and hoped that he'd respond to the encouragement in her smile and perhaps look at her with the eyes of the boy she had grown up with, not with the impassiveness of the man he had become.

Instead he finished his drink and stood up. 'Shall we eat? I'm starving.'

She turned her thoughts to dinner; anything rather than dwell on the hurt his coldness inflicted. 'Yes, the chicken pie will be ready by now.'

'Good. I want to tell you about my weekend.' His voice was injected with enthusiasm as he turned the conversation around to work. Grace took the pie out of the oven. She had no choice but to listen. There was no place in Freddie's life for sentimentality; somehow the war had taken that, too.

* * *

Trixie ran down to the beach. The party had already begun. A crowd of people were standing around a huge fire on the beach in front of the club wearing summer dresses and open-neck shirts, drinking sangria, their animated faces illuminated by the orange glow of the flames. She looked around for Jasper, but caught the energetic waving of her friend Suzie instead. 'So how much trouble were you in?' Suzie asked when Trixie joined her.

'I thought it would be worse. That Lucy Durlacher's a snitch!'

Suzie grinned triumphantly. 'But guess who chatted her up this morning in the diner?'

'George,' Trixie replied, grinning.

'Correct. I suggest we encourage that as much as we can.'

'Mrs Durlacher would have a fit if she knew.'

'Let's hope the relationship is given a chance to blossom before she finds out. That way the impact will be all the more horrible.'

'You're terrible, Suzie.'

'Don't pretend you don't want to inflict the greatest pain on Evelyn Durlacher!'

'My mom is a great believer in karma.'

'What goes around, comes around. Well, I'm just helping it along.'

'She'll reap what she's sowed, whether we help it along or not. Where are they anyway?' She scanned her eyes over the faces of people she had known all her life.

'They're coming. They promised they would. Oh, I'm totally mad for Ben. If he doesn't throw me up against a wall and kiss me soon, I think I'll die!' She tossed her sun-bleached hair and sighed melodramatically. 'English boys are so reserved, it's driving me crazy!'

'There's nothing reserved about Jasper,' said Trixie. 'In fact, he's voracious.'

'Don't make me jealous.'

'Then I won't tell you,' Trixie teased.

'OK, so how far have you gone?'

Trixie's eyes gleamed with jubilation. 'The whole way.' She took Suzie's hands and sprang up and down on the sand. 'He's amazing!'

'Calm down. I want details. How was it?'

Trixie stopped bouncing. 'He makes me feel like a woman,' she said seriously.

'That sounds like a bad song.'

Trixie shrugged. 'There's truth even in bad songs.'

'Was he better than Richard?' Suzie asked, referring to the lover Trixie had had the summer before.

'Oh, forget Richard, Suzie. He was part of my experimental phase. *This* is love.' She lowered her voice. 'Don't breathe a word to anyone. I'm going to go on tour with them in the fall.'

'Has he asked you?'

'No, but he will.'

'Then I'll come too, with Ben,' Suzie suggested.

'That's a great idea!' Trixie exclaimed happily. 'We can go together.'

'Oh, Ben! Where are you?' Both girls looked out over the growing number of people. Suddenly, Suzie pointed to a small group walking towards them up the beach. 'There!' she exclaimed. 'At last!'

'Play it cool, Suzie. Play it real cool!'

Suzie flicked her hair and pinched her cheeks. 'How do I look?'

'Irresistible.' Trixie giggled.

'Just think: you, Jasper, me and Ben, travelling around America in a tour bus. It's just too wonderful.'

'With Lucy and George?' Trixie raised an eyebrow.

'Oh, George will have tired of her by then!' said Suzie, wiggling her denim hot pants and striding off down the beach. 'Or her mother will have sent her to a convent!'

Jasper's face lit up when he saw Trixie. 'Hi, beautiful,' he said, hooking his arm around her neck and pulling her face close so he could kiss her. His guitar hung over his other shoulder, promising a rendition or two, and a cigarette smoked between his fingers. She pressed her lips to his and savoured the taste of beer and tobacco. Suzie walked alongside Ben, her hand slipped into the pocket on the back of his jeans. Ben put his arm around Suzie's waist and asked her how the party was going. Trixie sensed he'd kiss her friend tonight. The idea of travelling around America in their tour bus seemed more real than ever.

They reached Captain Jack's, where the boys started to set up their equipment on the terrace. The girls rushed off to bring them drinks. When they returned, the band was surrounded by miniskirted girls with heaving breasts and starry eyes. They were like bees around a honeypot, Trixie thought resentfully. 'Beers coming through,' she shouted, pushing past them to where George was arranging his drums while Jasper and Ben were soaking up compliments like a pair of happy sponges.

Among the miniskirts was Lucy Durlacher. She had pulled her ash-blonde hair into a ponytail and applied blue eyeshadow. Suzie seized the moment and Lucy's arm. 'Lucy, come over here. Have you seen these drums? They're incredible. Go on, touch one.' Lucy didn't need further encouragement. She stepped forward and put her hand out. George settled his eyes on her. She wasn't beautiful, but she had the appeal of forbidden fruit. When she looked at him her cheeks blushed the colour of cranberries. 'Hi, Lucy,' he said, and she returned his smile with a shy grin.

Suzie turned to Trixie and whispered, 'Well, that wasn't difficult!'

Trixie watched Lucy and George, but only for a moment. She was more concerned about keeping the other girls away from Jasper. He was much too polite to do it for himself.

It wasn't long before Joe Hornby appeared. He strode through the crowd in a flowery shirt and bright-red shorts, puffing exuberantly on a cigar, and took centre stage on the terrace. 'Right, boys, are you ready to play?' he shouted, pleased with the turnout. 'Let's see what the good people of Tekanasset make of you!' He waved his cigar, and somehow the voices hushed around the fire and people turned to listen.

'Ladies and gentleman, good folk of Tekanasset, may I introduce Big Black Rats. You haven't heard of them yet, but soon their names will be as celebrated as their famous countrymen, the Rolling Stones and the Beatles. A fine heritage, indeed. But they're going to go even further. Mark my words, you heard it here first. But enough talk, you can decide for yourselves. Jasper, Ben and George, let's rock!'

The boys began to play. The amplifiers weren't sufficient to carry the sound over the beach, and only those standing close got to hear them adequately. Those at the back gave up after a few minutes and resumed their conversations, while the grown-ups frowned at the unfamiliar sound of modern music. But the young gathered round and soon they were jumping wildly on the sand, arms in the air, bronzed bodies moving to the beat as if possessed.

'So this is what all the excitement is about!' said Evelyn, who had only come to the party to keep an eye on her daughter. She looked very out of place in yellow slacks, a matching yellow twinset and pearls.

'I rather like it,' said Belle. 'The boy's got a good voice.'

Evelyn screwed up her little nose. 'It's good, but not excellent. I think to make it in that industry, you have to be excellent.'

'I disagree, Evelyn. To make it in that industry you just have to be appealing,' Belle argued.

Bill wandered over with a beer, immaculate in blue trousers and pink shirt, his blond hair swept off his face like a schoolboy spruced up by his mother. He was in good spirits, having played tennis all afternoon and only conceded a set. 'Not bad,' he said. 'I've heard worse.'

'I wonder whether Trixie's here, or whether Grace had the good sense to ground her,' Evelyn said, searching the throng of dancing bodies for the girl.

'I meant to tell you I bumped into Freddie this morning, Evelyn,' said Bill.

'What did he say?' she asked, far too curious to bother reproaching him for not having told her earlier.

'It turns out he knew all along that they were going away for the weekend.'

'Really?' said Belle in astonishment. 'And he let her go?'

'Apparently,' Bill answered.

'Well, there's a simple reason for that,' said Evelyn. 'They're not like us.'

'How do you mean, Evelyn?' Belle asked, knowing from Evelyn's tone exactly what she meant.

'They've got no class,' she said, lifting her chin. 'I wouldn't want those boys for our daughter, but for people like the Valentines, those boys are *their* level.' She spoke as if *they* belonged to an entirely different, and inferior, species.

'I must say, I'm surprised at Freddie. I've always thought him a very correct man,' said Belle.

'I've always thought him a very cold man,' Evelyn added.

'He warms up on the golf course,' Bill interjected. 'There's nothing cold about him when he hits a hole in one!'

Evelyn rolled her eyes. 'Right, I've had enough of this music. I'm going home. Bill?'

He sighed his displeasure, but knew it wasn't worth arguing with his wife. 'I've told Lucy to be home by eleven.'

'Then you've got no reason to doubt that she'll be safely tucked up in bed by five past,' said Belle.

Belle enjoyed a good party. Her husband, John, was a great raconteur and loved nothing better than to hold an audience with his stories, usually grossly exaggerated. She wandered around the fire, talking to friends, while John held a small group in his thrall, laughing uproariously at his own punchlines. She watched the young dancing in the golden glow of the flames. They looked like savages, jumping up and down on the sand in bare feet, their naked limbs flailing about to the almost hypnotic rhythm of the drums. Her own children were in their twenties now with families of their own. She was relieved she no longer had to worry about her daughters. It was a hard time to be young, she reflected.

She remained at the party until midnight. By then most of the grown-ups had gone home, leaving only John, with a few of his closest friends, laughing at old stories told a hundred times before. By then the music had stopped. The boys now lounged on the sand with Trixie, Suzie and a few other girls, drinking beer and smoking what smelt suspiciously like weed. Belle looked a little closer. At first she didn't believe the evidence of her own eyes. No, surely not, she thought. It was way past her curfew. But yes, indeed, there was no mistaking the pale hair and pale skin of Lucy Durlacher.

Belle was at heart a *good* person and very aware of her reputation as such. However, Evelyn had offended her tonight. She had known Evelyn all her life, they had been at high school together, and she was well aware and endlessly tolerant of her faults. Yet tonight her snobbishness had grated. Evelyn had never met those boys and the Valentines might not be 'top drawer', as the English would say, but they were kind, *good* people – Belle was particularly fond of Grace. So, instead of doing her duty as a friend to Evelyn, she walked away with John, leaving Lucy on the sand to smoke and flirt into the early hours of the morning.

The small group of young people remained by the fire, which was now reduced to crimson embers revived every now and then by the wind that swept in off the sea. Surrounded by empty beer bottles and cigarette butts they laughed and chatted beneath the full moon, oblivious of the time that ticked towards dawn. The gentle sound of the ocean lulled them into the realm of the unreal, as the waves washed diamonds onto the beach.

George and Lucy sat a little apart from the rest, their heads together, her hair now falling down her back like that of a sleek mermaid. She looked quite pretty in the semi-darkness, her skin having taken on a silvery translucence. They talked in low voices, punctuated by her occasional soft laughter. Trixie inhaled a spliff then passed it on to

Suzie, who sat cross-legged beside Ben. 'Mission accomplished,' she said to her friend, nodding in the direction of George and Lucy.

'A job well done,' Suzie replied. 'Now it's my turn,' she added, passing the spliff to Ben.

Jasper put his hand around the back of Trixie's neck, underneath her hair, and pulled her close to kiss her. 'You look beautiful tonight. Did I tell you?' he whispered.

'No, you didn't,' she replied softly.

'Well, you do.'

'Perhaps there's a dune we can go hide behind,' she suggested, feeling emboldened by the alcohol and cannabis.

'I like the sound of that.' He kissed her neck. 'I'm not sure I can stand sitting next to you for much longer.'

'But if we leave, we'll break up the party.'

'If we leave, the party will get going,' he said. 'Come on.'

They stood up, but none of the others seemed to notice. He took her hand and they wandered up the beach, into the darkness. They fell onto the sand and began to kiss. Trixie felt the warm sensation of desire creeping over her limbs and writhed like a pleasure-seeking cat. Jasper swept her hair off her face and buried himself in her neck. He found her mouth and began to kiss her more ardently as his thumb searched for her breasts, which rose and fell with her excited breath. Trixie was not an innocent; she had lost her inhibitions with the various lovers she had taken since she had slept with her first at the tender age of seventeen. But none of them had aroused her like Jasper. Their chemistry was the perfect blend, rendering every touch exquisite, and she thought she would die for his teasing and slow-stroking. He caressed her belly, causing desperate flutters of anticipation beneath, and then up her thighs and under her skirt, where they traced the cotton of her panties. The flutters in her belly intensified with impatience, and she opened her thighs without reservation, inviting him in.

They made love for a long while, neither of them aware nor much interested in the time. When at last they lay sated and laughing at their daring, they were interrupted by a loud squawking coming from further up the beach. At first they thought it was a seagull, or some other bird in distress. But when they rolled onto their stomachs and looked over the dune to the remains of the fire, they saw the two couples sitting up and staring at a woman with wild hair, in a dressing gown, gesticulating in fury. 'Oh my God,' Trixie hissed. 'That's Lucy's mother!'

'Are you serious?' Jasper checked his watch. In the moonlight he could just make out the hands. It was half past three in the morning.

'I'm telling you. That's Evelyn Durlacher with her hair standing on end!'

Jasper laughed. 'Oh dear, poor Lucy's been caught in flagrante!'

'Her mother's crazy!'

'She *looks* crazy!' Jasper agreed. 'I'm glad I'm not on the receiving end of that.'

They watched as Lucy was unceremoniously pulled up the sand by the arm. Trixie imagined Evelyn had seen all the empty beer bottles. She wondered what else she had seen. Had Lucy and George been making out? It was fortunate that she and Jasper were hidden behind a dune; she couldn't afford to be in any more trouble. 'I think you'd better walk me home,' she said, standing up and wriggling into her panties. When she looked back at the fire she saw that George had disappeared, leaving Ben and Suzie to resume from where they had left off. She took a moment to savour the sight of her friend being kissed by the man of her dreams. She smiled at the thought of their tour. It was all going to be such fun.

Jasper picked up his guitar. 'I've written a song for you,' he said, strumming a few chords. 'Do you want to hear it?'

'I'd love to. I've never inspired a song before.' Trixie sat on the dune and hugged her legs. 'What's it called?'

'Trixie,' he replied and laughed at himself.

'I love it already,' she enthused.

'Sometimes simple is best.' He began to play. She watched, eyes shining with emotion, as he sang to her softly. In that moment, as he sang of longing and desire, she believed she loved him more than she could ever love anyone.

When he finished, he looked at her dreamily. 'So, what do you think?' he asked.

'It's the most beautiful song I've ever heard.'

'Really?' He was incredulous. 'Are you just saying that because it's about you?'

'Well, you *were* truly inspired when you wrote it.'

He laughed and the lines creased around his mouth and eyes. 'You're not wrong, Trixie Valentine.'

'I think I should be your band mascot.'

'I would be honoured,' he replied, standing up and slinging the strap of his guitar over his shoulder. He picked up his jacket. 'Now I'll walk you home.'

'Jasper,' she began.

'Yes?'

'Can I come with you in the fall?'

'Will you parents let you?'

'If they don't, I'll run away with you,' she replied confidently, gazing at him with a starry look in her eyes.

He frowned. 'Do you really mean that?'

'I've never been more sure of anything,' she replied, taking his hand. 'You know, I'd run away with you in a heartbeat.'

'Then you can be my mascot and I'll compose songs for you,' he said. 'All the greatest songs have been inspired by love.'

She looked at him steadily. '*Do* you love me?' she asked.

He nodded slowly. 'I think I do, Trixie.'

'You *think* you do?'

'No, I *know* I do,' he said with certainty. 'I'm just surprised by it, that's all. This is a first time for me.'

'And me,' she replied, suddenly bashful. 'But I know I love you, too.'

They walked up the beach hand in hand, feeling unexpectedly vulnerable for having disclosed the contents of their hearts. A shyness had come over them which, as well as being unfamiliar, left them both feeling a little afraid. Suddenly the playfulness of their relationship was overshadowed by the very adult implications of love.

When they reached Trixie's house, their parting kiss was almost awkward. 'It was fun tonight,' she said, grinning at him in the hope of recapturing their earlier light-heartedness.

'I had fun, too,' he agreed, smiling down at her.

'Now I'm going to scale the wall and climb in through my bedroom window so I don't wake my parents.'

'Are you sure? Don't fall and kill yourself. I've just found you.' The caring tone in his voice made her feel cherished and her heart was once again filled with bubbles.

'I won't,' she replied. 'Now watch how it's done.' She began to climb with enthusiasm, keen to show off her skill. She reached her bedroom window and slipped inside. Then she leaned out and waved down at him. 'Sleep well!' she hissed. He waved back and blew her a kiss. She watched him walk off into the dark, her heart bursting with happiness. 'He loves me, he loves me not. He loves me . . .' And she closed the curtains and fell into bed.

Chapter 8

The following morning it rained. Tekanasset was shrouded in a thick white cloud that drenched the island, washing it clean. Trixie would have liked to sleep in, but her father was always very strict about breakfast. The family convened in the kitchen at eight, no matter what. When she was small her mother would cook eggs, bacon and toast – a very English breakfast. Now there were pancakes, too, because Trixie had rebelled against her parents' determination to hold onto their roots and insisted on having an American breakfast like all her friends. That meant pancakes with maple syrup.

When she appeared with long, dishevelled hair falling over eyes smudged with kohl and full of sleep, her father looked her over with displeasure. 'Trixie, you're a sorry sight this morning.'

Grace agreed. 'Darling, go and wash your face and brush your hair. You can't come down to breakfast like this!'

But Trixie flopped into a chair and poured herself a cup of tea. 'I'm tired,' she complained. 'Come on, one morning without washing my face won't kill anybody.'

'It's a matter of discipline,' said her father, closing the newspaper.

'Yeah, yeah, civilization is about standards. I've heard it a hundred times. Let's just lower the standard this once, please.' She added a spoonful of sugar and a dash of milk to her tea and stirred it sleepily.

'So, did you have a good time last night?' Grace asked, placing a plate of eggs in front of her husband, in the knowledge that food, more than anything else, would distract him from his daughter's lack of discipline.

'It was really fun. Jasper played and we all danced. The grown-ups disappeared pretty quickly after that.'

Grace laughed. 'I don't suppose their music is for us.'

'I don't know,' she shrugged. 'I think you'd like it, actually, Mom. You're never one to follow the crowd. In fact, I think you'd pretend to like it even if you didn't, just to be different.'

Trixie sipped her tea thoughtfully. She wanted to tell them about Evelyn Durlacher coming for Lucy at three in the morning, but didn't want them to know that *she* had been out at that time, too. After all, her curfew was midnight. Fortunately her father was a deep sleeper and she could rely on her mother, if she had heard her creep in, to turn a deaf ear. Trixie wondered how they'd take the news that she was going to go on tour with the boys in the fall.

She watched her father tuck into his breakfast. His face was serious, his back rigid, his shoulders straight – everything about him exuded discipline. Sometimes she wondered what he had been like before the war. She never noticed his eyepatch or the scar down his face, because she was so used to them. But now she looked at him with the eyes of a young woman in love for the first time and wondered what it was about her solemn, distant father that her mother had fallen for. What had he been like as a young man? Had he been playful like Jasper? Or had he always been so humourless and inflexible? She looked at her mother, making pancakes at the stove. She was a curvaceous, sensual woman with deep, dreamy eyes and a sweet, kind face. She loved novels, romantic movies, flowers and bees. Her father hated bees and cared little for flora and fauna. He loved golf and books on military history. He liked things to be neat and tidy. He liked routine. Her mother was by nature as carefree as a bird. As she drank her tea Trixie wondered how on earth they had lived together all these years, having so little in common.

'Mom, what was it about Dad that you fell in love with?' Trixie asked her mother when her father had left for work.

Grace sat down and put her elbows on the table. She rested her chin on her hands. 'Your father was my best friend,' she began softly. 'We'd known each other all our lives.'

'But what was he like?' Trixie persisted.

'He was very handsome. He was cheerful and mischievous and full of fun.' She said those words with wistfulness, reflecting on what he had brought to the marriage and then taken away.

Trixie pulled a face. 'Dad, cheerful and mischievous!' She laughed sceptically. 'Are you sure we're talking about the same person? So what changed?'

'The war,' her mother replied.

'Really? Can a person change so much?'

'He's still my Freddie underneath,' said Grace, a little defensively.

'Does it make you sad?' Trixie asked, trying to imagine how she'd feel if Jasper fought in a war and returned home a different man.

Grace stirred milk into her coffee. She didn't want to answer Trixie's question directly. It wasn't right for children to know too much about their parents. 'I'm not sad, darling. How can I be sad when I have you?' Her smile was so tender that Trixie felt her heart flood with guilt. She smiled back and picked up the maple syrup.

Later Trixie went upstairs to change for work. She had to be at Captain Jack's at eleven. Grace walked over to Big's house with a basket of honey. It was not far from Sunset Slip if she took the path over the bluff. It had stopped raining and the sun had come out. Grace could make out the pointed gables of the house long before she reached it, like the sails of a massive ship in dock. So large and imposing was it that sailors used it as a guide for navigating their way to land. Being the first home to be built on the island, it enjoyed the very best location, on the eastern side, with a three-hundred-degree view of the ocean. It boasted the largest lawns and gardens of any house on Tekanasset, and was sheltered from the wind by tall trees as ancient as the house, and wild woodland where once they hunted boar, brought over from Europe for sport. Now there were no boar, just a pack of dogs, a giant cat called Mr Doorwood, a few exotic-looking hens and a cockerel that crowed on the henhouse every morning at dawn.

Grace rang the bell and spoke her name into the intercom. The grand gates opened in a suitably stately fashion and she stepped onto the gravel driveway with a sigh of pleasure. Through the trees she could see the bright-blue shutters and white porch of Big's magnificent house. Grace had planted the hydrangeas, the climbing roses and shrubs that gave the house a somewhat Cornish appeal, and created herbaceous borders that lined the lawns on the other side because Big had wanted a quintessentially English garden. Grace had learned all about horticulture from her father. Working among the flowers and creatures he so loved kept her close to his memory.

She found Big playing croquet on the glistening lawn with a trio of ancient friends in tennis shoes and white hats. When she saw Grace, Big waved vigorously. 'Grace, come and watch me win.' She lined up her mallet and sent her opponent's ball flying across the grass. 'Sorry, Betty-Ann, needs must.'

'I'll accept defeat with good grace,' Betty-Ann replied, walking over to stand by her ball. Grace sat beneath the veranda and watched them finish. She marvelled at the way Big managed to play croquet, using her mallet as a walking stick. The butler brought her a glass of lemon juice and she stroked Mr Doorwood, who had taken it upon himself to jump onto her lap. She swept her eyes over the garden in satisfaction. The borders were bright with the flowers she had planted. It was fortunate that Big had a couple of full-time gardeners to keep them all weeded and trimmed.

When the game was over, Big and Betty-Ann joined her at the table, while the two other friends shook hands briefly with Grace then left for some other pressing engagement. 'If Mr Doorwood is a nuisance, just throw him off,' said Big, sinking into a chair with a sigh.

'I like him,' Grace replied.

'He's enormous,' said Betty-Ann. 'You must have giant mice beneath your floorboards.'

'He's a terrible mouser,' Big complained, pouring herself and Betty-Ann some juice. 'The laziest cat on the island. Believe me, the mice have it good over here.' She turned to Grace. 'I suppose you've heard about Lucy Durlacher.'

Grace shook her head. 'No, I haven't heard anything.'

Big smiled. 'I hate to take pleasure in the misfortunes of others, but Evelyn's had it coming for some time.'

'Oh?' Grace raised her eyebrows expectantly.

'Evelyn dragged Lucy away from the party in her nightdress at three in the morning.'

Grace was astonished. 'Really? In her nightdress?'

'I kid you not. She went crazy. Lucy was canoodling with one of those boys and the place smelt strongly of marijuana. Poor Lucy, I doubt she'll ever be let out again.'

'But how do you know?' Grace asked.

Betty-Ann grinned guiltily. 'My maid's sister works for Joe Hornby and heard them all talking about it over breakfast this morning. She came scuttling round under some pretence and relayed the gossip.'

'The Island grapevine is well and truly working, then,' said Grace.

'It's never been in better shape,' Betty-Ann laughed.

'I presume your Trixie was tucked up in bed by then,' said Big.

'I hope so,' Grace replied, biting her lip. 'But I couldn't guarantee it. I didn't hear her come in.'

'You must tell her. She'll be highly amused,' said Betty-Ann.

'Oh, she'll know already. The island must be buzzing with it,' Big added, waving her bejewelled fingers dismissively.

'Fancy going out in your nightdress. I wouldn't be seen dead in mine,' Grace laughed.

'You can bet Evelyn's is made of the finest silk and lace,' said Big. 'I'm only surprised she didn't send that husband of hers in her place. I'm sure his pyjamas are just as exquisite.'

'He's as perfect as a shop dummy,' interjected Betty-Ann scornfully. 'And just as shallow. I've never liked the man, he's much too pleased with himself. Just like his father was.'

Big smiled in amusement. 'What did *you* have for breakfast this morning, Betty-Ann? You're on fire!'

'Oh, nothing unusual. There's just something about those two that gets my goat.'

'That makes two of us,' said Big.

'*Three* of us,' Grace added. Then in response to Big's astonished look, she picked up a jar from her basket and added: 'Perhaps it's something in the honey!'

Freddie worked hard all day making preparations for the harvest. There would be a wet harvest for berries used in juices and sauces, when they'd flood the bog so that the cranberries floated to the surface to be rounded up with brooms, and a dry harvest where the berries were hand-picked for the fresh fruit market. He threw himself into his job with enthusiasm, as he did every day, and forgot about Grace and the children. At the farm he was free of resentment. He liked who he was when he was there. At home he was aware of his shortcomings but unable to do anything about them. Grace was a constant reminder of his hurt, and the love he felt for her had been so heavily wrapped in self-defence that he was no longer sure if it still had a pulse. He didn't like to think about it. It was better that he kept to his routine and didn't raise all those old, unanswered questions. He had lost himself down the years and now it was too late to find himself again. He had created a bitter casing and imprisoned himself inside it. He might as well accept his life as it was, and himself as he had become.

It was at work that he overheard a couple of the men discussing Joe Hornby and the band he was busy promoting. 'You know there's no money there,' said one.

'Yes, but apparently one of the kids is very rich.'

'Well, that explains it, then.'

'I wouldn't put my money on old Joe, though. You know what he's like.' They both laughed.

'A flake.'

'Yes, or a lot of hot air as my mother used to say.' More laughter.

'That Jasper Duncliffe is a talented boy, though. Great vocals. He could go far, if it wasn't for that idiot. Someone should tell him.'

Freddie walked away, the blood rising to his temples. Jasper *Duncliffe*. Surely it must be another family? Duncliffe must be a very common name in England, he thought anxiously. He went into his office and closed the door. He wanted to telephone someone, but didn't know who. He couldn't share this with Grace. He couldn't share it with anyone. He sat down and put his head in his hands. All the old feelings of jealousy, betrayal and hurt rose in a giant wave, invading the serenity of his workplace. *Discipline*, he told himself. *Discipline*. But the thought of his beloved daughter with a member of *that* family made him want to throw something against the wall.

Trixie finished her shift at four. People liked to linger over their lunches. They enjoyed sunbathing all morning and eating later, which meant she found herself working five hours, sometimes more. She thought about Jasper as she worked. The anticipation of seeing him that evening gave her step an extra bounce and her good mood was infectious, making the other waitresses smile with her.

She changed out of her uniform and put on a short, floral sundress that barely reached mid-thigh, and a pair of sandals. As she passed the bar, Jack put down the telephone.

'Message for you, Trixie,' said her boss. 'Someone called Jasper needs to see you urgently.'

Trixie frowned. 'Really? Did he say anything else?'

'No, but he sounded serious.'

She felt uneasy. 'OK. I'll go now.'

He smiled. 'So he's called Jasper, is he?'

'He's called Jasper, Jack. I think there must be something special about the initial J, don't you?'

'Off you go, Trixie. Don't do anything I wouldn't do.'

'Leaves me more than I can handle!' She laughed and left the restaurant, but as soon as she was on her way to Joe's the uneasy feeling returned and she quickened her pace. It must be something important if Jasper had called Captain Jack's. She hoped it wasn't anything bad.

As soon as she opened the door of Joe's home her fears were confirmed. It *was* something bad. Joe was puffing his cigar, talking on the telephone in a loud voice, explaining that the band wouldn't be playing. She could see through the glass to where the boys were huddled around a table on the lawn looking grave. She felt the blood drop to her feet.

She strode outside and immediately registered Jasper's ashen face. His eyes were red, his mouth set into a grimace as if his entire world had just imploded. When he saw her, he took a deep breath. 'Trixie,' he said.

'What's going on? What's happened?'

His face grew taut as he strained every nerve to control his emotion. 'My brother's been killed in a car crash. I have to go back to England. I . . .' His voice trailed off and he took a drag of his cigarette with trembling fingers. The ashtray and empty beer bottles in the middle of the table revealed an afternoon of chain-smoking and drinking.

'I'm so sorry,' she cried, falling onto her knees and wrapping her arms around him.

Embarrassed by her affection, he patted her then disentangled himself. 'Life's a bummer,' he replied, and the leaden sound in his voice made her heart buckle.

George got to his feet, put his hands behind his head and started to pace the lawn. 'We'll wait for you, mate,' he said. 'As long as it takes.'

Jasper shot him a look that told him he was being ridiculous, but Trixie didn't understand why. 'I don't know,' he mumbled. Then he stood up angrily. 'It was all going so well, and now *this*!'

'How old was your brother?' she asked.

'Older than me, and that was the best thing about him,' Jasper said harshly, then looked like he was going to burst into tears. 'No, that's unfair. I loved him. He was a good man. The best. Better than me, anyhow, and now I have to fill his shoes and I'm totally inadequate. In every way, I'm inadequate.'

'So what will you do?' she asked.

'Go home.'

'But you'll come back?'

He looked at her steadily. 'Walk with me, Trixie. I need to get out of here.'

Ben drained the beer bottle. 'Take as long as you want. We'll hang here. George, roll one, will you?'

They set off up the beach. He took her hand. For a long while they walked in silence. Trixie had so many questions, but she didn't want to press him until he was ready to talk. Finally he stopped and turned to face her. She could barely look into his eyes for the desolation there.

'I love you, Trixie. I love you with all my heart.' Jasper placed his hands on her shoulders. 'I love you more now that I know I might lose you.'

'What do you mean?' Her heart began to hop about like a frightened cricket.

'I have to return to England and I might not come back.' His words winded her and her eyes filled with tears. 'Don't look at me like that, my darling. I can't take it,' he groaned.

'You can come back, surely? Why wouldn't you?'

'Because my destiny is no longer to be a rock star, but to run a great estate.' He said it as if it wasn't a great estate but a great curse.

She screwed up her nose. 'I don't understand.'

He smiled and traced her jawline with his thumbs. 'Of course you don't. How could you? You know nothing about me. My brother was . . .'

'I'll go with you,' she interjected suddenly.

It was his turn to look bewildered. 'You mean that?'

'Of course I do. If you want me to come with you, I will.'

A look of relief momentarily swept the shadows away. 'Are you serious? You'd give up everything for me?'

'I'd follow you to the ends of the earth, Jasper. I know we're meant to be together. I feel it.'

'Then we must marry. I can't expect you to come all the way to England without a promise of commitment.'

Her spirit soared with happiness. 'If you want me as your wife, I'll marry you.'

'I want you, full stop, Trixie.' The shadow of doubt darkened his features once again. 'But you're so young. You want to work in fashion and travel the world. I couldn't ask you to give all that up for me. You don't know what sort of life awaits you in England. I'm not entirely sure you'd be suited to it. I'd hate to make you miserable. You'd only end up loathing me.'

'What are you talking about, Jasper?'

'Being my wife would mean you'd have to give up all your dreams. You wouldn't be able to work in fashion and travel the world to attend the fashion shows. You'd be holding meetings to raise money for the church roof and throwing dinner parties for the High Sheriff and his wife. It's a commitment I'm not sure you'd relish. I don't think it would make you happy.'

'I'll be happy to be with you, wherever that may be.'

He sighed and cast his gaze out to sea. He seemed to weigh up the possibilities. 'OK, here's the plan,' he said, turning back to her. 'I'll go home and attend my brother's funeral. Then, when I've sorted everything out, I'll send for you.'

Trixie felt the world adjust into sharp focus. Her nerves tingled as she began to sense everything more intensely. This was drama at its most exciting. It was what one read about in novels but never actually lived. Now she was really living. She always knew she was too big for a small island like Tekanasset. 'I'll wait for you, then,' she replied.

He bent down and kissed her passionately. 'My career might be in shreds but I still have you, Trixie.'

'You'll always have me, Jasper. I'll wait as long as it takes.'

Chapter 9

Grace was putting the pastry on top of an apple pie when Freddie arrived home. She heard the screen door bang and his familiar footsteps in the hall as he put his briefcase on the floor, hung up his jacket and patted the dogs, who rushed in to greet him. She could sense his anger and her heart contracted. She had grown used to his distance, and her memories and the gardens compensated for that, but his anger hurt her every time anew.

She dipped the brush in the melted butter and glazed the top of the pie, anticipating his entrance at any moment and preparing herself for whatever it was that was upsetting him. She heard him go into his study and the clinking of the decanter told her he was pouring himself a whiskey. A moment later she heard the light tapping of dog paws on the wooden floorboards in the hall and Freddie strode in.

She could tell from his face that he was hurt more than angry and she couldn't imagine what had caused it. 'What's happened, Freddie? Are you all right?'

He walked through the kitchen and out onto the veranda where he put a hand on his hip and gazed out to sea. Grace took off her apron and followed him. 'It's Trixie,' he said at last, without looking at his wife.

'What about her?'

'It's this young man she's seeing. I don't like it at all.'

Grace's anxiety lifted. 'You have to let her go, darling,' she said. 'She's nineteen.'

'I don't like the boy.'

'Have you met him?'

He shook his head and took a swig of whiskey. 'I don't like the sound of him.'

She sighed, a little impatiently. 'Then you must meet him and judge him from having met him rather than what you hear about him.'

'We come all the way out to America, thinking we've left England behind, and it finds us, all the way across the Atlantic. Can you believe it?'

'What are you talking about?'

'This Jasper . . .'

'Yes?'

He took another swig. 'I'm not sure. I could be wrong. After all . . .' They both heard the front door open and the rattling of the screen door banging shut. He glanced fearfully at his wife.

'After all, what?' she whispered. But it was too late. Trixie was marching through the kitchen, her jaw set into a determined scowl.

'I need to talk to you both,' she said, joining them on the veranda. Grace suddenly felt weak in her legs and sat down on the swing chair. She noticed her daughter's white face and the purple shadows beneath her eyes that betrayed tears shed and wiped away. 'Jasper is going to England and he won't be coming back,' she announced dramatically. Grace and Freddie were both taken aback. Having imagined endless possibilities, Jasper leaving Tekanasset was the only one they hadn't thought of. Grace felt the impulse to reach out and embrace her daughter. But there was something about Trixie's determined jaw that told her there was more and that she wasn't going to like it. She remained in her seat and braced herself for what was to come.

'I'm going with him,' Trixie declared. 'He's asked me to marry him.'

Freddie's face flushed such a deep crimson Grace thought he was about to suffer a seizure. 'You're not marrying him, Trixie,' he said, and his voice was as hard as granite.

'Wait a minute, everybody. You're both one step ahead of me,' said Grace, struggling to keep calm. 'Darling, why is he going back to England? I thought he wanted to be a rock star.'

'His brother has died,' Trixie replied.

'Oh, I'm so sorry,' said Grace. 'How terrible. How did he die?'

'In a car crash.'

Freddie drained his glass and turned to his daughter. The way he looked at her made Grace's heart freeze over. 'Tell me, why can't he come back?'

'Because he has to run his estate, apparently.'

Freddie nodded slowly. 'Because he has to run his estate.' He glanced at Grace, almost accusingly. 'What's his full name, Beatrix?'

'Jasper Duncliffe,' Trixie replied. Now *she* was beginning to feel uneasy. 'Why? Do you *know* him?'

Grace felt the ground spinning away from her. Jasper *Duncliffe*. Her mind began to race as the blood shot to her temples, where it pounded painfully against her skull. If he was who she thought he was, then the brother who died would be his *elder* brother, which was why the responsibility now lay with him to run the estate. If *he* had to run the estate that would mean his father was also dead. She took a sharp breath as if her own heart had been stabbed. Her hand shot to her chest. *Not necessarily. Not necessarily*, she thought, searching desperately for another possibility. She stood up. 'I'll be back in a moment,' she gasped, hurrying into the kitchen.

She leaned against the counter and stifled a sob. She could see Freddie and Trixie talking on the veranda. She had to remain calm. There was no way that after all these years she was going to let down her defences and give in to the pain. She opened the fridge and pulled out a bottle of wine. With a trembling hand she reached into the cabinet for a glass and poured it unsteadily. She took a large swig. Her neck felt sore from straining against the incoming tide of emotion that threatened to break through the barriers that had remained steadfast and strong for nearly thirty years, and her head was now throbbing. She wanted to run to her bed and cry beneath the covers, but she couldn't. She had to return and continue the conversation as if this had nothing to do with her own broken heart, with her own grief, with her own past.

She took three deep breaths and wiped the sweat off her brow with the tea towel. Then she lifted her chin and walked outside. 'He *will* send for me,' Trixie was saying, and her voice was thin as if she, too, was struggling against her own tide of emotions.

'Beatrix, you know nothing about what it means to marry a man like Jasper. He'll return to England and once the funeral is over and reality dawns, he'll realize that he can't marry a flighty young girl like you. A man like Jasper will put duty before his own desires.'

Grace sat on the swing chair again, but this time her body was stiff, as if it belonged to someone far stronger than she. 'Your father is right,' she said. Freddie wasn't expecting the support of his wife. Neither was Trixie, who began to cry. 'He will put duty before his own desires and marry one of his own kind. That's what men like him do. They put family first. If he inherits a great estate he will take his responsibility very seriously.'

'I don't understand you British,' Trixie snapped. 'You're not human.'

'We're only trying to prevent you from being hurt, you foolish girl,' Freddie growled.

'Because we love you,' said Grace and her eyes began to well with tears at the mention of the word *love*.

'Well, I'm going to wait for him. I'll wait as long as it takes, but I *will* marry him.'

Encouraged by his wife's surprising support, Freddie decided to strike a deal, one that he was sure would turn out to his advantage. 'If he sends for you, you have my blessing,' he said slowly.

Grace swallowed hard. 'And you have mine, too,' she added.

Freddie nodded and there was a glimmer of warmth behind his eyes. 'Then that's settled.'

Trixie was reassured. The colour returned to her cheeks. 'You mean that?' she asked. 'You really mean that?'

'I mean that,' her father confirmed. He took a cigarette out of his breast pocket and lit it, then he turned and leaned on the balustrade and looked out over the sea. 'If he sends for you I will admit that I'm wrong and that I've misjudged him.'

Trixie was suddenly filled with excitement. 'Then I must go and tell Jasper right away!' she exclaimed, her face now pink and smiling elatedly. She ran into the kitchen, grabbing an apple from the fruit bowl on the way, and out through the hall. The screen door rattled then slammed and the house was left silent and still.

Grace and Freddie remained on the veranda. The dogs, who had sought refuge in the kitchen, now wandered out sheepishly, sensing perhaps that the air was strained with thoughts too anguished to articulate. Freddie smoked pensively, Grace sipped her wine. They had united briefly and yet, still, they felt oceans apart. Grace tried not to think about herself. She thought of her daughter, setting out on the first adventure of her life, her heart filled with love and optimism, just as hers had been all those years ago. Trixie believed, as Grace once did, that love has the power to burn away all obstacles, that it is a virtue that negates any wickedness committed in its name. Grace could tell her she was wrong, as she herself had been, but what was the use? Her father had told her that wisdom cannot be taught. 'Knowledge can be taught, but wisdom must be learned through experience,' he had said. Trixie had to make her own way and learn from her own mistakes. That was the purpose of life.

'What's for supper?' Freddie asked, turning away from his melancholic pondering.

Grace looked at her watch. 'The apple pie will be ready now,' she said.

'Apple pie? That's good,' he replied.

'I've made chicken escalopes to fry.'

He smiled. 'Good. I don't imagine Trixie's going to come home to eat.'

'No, she'll be eating at Joe's, I should think.' She stood up and followed him into the kitchen. 'How sad for the boys. Do you think their dream of being a famous band is now over?'

Freddie nodded. 'I think so. From what I heard, Jasper has the voice.'

'And the money to finance it,' she added quietly.

'Indeed. I think the most disappointed will be Joe. He must have seen Jasper as a pot of gold.'

'Poor boy. He came all the way out here to escape his family and live his dream and it's all shattered.'

'They're different from us, Grace.'

'I know,' she replied softly.

'We're going to have to be strong for Trixie.'

'Yes, we are.'

He smiled at her sadly. 'He's never going to send for her.'

'Men like him never do.' She took the escalopes out of the fridge and put the pan on the stove. 'Duty first,' she added, careful to keep the bitterness out of her voice.

'Duty first,' he agreed. 'Trixie will have to learn the hard way that her parents know best.'

'And that we love her very much,' Grace added firmly. *That* was the only form of love she was totally sure of.

Trixie and Jasper snuggled into the little rowing boat in Joe's boathouse. It was the only place where they could be totally alone and undisturbed. They had lined it with anything soft they could find and lay entwined, aware of every minute that brought them closer to saying goodbye. They didn't make love. Neither felt like sex. It seemed somehow inappropriate to reduce their relationship to the merely physical, when what they felt now, in the face of such uncertainty, was much more spiritual.

In spite of Jasper's reassurances that he'd send for her when he was ready, at the back of Trixie's mind lurked a small smudge of doubt. Contained in that small smudge was the memory of Jasper telling her that his mother wouldn't approve of her and of her father warning her that, for a man like Jasper, duty to his family would always come first. She didn't voice her fears because she was afraid that if she brought them out into the open they might come true. While Jasper was promising her a life together she wanted to believe him.

Trixie wished she could spend the whole night wrapped in his arms, but she knew she had to leave. Soon they'd be married and she'd have every morning to wake up with him for the rest of her life. Reluctantly, she asked him to walk her home. They set off up the beach, hand in hand. The water lapped the sand with waves so quiet they were barely audible. The sky was studded with stars as bright as quartz and in the midst of it all was a luminous moon encircled by mist. It was beautiful and Trixie felt all the more moved to be parting from her lover surrounded by such magnificence.

He kissed her beneath the porch and plucked a rose as he had done before. 'You'll come and see me off tomorrow, won't you?' he asked, slipping the flower behind her ear.

'You know I will.'

'God, I'm going to miss you, Trixie,' he groaned, gazing down at her.

'And I'm going to miss you, too. But we'll be together very soon.'

'Yes, we'll be together soon,' he reassured her. '*Very* soon.' This time she didn't scale the wall. It didn't seem becoming for a girl on the brink of marriage to be sneaking in through the window.

She opened the door and kissed him one last time. 'Until tomorrow,' she said.

Jasper watched her disappear inside, then he walked back down the beach. A terrible emptiness engulfed him. The world seemed somehow less friendly now that his brother was no longer in it. He imagined his mother's grief and felt a yearning for home. He'd have to step into his brother's shoes now and be the man. He wasn't sure how to do that. He'd always been the rebellious boy of the family. His two sisters would need him, too – they'd *all* need him and yet he was so lacking in every quality now required of him. He cursed Edward for dying and leaving him in the dreaded position of having to take over. He cursed him for dying and leaving him broken-hearted.

But Trixie was a lifeline. She was the part of Tekanasset and his dream that he could cling to. For a man drowning in a sea of impending responsibility, she was the little raft that promised to preserve Jasper Duncliffe. As long as they were together his dream was still afloat. Perhaps he couldn't ever be the musician he longed to be and he would never tour the world with George and Ben, but he and Trixie would live their dream in the English countryside and he'd play his guitar and she'd listen and somehow she'd keep his creative spirit alive. He truly felt he could be happy if Trixie was by his side.

Of course, his mother would disapprove. Trixie was not the sort of girl she could ever warm to, for reasons which were too small-minded and petty to contemplate. His mother was a superficial, prejudiced woman who would certainly consider a girl like Trixie to be beneath her in every way. Jasper wished he were wrong and that his mother would surprise him and embrace the girl he loved, but he knew in his heart that acceptance and compassion were not included among the few redeeming qualities she possessed. However, he would insist; after all, he was the man of the family now and no one could tell him what to do. That thought uplifted him a little.

* * *

Trixie slept fitfully. She drifted in and out of sleep and was plagued by confusing dreams of losing things and shouting and not being heard. She woke as dawn broke over the sea and her heart lurched as memories of the day before closed in and covered the sun with cloud.

She got up and threw on her dressing gown. The kitchen was quiet. The dogs weren't there. She smelt coffee. The weak light streamed in through the windows. Outside the sea was as calm as a lake. Then she heard the soft squeaking of the swing chair on the veranda. She padded outside to find her mother, alone, in her dressing gown, her hair dishevelled and falling over her shoulders, her rough gardener's hands hugging a mug of coffee. Her face, devoid of make-up, was pale and drawn, but she looked younger, like a girl, in her desolation. When she saw Trixie she raised her bloodshot eyes and pulled a frail smile. 'Hi,' she said. 'You're up early.'

'I'm too nervous to sleep,' Trixie replied, sitting beside her.

Grace put an arm around her child and pulled her close. 'I know,' she said, pressing her cheek to Trixie's hair. 'I'm sorry this terrible tragedy has ruined your happiness.'

'It's going to be OK,' Trixie replied firmly. 'We love each other. There's nothing that can keep us apart.'

'I hope you're right,' said Grace.

'I have no doubt,' Trixie lied. 'It's just all happened much quicker than we anticipated.' She laughed bitterly. 'I was intending to go on tour with him in the fall. It was going to be a challenge to get that past Dad, but now, as it happens, I'll be going to England instead and Dad has given us his blessing. It's turned out much better this way. I won't have a fight on my hands. You'll have to come over. I can't imagine Jasper's family will schlep out here for the wedding.'

Trixie felt her mother tense and sat up. 'Are you all right about this, Mom? I know I'm going to the other side of the world, but it's your home. Surely that's a good thing. I mean, it's not like I'm going to live in Australia.'

'I know, but it's all come as a bit of a surprise. I just need time to get used to it.'

'Oh Mom, you know I love you,' said Trixie, pulling a sad face.

Grace chuckled. 'I know you do, darling, and I love you so much.'

'You won't be losing me.'

'You'll be very far away, though.'

'But you can come and visit.'

Grace nodded, but her eyes began to sting so she turned her gaze to the ocean and blinked hard. 'Tell me, darling, does Jasper . . .' She paused and cleared her throat. 'Do Jasper's parents know about your plans?'

'I don't know. I mean, he hasn't mentioned them.'

'At all?' Grace was almost too frightened to breathe.

'Well, his father is dead and although he said his mother would disapprove of me, I'm sure once she meets me she'll like me.'

Grace continued to stare out over the water. 'His father's dead?' she asked, and her voice was as calm and steady as the sea.

'Yes, that's what he said.'

'How did he die?'

'I don't know. He didn't say.'

Grace nodded, but she didn't turn to look at her daughter. If she had, Trixie would have seen the raw pain in her eyes and the tight muscles in her neck as she fought back her tears. Trixie continued to talk, which gave Grace time to suppress her grief. A little bee buzzed about one of the balls of hydrangeas. Grace was distracted a moment and turned to watch it. A second later it flew towards her and settled onto the lapel of her dressing gown, the exact same place where she always wore her bee brooch. She caught her breath and remained very still.

'Mom, there's a bee on your dressing gown,' said Trixie. Grace was too moved to do anything but nod. 'Are you all right?' Trixie now noticed her mother's strange expression. She looked as if she was about to burst into tears. She put her arm around her and the bee flew away. 'Mom?'

Grace let out a howl of pain. It came from deep in her core and frightened Trixie with its brutal, primitive sound. 'Mom, what's the matter?' she asked, but Grace couldn't explain. Not to her daughter, not to her husband, not to anybody. Where would she begin? How could she translate into words the sheer depth of her love? How could she describe the devastation of her loss? So she didn't.

She pulled herself together and dried her eyes, then she kissed her daughter tenderly. 'I hope it works out for you, Trixie,' she said softly, smoothing away the lines of confusion on her daughter's face. 'I hope you both have a love that lasts. You deserve nothing less.'

'Thank you, Mom,' Trixie replied. 'But I'm sure it will.'

Grace patted her daughter's knee. 'Why don't you go and put some clothes on and I'll make you breakfast. You need all your strength today.'

Trixie left her mother on the veranda and went upstairs to dress. As she pulled on a pair of denim shorts and a casual sweater she heard the muffled sound of crying again. She had never heard her mother sobbing like this before and it cut her very deep to think that *she* was the cause of her unhappiness.

She wondered whether to go down and comfort her, but something told her that Grace could not be comforted.

Later Trixie stood on the quay and kissed Jasper goodbye. 'If you cry tears into the water of this harbour, it means you'll come back,' she told him, her eyes glassy with emotion. 'Make sure you do, because mine won't count.'

'I'll do my best,' he said. 'But you're coming to me first. Promise you'll wait?'

'I promise.'

He embraced her fiercely and pressed his lips to hers. 'I love you, Trixie Valentine.'

'And I love you, Jasper Duncliffe.'

As he boarded the boat, her words rang in his head like a melody that was already outdated – a melody that belonged in a world which was no longer real. He waved goodbye to Trixie, to George and Ben and Joe. He waved goodbye to Jasper Duncliffe, musician, free spirit, boy, and he waved goodbye to Lord Jasper Duncliffe, too, because neither of them existed any more. He was Lord Penselwood now, the new Marquess of Penselwood, and he was going home, to Walbridge Hall.

PART TWO

Chapter 10

Walbridge, England, 1938

The first time Grace cried for Rufus was on the day of his engagement in the spring of 1938. It would not be the last.

She hadn't seen him since that July, five years before, when he had driven her back to the Beekeeper's Cottage in his gleaming Alfa Romeo. Although she had looked out for him in the ensuing years from her secret vantage point just below the woods, she had never seen him, or his motor car. If he had spent time at home she had been unaware of it.

Of course, there was no reason why he should have sought her company. Although she was a young woman now, from a class point of view they were quite literally worlds apart. Nevertheless she yearned for him. She kept the memory of his face, captured that day in the open-topped motor car, like a picture postcard held against her heart, and the wonderful thing about memories is that they never fade. Photographs get damaged, sun-bleached, tarnished and curled, but memories are always as new as the day they were made. Rufus's dark chocolate eyes, smiling at her fondly, were as bright as if it had been only yesterday.

She'd share her dreams with her mother, knowing that although she couldn't see her she was close, listening with interest and loving her unconditionally. Sometimes she'd cry onto her pillow because she feared her love for Rufus would prevent her from ever enjoying a *real* love. She worried that no one would be capable of inspiring in her the intoxicating mixture of happiness and longing that Rufus inspired. Although she accepted that he would never, *could* never love her, she harboured a secret desire in her heart, so small she was barely aware of it, that by some magic the world would change and he would one day love her as he would love a woman in his own world.

But then she heard the news that he was getting married and all her dreams shattered in one terrible, devastating moment.

It was a Saturday night at the Fox and Goose. Grace had just turned nineteen. She sat in the pub with her father, Auntie May and Uncle Michael, Freddie and his younger sister, Josephine. Grace didn't much like Josephine. She had a sour mouth and a sharp tongue, and other people's happiness irritated her to the point of rudeness. Freddie now worked on the Walbridge estate full time. Mr Garner was still very much alive, so Freddie's dreams of managing the farm were yet to be realized. Grace was employed four afternoons a week by a retired colonel who lived alone in a manor house on the edge of town. Reverend Dibben had recommended her and the old colonel paid her well for the simple task of reading to him, because his eyesight was rapidly deteriorating and he loved books more than anything else in the world. So Grace, with her sweet voice and intelligent narration, was the perfect companion, bringing much pleasure and satisfaction to a grateful old man.

Everyone wondered why Arthur Hamblin had never married again. Not only would marriage have given him companionship, but it would have freed his daughter from the responsibility of looking after him. Some said it was because he still mourned his wife, others claimed it was because he never wanted a stepmother for Grace. Whatever the reason, Grace cared for him as a dutiful daughter should. She washed and ironed his clothes, kept the house clean and tidy, cooked his meals and kept him company. Her afternoons with Colonel Redwood were a welcome respite from domesticity. She was able to indulge her love of novels, for Colonel Redwood's favourite books were the greatest love stories every written. While she read Tolstoy, Dumas and Austen, the tales of broken hearts and longing fuelled her own fantasies and the secret hope that like the heroes and heroines of those novels, she and Rufus might, by some wonderful twist of fate, love each other too.

But then Michael Valentine came back from the bar with a trio of beers for himself, Freddie and Arthur, and the happy news just relayed to him by the publican. 'Lord Melville has found himself a bride,' he announced cheerfully, sitting down.

'How wonderful,' gushed May. 'Who is the lucky lady?'

'Some duke's daughter. I don't know.' Michael shrugged and sank his lip into the foamy head of his beer.

Josephine blew a stream of smoke out of the side of her scarlet mouth like a dragon. 'How dreary,' she sneered. 'There's nothing *wonderful* about an arranged marriage, Mum. Their lot are all so dry and unemotional. It'll be a very dull wedding, I suspect.' Grace watched them discussing the news through the cloud of smoke, as if she were a ghost. She remained very still, internalizing her misery so that no one would know that the news had just broken her heart.

'You're wrong, Josie,' said Arthur. 'Lord Melville's not at all like his father. He's a fun-loving and witty fellow, straight out of a Noel Coward play.'

'I'm not saying he's not amusing, Arthur. He's certainly handsome. I'm rolling my eyes at his obvious choice of bride.' Her pointy lips extended into a thin smile. 'I'd admire him more if he eloped with a barmaid or something. Marrying the daughter of a duke is so bloody predictable.'

'So what?' Freddie cut in. 'He has to marry one of his own.'

'Why? So that when the Marquess dies and he inherits the estate, she can hold big garden parties as graciously as her mother-in-law. Well, you're right about that, I suppose; a barmaid wouldn't know how to behave like a marchioness.'

'*You* wouldn't know how to behave like a marchioness, Josie,' Freddie laughed. He turned to Grace, who was sitting quiet and still beside him, as if the news had turned her to stone. 'What do *you* think about it, Grace?' His question sounded more like a challenge than an enquiry.

'I don't really have an opinion. I mean, I don't know either of them, so . . .' Her voice trailed off and she gave a little shrug and a sniff to hide her awkwardness.

'You see, Grace is right,' interjected Josephine. 'Why is it that people get overexcited about a wedding when they don't even know the people getting married? It's the same madness as when a member of the royal family gets married, but at least they're public figures and we all know a bit about them. I admire the King for abdicating in order to marry naughty old Wallis. Now that showed a lot of spunk! Lord Melville should have found himself a wicked American divorcee like her!'

Freddie elbowed Grace in the ribs. 'Do you remember when you had a crush on Rufus, as you called him?' He laughed scornfully.

'You called him Rufus?' Michael asked, raising his eyebrows in surprise. 'That's familiar.'

'Really? Did you have a crush on him, Grace?' Josephine joined in, narrowing her eyes. 'Lord, I didn't know you had it in you!'

'I'm sure I don't know what you mean,' Grace replied, feeling her face grow hot.

'Yes, she did. He chatted her up after church once,' Freddie told them.

'And then he brought his grandmother to our home to be stung by a bee to cure her arthritis,' Arthur added proudly.

'Now I've heard everything!' Michael chuckled.

'The Dowager Marchioness in your little cottage?' said May, impressed. 'Why ever didn't you tell us?'

'She'd never been to the cottage before. It was a great honour,' said Arthur.

'What was she like?' May asked. 'I've only ever seen her from a distance at church.'

'She was as deaf as a post,' Arthur added, warming to the subject. 'We had to shout, didn't we, Grace?'

'You never told me that,' said Freddie grudgingly, turning to Grace.

She shrugged. 'It wasn't important.'

'Then the following day she sent her chauffeur for Grace,' Arthur continued, directing his speech at May, who gazed at him wide-eyed with fascination.

'Why? Did it work?' May asked in delight.

'It worked so well, she wanted to be stung on the other hand,' he said. They all roared with laughter. 'So, my Gracey goes off in the Bentley and Lord Melville shows her around the house and garden – *my* garden. I think he took a shine to you, Gracey,' he added tipsily.

'If he saw you now, I think he'd call off his engagement,' Michael added with an appreciative nod. Now it was Freddie's turn to go quiet and internalize his resentment.

'Those gardens are the loveliest in the whole of England. Don't you think, Grace?' said May. 'Your father's a wonderful gardener. You only have to look at your garden to see what a magician he is with flowers. Arthur's got green fingers *and* toes!' She smiled affectionately at him.

'Yes, he has,' Grace replied, fighting tears that began to prickle behind her eyes.

'So, did he kiss you behind the garden wall?' asked Josephine, glancing irritably at a chip on her crimson nail polish.

'Of course not,' Grace retorted, appalled. 'I was fourteen.'

'That never stopped anyone having a kiss,' said Josephine.

Freddie baulked. 'What, you think he'd have kissed you if you'd been twenty?'

Grace felt she was drowning in his teasing. 'That's silly,' she replied unhappily, trying to keep her head up.

'He might have. You're a pretty girl, Grace. Men like Lord Melville can have anyone they want.' Josephine's ice-grey eyes bored into hers through the ribbon of smoke that wafted up from the cigarette poised in front of her mouth. 'Would you have let him, then?'

Grace didn't like her bullying tone. 'I was fourteen, Josie,' she repeated.

'Oh, I'd have let him, all right,' Josephine declared nonchalantly. 'I think he'd make a lovely kisser. He's got a good mouth. Shame he's wasted on some frigid duke's daughter. He'll never know true passion.'

'How do you know his lady's not passionate, Josie?' her mother asked. 'You don't know anything about her.'

'I'm jumping to wild conclusions,' Josephine replied with a wicked grin. '*Much* more fun to be cynical. What are the aristocracy for if not to be made fun of?'

When they all left the pub at ten, Freddie didn't even say goodnight to Grace. May and Michael waved to Grace and Arthur as they cycled off up the lane, while Josephine linked arms with her brother and inclined her head to share a joke, which, coming from her, was bound to be at someone else's expense.

Grace pedalled furiously, longing to be alone with her unhappiness. It was too dark to cycle through the woods, so they went the long way round up the lane, their bicycle lights showing the way. She seethed with fury at Freddie for being unkind, and for ignoring her for the rest of the evening, after having teased her so meanly about Rufus. Fond as she was of Freddie, he could be very cruel. She fought back tears.

Once in the privacy of her bedroom she threw herself onto the bed and sobbed. She knew she should never have hoped, she should never have dreamed. Hoping and dreaming only gave the heart false expectations.

Assuming his daughter was simply tired, Arthur went into the sitting room to read on his own. The nights were still chilly so he lit a fire and sat in his chair, reading and puffing on his pipe, as he did every night. He didn't imagine that his daughter was crying herself to sleep, wishing she had a mother to share her grief with. He didn't guess that she could be anything other than entirely happy. Pepper snoozed at his feet. He turned the page. He thought no more of Lord Melville and his engagement.

Until a hand-delivered invitation arrived the following week. The envelope was addressed to Mr Arthur Hamblin, but on the stiff white card inside, Mr Arthur Hamblin's name was followed by Miss Grace Hamblin, which was a novelty because until that moment Arthur had only ever been invited to the Hall on his own. Now that Grace was a young woman, however, she was invited to accompany her father in the place of a Mrs Hamblin. The pleasure of their company was requested on Saturday 7th May at 4 p.m. at a tea to celebrate the engagement of the Earl of Melville and Lady Georgina Charlton. Arthur soon discovered that all the men and women who worked on the Walbridge estate were invited to meet the lady who would one day be the new Marchioness of Penselwood.

Grace received the invitation with a mixture of elation and dread. The thought of seeing Rufus again filled her with a sharp and painful yearning, yet the knowledge that beside him would be the woman he had chosen to spend the rest of his life with cut her to the quick.

Freddie was invited, too, but he grumbled about it and pretended he really didn't care and was only going out of politeness. May set about helping Grace find a suitable dress. 'You have to look your very best,' she gushed, dragging her into the only shop in town which sold dresses smart enough for an occasion such as this.

'But I don't have the money to buy a new frock,' Grace protested.

'Michael and I are going to buy it for you,' May insisted. 'I'm the nearest thing to a mother you've ever had, so it's my treat. Fortunately, summer frocks are less dear than winter ones.'

Grace tried on a number of dresses and settled on a pretty blue-and-yellow floral tea dress with buttons down the front and on the short, puffed sleeves. 'I have just the hat to go with it,' said May, giving it a tweak here and there. She stood back and admired her. 'You look like a real lady,' she added, moved. 'It's a shame your mother isn't around to see you. She'd be as proud as punch, she would. Still, you've got Arthur and I can't wait to see his face when he sees his little girl, all grown-up.'

'It's a beautiful dress, Auntie May,' said Grace, looking at her reflection in the mirror. May was right, the dress made her look sophisticated. Her spirits lifted. Perhaps when he saw her . . .

The day of the tea, May spent most of the morning curling Grace's hair and pinning it back on one side in a loop. Her hair was thick and glossy and took May much longer than she had anticipated. She then positioned her hat at a coquettish angle on her head. Josephine brought over her vanity case of make-up and insisted on applying it herself. Grace looked at her overplucked eyebrows and the bright scarlet lipstick, painted on in the famous 'Crawford smear', and shuddered. She had never worn make-up in her life and the thought of looking cruel and fake like Josephine filled her with horror. But May intervened and a pretty rose-coloured lipstick and a smudge of rouge for her cheeks were decided upon. Her eyelashes were left alone and the blue eyeshadow that Josephine lifted out of the case was promptly put back again.

When Arthur came in from the garden to change, he was astonished by the sight of the young woman in the hall, who looked so like his late wife. He was lost for words and his eyes shone with a mixture of pride and sorrow. May jumped to the rescue. 'Doesn't she look lovely, Arthur?' she gushed. 'She'll be the belle of the tea party, for sure.'

'Not a lot of competition,' said Josephine sourly.

'Oh, I don't know, when the ladies doll themselves up, you'd be surprised how pretty some of them can look,' May retorted.

Arthur managed a small smile. 'You look beautiful, Gracey,' he croaked.

'There, I told you your father would be proud. You have every reason to be, Arthur, with Grace on your arm.' She laughed. 'Freddie will be jealous, won't he, Josie?'

'He's not going to be jealous of Arthur, Mum.'

'He'll wish she was on *his* arm.'

'Then he should have asked her, rather than bottling it all up like a bashful child.'

May swept Freddie aside with a deliberate smile. 'You're going to have such a nice time. I want to hear all about it. Every detail. You won't forget anything, will you? I'll be longing to hear.'

'I'll leave the details to Gracey,' said Arthur. 'But I'll tell you all about it in the morning.'

May clapped her hands. 'Well, I'd better go and see how my Freddie's getting on.' She picked up her bag to leave, but hesitated by the door. 'Have a lovely time, won't you.' She smiled at Arthur and her expression was full of wistfulness. Grace knew she was thinking about her mother and wished she had known her as they had.

Josephine followed May outside, tossing back a casual 'have a nice time' as she left.

'Well, I'd better go and smarten up, or I'll let you down, Grace,' Arthur said, making for the stairs. Grace wandered into the sitting room and stood in front of the mirror which hung above the fireplace. The glass was tarnished and the light was dim, but she could see enough to be surprised by the transformation. From the photo of her mother, even *she* could see the resemblance. She stared hard and little by little she detached herself from the reflection and saw, in her place, the gentle countenance of her mother, gazing lovingly back at her. She felt her heartbeat quicken and the sweat begin to break out on her skin. She smiled and her mother smiled back. Her heart overflowed with love for the woman she had never known, but always felt close to, and as her eyes glistened so glistened the eyes of her mother. It didn't matter that the thoughts she tried to assemble were too tangled to communicate, because her mother understood the feelings behind them.

'Are you all right, Gracey?' It was Arthur, standing in the doorway.

The vision quickly disappeared as Grace was wrenched out of her trance and the face in the mirror was hers once again. 'I wish my mother was here,' she said softly.

'So do I, Gracey,' Arthur replied. 'She'd have loved getting you ready. She loved dressing up.'

'Am I like her, Dad?'

His face turned pink with pleasure and he nodded. 'So very like her.'

'I feel her sometimes. I know she hasn't left us.'

'She wouldn't leave us, Gracey. I know that, too. And today, of all days, she'll be watching from wherever she is. Come, we don't want to be late, do we?'

'No, we don't.'

'I hope there'll be Victoria sponge.'

'Oh, Dad,' she laughed. 'You're always thinking of your stomach!'

* * *

Arthur and Grace cycled to Walbridge Hall. They took the shortcut through the woods and arrived at the house down the back drive. The mansion was bathed in sunshine and guests were already walking through the gate in the hedge, onto the lawn. Grace recognized most of them, even though some of the women were almost unrecognizable in smart tea dresses and lavish hats. There was a receiving line and Grace craned her neck to see beyond the crowd to where Rufus stood with his fiancée, shaking hands and greeting the guests. Everyone would get a chance to meet his bride, but Grace hadn't thought a great deal about *her*. Seeing Rufus again was all that had occupied her mind since the arrival of the invitation. Now she felt the butterflies grow agitated in her stomach as they neared the front of the queue. She felt, too, the unfamiliar pain of jealousy as she glimpsed the tall, white-skinned woman with thick blonde hair cut into a fashionable bob. Grace's head swam. Lady Georgina was a beauty, but more than that, she had the poise and elegance of a woman born into the highest echelons of society – attributes that Grace, however hard she wished for them, could never possess.

Arthur began to speak to the couple in front, but Grace didn't listen; she kept her eyes trained on the striking figure of Rufus, who smiled politely and looked genuinely pleased to see everyone. He hadn't changed at all. If anything, the lines that age had carved into the skin around his eyes and mouth only served to enhance his good looks. She wondered whether he would even remember her, and tried to prepare herself for the disappointment if he failed to recall her name.

At last it was their turn. At first Rufus didn't recognize her. He shook Arthur's hand and then hers and it was only when he was about to introduce them to Lady Georgina that he turned back swiftly, his expression softening suddenly, and the Rufus she had fallen for that day outside the church smiled at her warmly. 'Goodness me, you've grown up, Grace,' he said and he seemed to drink in her features as if aware that he didn't have enough time to savour them.

'A little,' she replied, conveying a confidence she didn't feel.

He stared at her longer than was comfortable, as if ensnared suddenly by a spell. She felt the colour flood her cheeks and didn't know where to look. But she was unable to tear her eyes away, as if she, too, had been caught by the same magic.

'Darling, aren't you going to introduce me?' It was Lady Georgina, now smiling down at Grace expectantly.

'Of course, Georgie.' He shook off the spell. 'This is Arthur Hamblin's daughter, Grace, who is a very proficient beekeeper.'

'Indeed,' said Lady Georgina, extending her hand. 'How fascinating.' Grace felt herself wither beneath the woman's cool gaze. She shook her hand. It was thin and cold and very soft. Her scarlet lips curled into a polite smile and she nodded briefly before turning her sea-green eyes to the couple who waited behind Grace. Arthur moved on and Grace, feeling the chill of Lady Georgina's smooth dismissal, glanced quickly at Rufus, who was still looking at her with a bewildered expression on his face. She gave a hesitant smile then followed her father onto the lawn. Her heart was pounding so hard against her ribcage she was afraid the whole tea party would hear it.

'What a smasher!' Arthur exclaimed. 'A real looker!' He didn't wait for Grace to reply, but continued enthusiastically as if he had been bound by an entirely different kind of spell. 'She's a real lady, she is. What a pleasure to meet her. I don't think I've ever met anyone so stunning in all my life. They make a handsome couple. We'll have to remember every detail to share with May tomorrow. She'll be disappointed if we don't.'

Grace listened to her father, but her thoughts were with Rufus. She turned to look back, but instead of Rufus's long face she saw Freddie's freckly one, gazing at her with ill-concealed admiration.

Chapter 11

'Wow, you look different,' said Freddie. But Grace could tell from his expression that he was trying to pay her a compliment.

'Thank you, Freddie,' she replied, longing to glance at Rufus over his shoulder but instinctively knowing it would enrage Freddie if she did. 'You brush up well yourself,' she added.

'Isn't she a corker, Lord Melville's bride-to-be?' interjected Arthur, barely able to take his eyes off the willowy Lady Georgina.

'She's in a class of her own,' Freddie agreed. 'They don't come better than that. In fact, I'd go so far as to say that I've never met a more beautiful woman in my life.' He blushed, as if suddenly aware that his remark, said out of spite, had exposed him.

Grace didn't flinch. 'It's true, she's very pretty,' she said. 'She's like a rare orchid. They make a fetching couple.'

'Well, she's a looker but she's icy,' he added, lowering his voice. '*I* wouldn't want to marry her.'

'I don't suppose she'd want to marry you, either,' said Arthur, scanning the tables set up beneath an ancient cedar tree for Victoria sponge cake. 'Do you think it would be rude to go and have a look at the food?' he asked.

A butler approached with a tray of drinks. 'Ah, what have we here?' Arthur exclaimed, sweeping his eyes over the tray of exotic-looking beverages.

'Champagne, ginger beer cocktail, sherry, and punch and soda,' the butler replied politely. 'If you would prefer tea, Mrs Emerson is serving it under the tree.'

'I think I'll have a cocktail,' said Arthur, helping himself. 'Grace?'

'That punch looks lovely,' she replied, reaching onto the tray. As she did so she caught a glimpse of Rufus over the butler's shoulder. He was still meeting and greeting the guests, his face aglow with pleasure, as if he really enjoyed shaking hands with the loyal staff who, like an army of ants, kept his father's great estate in working order. Beside him his frosty fiancée was beginning to wilt in the sunshine. She was barely able to muster a smile and Grace was sure her throat was strained to suppress a yawn.

Suddenly, Rufus lifted his eyes and they locked into Grace's with a jolt, as if hers had a strange magnetic pull that left him powerless to resist. So surprised was she to be caught watching him that she remained frozen, staring at him with a wide and startled gaze. For a brief, eternal moment, Grace felt the world still around her. There was only Rufus and his dark, enquiring eyes, finding their way into her soul as if they had always known the way.

Then the moment was lost. The people about her sharpened into focus and her father's voice penetrated her consciousness. 'Gracey?' he said. The blood rushed to her cheeks in a flood of embarrassment and with a monumental effort she wrenched her eyes away. 'Are you all right?' he asked.

She took a sip of punch. 'Shall we go and inspect the tea?' she suggested, trying to steady the tremor in her voice.

'Now you're talking,' he replied. 'Freddie? Shall we go and see what's on offer? I bet they'll have some mighty good cakes, don't you?'

The three of them walked across the lawn to the tables. Arthur chuckled with pleasure at the sight of all the cakes and scones and biscuits laid out on pretty china plates. He wandered up and down, shaking his head in astonishment, his cheeks aglow with pleasure.

'Look at all this!' Freddie exclaimed. 'And we're the first.'

'Someone has to be,' said Grace. 'What'll you go for?'

'Chocolate,' Freddie replied. 'You?'

'Coffee.'

'Let's share. You have a bit of mine and I'll have a bit of yours.'

She laughed. 'You're a greedy man, Freddie!'

'Why settle for a taste of one when you can have a taste of two?'

The sight of the three of them at the tables drew others and soon the cakes were surrounded by eager guests, all chatting to one another and commenting on the delicious feast and the delicate beauty of the soon-to-be Countess of Melville. Mrs Emerson, a rotund lady with breasts as large as balloons and hips as wide as the table, merrily talked to everyone, handing out Earl Grey tea in delicate china cups. Arthur had known her since he was a boy growing up in Walbridge and he lingered, sharing a joke or two, while he finished his cake and decided on which spongy treat he'd try next.

The air was infused with perfume as the ladies grew hot in the sun. Grace mingled with Freddie, talking to all those she knew, from the farm labourers who worked with Freddie to cheerless Mr Garner, whom Freddie hoped to supplant one day. Everyone was there. Gardeners and foresters, maids and kitchen staff, butlers and valets. Grace noticed that the Marquess and Marchioness of Penselwood had emerged to mingle. The Marchioness was standing with a couple of smartly dressed ladies Grace didn't know. They seemed very pleased to be speaking to her, and she was nodding with her head slightly bent, giving them her undivided attention, making them feel that they were the only people on the lawn she wanted to talk to. The Marquess was laughing heartily with Colonel Redwood, whom Grace hadn't expected to see at the party, and Reverend Dibben, who was at *every* party. She shared her cake with Freddie, who then went back to the table to grab another slice of the coffee cake. Finding Arthur hovering in front of the Victoria sponge, he was detained for some time chatting with him and Mrs Emerson, who enjoyed cheeky young men like Freddie more than she enjoyed cake.

'Hello, Little Bee,' came a voice behind Grace. She turned around to find Rufus standing over her. Her heart gave a startled flutter and she blinked up at him in surprise. 'How are your furry friends? Not stinging anyone, I hope?' he asked.

She smiled and blushed. 'No, they're quietly going about their business.'

'Good.' His eyes took in her features and he seemed surprised by what he saw. 'It wasn't so long ago that you were a girl. Look at you now. How time has flown.'

'Yes,' she replied, trying to think of something witty to say, but finding nothing but a mind blank with confusion. 'Congratulations on your engagement,' she said, remembering she had already congratulated him with her father on arrival.

'Thank you,' he replied. 'And you?' His eyes seemed to dig beneath her skin. 'Are you spoken for?'

She laughed and pulled a face. 'No, no, I'm . . .' She looked over at the table where her father was still engaged in conversation, polishing off a slice of Victoria sponge. 'I'm still with my father. The two of us against the world.' Her face softened as she watched him. 'He likes your cake.'

'Ah, that's Mrs Emerson's department. She's a terrific cook. If I lived here full time I'd be the size she is.' He laughed bashfully. 'That's awfully rude of me, but when I was a boy her nickname was Lardy.'

Grace put her hand to her mouth. 'Oh, that's awful.'

'Yes, rather. Still, I'm very fond of the old girl.'

'How's your grandmother?'

'Alive, astonishingly. Every year Mama says will be her last and every year she proves her wrong. If there's another war, I shall suggest she sign up. Put her on the front line and she'd show those Boche a thing or two.'

Grace looked anxious. 'Do you really think there will be another war?'

'I'm afraid Hitler's pushing for war. He's increasing his armies. He's swallowed up Austria and now he looks set to swallow up the Sudetenland as well. I'm afraid it looks certain.'

'But we've only just recovered from the last one,' she protested.

'I know, but I don't think people learn from history.'

'Don't say that.'

'Human beings are really very stupid, Grace.'

'Not stupid enough to send young men to their deaths.'

'They've done it before and they'll do it again and again. It's all about power, and people will do anything for that, even sacrifice their young men.'

Her eyes clouded with anxiety. 'Even you?'

His face grew tender and there was something very intimate in the smile he gave her. 'Would you mind?'

'Yes, I would.'

'You're very sweet, Grace. Really, I don't think I've ever met anyone as sweet as you.'

She blushed again. 'Not at all. I'd have a very hard heart if I didn't care about young men going off to die.'

'It will happen, but God willing it shall not last as long as the Great War. I shall end my days here at Walbridge, doing what my father has always done and his father before him. Eton, Oxford, Sandhurst; I've already ticked those boxes. There's a rather satisfying sense of continuity in it, though between us, I do dread the monotony. It's all very predictable. I rather long for twists and turns in my life that haven't been negotiated at my birth. You know, in a strange way I might even welcome a war. At least it will break up the tedium.' He sighed. 'Still, one can't complain. I know my future; many people don't have the luxury of such security.'

'I can't think of anything nicer than living in this beautiful place.'

'You'd hate it, Grace. It's much too big.'

'But the gardens . . .'

'Yes, the gardens, they're special. Full of bees.' He grinned. 'Grandmama's arthritis improved for a while but then it got bad again. She demanded to see you, but I put her off. I knew you'd be upset at having to send more of your favourite creatures to their deaths.'

'I would have done it for her. Those poor hands looked so painful.'

'They're more claws than hands. I'm surprised she hasn't come out looking for you.' He made his hands into claws and pulled a face.

She laughed. 'You're wicked, Rufus!'

'If she knew you were here she'd have you in the borders looking for bees. But she hates people, generally speaking, so a party like this is a nightmare to her. I'm not even sure she'll make our wedding.'

Grace's stomach plummeted at the mention of his wedding. 'When is it?'

'Next May. It's a long way away, but Georgie wants to get married when the bluebells are out, and I can't deny her that. I'll be taking her away from her home and settling her into a house in London where bluebells never grow.'

'That's a lovely time of year to get married.'

'Yes.' He suddenly looked sad and his forehead creased into a frown. 'I sometimes wonder . . .'

At that moment Arthur and Freddie joined them. Arthur was having an exceedingly good time, but Freddie's face had darkened with irritation and Grace wondered who had offended him.

'Now your father's here, I shall leave you and mingle.' Rufus glanced at Freddie and smiled. 'It's not polite to leave a lady standing on her own.' He moved away and was immediately caught by Mrs Garner and a couple of her heavily powdered friends.

'What was he on about?' Freddie demanded.

'He was asking me about the bees,' she replied. 'Reminding me of the time he brought his grandmother to our house.'

'He remembers you, Gracey,' said Arthur proudly.

'Not really,' she lied. 'He was just being polite.'

'I suppose they have to make their way around and talk to everyone,' said Freddie. 'He's right, though, I shouldn't have left you on your own. It made it impossible for him to move on and talk to someone else.'

'If Lord Melville had not wanted to talk to me, he would have had no trouble in introducing me to somebody else,' said Grace, and then she did something very out of character. She walked away. She simply turned on her heel and disappeared into the crowd. How dare Freddie make her feel small and inadequate all the time, she fumed? Talking to Rufus had given her a sudden burst of confidence. If *he* could treat her kindly, then so should Freddie. She needn't put up with spitefulness from anybody, least of all from someone she had known all her life.

As she strode into the throng she felt a surge of triumph. She didn't look back but she knew her small gesture of defiance would have taken Freddie by surprise, as much as it had surprised her. For a moment she worried about who she was going to talk to – she didn't want to bump into Lady Georgina – but there, his face beaming with pleasure, was Colonel Redwood.

When it was time to go, Grace was engulfed by a terrible sense of defeat. Rufus was getting married. She might never see him again. He had said he would die here at Walbridge when he was old; he hadn't mentioned that he'd live here *now*. He had told her he'd live in London and she assumed he'd remain there until his father died and he inherited the estate. It might be years before she laid eyes on him again. Years and years. She felt a rising desperation in her chest and a tightening sensation in her throat. If she had been alone she might have given in to tears, but as it was she had to smile even though her heart was flagging.

Lord Melville and Lady Georgina were at the gate, shaking hands with the guests as they left. It wasn't a formal line and some were simply waving and thanking them as they passed. But Grace found herself in front of Rufus once again, alongside Freddie and her father. This time Rufus did not allow his eyes to linger. He said goodbye politely and Lady Georgina told her how delicious the honey was. 'I'll make sure Mrs Emerson sends a box of it up to London,' she said, shaking Grace's hand with her cold, thin one.

'I wish you many happy years together,' said Arthur, now lightheaded and garrulous from the cocktails. 'I look forward to your return to Walbridge.'

'So do I,' said Lady Georgina graciously. 'You'll have to keep sending us your honey. It will be nice to have a little bit of Walbridge Hall in Edgerton Place.' Grace swallowed her despair and moved on through the gate. She was overcome by a wave of sorrow and hurried over to her bike, which was leaning against the house where she had left it. She didn't say goodbye to Freddie and she didn't wait for her father. She pedalled hard for home, tears streaming down her face, ruining her make-up and her newfound confidence, now in tatters.

When Arthur arrived at the cottage he found Grace beside the hives, sobbing. 'Gracey?' he asked, hurrying over. 'Whatever's the matter?'

'I'm just terribly unhappy,' she replied.

'Unhappy? Why?' He studied her blotchy face in bewilderment.

She was about to blurt out the truth, but something stopped her. A man like Arthur Hamblin would never understand her love for Lord Melville. To him, love between two people of a different class was inconceivable and foolish. She'd discussed Jane Austen with him enough to be sure of that. 'Freddie was so cruel,' she said instead.

Arthur's face softened and he nodded. *This* was a situation he could deal with. 'He's only cruel because he's sweet on you.'

Grace stared at him, genuinely surprised. 'Sweet on me?' she repeated.

'Can't you see it? I can. So can May.' He laughed. 'In fact, I think everyone can see it but you.'

'Then why is he so horrid?'

'Because he's jealous.'

'Of who?'

'Of Lord Melville, of course.'

'Why would he be jealous of Rufus?'

'Because he thinks you've taken a shine to him.' Before Grace could protest, he continued. 'Of course, *I* know you haven't. He's a gentleman and nice girls like you will always admire and respect a gentleman, but Freddie is young and he's wildly jealous of any other man who goes near you.'

'Are you sure?'

'I know more than you think. Freddie's always been like a brother to you, but now you've grown into a pretty young woman he's struggling with his feelings. He's a man looking at you with a man's eyes and it's all very confusing. Of course, it wouldn't be so confusing if you gave him a little hope.'

'Hope?'

'He'd be good for you, Gracey,' he told her seriously. 'One day, when Mr Garner retires, he'll be running the farm. He's naturally clever and he understands the land with a peasant's instinct. Besides, everyone likes him. He's a good lad. You'd do well to marry a man like Freddie, who'll be able to look after you – and you won't have to leave Walbridge.'

'Or you,' she replied, granting him a small smile.

'Well, I don't want you to leave me, Gracey, but you will, one day. It's natural. You'll marry and move out and I'll be left on my own.'

'Why have you never remarried, Dad? You're a good-looking man and you're kind and funny; any woman would be lucky to have you. Besides, you're not old.'

He shrugged, and then turned his eyes away. 'I never wanted to replace your mother,' he replied, resting his hand on the top of the beehive.

'It wasn't because of me?'

'No, you would have thrived with a nice step-mum to look after you.'

'I like being with you, just the two of us. We're a team.'

He grinned. 'A *good* team.'

'If one day I marry, you know I'll never move far away. I just couldn't be far away from you, Dad.'

'Don't make promises you can't keep, Gracey. But I'm grateful for the thought.'

He patted her gently. 'You're a good girl. Don't let Freddie upset you. He's just immature. Maybe you could look at him with different eyes, now that you're a woman. Life is a long road, and it's sometimes hard. To choose to travel that road with a man who knows you, understands you and shares the same culture, would be a wise choice indeed.'

'But what about the breathless, all-consuming love that writers have described over the centuries? Shouldn't I hold out for that?'

'Passion doesn't last, Grace. Look at Vronsky and Anna Karenina. That kind of passion is all part of forbidden love.'

'Elizabeth Bennet and Darcy, then?' she suggested instead.

Her father smiled. 'How dull *their* lives would have been after marriage. Darcy had no sense of humour. Elizabeth Bennet was much too good for him.' He looked at her seriously now. 'What you need is love, of course, but the steady, loyal, constant love of a friend. I think you might already love Freddie, but not know it. Here you are looking over his shoulder when the man for you is standing right in front of your nose.'

'I've never thought of Freddie in that way.'

'Then I have sown the seed. We don't need to speak about it any more. I would never push you to marry anyone you didn't want to marry. But I can guide you. Now, let's go and let the dog out. We could take him for a walk in the woods, if you like. He could do with a run and I could do with some exercise after all that cake. I'll tell you about the book I'm reading. I think you'd enjoy it. It's a wise and uplifting tale.'

That evening, as her father settled into his easy chair and opened his book, Grace's thoughts wandered to Freddie. She certainly hadn't guessed that his unkind comments were made out of jealousy. Freddie as a suitor had never entered her mind. Freddie as a husband was even more inconceivable, but it was a sobering thought. Was that *all* she could hope for? She recalled Rufus's comment about the monotony of his predictable life and she realized that she knew what he meant. Predictable, for her, was to marry Freddie. She'd spend the rest of her life in Walbridge. Their children would be born here and grow up here and she'd end up in the village cemetery like those who had lived the same sheltered life and died before her. It was a lonely thought and the more she dwelt on it, the lonelier she became. But what was the alternative? To live a life dreaming of a man she could never have? It was over. She had to erase Rufus from her heart or there would never be space for anyone else, and the thought of a life without love was unbearable.

At least if she remained here in Walbridge she might glimpse him from time to time. Their lives would run on parallel lines, and occasionally, as they turned the odd corner or climbed the odd hill, she'd see him and that would be something.

Chapter 12

Grace tried to forget about Rufus. She went back to her life – reading for Colonel Redwood, looking after her father, meeting her friends in the Fox and Goose – and pushed into the recesses of her mind her brief moment on the lawn with Rufus. She discovered that by focusing on the present, she was able to prevent her mind from wandering into the past. When she wasn't busy, she watched the bees. Every time Rufus's face surfaced, she concentrated all her attention on the small creatures she so loved. She watched them working in the flowerbeds and she watched them coming in and out of the hives. She listened to their low buzzing, and as the summer days grew shorter and the evenings chillier, she found that if she applied herself to her task, it worked. But it required a monumental effort, and at night, when she lay in bed with nothing but her will to control the determined wandering of her mind, she gave in. She was too tired and too unhappy to fight it.

Freddie was busy with the harvest. He was up at dawn and spending all day in the fields, thatching ricks, cutting the wheat and barley, tying them into stooks to dry in the sun. May made him sandwiches, which he ate in the shade with the other labourers, and fed him supper when he returned after dark, his clothes full of dust, his face smeared with sweat and dirt, worn out and ready for bed. Grace barely saw him. She barely saw her father, either, for he was busy in the vegetable garden, picking fruit and vegetables to feed the large house parties being held at the Hall. She took over the beekeeping and spent hours in the shed washing jars, sticking on new labels and preparing for the harvest. Once they'd extracted the honey in early September they'd take it up to the farm office in crates. She wondered whether Lady Georgina would really send for some from London and whether the jars she held in her hands would eventually be held in Rufus's. It was a thought that caught her off guard and consequently broke through her resistance. Holding the glass in her hand, she could almost feel the warmth of his fingers on top of hers. As she prepared each jar she took her time, placing them carefully in rows along the shelves of the shed with a silent prayer for Rufus.

At the end of the summer the village celebrated the harvest festival with a church service. Grace found herself sitting next to Freddie. He was tanned and slim, his auburn hair bleached in the sun and falling over his forehead in thick chunks. His eyes shone bluer against his brown skin and his freckles had multiplied and spread across his nose and cheeks. The hard work had made a man out of him and Grace noticed for the first time how handsome he was. 'How have you been, Grace?' Freddie asked in a low voice.

'Fine,' she replied. 'Busy preparing for the honey harvest and reading to Colonel Redwood.' She noticed Freddie's legs were longer. He seemed to take up more space in the pew. She also noticed his smell. 'What have you put on yourself?' she asked, giving a sniff. She felt him grow hot and wished she hadn't asked.

'Shaving foam,' he replied, rubbing his chin self-consciously.

She glanced at him and noticed his cheeks were red. 'It smells nice,' she said, then laughed at herself for giving him a compliment. She'd never told Freddie he smelt nice before.

She waited for him to put her down or to make her feel stupid for such an uncharacteristic comment, but he didn't. To her surprise he smiled at her with affection.

'You smell of a summer garden,' he said. His blush deepened.

'Really?'

'Yes, when I think of you,' – he looked embarrassed – 'I think of flowers.'

Grace stared at him in astonishment. 'That's nice,' she said, wanting to be more effusive but not finding the words.

At that moment the Marquess and Marchioness of Penselwood walked down the aisle in a stately procession with the frail and shrunken Dowager Marchioness beside them, and took their places in the front pew. The congregation hushed. Grace was not surprised that Rufus was absent. He was never at Walbridge these days. She found herself searching the faces of the Marquess's party, for he seemed always to be accompanied by an entourage of house guests, but Rufus's was definitely not among them. She *was* surprised, however, to find that she didn't suffer the habitual pang of disappointment and was easily distracted by Freddie's knee pressing gently against hers. She didn't move her leg away but let it rest there, feeling a strange and unfamiliar thrill as the warmth seemed to travel all the way up her body and cause her spine to tingle. If Freddie felt the same sensation, he didn't let it show. But Grace noticed that every time they sat down after singing a hymn, his knee returned to touch hers, and every time she felt the pressure of his proximity, the warmth between them intensified.

After the service they all flooded into the churchyard to mingle and chat. Freddie was eager to talk to her. 'Will you come to the river this afternoon?' he asked, gazing down at her hopefully. 'I feel I haven't seen you for months.'

'*You're* the one who hasn't had time for *me*,' she replied.

'I know, it's been mad.'

She smiled, unsure of the strange new energy that vibrated between them. 'You've been working hard,' she said, looking him up and down and thinking how thin he'd become. 'Isn't Auntie May feeding you?'

'I've never worked so hard in my life, but I love it, Grace.' His eyes shone with enthusiasm. 'I love being out in the fields. I love the physical challenge of it. It's the best thing I ever did.'

'That's nice, Freddie. Mr Garner really better watch out, then.'

'He'd better. One day I'm going to be running the whole estate.'

'I bet you will, too.' Her cheeks burned with admiration. The dynamic between them had changed in just a few months. She no longer felt older than him. He had caught up with her and run on ahead, turning from a boy into a man in a few giant leaps.

'Will you come?' he asked.

'Yes, I'll come,' she replied, and the smile her answer induced gave her an unexpected frisson of pleasure.

A while later she was taking the shortcut home with her father. The leaves were yet to turn but the light was the softer, golden hue of early autumn. The fields were all cut and the stubble gleamed in the sunshine. She thought of Freddie and the hours he had spent in those fields. The labour had strengthened his shoulders and toned his body and given him a certain vivacity which she found very attractive. She glanced across at her father and thought how, for him, the physical work just wore him out. He looked tired.

'Dad, what are you thinking about?' she asked.

'Oh, nothing,' he replied, shaking himself out of his thoughts.

'I was just thinking how lovely the woods look in this light. Besides spring, early autumn is my favourite time of the year.'

He smiled now and looked around him. 'We have a lot to be grateful for.' He nodded. 'Harvest festival reminds us of that.'

'That's true. We have everything we need,' she added.

'Happy people aren't necessarily those who have everything, but those who make the best of everything they have,' he said wisely. 'We do all right, you and I, don't we, Grace?'

'We do better than all right. The things that make me happy aren't the things that can be bought, Dad. Happiness comes from accepting what one has. You taught me that.'

'I'd like you to have had a mother,' he said, his face becoming solemn again. 'But God had a plan and that wasn't part of it.'

'Auntie May has been a mother to me,' she replied.

His expression softened and he turned his face to the sun and sighed. 'She's always been there for you. I don't think I could have done without May.' He thrust his hands into his trouser pockets.

'She's been there for you, too, hasn't she?'

He glanced at her and frowned. 'She's been a steady friend. It's hard bringing up a daughter on one's own. Your grandma and aunt tried to help in the beginning, and they did for a while, but they wanted to take over, not just you but the house too and me with it! I sent them both packing. I don't know anything about women's things. If May hadn't been there to step in, I don't know what I'd have done.'

'You'd have done just fine, Dad. We'd have muddled through.'

'I wanted more for you than muddling through, Grace. May's a fine role model. She's kind, gentle, hard-working and funny. I remember thinking, when you were a little girl, that if you grew up to be like May, you'd make me and your mother proud. May was the closest friend your mum had and I know she'd approve of her taking over and setting an example for you to follow.'

'And how have I turned out?' She gave a little smile, but her father took her seriously.

'I'm proud,' he replied. 'I know I can speak for your mother. She's proud, too, wherever she is.'

'Not far away, I don't think,' said Grace.

'She's always with us, Grace. Don't ever forget that. Just because you can't see her, doesn't mean she's not here in spirit. The body's only a shell and she doesn't need it where she is. She can be anywhere at any time, in a single thought.'

'That's a nice idea.'

'It's true. We're here to learn, Gracey. To grow in love. That's all there is to it. It's not complicated. And the way to grow is through selflessness, forgiveness and compassion: love. That's all there is. Putting oneself second, not first. Looking out for one another, like the bees.'

He glanced at her and smiled. 'Do you think the bees are ready for harvest?' he asked.

'They're still foraging a bit, but it's getting chilly now, especially in the evenings.'

'I suggest we start next week.' He stepped up his pace. 'Let's have a look when we get home. But I hazard a guess that the time has come to extract the honey.'

'Everything's ready. I've prepared all the jars.'

'You're a good girl, Gracey. I could have had a rebellious or difficult child, but I got you.'

'Made in your image, Dad,' she laughed.

'Perhaps on the inside, Gracey. But on the outside, you're the image of your mother.'

After lunch, Grace cycled to Freddie's house. Her heart inflated and began to beat faster as she approached his home. All this for Freddie, she thought, laughing at the absurdity of feeling nervous about the boy who was like a brother to her. But when he stepped out into the street, it was a very different Freddie from the lad who'd always anxiously waited for her to come and spend time with him. This Freddie made her feel awkward and a little shy. His gaze was heavier, his manner more confident, his smile wiping away the old sneer of resentment she had never understood. When he suggested they cycle to the river, her skin rippled with a mixture of apprehension and excitement. She didn't realize that she no longer had to concentrate on keeping Rufus out of her thoughts; Freddie had taken up all the space there.

As they raced down the path that wound its way alongside the river, she began to feel less uncomfortable. He cycled in front of her, throwing back the usual banter as their bicycles sped over stones and tree roots crossing the track. He was faster than before and she had to shout for him to slow down. He teased her for being a girl, but the tone of his voice and the way he laughed was full of affection, and she was aware, as never before, that he was a man and she was a woman. He was suddenly more than just *Freddie*.

They reached their usual place and leaned their bicycles against the tree. Freddie untied the rug off the back of his bicycle and laid it on the grass. 'Are you going to swim?' she asked.

'Might do, if I get hot,' he answered.

'Do you remember how you used to dive off that bridge?'

'And nearly kill myself in the process.'

'No, you were much too good. You skimmed the surface like a swan.'

He grinned and sat down beside her. 'You were always a fine audience, Grace.'

'Well, I was always impressed,' she replied truthfully. She hugged her knees.

Freddie lay back and propped himself up on his elbows. 'They were halcyon days.'

'They still are. In fact, I'd say they just get better,' said Grace happily.

'They won't get better if there's a war.'

'War? There's not going to be a war,' she retorted, feeling suddenly afraid. 'No one wants another war.'

'I don't think we'll have any choice, Grace.'

'Don't say that.' She gazed out over the water. 'Let's not talk of sad things. Entertain me instead.'

'How?' He laughed.

'I don't know. Go and dive off that bridge again.'

'OK, I will,' he replied, rising to the challenge. 'Anything for you, Grace.'

Suddenly, she caught sight of what looked like her father standing on the other side of the river. She shielded her eyes against the sun and squinted. 'Dad?' She frowned.

Freddie followed her line of vision. 'Arthur, where?' he asked.

She pointed. 'There, on the bank.'

'I can't see anyone.'

'It's Dad.'

Freddie chuckled. 'It's just the light and shadow, playing with you.'

The vision disappeared. 'I'm sure it was him,' she said quietly.

'What would he be doing on the river bank?'

'I don't know.'

'You're seeing things.'

'Or someone else, spying on us. What do you think, Freddie? Do you think we're being spied on?'

'You're mad. There's no one there. There never is. It's just you and me.'

'I hope so.' She laughed uncertainly. 'It just looked like him.'

'Do you want me to jump off that bridge or not?'

'Yes, I do. But be careful.'

He got up and stripped down to his underpants. She forgot all about the sight of her father on the bank and laughed nervously as Freddie tossed aside his clothes and stood before her, tanned from the waist up, broad and muscular. 'Are you going to come in?' he asked, smiling down at her.

'No, much too cold.' She shooed him away with her hand. 'Go on!' He walked through the trees and appeared a moment later on the bridge. She could see him watching her to make sure she didn't take her eyes off him. He didn't realize that she *couldn't* take her eyes off this dashing new Freddie, even if she had wanted to.

Her heart was suddenly filled with panic as he climbed up onto the balustrade. She changed her position and knelt up on the rug, praying that he didn't do something stupid and hurt himself. It had been a long time since he'd jumped off that bridge and he was bigger and heavier now.

He put his arms above his head and took a deep breath. 'Ready?' he shouted.

'Be careful!' she shouted back. As he pushed himself off into the air she placed her hands over her mouth and gasped. He jumped very high then came swooping down like a swallow, arms out like wings, before putting them together and skimming the water, just below the surface. He then disappeared, leaving the water rippling gently where he had broken through.

She was poised, ready to clap, but he didn't come up. She leapt to her feet and anxiously searched the river. He still didn't come up. Her heart seemed to stall and fear rose to blacken the happiness that had, only minutes before, filled it to the point of bursting. 'Freddie!' she cried. She was about to choke on her fright when Freddie stood up, only a few feet in front of her, smiling jubilantly.

Grace burst into tears. 'You idiot!' she shouted furiously. 'You scared me!'

'Grace, I didn't mean to frighten you.' Freddie waded out of the water, his face contorted with remorse. Then, before she could reply, he had pulled her into his arms and was kissing her so passionately that she didn't know whether to be angry or pleased. His mouth was warm and wet and surprisingly exciting. He pulled away a moment. They stared at each other, both surprised and a little afraid. Grace had stopped crying. She was calm now, too astonished to be cross. She felt the rising swell of desire and edged forward a step. It was barely perceptible, but it was enough to encourage Freddie. He wound his hands around her neck and kissed her again.

Lying in Freddie's arms felt like the most natural thing in the world. They were on the rug, Freddie's wet body drying slowly in the sun and against Grace's summer dress. He ran his lips over her cheeks, across her jawline and down her neck, and she laughed softly as the sensation caused her body to tingle, right to her toes. This was her very first kiss. She had often imagined being kissed, but the reality far exceeded her expectations. It stirred feelings in her she never knew she had, and she recalled with tenderness how Freddie had said that when he thought of her he thought of flowers.

Her father was right: perhaps she had loved Freddie all along and just never realized. She had been so busy looking over his shoulder that she hadn't noticed him, until a summer on the farm had made him man enough to attract her attention.

They lay kissing for what felt like hours. Intoxicated by the smell and feel of each other's skin, they kissed and touched with an unquenchable thirst for more. But the end of the day came and the shadows lengthened and the air turned cold. Freddie got up and put on his clothes. 'Don't frighten me like that again,' she said, watching him buttoning up his shirt.

'I'm glad I did,' he replied. 'If I hadn't I might not have had the courage to kiss you. I've wanted to kiss you since I was fifteen,' he confessed.

'Really? For that long?'

'You've always been the girl for me, Grace. Always.' He sat down beside her and swept her hair off her face. His eyes were heavy with emotion. 'I've loved you for as long as I can remember. I feared you'd never love me back.'

'I didn't know I loved you until today.'

He beamed happily. 'So you love me, Grace?'

She smiled shyly. 'Yes, Freddie. I do. You're different. You're not a boy any more.'

'And you're not a girl, either.'

'Our games have got much more exciting,' she laughed.

'Let's play a little more, then. I'm not ready to take you home.'

'*Are* you going to take me home, Freddie?'

'You're my sweetheart now. I'm not going to let you cycle home on your own. I'm going to take care of you from now on.' She smiled with pleasure and lay down so he could kiss her again. 'You're my sweetheart, Grace,' he repeated. 'I love the sound of that, and I love the sound of "I love you." I've only ever said it in my head.'

'To me?'

'To you.'

'And I never knew.'

'You do now.' He kissed her. 'I love you.' He kissed her again. 'I love you.' And presently he kissed her again . . .

Chapter 13

It was almost dark when Grace and Freddie cycled back to the Beekeeper's Cottage. They pedalled side by side, laughing and chatting merrily, trying to bicycle and hold hands at the same time. They wobbled and weaved, and when Grace nearly fell off, Freddie steadied her by taking hold of her handlebar and guiding her back onto the track. There were no barriers between them now, nothing to prevent them from feeling entirely intimate with each other. They had declared their love and the evening looked more beautiful because of it.

They reached the cottage. The windows were dark. Grace leaned her bicycle against the wall and wandered into the garden. 'Dad!' she called. There came no reply from the borders. She could see no activity about the hives. 'Where is he?' she asked Freddie, who was striding across the grass behind her. A moment later Pepper appeared. He wagged his tail, happy to see them. Grace bent down and stroked his ears. 'Where's your master?' she asked, but the dog looked back at her with big, shiny eyes, communicating nothing but his desire to be petted.

'Let's try inside,' Freddie suggested. They walked into the cottage and switched on the light. Grace could tell immediately from the feel of the place that her father wasn't there. It was quiet and empty, like a tomb. She began to feel anxious. If he had gone out he would have left her a note. He certainly wouldn't have left Pepper to roam freely about the garden.

'Oh, Freddie, I'm worried,' she said.

'Don't be. He'll probably be at the pub.'

'He would have let me know. He would have shut the dog in the kitchen.'

'Perhaps he's gone looking for *you*.'

'Maybe,' she replied, feeling a little better. 'He's probably at your house.'

'Let's go and see. I don't know about you, but all that kissing has made me hungry.'

'You boys only ever think of your stomachs.' She laughed despite her concern.

He drew her into his arms. 'How can I think of my stomach when I'm with you?' He kissed her nose. 'How ungallant.'

But something tugged on her gut. 'Let's have another look in the garden.' She pulled away and hurried back outside.

Grace walked about the flowerbeds, sensing something strange but unable to decipher what it was. Pepper sniffed the grass then took off towards the hives. Instinct told her to follow him. Her heart heavy with dread, she watched the dog disappear into the shrubbery. Then she saw a pair of feet peeking out from beneath a bush. The shoes and socks were unmistakable. 'Dad!' she cried and ran over to where her father lay inert on the ground. Freddie was beside her in a moment. Grace let out a howl and fell onto Arthur's chest. There was no heartbeat beneath. No sound of life. Nothing but a limp and vacant shell. 'He's gone!' she exclaimed in horror. 'He's gone!'

Freddie knelt down and felt Arthur's neck for a pulse. Then he put his cheek to his nose and mouth to feel for a breath. There was nothing. No whisper of the man, just the still silence of death. 'Oh, darling Grace, I'm sorry,' he said. Grace was overcome by an assault of grief. It knocked her sideways, into Freddie's arms. She clung to him in despair and all he could do was hold her tightly and wait for the sorrow to make its way through her.

Grace held onto Freddie with all her strength. She squeezed her eyes shut and let the terrible sense of loneliness engulf her. Her father had been everything to her: father, mother, brother, sister, friend. Without him, she didn't know how she could go on. Like a ship lost at sea, she had been robbed of her rudder and her sails, and she no longer knew which direction was home. 'He was there on the riverbank, Freddie,' she whispered. 'He had come to say goodbye.'

'What do we do?' she asked finally.

'You stay here while I go and get help.'

'How did he die? Why . . . ?'

'I don't know, my darling. Only a doctor can tell you that.'

Her eyes filled with tears again and her chin trembled. 'He was all I had,' she choked.

Freddie held her face firmly and looked into her eyes with conviction. 'No, Grace. You have me. You'll always have me.'

When Grace had calmed down, Freddie disappeared on his bicycle to get help. He promised to be as quick as he could. She watched him go, afraid to be left on her own, then turned her attention back to her father, barely able to believe that he had been taken from her so suddenly, without any warning. She hadn't had a chance to say goodbye. That thought made her cry again. She took his hand and held it against her cheek, silently cursing God for taking the only parent she had ever known.

She remained on the grass, her light cardigan inadequate against the chill of evening and the cold that now seemed to come from the very marrow of her bones. Her father's spaniel curled up against his body and gazed at Grace with eyes full of resignation. 'You're mine now,' she told him. The dog sighed heavily, as if to let her know that he was settling for second best. She glanced at the hives then back at her father. There was no sign of stings on his skin. The bees hadn't killed him. She swept her eyes over his face. His expression was serene, as if he had simply fallen asleep. If she hadn't been holding his icy hand she might have expected him to wake up at any moment and ask what all the fuss was about. She recalled walking home from church that morning, and how tired he had looked. He didn't look tired now, or old. His skin was translucent and the lines had softened around his mouth and eyes. The deep furrows in his forehead had relaxed and melted away. He resembled a boy again. However he had died, he hadn't suffered. She was sure of that. Perhaps he had simply reached out and taken her mother's hand.

Freddie returned with his parents and the vicar, all squeezed into Reverend Dibben's little Austin. When May saw Arthur, she gave a gasp and burst into tears. She helped Grace off the grass and gathered her into her arms. 'You're freezing, my dear. Let's get you inside at once. You'll catch your death out here.' Her voice was reassuringly maternal, firm and capable, and Grace let her usher her into the house and settle her on one of the spindle-back chairs in the kitchen. 'It must have been a heart attack,' said May as she bustled about, taking cups down from the cupboards and filling the kettle with water. She was efficient and knew the kitchen well. Her warm presence pervaded the room and thawed Grace's cold bones, lifting her despair like sun on mist.

The men carried Arthur into the house and laid him onto his bed, folding his hands across his chest. May lit a candle and Reverend Dibben said a prayer. They all bowed their heads and Grace cried softly at the sight of her father lying there, never to wake up again.

They crowded into the small kitchen and drained May's pot of tea.

'I'll organize an ambulance to collect your father tomorrow,' said Michael. 'Don't worry, Grace, we'll see to all the arrangements so you don't have to worry.'

'Why don't you come and stay with us tonight, dear?' May suggested. 'I don't think you should be here on your own.'

'I'm not on my own,' Grace replied.

May smiled sympathetically. 'You know what I mean, dear.'

'I can't leave Dad,' she protested.

Michael caught his wife's eye. 'He'll be fine here. You don't need to worry. It's *you* we're concerned about.'

'I'll stay,' Freddie suggested. 'I'll sleep on the sofa. If Grace wants to be here with Arthur then I'll stay with her and keep her company.'

This idea appealed to May although Reverend Dibben's lips pursed. 'Your father is with God now, Grace,' he said.

'I'm not having him being here on his own. I couldn't bear the thought of him . . .' Her voice trailed off.

May patted her hand. 'Don't upset yourself, dear. If you want to stay here, then here you shall stay. Freddie will keep you company.'

Grace smiled gratefully at Freddie. 'Thank you,' she said and their eyes were full of affection for each other which no one else could see.

Before leaving, Michael lit the fire in the sitting room and May brought a spare blanket down from the cupboard on the landing and spread it on the sofa for Freddie. She went to the icebox and laid out bread, cheese and ham on the table for supper and popped a couple of potatoes in the oven. 'We'll be OK, Mum,' said Freddie, watching his mother in amusement.

'I just want to make sure you both eat, especially Grace. Make sure she eats, won't you?'

'I will.'

'You're a good boy to stay and look after her.'

'I'm very happy to.' His mother couldn't know *how* happy.

May put the salt and pepper pots on the table then stood up with a sad face. 'What a dreadful business. Poor Grace, she never had a mother and now she loses her father. It's so unfair.'

'She's got us, Mum,' said Freddie.

May nodded. 'She's got us. Indeed she has. We'll take care of her.' She lowered her voice. 'She can't stay here on her own, you know.'

'Don't say that.'

May pursed her lips and said nothing more about it. 'We'll leave you now. I hope you'll both be all right.'

'We're not children any more, Mum.'

'I know, but I'll never stop being your mother.' She had to stand on tiptoe to kiss his cheek. 'Be good, now.' Freddie watched her leave.

He found Grace in her father's chair. The golden glow from the fire skipped and jumped across her face, which remained pale in spite of the light. When she saw him she tore her eyes away from the flames and smiled. 'Thank you, Freddie,' she said softly. He sat on the sofa and she came to curl up against him, resting her head on his shoulder.

'We're alone now,' he said, pulling her close and kissing her head.

'Except for Pepper,' she replied.

'Except for him.' They both looked at the dog sleeping peacefully in front of the fire.

'We have to make the most of every day, Freddie,' Grace said firmly. 'We never know when we'll be called back. One minute Dad was in the garden, weeding, and the next he was gone. How strange that one man was taken from me just as another was given to me.'

'That's a nice way to look at it. It'll make it easier for Arthur to leave knowing that you're not alone.'

'I'm going to have to get a proper job, Freddie. I'm going to have to . . .'

'Hush, don't think about that now. You're upset. When Arthur's been laid to rest we'll discuss your future. Thinking about it in your state of mind will just upset you more.'

She sighed and relaxed again, knowing that she would have Freddie to help her make decisions. She didn't feel quite so alone any more. 'This afternoon was such fun,' she told him. 'I wish Dad could have seen us together. You know, he was very fond of you, Freddie. He said I couldn't do better than a man like you. He thought the world of you.'

'I thought the world of him, too.' He chuckled. 'And I respect him even more for his wisdom. He was right, of course. You'll never do better than a man like me.'

'Freddie?'

'Yes?'

'Are you still hungry?'

'Yes.'

She sat up and grinned at him. 'Shall we have our first supper, then?'

He took her hand. 'It's our first *date*, you know.' He smiled tenderly and she gazed back at him with equal affection. The flames danced in her eyes and he wound his arm around her neck and kissed her lips. Grace realized then that it was possible to feel happy in the wake of such unhappiness.

They dined at the kitchen table and Grace lit a candle and placed it in the centre. They drank ginger beer and tucked into the supper May had prepared for them. They talked a lot about Arthur. Grace shared her memories and Freddie held her hand when she cried. But they laughed, too, and in spite of the tragedy, or perhaps *because* of it, Grace felt her heart overflow with love for Freddie.

It was past midnight when they decided to go to bed. Freddie lingered at her bedroom door and kissed her gently. Grace didn't like the idea of going to bed alone. She hesitated and let him kiss her until she was forced by sheer weariness to let him go. She heard him downstairs as she undressed and prepared for bed. It was a reassuring sound, but strange, too, for she was used to her father's habitual routine and his slow, familiar tread. She lay beneath the sheets and thought of Freddie downstairs on the sofa. She hoped he was warm enough with the blanket and the dying fire. She strained her ears and listened out for his movements, but she could only hear the regular ticking of the grandfather clock in the hall. After a while the house went quiet as if it, too, had succumbed to sleep.

She closed her eyes and tried not to think of her father down the corridor. She tried not to think about her future without him. She tried not to think of all the things she'd miss. If only she could cease thinking altogether – but her mind whirred unhappily in the darkness as her exhausted body waited for the relief of slumber.

She must have fallen asleep eventually, for she was awoken by a bright glow filling the room. She opened her eyes and saw, to her bewilderment, her father standing at the end of her bed, surrounded by a white light, like mist. He looked younger and more handsome and was smiling at her with joy, as if he wanted her to know how happy he was. She blinked, certain that she was dreaming, but he remained, radiating a deep and powerful love. Her heart began to beat frantically but she instinctively knew that if she felt afraid he would disappear, that somehow her fear would prevent her from seeing him. So she remained perfectly still, eyes wide, heart open, absorbing his love like a dry sponge. Then slowly he began to fade, either because of her weariness or his, she wasn't sure. She willed him to stay, but a moment later the room was filled with darkness again and she was once more engulfed in loneliness, wondering whether grief had induced her to dream the whole thing up.

She climbed out of bed and tiptoed lightly down the stairs. The embers were still glowing in the grate and Freddie was asleep beneath the blanket. She stood in the doorway not knowing what to do. She didn't want to be alone, but it was inappropriate to sleep with Freddie. But it didn't *feel* inappropriate. She had known him all her life. Up until that afternoon he had been like a big brother to her. She bit her fingernails as her feet grew cold. Then she took a deep breath and climbed beneath the blanket to snuggle up against him. She woke him up, but his head was heavy with sleep and soon he was breathing deeply again and Grace felt warm and comforted against his body. She closed her eyes and felt a reassuring sense of security wash over her.

In the morning, she awoke before he did. She lay against his stomach. One arm was casually falling about her waist, the other pillowed her head. She longed to remain there, but she knew it was very possible that May would come over early. Reluctantly she crept out, disturbing him as little as possible. He stirred but did not wake. She crept across the floorboards, wincing every time they creaked.

She went upstairs to her bedroom and opened the curtains. Outside, the sun was shining brightly as if it didn't know her father was dead. She slipped into a dress, pinned her hair up and applied a little rouge to mask her dreadful pallor. She let Pepper out of the kitchen and he scampered across the hall to be released into the garden. The noisy latch awoke Freddie, who sat up with a start, unsure of where he was. His auburn hair was sticking up in tufts and his cheeks were pink. His dark-blue eyes shone brighter against his blushes. 'Did you sleep here last night, or did I dream it?' he asked, raking fingers through his hair.

'You dreamed it,' she replied.

He tilted his head and grinned. 'No, I didn't.'

Suddenly May appeared at the door, carrying a basket of bread rolls, her daughter Josephine a few paces behind. 'We've brought you breakfast,' she said briskly. 'My dear, you look very pale. Freddie, did you make sure Grace ate last night?'

'She ate plenty, Mum,' he replied sleepily, stretching the arm that was stiff from where she had laid her head.

'I'm fine,' Grace interjected.

Josephine caught up. 'You poor thing, Grace. What a shock! What a terrible shock. I can't bear to think of you all alone in this house without Arthur. It's simply dreadful.' She pushed past her mother and Grace and strode into the hall. 'It feels so empty now, doesn't it?'

'I've brought you some rolls,' said May. 'They're fresh from my kitchen. I was up baking at dawn. I couldn't sleep.' She joined her daughter in the small hall. 'The ambulance will be here this morning to take Arthur. Michael called them as soon as he could. You should eat, though, the two of you. You can't do anything on empty stomachs. Grace, come with us.' May and Josephine led the way into the kitchen.

Grace followed them and set about making a pot of tea. It seemed that Auntie May was hiding her grief behind a mask of efficiency and activity. She had applied make-up, but lipstick and eyeshadow could not conceal the evidence of tears shed throughout the night. Josephine wore her Crawford Smear in deep crimson. She looked more radiant than ever, excited no doubt to be involved in a drama. Grace laid the table and gave Pepper his morning biscuit. Freddie wandered in, having dressed and wet his hair. He was flushed from the cold water he had splashed on his face.

'Now, sit down, both of you, and put something inside you,' said May. Freddie caught Grace's eye and without saying a word they both communicated their concern. May was acting very oddly, even for a woman who had just lost a dear friend. Josephine lit a cigarette and appraised her nail polish. Freddie and Grace ate the rolls and drank their tea. May didn't sit at all. She paced the room, pretending to be busy.

'Mum, you have to tell her,' said Josephine, flicking ash into the ashtray her mother had placed in front of her. 'All your bustling about is making me dizzy.'

'Tell me what?' Grace looked searchingly at May.

May pulled up a chair and sat down. 'You will have to come and live with us,' she said firmly.

'We'll be a big, happy family,' said Josephine. 'You can share my room until we kick Freddie out.' She grinned at Freddie provocatively. Freddie didn't seem to hear her.

Grace stared at May in shock. 'Why can't I live here?'

'You can't live here on your own!' Josephine interrupted. 'It's creepy living in an old cottage alone.'

'It's not creepy at all. It's my home. I *want* to live here. I'm not a child any more.'

'I'm afraid Mr Garner won't let you.' May looked at Grace and pursed her lips with fury directed at Mr Garner. 'This cottage was tied to your father's job. As he's no longer working on the estate, they won't let you stay.'

'It's a man's world,' said Josephine with a sigh. 'If you were a man they wouldn't dream of kicking you out.'

Grace blanched even more. 'But who will look after the bees?'

'I don't know, my dear. That's *their* problem,' said May.

'I would have thought the bees were the least of your worries,' interjected Josephine.

'Someone will have to look after them, surely?' Grace gasped. 'We were going to harvest the honey this week.' She stifled a sob.

'They'll find a new beekeeper,' said May.

'But I know more about bees than anyone.' Grace's voice thinned to a whisper and her eyes filled with tears. 'They can't throw me out of my own home. Dad hasn't even been buried yet. I'm not leaving.'

'Michael spoke to Mr Garner this morning. They won't do anything in a hurry, of course. But you won't be able to stay indefinitely. Ultimately, you will have to find accommodation elsewhere. But don't worry, Michael and I will see to it all.'

'Until then you can come and live with us,' said Josephine gleefully.

'Thank you for the offer, but I'm staying here. This is my home.' Grace turned her feverish eyes on Freddie. 'They can't make me leave my home! Please, don't let them make me leave.'

Freddie's face was now red with indignation. 'I'll go and talk to him,' he said, jumping up.

'What can *you* do about it, Freddie?' Josephine asked, giving a sceptical little sniff. 'You're about as useful as a whisper in a wind.'

'And you haven't finished your breakfast!' May exclaimed.

He glanced at his watch. 'I haven't got time for breakfast. I have a job to do.' He smiled at Grace and his eyes shone with intent. 'Make that *two* jobs. The most important one being rescuing you, Grace. Don't worry, Mr Garner's not going to know what's hit him.'

'Oh Freddie, don't do anything stupid!' said Grace, fiddling with her hands.

'Not stupid, Grace. It'll be the best thing I've ever done in my life.'

The three women watched him leave, wondering what on earth he could do to change Mr Garner's mind. But Freddie knew. There was only one thing he *could* do, and, as he climbed onto his bicycle and set off up the track, he realized with a buoyant heart that he had never been surer of anything since the day he was born.

Chapter 14

Arthur Hamblin's funeral was a subdued affair. There was a small afternoon service at the local church where Reverend Dibben droned on and on and even Grace's mind began to wander. May dabbed her eyes and blew her nose throughout while Josephine comforted her noisily, never shy about drawing attention to herself. The pews were full of friends and people Arthur had worked with and it was heart-warming for Grace to know that her father was loved by so many people. Even Mr Garner had deigned to come and pay his respects, and Arthur's mother and sister had taken the train from Cornwall, although after the initial pleasantries Grace didn't know what to say to them. Grace sat in between Freddie and Michael and resisted the temptation to take Freddie's hand. But he pressed his knee against hers and only they knew its significance.

Arthur was laid to rest in the churchyard beside his wife, and alongside all the flowers Grace had placed a jar of honey and a copy of 'The Bee-Boy's Song' by Rudyard Kipling, which he was so fond of. The headstone was yet to be made, but Michael had arranged for a temporary wooden one until the marble one was ready. It simply stated his name and the dates of his birth and death. Grace stared down at those numbers and thought how fleeting life was when viewed in that basic way. The cold figures carved into the wood told nothing of the warmth of his being, the love he had given and received and the valuable contribution he had made to their small world. Suddenly it seemed desperately important that people remembered him, for without memories Arthur would cease to exist altogether and, for Grace, that was unbearable. She swept her eyes over the faces of those she had known all her life and felt a swell of affection for every one of them, for in each mind there glimmered small fragments of her father's existence, and in a strange way Grace felt that, as long as they continued to shine, Arthur lived on.

She felt Freddie's strong presence beside her. He now stood like a rock, sheltering her against the wind. While he was here, she would be safe – and she wouldn't be alone. She shifted in her seat and gently pressed her arm against his. The warmth of his skin burned through his jacket and the comforting vibration he gave off enveloped her like a cloak. She didn't need to look at him to know what he was thinking, for she felt his love as if it were a physical thing.

Once the funeral was over everyone went to the Fox and Goose for a drink. Mr Garner had arranged for the estate to cover the costs and soon the pub was heaving with people overflowing into the beer garden behind. The sun was bright and warm, bouncing off the river, although with every day that passed it sank a little lower in the sky and cast ever longer shadows across the grass. A few crisp brown leaves lay scattered, shuffled every now and then by a chilly wind that brought autumn on its breath.

Grace spoke to everyone, grateful for their sympathetic words and the memories they shared. Each time she lifted her eyes they somehow fell on Freddie, who was watching her from the other side of the garden. When their eyes locked she felt a frisson of pleasure and the reassuring sensation of being truly looked after. She longed to be down on the river-bank, just the two of them, and wished she could turn the clock back to that afternoon when her life had seemed as serene and idyllic as that grassy clearing in the wood.

'Lord and Lady Penselwood send their condolences,' said Mr Garner, limping over. He was a dour man with a bulky body, short neck and small, weaselly eyes.

'Thank you,' Grace replied. At once she thought of the cottage and the fact that Mr Garner had told Michael she would have to move out. She waited anxiously for him to mention it.

'Your father was a valuable man on the estate. He'll be sorely missed. Hard-working, loyal men are difficult to find.'

'Thank you,' she said again.

'Freddie tells me you're a proficient beekeeper. I suppose your father taught you all he knew?'

'Yes, he did, Mr Garner.' She barely dared breathe. Could it be possible that Mr Garner was going to let her stay? 'During the summer months he was so busy in the gardens at the Hall, *I* did the beekeeping. There's nothing I don't know about bees.'

'Walbridge Hall has always had a beekeeper. That's going back about four hundred years, Miss Grace. The Marquess is very keen that the bees flourish. I think I can count on you to see that they do.'

Her heart filled with happiness. 'You definitely can, Mr Garner. I won't let you down.'

His little eyes darted to Freddie, who was watching them while pretending to listen to his father and Colonel Redwood. 'Mr Valentine is a good man,' he said.

'Yes, he is,' Grace agreed.

'He's got a natural instinct for the land. I see a bright future for him here at Walbridge, Miss Grace.' He took a sip of beer. 'A dark horse, he is. I wouldn't have put my money on him this time last year, but he's grown into a fine young man, full of ambition and promise. You can be proud.'

'I'm so glad,' she answered, wondering why he was telling *her* and not Freddie's mother.

'So, I suggest you come to my office tomorrow morning and we'll discuss the finer details of your employment.'

'Thank you, Mr Garner.'

'Don't thank me, Miss Grace, thank Mr Valentine. He's saved me the trouble of having to find another beekeeper. Like hard-working, loyal labourers, beekeepers are difficult to find.'

Mr Garner hobbled away and Grace weaved through the crowd towards Freddie. She was detained a couple of times by people wanting to share their sympathy, but she finally reached him, and dragged him away to a quiet spot by the wall. 'Oh, thank you, Freddie!' she exclaimed. 'I want to throw my arms around you, but I can't.'

'So you're official beekeeper now.' He grinned triumphantly.

'Yes. At nineteen, I'm in charge of the hives, and I can stay in the cottage. It's too good to be true and it's all because of you.'

'I wasn't going to let him turf you out of your home, Grace.'

'Dad would be so proud.'

'You deserve it. I can't say I'm very keen on the little creatures, but they make you happy.'

She laughed. 'Oh, Freddie, you wouldn't mind a bee sting now you're a grown-up.'

'Don't be so sure. I'm still traumatized.'

'You're being silly!'

He grinned and his freckles spread across his cheeks. 'The only good thing about bees is the honey they make. I won't say I'm not keen on that.'

'I shall put aside a jar next week, then. A special one for you.'

He looked shifty a moment and glanced furtively around the garden. 'Meet me down at the river as soon as this is over?'

'Why the whispering?'

'I've got a surprise for you and I don't want anyone to know, especially Josephine. If she knows we're going she'll want to come, too. I'm afraid you're going to be her pet project now. She wants to be chief mourner and that involves being in the know about everything. She's furious that you're not coming to live with us.'

'I don't know why. I've never felt she really likes me.'

'She's jealous of you, that's all.'

'Well, she has no reason to be jealous.'

Freddie gazed at her fondly. 'She has *every* reason to be jealous.' He noticed the Colonel making his way slowly towards them. 'Meet me at five,' he hissed. 'And don't be a minute late!'

At ten to five she cycled off with Pepper running along beside her. As soon as she took the path through the wood, with the river on her left, the dog disappeared into the undergrowth. The odd panic-stricken pheasant fleeing into the trees was the only indication of where he was. She thought of Freddie waiting for her on the bank where they had so often met. Her excitement mounted as she approached. Up ahead, through the trees, she could see him setting out a picnic. He had brought a rug, a bottle of wine and two glasses.

When he saw her, he waved vigorously. She forgot about the shadow of grief that constantly threatened to smother any pleasure, and waved back. This clearing seemed detached from the tragedy of Arthur's death, as if it were a magical place where unhappy thoughts were dissolved on entering. It was a relief to leave her sorrow outside.

He helped her climb off her bike and leaned it against the tree with his. Then he pulled her into his arms and kissed her fiercely. 'I've been wanting to do this all day!' he exclaimed. She closed her eyes and let his love wrap her in a warm blanket of security and familiarity. Finally, when he gave her room to speak, she laughed.

'Dad always said to avoid unhappy thoughts you have to completely focus on the moment. It's easy to do that with you. When I'm with you, Freddie, I don't want to be anywhere else. And I don't think about anything else, either.'

Freddie's face was radiant with pleasure. 'I've been longing to have you to myself all day. Tell me truthfully, did you sleep with me on the sofa the other night?'

She grinned bashfully. 'I didn't want to be alone.'

'I thought so. Lucky you weren't there when Mum and Josephine appeared.'

'I missed them by a minute!'

'I wish I hadn't slept through it.'

'You were fast asleep,' she said. 'Which was probably just as well.'

'Pity.'

'I don't suppose we'll be able to do that again.'

He smiled, then ushered her to the picnic rug. 'Let me pour you a glass of wine.'

'Wine?' She picked up the bottle. 'How very grand.'

'Yes, and a picnic. Mum made it for us, so don't congratulate me.' He opened the basket to reveal sandwiches and cake.

'You told her we were sneaking off?'

'Don't worry. She's very discreet. She's made a *special* picnic, and she promised not to tell Josephine.'

He poured her a glass and she bit into a chicken sandwich. It tasted delicious. She had forgotten how hungry she was. They clinked glasses and Grace sipped the slightly warm Sauvignon. In spite of its temperature, she savoured the exquisite flavour and felt a pleasant tingling in her stomach.

Pepper returned from the woods with his tongue hanging out, panting heavily. He trotted down to the river to lap at the cold, limpid water. Freddie chattered away as normal, but he looked a little tense. His movements were slightly jerky and his hands trembled as he passed her things from the basket. Grace wondered why he was so nervous. If anything, she thought the wine would relax him. After they had eaten the cake and enjoyed another glass of Sauvignon he seemed to settle down, but his cheeks were flushed and he was still looking at her with a strange, almost bashful, expression. Then she remembered he'd mentioned a surprise and she began to feel a nervous buzzing in her stomach and her hands began to tremble, too, as she sipped from her glass.

As the tension built between them, the sun began to set and cast long shadows across the grass, but their patch remained warm and golden as the last of the light refused to be consumed. At last, Freddie stood up and walked behind the tree where they had leaned their bicycles. He reappeared with a bunch of bright-red roses. 'These are for you,' he said, sitting beside her and placing them in her hands.

'Freddie, they're beautiful,' she gasped, pressing them to her nose. 'Is this the surprise?'

'No,' he replied. '*This* is.' He pulled something out of his breast pocket. He opened his fingers to reveal a ring made out of woven straw. It was exquisite.

'What's this?' she asked in astonishment. 'Did *you* make it?'

'I did,' he replied, and his hands began to tremble again. He lifted it off his palm and took her hand, shifting himself into a kneeling position.

'Oh, Freddie!' she whispered as the tears blurred her vision.

His voice was solemn. 'Will you, beautiful Grace Hamblin, marry me, Freddie Valentine, your oldest and most devoted friend?' He slipped the makeshift ring onto the third finger of her left hand.

'Oh, Freddie, yes, I will . . .' she laughed, flinging her arms around him. 'I mean, I do.'

Freddie was now shaking as much as she was. They clung to each other in amazement and joy. 'You said yes!' he exclaimed, squeezing her.

'Did you think I wouldn't?'

'I wasn't sure.'

'We're meant to be together, Freddie. We've always been together, haven't we?'

He laughed. 'Yes, we have. I hope we grow old together.' He kissed her tenderly and she wondered why it had taken her so long to notice him when all the time he had been by her side, patiently waiting.

'I love the ring!' she said, lifting her hand.

'I didn't have time to buy you a real one.'

'This is more perfect than a real one because you've made it yourself.'

'I'll buy you a real one as soon as I can afford it. I want to buy you something special.'

'This is special! How can anything from a shop be more special than this?'

He laughed. 'I love you, Grace. It's so good to be able to say it. I love you!' he shouted into the trees.

'I can't wait to tell Auntie May!'

'She'll be so pleased. Now you'll be a real daughter to her.'

She looked at him seriously. 'You will come and live with me in my cottage when we're married, won't you?'

'Of course.'

Then she narrowed her eyes as she recalled her strange conversation with Mr Garner at the funeral. 'You told Old Peg Leg that you were going to ask me to marry you, didn't you?'

He blushed guiltily. 'I did, Grace, because that way he'd allow you to stay in your home.'

'But you're not just marrying me to be kind?'

He frowned. 'My darling Grace, I've loved you for years. There's never been anyone else for me but you. I didn't ask you to marry me to be kind. I asked you to marry me because I want to spend the rest of my life with you and only you. I might have waited until you'd had time to grieve for your father, but when Mr Garner threatened to kick you out of your home, I had to act fast. It's all a bit sudden, but it's right.' He grinned mischievously. 'I liked you lying next to me on the sofa. I want to lie next to you again. Why wait?' Now she blushed, too. He curled her hair behind her ear. 'I'm going to take great care of you, Grace.'

'I know you will,' she replied softly and lowered her eyes, embarrassed.

* * *

A little later they were bicycling back towards town, their hearts bursting with an unfamiliar kind of exuberance. They ran into Freddie's house and broke the news. Auntie May dissolved into tears. Uncle Michael went red in the face with pleasure, patted his son heartily on the back and drew Grace into his bear-like embrace. Josephine was so surprised she threw her arms around Grace, pressing her sticky lips on her cheek and leaving a crimson smear. 'A wedding! Oh, how exciting. What am I going to wear?'

Grace stayed for dinner and they all made plans around the dining-room table. May tried to persuade Grace to stay the night, but she firmly refused, insisting again that she was quite happy on her own at the cottage. In fact, she felt happier there than anywhere, because every corner of that little house echoed with memories of her father. It had been such a busy day she had barely had time to think. Left alone in her room, she would revisit all the good times and try not to mourn his loss.

Later, after Uncle Michael had driven her home, Grace lay in bed with Pepper curled up against her feet. She toyed with the makeshift ring and thought of Freddie. She couldn't believe she was getting married. In the silent darkness of her room she smiled at the thought of her wedding. Auntie May would help her with the dress and she would cut some berries from the garden for the bouquet. It was all so exciting until she thought of walking down the aisle. Who would give her away? Then she wept quietly into her pillow.

The following morning she awoke to the sound of rain on the window panes. She got up to avoid wallowing in her bed with the empty feeling gnawing at her stomach. The sooner she got on with her day, the better she'd feel. She didn't glance down the corridor as she went to use the bathroom and she tried not to let her eyes linger on her father's shaving soap and razor. Downstairs, she let Pepper out into the garden and put the kettle on the range. Then she sat alone at the kitchen table, staring at the walls, which seemed so much bigger now that her father wasn't in the house. She longed for Freddie, for the familiar sound of another human being shuffling about the house. She longed for company to chase her loneliness away.

Suddenly there was a knock on the door. She imagined it might be Auntie May with another breakfast hamper. But when she opened it she found grumpy Cummings in his chauffeur's hat, holding a stiff white envelope. 'This is for you, Miss Grace,' he said solemnly. She looked over his shoulder at the gleaming black Bentley and wondered why she hadn't heard it arrive. Pepper was busy sniffing the wheels. She hoped Cummings wouldn't turn around and see him cocking his leg on the rubber tyre.

'Thank you,' she replied. He nodded curtly and left. She called the dog, then retreated into the hall, closing the door behind her. She ran her fingers over her name, which was neatly and rather flamboyantly written in black ink. Her heart began to thump as she saw the Penselwood family crest of a lion and dragon embossed in gold on the back of the envelope. She lifted the flap and withdrew the correspondence. She noticed immediately that it was headed with the letter *R*, also embossed in gold. She sank onto a chair and began to read.

Dear Grace,

I'm so terribly sorry to hear the sad news about your dear father. You must be devastated. Arthur was a very good man, highly respected and loved by those he worked with here at Walbridge, and the many friends who were fortunate enough to have known him. I hope you are bearing up, Grace, and seeking consolation in those charming little bees you love so much. I do hate to think of you alone in that cottage but hear from Mr Garner that you are going to remain there to look after the hives. That fills me with joy, because to lose your father and *your bees in one moment would be unbearable.*

If I can do anything, please let me know. I will be spending much more time at Walbridge now that I have joined the tank regiment in Bovington and will be living at home. Papa is getting older and is keen for me to learn the ropes, so that one day, on his demise, I might take over (and do an adequate job of it, so as not to make the old man turn in his grave!). I do hope to see you, and to see a sunny face and not a sad one. Your sorrow will pass, Grace, and you will be left with all the lovely memories of a very fine father. At least, that's what Grandmama says, and she should know.

My warmest wishes, Rufus

Grace read it again, this time more slowly. She felt his sentiment reverberate off the page like a warm, familiar fire, and her heart contracted, slipping into a well-established pattern of behaviour. But the yellow ring caught her eye and she held up her hand to look at it. *That* was real; *Rufus* was not, at least not an option. She closed the letter and replaced it in its envelope. Then she went upstairs and put it away in her dressing-table drawer and pushed it shut. She opened her bedroom window and leaned out to breathe the damp air. Freddie was her future. Freddie was the man she *really* loved. Rufus had just been a fantasy. A *childish* fantasy she had now grown out of. She took a deep, satisfied breath.

At that moment a bumblebee came buzzing in from the climbing roses on the wall outside her window. It settled on her yellow cardigan. She watched its fat, furry body as it clumsily clambered over the wool. Then she lifted it gently and put her hand outside. It was still raining and the little bee didn't appear too pleased about it. But it eventually toddled off and, astonishingly for such a rotund creature, was carried upwards by its impossibly tiny wings, until it disappeared into the mist.

Chapter 15

Tekanasset Island, Massachusetts, 1973

After Big's house, the largest private home on the island belonged to Bill and Evelyn Durlacher. It was a gleaming white clapboard house built in the 1800s, with a grey-tiled roof, tall sash windows and a veranda that ran along almost the entire southern wall, its trellis roof covered in pink climbing roses. The interior had been decorated by a famous designer, flown in from New York, who had got so carried away with his nautical theme that the rooms looked as if they belonged on a ship rather than on land: shiny wooden floorboards, blue-and-white-striped upholstery, furniture gleaned from old boats. The bookcases were full of glossy hardbacks, bought in bulk, and the coffee tables laden with giant tomes on art and history, chosen for their distinction rather than their content, neither of which was of any interest to Bill and Evelyn. Every wall was hung with pictures, mainly of boats, and every table adorned with expensive knick-knacks chosen by the designer. In fact, when the house was finished there was barely anything in it that Evelyn had seen before. But she was delighted because the place looked 'done' – heaven forbid that people should think she had been so common as to put it together on her own.

The gardens had been nothing special until Grace Valentine had transformed them twenty years ago. Evelyn had told her in no uncertain terms that she wanted 'grand', not 'quaint', so Grace had divided the grounds into three separate gardens. In one she had placed a stone fountain in the centre and planted boxwood and roses in a geometric arrangement around it, creating the most splendid rose garden on the island. In the second, she had designed a very English garden with a brightly coloured herbaceous border that was the envy of all, and in the third she had worked an orchard around the tennis court, planting cherry trees that blossomed in the spring and looked like snow.

Now Evelyn, Belle, Sally and Blythe put down their tennis rackets and left the court to Bill and his highly competitive men's four. Bill rarely deigned to play with his wife because he didn't consider women to be enough of a challenge, and when he did, Evelyn complained of the patronizing way he patted the ball at her, and usually ended the match before it had finished by storming off in a rage. Now he strode onto the immaculately clipped grass in his dazzling tennis whites and opened a new box of Slazenger balls.

'Let's go and have a drink on the terrace,' Evelyn suggested, leading her ladies up the path towards the house. Belle admired the gardens but Evelyn didn't notice the vibrant colours and the little bees that buzzed about them, because she was so busy deciding which dress she was going to wear to dinner that night.

'I think you have one of the prettiest gardens on Tekanasset,' said Belle, knowing that the only compliment Evelyn would appreciate was one delivered in the superlative.

'Well, I told Grace I wanted Versailles, not Le Petit Trianon,' Evelyn replied with a little sniff. 'I think she got the point.'

'She certainly did,' Sally interjected. 'I must say, it's looking spectacular.'

'I fear everything goes a little mad in August,' said Belle. 'At least, mine grows out of control and I have to throw my hands up and give in to nature.'

'Not here,' said Evelyn. 'Old Tom Robinson and his son Julian are weeding away like dervishes. You know Tom is nearly seventy?'

'It's the oxygen in the greenery that keeps him young,' said Belle.

'Then we should all put more plants indoors,' Evelyn suggested.

'Or give in to a little nip and tuck,' Blythe added.

'You wouldn't dare, would you, Blythe?' Belle asked.

'Oh, I'd sell my soul for eternal youth,' she laughed.

They sat on the terrace. Evelyn crossed her tanned legs. Her white skirt barely covered her skinny thighs. She wore white tennis shoes with little socks held in the right place by the pale pink balls at the back. She had barely sweated into her white tennis shirt and the pale pink sweat bands on her wrists were dry. It was Evelyn's priority to look 'done' whatever the circumstances. She rather regretted being seen on the beach in her nightdress at three in the morning.

'Have you heard that Joe's rock band has broken up?' said Evelyn as a butler appeared in his tailcoat to pour the drinks. The three women looked him up and down in astonishment. The poor man was very hot in his uniform, not least because he was overweight and unfit. 'Well, let me tell you. Jasper, the one Trixie's in love with, has had to return to England because his brother was killed in a car crash.'

'Yes, I heard,' said Belle sadly. 'Poor boy. What a dreadful tragedy.'

'I gather he's not coming back, either. He has a vast estate to run, apparently,' Blythe added.

'Who would have known he came from *that* sort of family?' said Sally, lighting a cigarette.

'Oh, I'm sure if we had met him properly we would have noticed that he was well bred. Lucy did say he had impeccable manners,' said Evelyn.

Belle watched the butler retreat inside. 'Who's *he*?' she hissed to Evelyn.

Evelyn smiled smugly. 'He's my new butler. He's called Henderson and used to work in the British royal household.'

'What does that mean?' Blythe asked.

'He worked for the royal family.'

Belle took a cigarette from the packet Sally held out for her. 'How did you find him?' she enquired.

'From a wonderful agency in New York,' Evelyn replied. 'When he's got to know me a little better, I'll ask him for all the gossip.'

'Ooh, do pass it on,' said Sally excitedly, blowing out a cloud of smoke.

'You can always count on me,' Evelyn replied. She brought her cocktail to her crimson lips, making sure she didn't leave a mark on the glass.

'So, is their career truly over?' Belle asked. 'Poor boys, what a disappointment.'

There was no such sympathy in Evelyn's voice. 'Lucy told me that Trixie expects to go and join him in England. Now, what do you think the chances are of that? Hmm?' She gave a little sniff. 'I imagine she'll grow old waiting for him to make an honest woman of her. Trixie is the sort of girl a man has fun with but doesn't marry.'

'I agree,' echoed Sally. There had never been a time when she hadn't agreed with Evelyn. 'Men marry the nice girls, not the naughty ones.'

'Poor Trixie,' Belle sighed. 'She must be broken-hearted.'

'More broken-hearted now she knows that he owns a vast estate. Do you think he's titled?' Blythe asked. 'I mean, don't estates come with titles?'

'Most certainly,' said Evelyn. 'I'll ask Henderson. He's bound to know that sort of thing.' She glanced at her manicure. 'He would have done better to have fallen in love with Lucy. She'll make some man a very good wife one day.'

'Oh yes, she will,' Sally gushed. 'You've brought Lucy up to be a *nice* girl.'

Trixie waited. She trusted that Jasper would send for her eventually, and her sorrow at their parting was replaced by a blind optimism for their future. He wrote her letters from England, which took over a week to arrive. She was impressed by the stiff white envelopes, embossed on the back with the crest of a lion and dragon, and she was thrilled by his writing paper, headed with the letter *J* in gleaming crimson. His handwriting was flamboyant but the contents of his letters were depressing. He wrote of his mother's despair, his sisters' fighting and the struggle he was having stepping into his brother's shoes when he knew nothing about how to run an estate. He wrote about the high expectations everyone had of him and his fear that he would disappoint.

Trixie began to feel apprehensive. Judging by the grand stationery and the fact that the estate was passed down the generations through the male heirs, it was clear that the

Duncliffes must be a grand and important family. While Jasper doubted he could run the estate, Trixie doubted she'd be good enough for his family. He had said his mother would disapprove of her and she now knew why. Trixie wasn't from a wealthy family. Her father was a farmer, her mother was a gardener and she was a waitress. Her confidence deflated like a balloon the morning after a party. It was Jasper's duty to marry one of his own sort. Even he had said she'd be ill suited to his life in England. She began to wonder if he wasn't right.

While her optimism about their future flagged, her confidence in their love remained strong. She longed for his physical presence with such vigour that her whole body ached. She wrote him emotional letters but kept her reservations to herself. Jasper always ended his with a paragraph about how much he loved her and missed her and yearned for the day when they would be reunited. Those parts she read and reread, wearing his name out with her kisses, replacing her fears with the hope that everything would turn out all right in the end.

Jasper had been gone four weeks when he telephoned. Grace shouted up the stairs with urgency and Freddie came out of his office to see what all the excitement was about. 'It's Jasper!' she exclaimed. 'He's calling from England!' Trixie ran down the stairs and into the kitchen where her mother was holding out the receiver, looking as surprised as Trixie felt.

'Hello?' she said.

There was a short delay, then Jasper's voice could be heard faintly down the crackling line. 'Trixie. I just wanted to hear your voice.'

'Oh, Jasper, you sound so far away!'

'I *am* far away.'

'I miss you!'

'I miss you, too. You have no idea how much. I wish I was in Jack's boathouse with you in my arms.'

'So do I,' she breathed into the receiver. 'Is it getting easier?'

'A little. I'm learning the ropes. I have a lot of good people around me who know what they're doing, thankfully. It's my mother who's driving me mad.'

'How is she driving you mad?'

He hesitated. 'She's just making life very difficult for me.'

'Have you told her about us?'

'Of course I have.'

There was a long pause. Trixie could feel his anxiety through the wire. 'You can't expect her to like someone she's never met, and she probably isn't too happy about me being American. Have you told her my parents are English?'

He sighed. 'It'll be fine. Don't worry. I love your letters.'

'Oh, I love yours, too. Did *you* put the lion on the back of the envelope?'

He laughed. 'No, the lion and dragon is our family crest, Trixie.'

'What's that?'

'It'll be your family crest when we're married.'

'Oh, good, so I'll get to have elegant stationery, too, with the letter B on the paper?'

'Yes, Beatrix, you will.'

'I'm so excited. Please send for me soon. I'm going crazy here missing you.'

'I know. Just a little longer. Keep writing to me, won't you?'

'You bet.'

'I think of you all the time, Trixie.'

'And I think of you, too.' Her throat constricted with emotion. 'I love you, Jasper.'

'And I love you, too. Don't ever forget it.'

'I won't.'

'I kiss you all over.'

She laughed through her tears. 'And I treasure every one.'

Grace sat on the swing chair and strained her ears to hear her daughter's conversation. From the little she picked up, it sounded positive. Since the news that Rufus had died she hadn't been able to sleep. Her nights had been spent here on the swing chair, gazing out over the ocean, remembering. She never felt alone. There was always the silent presence of her invisible companion. Somehow, in the darkness, she felt him stronger, closer, and there was something about his company that she found soothing.

If Trixie married Jasper, she would have to return to Walbridge and confront her past. She'd have to revisit the cottage, the scene of her father's death, the river where Freddie proposed, the church where they were married – and she'd be faced with having to unravel all that came after.

When Trixie hung up the telephone, Grace went back inside. 'He says I have to wait a little longer,' she told her mother.

'Oh, darling, I'm sure it won't be much longer,' said Grace.

'I sense his mother is being very difficult, but I'm sure she'll like me when she gets to know me.'

'Of course she will,' said Grace, remembering the icily beautiful Lady Georgina with a shudder. She didn't suppose she was any less formidable now, over thirty years later.

'It's going to be OK,' said Trixie happily. 'Jasper loves me. I mean, he telephoned all the way from England just to hear my voice.'

'I don't doubt that he loves you, darling. Poor thing, having to deal with a death in the family as well as a sudden change in his career plans. His life really has been turned upside down.'

'But I'm going to fly over and put it the right way up again.'

'I'm sure you will.'

'Don't look so sad, Mom. *I* don't doubt that it's all going to work out fine, so neither should you.' Trixie put her arms around her mother. 'I'm going to be Mrs Jasper Duncliffe. How does that sound?'

'Different,' said Grace, fighting her impulse to tell her the truth. But if she did, she'd have to confess how she knew. If she confessed how she knew, Trixie would wonder why neither parent had mentioned the coincidence. If she *did* marry Jasper, they'd have to tell her that they, too, came from Walbridge and hope that Trixie wouldn't be hurt. And she'd have to tell her about Rufus.

She could feel her daughter quivering with excitement. Why hadn't Jasper told her? Did he think Trixie would love him less if she knew he was the Marquess of Penselwood? Or did he know in his heart that a man of his background could never marry a girl like Trixie?

The days passed, growing shorter as summer slipped into autumn. Grace extracted the honey from the hives. Trixie worked hard at Captain Jack's. August was busy with tourists and city-dwellers flooding the island for their summer break. Trixie worked long hours, serving demanding clients with an unwavering smile. She didn't have much time to pine for Jasper. But once everyone had gone, the island was left slightly shaken, like a city after carnival. The first leaves began to turn. The wind blew in chilly and damp and Trixie felt the first niggle of doubt about Jasper.

At first Grace didn't realize it, because Trixie was working, or out with Suzie, but as September was swallowed into October and Jasper still hadn't sent for her, she noticed her daughter becoming withdrawn and uncharacteristically solitary. She would sit for hours on the beach, staring out to sea, smoking endless cigarettes, or wander the shore like a solitary gannet, searching the sand for sea glass. She stopped going out with Suzie and went to bed early, hiding beneath the quilt, sleeping until midday on Sundays. Grace tried to be encouraging but even she noticed that Jasper's letters grew fewer and shorter just as Trixie's grew more frequent and desperate.

Freddie was concerned but resigned. He didn't say 'I told you so', because he didn't have to. Grace knew as well as he did that Jasper's will was weakening. He wasn't going to send for Trixie. He was going to put duty before happiness, as his sort always did. Grace thought of Rufus. Why had she ever thought Jasper would be any different? Her heart went out to her daughter. If she had been able to wave a wand she'd have granted Trixie the life with Jasper that she craved. She'd do anything for her daughter's happiness. She'd return to Walbridge if she had to and walk among her memories, even though every step would hurt. But there was no magic wand, only a terrible not-knowing, until in early November Trixie received a final letter from Jasper.

Trixie was too upset to read it out. She handed it to her mother and ran onto the veranda to cry on the swing chair.

Freddie looked over Grace's shoulder and read the words he had anticipated seeing for a long time.

My darling Trixie,

This is the hardest letter I will ever have to write. Things have been very difficult over the last few months. I have fought endlessly with my mother and tried desperately hard to make it work for us, but I fear the battle is lost. I cannot bring you here, my love, knowing how unhappy you will be. I cannot let you sacrifice your life for me. I have given up singing and put my guitar away because the sight of it and what it represents only makes me miserable. I love you with all my heart and treasure the memories of those precious weeks together on Tekanasset. I won't ever forget you. But please forget me. You deserve better.

With love always, Jasper

'Just as I thought,' Freddie groaned. 'How I wish I'd been wrong!'

'How could he?' Grace exclaimed. 'He's gone and broken her heart, just as you predicted.' She turned to face him. 'Oh Freddie, could I have done anything to prevent it?'

'She's a wilful girl, Grace, you know that. I tried to warn her but she wouldn't listen.'

'What's she going to do?'

'She's going to do what we all do when we are let down or disappointed or broken-hearted. We carry on.' He clenched his teeth and frowned. 'We get up, dust ourselves down and try to make the best of it. She'll go to college and she'll get over him – and perhaps we shall never hear the names Duncliffe or Melville or Penselwood again.'

Grace felt her face flush. 'I'll go and talk to her,' she said and went outside.

* * *

She sat beside her daughter and pulled the sobbing girl into her arms. 'I'm sorry,' she said gently.

'I should have listened to Daddy. He knew. Why didn't I listen?'

'Because you were in love,' Grace replied.

'I hate him!'

'No, you don't. You should, but you don't.'

'You don't understand, Mom. You've never been there. You've only ever loved Daddy. You don't know what it's like. I hate him with all my heart. I never want to hear from him or see him ever again.' Trixie buried her face in her mother's sweater, and Grace smiled sadly because in spite of the most terrible suffering, the heart goes on loving; that is the beauty of love.

Chapter 16

There are many ways to break a heart because wherever there is love there is the possibility of pain. Trixie had suffered a direct hit to hers, but Evelyn Durlacher's heart would be broken in a different way. While Grace made sure that her daughter's unhappiness did not become fodder for the gossip-mongers, Crab Cove golf club was awash with the news that Lucy Durlacher had run off with one of the two remaining band members. And it wasn't the one she had *supposedly* been seeing, but Ben, the one who had *supposedly* been seeing Suzie Redford.

Big claimed she had seen it coming. 'I feel a certain sympathy for Evelyn; one would have to be very hard-hearted not to, but at the same time I feel the silly woman brought it upon herself. If she hadn't pounced like a greedy old vulture onto the lame and wounded, she might not have attracted such disaster. What goes around comes around. There's a lot of truth in that.' Big and Grace sat in the tea room at the golf club, and although most people spoke in hushed voices, Grace sensed they were all talking about Evelyn and Bill.

'I suppose she has always fed off the misfortunes of others,' said Grace.

'She most certainly has. But still, her daughter has run off and Bill and Evelyn have no idea where she is. The girl left a note, but she didn't say where she was going. You see, she doesn't want to be found and she certainly doesn't want to come back.'

'Poor Suzie.' Grace sighed. 'Trixie and she make a sorry pair, don't they?'

Big pulled a face. 'Oh, Suzie will recover; she has a very shallow heart, but Trixie, now *she's* the one I feel most sorry for.'

'She's desperate, Big, and it grieves me so much to see her like that.'

'What a cad to promise marriage and then let her down.' Big's face hardened. 'If I were his mother . . .'

'I'm afraid I think it's his mother who has prevented the marriage,' Grace interrupted.

'Really? Why would she do that?'

Grace put down her teacup. 'Because they are a very grand family and it's his duty to marry one of his own.'

'What's the name?'

'Penselwood. Lord Jasper Duncliffe's elder brother died without an heir, so the title has passed to his brother. Jasper is now the Marquess of Penselwood.' Grace dropped her gaze into her tea.

'Now, I know that name,' said Big slowly, narrowing her eyes.

'You do?' Grace asked, surprised.

'Of course I do. My father knew the Marquess of Penselwood. What was his name? It was a funny one.'

'Aldrich?'

'That's the one. Aldrich Penselwood. You know, he had a house here on Tekanasset. He used to summer here with his wonderfully eccentric wife, Arabella, and their children. I remember about three or four mighty beautiful children. One of them was very naughty. A darling little boy called Rufus. Yes, Rufus, I remember now. He was delightful.'

'Jasper is Rufus's son,' said Grace. 'What a coincidence that they used to summer here.'

'Coincidence? I don't think so. Surely that's why Jasper was here in the first place.'

Grace felt as if she had just been stung. Why hadn't she thought of that? 'Why did they stop coming?' she asked.

'The war, I imagine. I don't know. They never came back after that and we lost touch with them. My father was very fond of Aldrich. They were both keen golfers, and if I remember rightly, Aldrich loved boats. He used to collect them, proper ones, expensive ones, and have them shipped to England in crates. And he used to make model boats, too. I felt sorry for Arabella. I don't imagine he gave her much attention.' She shrugged. 'Then again, perhaps she was very frosty in the bedroom and that drove him to seek solace in his boats. I don't remember her smiling very much. But *he* had a twinkle.' She summoned a waiter and ordered two slices of cranberry pie.

Grace's mind was busy making sense of the fact that Rufus had been to Tekanasset. She recalled the time she had gone to Walbridge Hall and momentarily glimpsed his father's study with all those model ships and paintings of the sea. She realized he must have bought them *here*.

'You know, I'm sure I have photos of Aldrich. My father was a keen photographer and my mother was very scrupulous about keeping his photographs,' Big continued. But Grace wasn't listening. Was it a coincidence that Freddie had chosen to move here? 'Grace, what are you thinking about?' Big asked, staring at her with narrowed eyes.

Grace blinked and reddened. 'Oh, nothing. Just that Trixie doesn't know Jasper is titled,' she said.

'Why not? What does he have to hide?'

'I think he knew all along that he would never be able to marry her.'

'Then why put her through the agony?'

'Because he *wanted* to, and while he was here it seemed possible. Once he got home and faced his mother, who I imagine is as formidable as her mother-in-law was, he realized it wasn't going to work.'

'Look, I'm old-fashioned, but surely gone are the days of arranged marriages?'

'You're right, they *are* gone, but still the aristocracy retain a sense of duty. Jasper will need to find a partner who can help him run the estate. She'll have to hold grand dinners for the county bigwigs, arrange charity functions in their ballroom, the summer fête in their garden, lunches to raise money for the church. She'll have to rub shoulders with the royal family at Royal Ascot and hobnob with dukes and duchesses during the London season. Can you imagine Trixie living that sort of life? She'd loathe the formality and the duty.' Grace's spirits deflated as Rufus's voice seemed to reverberate across the decades. 'The only women capable of that are the ones who are bred for it,' she added, but it could have been Rufus, speaking through her.

'Then Trixie has had a lucky escape,' said Big firmly.

'I think she has, but right now she believes she'll never love anyone again.'

'She will, and if she doesn't she'll end up like me and I haven't done too badly.'

Grace smiled fondly at Big. 'Did you ever come close?'

'Oh yes.' Big's eyes sparkled and she cut the corner of her cranberry pie with her fork. 'I had many suitors.'

'But none of them was good enough?'

'None of them came close to my Pa.' She popped the piece of pie in her mouth and chewed enthusiastically. 'They were all diminished by him. He was such a great man, he made them look inadequate. But I have no regrets. My Pa was God's greatest gift to me and not a day goes by when I don't miss him.'

Grace thought of her own father and felt a pang of homesickness. 'I miss mine, too, Big. Do you think we ever grow too old to miss them?'

'Never!' Big was certain. 'They're our first loves, and in my case, my *only* love – although poor Pa was always trying to marry me off. He and Ma wanted grandchildren. They despaired. But that's just the way it was. I wasn't going to budge an inch.' Big patted Grace's hand and chuckled. 'Enough about me. Trixie will love again and one day she'll look back on her past and thank the good Lord she didn't marry Jasper, because she will have found happiness with someone better. One has to be philosophical.'

'Trixie's not at all philosophical. She and Suzie are talking of going to New York. Freddie would like her to go to college, but she doesn't want to go. She wants her life to start right away.'

'I suppose it's time they made their own way in the world.'

'Trixie wants to work for *Vogue*. If she's lucky enough to get a job, she'll start at the bottom making the tea. But she'll work her way up, and if she's clever enough, she might end up where she wants to be.'

'Which is?'

'Editor, probably, but more likely writing about fashion and seeing a bit of the world.'

Big's steely eyes glinted. 'Is she serious about wanting to work in fashion?'

'Yes, she's a bright girl and she writes well.'

'Then let me see what I can do for her. I know one or two people who might be useful to her.'

'Thank you, Big. That would be wonderful.'

'Think nothing of it,' said Big. 'It's what friends do.'

When Grace returned home it was getting dark. She called for Trixie, but the house was silent except for the excited panting of the dogs. She looked at her watch. She had just enough time to take them for a walk up the beach before sunset. They wagged their tails and bounded onto the sand. There was a strong wind and Grace wrapped her coat tightly around her. She thought of Evelyn and her heart went out to her, for she knew what it was to suffer. As much as she disliked the woman, she wouldn't wish that kind of heartache on anybody.

As she strode up the sand she thought of Rufus. When she left England after the war she had assumed she was leaving every shadow of him behind. For each corner of Walbridge was haunted by his memory, and as long as she was there she knew she'd never be free of him. But now she realized his shadow reached Tekanasset. Perhaps he had walked up that very beach. He would most certainly have gone to Crab Cove golf club. How strange that all these years she felt so far away from him, she was actually walking in his footsteps.

The fact that his family had once taken a house here explained why Jasper had come to the island with his band. Maybe Rufus's parents had known Joe Hornby and given Jasper his details. She wondered when and how Rufus had died. In her memory he was still the young man she had fallen in love with. She couldn't imagine him older. She certainly couldn't imagine him dead. The thought made her go cold and she put her head down to walk against the wind.

It was getting dark now. She could barely see the dogs. She turned around and walked with her back against the wind, which was much easier. She mulled over these new, troubling revelations as the dogs bounded over the dunes, frolicking in the long grasses. When she reached home she was greeted by Freddie, waving at her from the veranda. She quickened her pace, hoping that Trixie was all right. She had been so down lately. Grace was unable to see Freddie's expression from where she was, but as she approached she saw another person through the glass door, standing in the kitchen.

She rushed up the garden path, the dogs at her heels. Freddie opened the door to let her in. There, standing with her back against the counter, was Evelyn Durlacher. Grace was astonished. She didn't think that, in all the years she had lived on Sunset Slip, Evelyn had ever visited her home. 'Hello, Grace,' said Evelyn, smiling tightly.

Grace took in her immaculately coiffed hair, her perfectly applied lipstick and nail polish, her pearls and her fine cashmere twinset in the palest grey, and couldn't think of anything to do other than smile back. 'Hello, Evelyn. What a surprise.'

'I know, it's long overdue. Freddie has sweetly given me a drink. You must have heard the news about Lucy. I imagine the whole island is chattering about nothing else. I've never needed a drink more than now.'

'Shall we go into the sitting room? It's not very comfortable here in the kitchen.'

'Oh, I'm easy,' she replied, but Grace led her into the sitting room anyway. Evelyn was the sort of woman who was a stranger to kitchens, especially her own.

Grace had a flair for gardens, but she did not have a flair for interior decoration. The sitting room was undoubtedly the cosiest on Tekanasset, but nothing coordinated and in spite of Freddie's obsessional tidiness, it was pleasantly scruffy and disorganized. Freddie gave a grunt of irritation and disappeared into his study, where nothing was out of place. But this was Grace's room, full of potted plants, ornamental bees and books that overflowed from the bookcases onto every surface, along with newspapers, magazines and Grace's garden designs drawn on pieces of paper.

Evelyn moved a pile of sketches off the sofa and sat down. Grace chose the armchair and the dogs flopped onto the rug in front of the empty fireplace. 'What a lovely room,' said Evelyn, sweeping her eyes over it.

Grace knew she was just being polite. She had seen Evelyn's exquisitely decorated sitting room. 'Thank you,' she replied, all the same. She wasn't going to apologize for the chaos.

'I like your bees. You collect them, do you?'

Grace fingered the gold bee brooch that she always wore below her right shoulder. 'I've always loved bees,' she replied softly.

'Well, you're a fine beekeeper. Your honey is the best on the island.' Evelyn sighed and looked a little awkward. 'You must be wondering why I'm here.'

'Well, I imagine it has something to do with Lucy. Are you hoping I'll be able to help you find her?'

'Lord, no,' said Evelyn. 'I don't want to find her if she doesn't want to be found.' She gave a joyless chuckle and glanced down at her manicure. 'I must give up trying to control her. That's what Bill says and I'm sure he's right. If she wants to run off with a musician, that's her business.

That's what Bill said, too. Let her go, were his words. So, I have let her go.'

'Oh, Evelyn, I'm sorry,' Grace said, her voice full of compassion.

Evelyn's eyes began to shine with tears. 'I'm sorry. You sound so sympathetic.' She took a gulp of wine.

'You can only do your best. Lucy's a grown-up now. You can guide them but ultimately they will do exactly as they choose.'

'How is Trixie? Is she OK?'

'She's fine, thank you,' Grace replied cagily. She didn't want Evelyn spreading her daughter's misery around the island.

Evelyn sighed and her shoulders sagged. 'You might not feel very lucky, but you are lucky. You haven't lost Trixie.'

'I would have let her go, if she had been happy,' said Grace. 'That's all one ever wants for one's children, don't you think?'

'Of course,' Evelyn agreed quickly. 'The trouble is I thought I knew what made her happy. It turns out I didn't know at all. But what's going to become of her? I know nothing about this young man, except that he's English and plays guitar and keyboard. Lucy wrote me a note saying that she's in love and not to worry about her. She didn't say where she was going. She didn't take much with her, just a suitcase. I don't know what she's going to do for money. Bill is quite prepared to support her. She might get in touch when she runs out of the little cash she took with her.' She shrugged helplessly and sniffed. 'At least, I hope so.'

'How can I help you, Evelyn?' Grace asked, wondering when she was going to tell her why she had come.

'You're being a great help just listening, Grace.'

'I'd like to do more. Have you asked Joe where they've gone?'

'Yes, but he says he no longer has anything to do with them. I think Jasper was the one paying for his services, so he's checked out, so to speak. They're on their own.'

'Did she take her passport with her?'

'No.'

'So she's not expecting to return to England with him?'

'I don't think so.' She smiled sadly. 'You know, after that party in the summer I went up the beach in my nightdress to find Lucy there with the other one. What was he called?'

'George.'

'That's the one. George. They were smoking cannabis and getting up to all sorts of things, and I really lost my temper. You probably heard about it. I saw red. I didn't think about Lucy. I thought about *me* and what everyone was going to say when word got around that Lucy was getting up to no good. I had let everyone know that I disapproved of them, you see.' She took a white cotton handkerchief out of her sleeve and blew her nose. 'Excuse me,' she said politely. 'I didn't give them a chance. Silly, really, considering that Jasper was obviously from a very good family. I mean, he has an estate and all, so he must be well bred, mustn't he?'

Grace didn't want to comment on Jasper's pedigree. 'He was a very nice boy,' she said evenly.

'Well, I know we're meant to be living through a time of change, but I'm an old-fashioned girl and I brought Lucy up to be a lady. I fear she . . .' Evelyn could barely get the words out. She pulled herself together and gave a little sniff. 'She has fallen into disrepute,' she choked.

Grace wanted to laugh, but she managed to keep a straight face. 'It's the 1970s, Evelyn, not the 1870s. No one is going to consider Lucy spoiled goods because she's had a walk-out. I think it's a good thing to experiment a little. In our day we were much too constrained.'

'Do you really think so?'

'Yes, I do. I only hope she doesn't get her heart broken. Young hearts are very tender.'

'She's broken mine,' said Evelyn, dabbing beneath her eyes, trying not to spoil her make-up. The woman looked so pathetic that Grace went to sit beside her on the sofa.

She patted Evelyn's bony shoulder sympathetically. 'Don't be broken-hearted. You know what I think?'

'No, what do you think?'

'If you accept her the way she is, and truly let her know that you only want her happiness, I think she'll come back.'

'Really?'

'Of course. She's run away because you disapproved so much that she knew the only way to be with the man she loves is to run off with him.'

Evelyn swallowed. 'I think you're right.'

'It's going to be OK.'

Evelyn gave a wan smile. 'I hope so.'

'So, what did you come to see me about?' Grace asked again.

Evelyn looked sheepish. 'I'm sorry we're not friends, Grace,' she replied tightly. 'We have so much in common. My Lucy and your Trixie . . .' She faltered. 'With those English boys. We've both suffered as mothers. I just wanted to talk to you. I can't talk to my friends.'

'Why not?'

'Oh, I just couldn't be as candid. I can say all this to you. You understand, you see. They wouldn't.'

'I think you should give them the chance to prove you wrong. Belle doesn't have a mean bone in her body.'

'But I've been so . . . you know. I haven't been very kind about those boys.'

'Then tell them you were wrong. Friendship is about being honest with each other and sharing your troubles as well as your triumphs. You can't get close to someone unless you open up and expose yourself a little. I think you'll find they'll be very sympathetic. No one minds someone admitting they made a mistake.'

Grace felt Evelyn swell with gratitude. 'Oh, thank you, Grace. You've been so kind.'

'I'm sure it will all work out.'

'I hope it works out for Trixie, too. I hope she finds some nice man.'

'I'm sure she will.'

Evelyn slipped her handkerchief back into her sleeve and took a deep breath. 'You're a good woman, Grace. This island's full of complicated people, but I've always been sure about you.'

'What did she want?' Freddie asked when Evelyn had left.

Grace frowned. 'I think she came to apologize, in her own way, for being judgemental about those boys.'

'What did she say?'

'She talked about Lucy.'

'Did she think you could find her?'

'No, she just wanted to talk to someone who understands. She said she couldn't talk to her friends.'

'Of course she can't talk to her friends. She's too proud. But you're an outsider, Grace; she doesn't need to keep up appearances in front of you.'

'Then I'm flattered.'

'She looked cowed.'

'She's learned compassion, I think.'

He chuckled cynically. 'She's learned that the higher you fly the harder the fall.'

Grace wanted to ask him how he had made the decision to come to Tekanasset after the war, but it was so long ago she felt foolish bringing it up now. It didn't change anything; at least, she didn't *think* it did. He raised his eyebrows. 'Yes?'

'Nothing,' Grace replied.

'You looked as if you were about to ask me something.'

She shook her head. 'No. I was just thinking about Evelyn. It was a surprise to see her. I think she's always considered me beneath her.'

'Well, you're not,' said Freddie emphatically. 'This is America, thank goodness. Evelyn Durlacher is just plain Mrs Durlacher, just like you.' He withdrew into his study again.

But Grace couldn't stop thinking about the past. If Lord Penselwood had helped them settle in America, why hadn't Freddie told her? What was he hiding? She poured herself a glass of wine and went back into the sitting room. She had been working on a garden design for a young couple who had just bought a property on Halcyon Street. She sat on the sofa and picked up her sketch. Once she had worked out what she would do, she would transfer the idea onto a proper plan to present to her clients. But as much as she stared at the paper, she was unable to see anything but the gardens at Walbridge Hall. She put down her sketch and took a sip of wine. Then she curled her feet under her and rested her head on the pillow. When she closed her eyes the past was always there, right beneath her eyelids.

Chapter 17

Walbridge, England, 1938

May had suggested that Grace sort out her father's belongings before the wedding. 'This is going to be yours and Freddie's home soon. You don't want the only other bedroom in the house stuffed full of Arthur's things.' She had smiled at Grace knowingly. 'After all, it won't be long before you have little ones to think about.' Grace had smiled back, her eyes full of tenderness at the thought of children. 'You and Freddie will have such beautiful babies,' May had gushed. 'And I'll be a grandmother. Goodness, who'd have ever thought I'd grow to be so old!'

In his will, Arthur had left everything to Grace. Fortunately, he wasn't a man who hoarded things. His bedroom had been kept neat and tidy and anything of importance was stored in a chest of drawers at the end of the bed.

May and Grace set to work on a Saturday in late November. Rain clattered against the window panes and the sun never managed to penetrate the thick cloud that hung like stodgy porridge just above the treetops.

Grace made them both cups of tea. She had been so anxious about going through her beloved father's possessions that she hadn't slept at all. Pepper had snored loudly on the end of her bed, which was a great comfort to her, alone in the house, and as much as she longed for her father to appear, as she was sure he had done the night he died, she saw nothing but the usual shadows on the wall. She now felt raw from tiredness and emotionally fragile.

'Come,' said May, carrying her mug of tea up the stairs. 'Pepper will keep us company, won't you, Pepper? Just think, Grace, in just under a month you'll be Mrs Valentine. Mrs Freddie Valentine. I can't believe my boy is going to have a wife.' She rattled on and Grace knew she was trying to keep her spirits up. They reached Arthur's bedroom door and May gently pushed it. Her father's familiar smell enveloped her in a miasma of memories and Grace felt her sorrow rise up from her stomach in a great wave, but she sipped her hot tea and swallowed hard, managing to overcome it.

May switched on the light and swept her eyes over the room. 'Well, he was very organized, wasn't he?'

'Yes,' Grace replied. 'It won't take long. He didn't have much.'

May sat on the bed and looked at the black-and-white photograph of Grace's parents. 'She was a nice-looker, your mother. Just like you.'

'I wonder whether they're together now, in Heaven.'

'Of course they are,' said May, picking it up. 'I think you should keep this. It's precious.' She handed it to Grace, who gazed at it forlornly. 'Now, we'll start with his clothes. What would you like me to do with them?'

Grace looked uncertain. 'I don't know. What do *you* think? Would Uncle Michael wear any of his things? He had a nice jersey or two.'

'Let's see. Anything we don't want to keep can be given away.'

Once they'd sorted the clothes, they turned their attention to the chest of drawers. Grace opened the top drawer and pulled out a walnut box. Inside there was a silk scarf, a small velvet box, a notebook and a plain white envelope with her name on it. She carefully put the box down and opened the envelope. Inside, there was a letter.

My dearest Gracey,

As much as we like to think we will live forever, we are mortal and the time will eventually come for me to leave you. With this in mind I put pen to paper, although it grieves me very much to do so.

I leave everything to you, Gracey. It gives me pleasure now to think of you taking care of all my books. They, as you are aware, are my most treasured possessions, besides the contents of this box and my beehives. The only thing dearer to me is you.

As you know, I loved your mother very much. She hadn't had time to accumulate much during her life so these are the few possessions of hers that I treasured. I write this letter as a precaution because I hope to be alive to give you these things personally. I hope to see you married to a nice man who will take care of you. I hope to enjoy grandchildren one day, but only God knows when it's time, so I take nothing for granted. It seems macabre to be writing to you like this, when I'm upstairs and you're outside in the garden with the bees. But one must be practical.

If the worst happens and I die before you are married, I am aware that you will no longer have a roof over your head. Uncle Michael and Auntie May will look after you, so please don't be too proud to ask for help. Don't be so far-sighted that you're blind to what's under your nose, either. Freddie is a kind young man. I believe that kindness is a quality much underrated these days. I don't know much about romance, but I know enough about friendship, respect and love to know that you and Freddie have the necessary qualities to make a happy union. I'm not telling you what to do, just nudging you in what I believe to be the right direction. If I'm dead, you won't be able to tell me to mind my own business!

My dearest, I leave you this box, with my love and your mother's love. Don't forget that we'll always be with you.

Your loving Father

Grace could barely read the final lines for the mist in her eyes. She handed May the letter then pulled the silk scarf out of the box and held it against her nose, closing her eyes as she inhaled. She was sure she could smell the faintest scent of rose in the fabric. May folded the letter and slipped it back into the envelope. 'Here, let's put this on you,' she said softly, taking the scarf out of Grace's hands and tying it loosely about her neck. 'Blues, turquoises and greens are your colours, too, Grace,' she said. 'It suits you.'

Grace stood up and looked at herself in the mirror on the wall. 'It's lovely,' she replied quietly. 'I shall treasure it.'

Next she opened the notebook. There, in her mother's handwriting, were pages and pages of recipes. She flicked through them. 'Goodness, I could have done with these years ago,' she exclaimed. 'Dad would have been much better fed. Look, soufflés, meringue pie and honey cakes.'

'Freddie's going to be a happy man,' said May.

'Dad would be happy to know that Freddie and I are getting married, wouldn't he? It's what he wanted. He *did* know best. Freddie *was* right under my nose.'

'He must have written this recently, don't you think?' said May. 'This year, for sure.'

'I wonder why? He wasn't old.'

'No, he wasn't, and he was in good health. But as we grow older we become more aware of our mortality.'

'I wish he was here now to see how happy Freddie is making me.'

May put her arms around Grace. 'I wish he was here, too,' she replied, and Grace sensed her heaviness of heart as she rested her head against Grace's for an extended moment.

'Hello!' It was Freddie, downstairs in the hall. Pepper jumped off the bed and bounded away to greet him. They heard Freddie talking to the dog and the scuffle of the animal's paws on the stone floor.

'We're up here,' shouted May.

A moment later he was standing in the doorway. 'How's it going? Are you all right, Grace?'

'Read this,' she said, handing him the letter.

Freddie took it and quickly read it. His cheeks reddened a little at the mention of his name. 'It's as if he knew he was going to die,' he said.

'No, it isn't, Freddie,' retorted his mother. 'He was just being practical, like he said.'

'So what's in the box?' he asked.

Grace showed him the scarf and the notebook. 'There's only this left,' she said, lifting out the little velvet box. She opened it slowly to reveal two rings. One was a simple gold band, the other a small diamond solitaire. 'My mother's rings,' she gasped. 'Oh, Freddie, look!'

'What a pretty solitaire,' admired May.

Grace slipped it on the third finger of her left hand. 'It fits, Freddie. Can this be our engagement ring? Would you mind?'

'If it makes you happy, of course I don't mind.'

'You've been saving up for a ring, Freddie; now you can spend the money on something else,' said his mother happily. Freddie was struck with an idea. He knew exactly what he would spend it on.

The day before the wedding it snowed. Large fluffy flakes floated down from a white sky as if God was emptying the contents of his pillow and covering the world in goose feathers. Grace hurried out into the garden excitedly while Pepper leapt over the frozen ground with glee. Today was her last day as Grace Hamblin. She wouldn't be sad to give it up. Her wedding would be the start of a new life with Freddie and she looked to the future with optimism and hope. Everyone spoke of impending war, but she refused to let those negative thoughts invade the peace she felt within. Her father had died and she had survived; if there was a war, she'd survive that, too. Freddie and she were going to be together until the end of their lives. Nothing was going to tear them apart. She felt very strongly that God owed her nothing less.

'Grace!' It was Freddie, pulling up on his bicycle.

'Look at the snow!' she exclaimed. 'Isn't it marvellous?'

'We're going to have a white wedding,' he said, leaning his bicycle against the wall. 'I've bought you a present.'

'A present? What for? You shouldn't have.'

He hurried over to her with a parcel, wrapped in brown paper and tied with string. 'I was going to buy you a ring, but as you have your mother's I thought I'd spend the money on something else.'

'But I don't need anything,' she laughed.

'You might not need it, but I want you to have it.' He

kissed her. 'I've wanted to buy this for you since I was fifteen. Let's go inside. I don't want the snow to spoil it.'

Once in the kitchen, she pulled at the string. 'What could it possibly be? Oh, Freddie, you are something else.' His face was alight with pleasure, watching her unwrap it. She saw a flash of colour and pulled out a bright-red dress. 'Oh my goodness, it's a red dress. How did you know I've always wanted a red dress?'

'You told me. Down by the river. I've never forgotten. In fact, I wanted to go straight out and buy you one, but I didn't have any money.'

'It's beautiful. Shall I try it on?'

'I hope it fits. Mum told me your size and the lady in the shop knew it, too.'

'To think of you in a shop, Freddie.' She laughed and ran upstairs. 'You wait there. I'll only be a minute.'

But Freddie was too impatient. He pushed open her bedroom door just as she was doing up the buttons that ran over her breasts. His expression told her how good he thought she looked. 'Do you like it?' she asked, knowing that he did.

'I don't like it, I love it,' he replied. 'But I want to unbutton all those buttons.'

'Freddie, you have to wait,' she said, turning away.

'You have no idea how patient I'm being.' He swung her around and pulled her into his arms. 'Red is a wicked colour,' he said, eyes gleaming with lust.

'That's why I wanted a dress. I wanted to feel wicked for a change.'

'Grace, I never thought you had it in you to be wicked.'

'It's amazing what the colour red can do to a girl.'

He sat on the bed and pulled her onto his knee. 'This is my present,' he said, slipping his hand under the fabric and tracing his fingers up her stocking.

She pushed his hand away. 'Freddie, you have to wait,' she insisted.

'Then kiss me, at least. You're driving me mad.'

That evening Grace remained alone in the cottage. May had tried to persuade her to spend the night before her wedding at their house, but Grace had explained that she wanted to spend her final night as Grace Hamblin at home. From tomorrow, for the rest of her life she would share the Beekeeper's Cottage with Freddie.

She switched on the wireless in the sitting room. Ella Fitzgerald's rich voice resounded through the rooms, making her feel less alone. She lit a fire and watched Pepper make himself comfortable in front of it. She still hadn't got used to her father's empty chair. It seemed bigger without him in it. She had put his pipe and reading glasses in the walnut box with other personal belongings of his that she wanted to keep. It was easier to accept his death if those things weren't scattered around the house.

She read her novel for a while, but soon she realized she was just staring at the words without absorbing their meaning. Her mind was drifting off into the gardens of Walbridge Hall and to Rufus with his twinkling eyes and infectious smile. She rested her book on her lap and willingly set aside her self-control. Since her decision to marry Freddie she had barely thought about Rufus. She had successfully blotted him from her thoughts, closing the drawer on his letter and her dreams. But now the finality of her impending marriage forced her attention onto the man she had secretly loved since she was fourteen. There hadn't ever been the slightest possibility of Rufus reciprocating her feelings, but suddenly, as her existence as a single woman was about to expire, she found herself reluctant to extinguish her hope.

She turned off the wireless and went to her bedroom and pulled open the drawer where she had shut away the letter Rufus had written to her after her father died. She sat on the bed and slowly withdrew it from its envelope. She traced her fingers over the embossed *R* and read his words for what she believed would be the last time. For tomorrow she was to become Freddie's wife. Tomorrow she would turn her back on Grace Hamblin's hopeless wishes and accept her future as Grace Valentine without ever again looking back.

As she replaced the letter in the drawer something in the doorway caught her eye. She swung around with a flush of guilt, as if someone had caught her reading Rufus's letter. There was nobody there and all was quiet except for the habitual ticking of the grandfather clock in the hall. She wandered into the corridor. The door to her father's bedroom was open. She was sure she had left it shut. With a thumping heart she went to close it. As she put her hand on the doorknob she noticed one of his handkerchiefs lying on the carpet at her feet. How strange. She was certain it hadn't been there before. She peered around the door to check that no one had sneaked in, but his bedroom was empty and silent as she had left it. She picked up the handkerchief and saw the initials she had sewn onto the corner years before. *A. H. H.* Arthur Henry Hamblin. She brought it to her nose and stifled a sob.

The following morning Michael picked Grace up in his motor car and drove her through the snow to his house where May and Josephine were waiting to help her dress for the wedding. It was bad luck to see the bride on her wedding day, so Freddie had been awoken early and sent out to meet his friends in the Fox and Goose for a pre-wedding drink. Michael opened a bottle of sherry and poured four glasses. May put on the gramophone and music resounded through the house as they curled their hair, applied make-up and danced around the room excitedly. There was a spring feel to the house in spite of the thick snow covering the ground outside. Bouquets of flowers had been arriving since dawn, for Grace was very popular, and the air was saturated with their sweet perfume.

A few weeks before, Grace and May had taken the train to Dorchester and bought a dress at the department store. It was a simple ivory-coloured dress adorned with pearls. They had celebrated their purchase with lunch at the Regis Hotel before catching the afternoon train home. Now Grace put it on and May buttoned it up at the back. Grace stood in front of the long mirror and even Josephine was unable to find anything unpleasant to say. 'Oh, Grace,' she sighed. 'You look beautiful.'

'Yes, you do,' May agreed. 'Arthur would be so proud.' She fastened the final button and stood back to admire the girl who was about to become a real daughter to her, wiping her eyes with a handkerchief.

Grace stared at her reflection and for a fleeting moment she saw her mother's face gazing back at her. Her lips curled into a gentle smile and her eyes shimmered with emotion. Grace forgot to breathe as her mother's whole expression radiated a love that seemed to reach her through the glass and envelop her in a warm and comforting light. 'Don't look so surprised,' said May. 'You're a lovely-looking girl, Grace.'

'Freddie's going to be the one to look surprised,' Josephine cut in. 'He'll wonder who's the girl walking up the aisle.'

For once May chided her crossly. 'That's unfair, Josie. Why don't you go and see if there's any more champagne? I think Grace needs a refill and goodness, so do I.'

Grace reluctantly turned away from the mirror and the vision of her mother vanished as quickly as it had come. 'Thank you, Auntie May. I don't know what I'd do without you,' she said.

May chuckled. 'That's what your father used to say.'

'I do so wish he was here.' A sob escaped Grace's chest and she let out a whimper. May gathered her into her arms and the two women sought comfort in each other, trying hard not to let tears wash away their make-up.

'He is here, don't you think, Grace? That's what he said in his letter, right? "We'll always be with you." Well, Arthur knew about those things, didn't he? He had a wisdom we don't have. I trust he knew what he was talking about and you must trust him, too.'

'Then I wish I could see him. Believing isn't the same as seeing.'

'I know it isn't, but it's all we've got.' She pulled away and looked Grace in the eye. 'Now, you walk down that aisle with Michael and know that my Freddie is going to take care of you in your father's place and he's going to do his very best to make you happy. You have to think about the future now. You're a grown-up and you're going to start a family of your own one day. You look just right and Freddie is the luckiest man in the world to be marrying you.'

At last Michael announced that it was time to leave for the church. Josephine walked with her mother, leaving Grace to travel in the motor car with Michael. Just as they were about to depart, the Marquess's black Bentley purred into the narrow lane, making it impossible for them to leave. It stopped and Cummings, the chauffeur, stepped out, went round to the back and withdrew the most enormous bouquet of flowers Grace had ever seen. 'Good day, Mr Valentine,' he said to Michael. 'These are for you, Miss Grace.'

Grace knew at once that they were from Rufus and a lump lodged itself at the bottom of her throat. Michael took the flowers inside and Cummings handed her the note. It was written in Rufus's distinctive hand: *Miss Grace Hamblin*. With trembling fingers she pulled out the little card. It was embossed with the now familiar gold *R* at the top, then below, he had written in black ink:

My dear Grace,
I wish you all the luck in the world on your wedding day. May you be blessed with many happy years of laughter and joy and the blessed buzzing of buzzy-bees.
Your friend, Rufus

She was so busy reading the note over and over that she forgot to thank Cummings, and when she remembered her manners and looked up, the motor car was reversing out of the lane and it was too late. Rufus would have said he was too sour to deserve a thank you and that made her feel a little better. She smiled as she recalled the expression on Rufus's face when he had decided to name him Lemon.

'That's a mighty bouquet of flowers, Grace. Are they from Lord and Lady Penselwood?' Michael asked.

The colour flooded Grace's cheeks. 'No, they're from Lord Melville. I once helped his grandmother's arthritis.'

'Ah, yes, so you did. I remember now. How kind of him to think of you today.'

'He's wishing me and Freddie good luck,' she said, slipping the card back into its envelope.

'I'll put that with the flowers in the kitchen.'

'Did you put them in water?' she asked, anxious for them not to wilt.

'I filled the sink. They'll be fine in there until you're ready to take them home. They've scented the whole house already. They must have come all the way from London. You don't get flowers like that in the middle of winter in Dorset! Must have cost a fair bit, I imagine.'

'He's very kind.'

'Very. Now, let's get you in the motor car. We mustn't keep everyone waiting.'

When Grace stepped into the church on Michael's arm, she thought of her father, then she thought of Rufus and finally, as she approached the end of the aisle and saw Freddie's eager face grinning at her with admiration and affection, she thought of the man whom she was about to vow to love and cherish until death did them part, and a small, inaudible voice cried out in her head: 'Run away, run away, you've only ever truly loved Rufus.' But she was now at Freddie's side and Michael was giving her away and she was repeating words without absorbing them because all she could think about was that beautiful bouquet of spring flowers in May's kitchen and the sudden realization that perhaps Rufus loved her a little, after all.

As Freddie slipped her mother's gold band onto her finger she was jolted back to her senses. Her eyes filled with tears at the sight of the ring her father had left for her in the walnut box and his words echoed loudly in her head, blotting out the voice that was telling her to flee. '*What you need is love, of course, but the steady, loyal, constant love of a friend.*' She trusted her father. She knew he had understood her needs better than anyone. She could never have Rufus. Freddie would make her happy. It was foolish to wish for more. She gazed into Freddie's eyes and saw the steady, loyal, constant love her father had recognized.

'I now pronounce you man and wife,' said Reverend Dibben happily. Freddie squeezed her hand between his reassuringly and she felt her body loosen and her mouth curl into a smile, rebelling against her heart which wanted to cry its longing into the vaults of the church.

'Hello, Mrs Valentine,' Freddie whispered, his indigo eyes bright with joy, and Grace didn't have time to mourn the loss of her name or to reflect on what that might mean before she was led to the back of the church to sign the register. She dutifully wrote her name, receiving congratulations from May and Michael with dignity and a strange numbness, as if she was under water. Then, to the resounding notes of the organ, she walked down the aisle on Freddie's arm – past the people she had known since she was a child and who would accompany her along the path to the end of her days – and out into her future as Mrs Freddie Valentine.

She knew she had done the right thing, but those flowers had shed light on the tiny seed of hope that lay hidden in the bottom of her heart. It now cracked open and a little green shoot burst forth, raising its head out of the dark.

Chapter 18

That night, alone at last in the Beekeeper's Cottage, Freddie unbuttoned Grace's dress and took her to bed. He was a gentle and sensitive lover and what he lacked in experience he more than made up for in enthusiasm. Small blunders induced laughter rather than a feeling of awkwardness, because they knew each other too well to be embarrassed. In Freddie's arms Grace made the transition from girlhood to womanhood without regret for her lost youth or her choice of husband. Beneath Freddie's stroking she forgot about Rufus and gave in to the heady range of new sensations that opened a door to a whole new world she had never known was there. Making love enticed her into the moment and she savoured it gratefully.

She soon settled into the rhythm of married life. Instead of cooking and washing for her father, she was baking and darning for Freddie. Without Arthur to cultivate the garden she attended to it herself. It wasn't long before she was weeding and planting, pruning and deadheading just as Arthur had done before her. She missed him dreadfully, but looking after his beloved bees and gardens made her feel connected, because if he lived on, he would surely be there, among the things he'd loved the most.

In the spring of 1939 Rufus married Lady Georgina at her family estate of Thenfold in Hertfordshire, the Dowager Lady Penselwood suffered a fatal heart attack in the vegetable garden, and Hitler marched his army into Czechoslovakia.

War was on everyone's lips, and the Fox and Goose vibrated with young men declaring loyalty to King and country with patriotic zeal and foolish naïvety. Among them was Freddie. 'Everyone's signing up,' he told Grace and his mother. 'Even your friend Rufus Melville is going to fight,' he added to Grace. Grace felt a cold and clammy dread in the pit of her stomach and didn't know whether it was on account of Rufus or Freddie. 'It's going to be exciting. I'm going to join the Dorset Yeomanry,' he declared proudly. 'We're not going to let the Germans invade. We'll sacrifice our lives for England's green and pleasant land.'

May had gone pale, for she remembered the first war and the fathers and sons who had gone off to fight with the same bravado, never to return. But Freddie knew nothing of war, and to him and other young men like him it promised adventure and excitement and a welcome release from the parochial monotony of their ordinary lives. Arthur had never spoken about the Great War and Grace knew from the way he had averted his eyes and drawn his lips into a thin line that war was unspeakable. She took Freddie's hand, but he was high on excitement and patriotic fervour and barely noticed it. Grace was suddenly gripped by a terrible fear. If she lost Freddie, she'd have nothing left.

As the clouds of war grew increasingly dark on the horizon, Grace tried to live as she always had, with joy and optimism. Yet the pleasure she derived from the trees and flowers, the birds and bees, was tinged with melancholy because war threatened everything that was beautiful. She felt vulnerable and afraid, and however much she focused her attention on the moment, as her father had taught her to do, the future invaded like the tentacles of an octopus, to drag her deep into her fears.

Then, one afternoon in early summer, Freddie cycled up to the cottage and shouted through the kitchen window with urgency. 'Grace! They need you up at the Hall. There's a swarm and you're the only one who knows what to do with it. Lady Georgina is beside herself. You must hurry.' Grace took off her apron, tied up her hair and shut Pepper in the kitchen. Freddie was waiting for her with her bicycle.

'She hasn't been stung, has she?' Grace asked, climbing on.

'No, but she's in a right panic.'

'Are you coming with me?'

'I'll come with you to the house, then I'd better get back to the farm.'

'We'll cut through the woods, it's quicker that way.' They cycled off together. 'Have they come to live down here now?' she asked.

'Lord Melville wants her in the country now there's going to be a war. It won't be safe in London.'

'I'm still hoping it won't happen.'

'Don't waste your energy, Grace. It's happening all right and it's going to be soon.' He grinned at her. 'You could join the Wrens.'

'Someone will have to keep the farm going while you boys are busy playing soldiers. I'll take your job, and then when the war is over they'll give me Mr Garner's job and you'll wish you never went off to fight.'

'I'd like to see you labouring away in the fields.'

'I think I'd enjoy it, actually.'

'Mr Garner's talking of getting in some livestock. Cows for milk and pigs for ham.'

'They already have chickens.'

'And you'll have to look after them all.'

'Me and Lady Georgina looking after pigs and milking cows!' She laughed heartily. 'Now that's a funny thought.'

When Freddie and Grace arrived at the house Mr Swift, the keeper, was waiting for them with the new head gardener, Mr Heath. Mr Swift had known Arthur for years and when he saw Grace he smiled affectionately. 'Ah, Grace, not a moment too soon. Her ladyship has withdrawn inside.' He chuckled, for Mr Swift was a wise and mellow man, as Arthur had been. 'You'd have thought the Germans had invaded,' he said in a quiet voice. 'A lot of fuss about nothing, if you ask me.'

'You'd better come round to the back of the house, Mrs Valentine,' said Mr Heath, his country accent wrapping itself around his vowels like soft squirrels' tails. 'There's a cloud of bees. A black cloud. Swarming all over the garden. Quite a sight, it is. Don't know what you're going to do with them.'

'Let's have a look and I'll tell you,' Grace replied.

Freddie disappeared to the farm and Grace followed the two men round to the back of the house. The gardens looked splendid. Fat flowers shone in the sunshine and the leaves on the trees were still a bright, phosphorescent green. The lawn had recently been cut, and cat's ear and chickweed grew among blue cranesbill and white campions on the bank leading up to the paddock. For a moment she forgot her purpose and slowed down to admire the magnificence of the gardens which had once been her father's domain.

At the back of the house was a large terrace where Lady Georgina had clearly been sitting only minutes before, for her magazines were strewn on the table along with a pretty china teapot, a delicate cup with its saucer and a little jug for milk, while the cushions had been placed on all the chairs and benches for her comfort. Music still resounded through the house from a gramophone inside, but the record was stuck and the notes kept repeating themselves.

The cloud of bees was still swarming in front of the wall where purple clematis grew in abundance and honeysuckle infused the air with its warm and fruity perfume. Grace put her hands on her hips and looked up to a place just below the second-floor windows. There, as she had anticipated, was a bundle of bees about the size of a rugby ball. To the untrained eye they looked as if they were simply climbing on top of each other in a desperate struggle to get inside the bricks, but Grace knew better. 'They're protecting the queen, trying to find a new nest for her,' she told the men. 'She'll be beneath that cluster.'

'Lady Penselwood won't want a nest in her wall, Grace,' said Mr Swift. 'You'll have to get rid of them somehow.'

'Lady Melville won't come outside until they're gone,' added Mr Heath. 'She's right scared of bees.'

Mr Swift took off his cap and raked his weathered fingers through grey woolly hair. 'They don't look like they're planning on going anywhere tonight.' He replaced his hat. 'So, what are you going to do, Grace?'

'I could do two things. I could rattle some tins to drown out the sound of the queen, which would make them all disperse. But I think I'll go home and return at sunset with my protective clothing. By then they will have formed a big ball of sleepy bees and I'll simply swipe them off the wall and put them in a basket. I might see if I can make a new hive. Just depends what sort of bees they are. We'll soon find out.'

She remembered one of her father's sayings: *A swarm in May is worth a load of hay. A swarm in June is worth a silver spoon. A swarm in July isn't worth a fly.* In which case the swarm would take to their new home very happily.

'Right, I'll tell Lady Melville,' said Mr Swift.

'She won't be coming out again this afternoon,' Mr Heath added.

'Then you can tell the maid that it's perfectly safe to come outside to clear away the tea. They're not going to sting anyone. They're far too busy with their nest,' said Grace. 'Right, I'll make my way home and return when it starts to get dark.'

Grace walked with Mr Heath back to her bicycle. 'Your father was a gifted man,' he told her gravely. 'I have great admiration for him.'

'Thank you, Mr Heath. He loved this place.'

'I can tell. The gardens have been cherished, that's for sure.'

'I'm the gardener at home now. Dad taught me well, but I've still much to learn.'

'If you'd like to come up here from time to time, I'd be happy to give you advice. What with the war coming and everything, the young men will be going off to fight and we'll be short of gardeners. I'll be grateful for your help as well.'

Grace's face lit up. 'I'd love to. Do you really mean that?'

'I really do,' he replied with a smile. 'Me, Mr Garner and Mr Swift will be the only men around, being old and not fit to fight.'

'I would think that was a blessing.'

'I fought in the Great War, Mrs Valentine, and I wouldn't want to fight in another, but my heart cries out for those young men who don't know the horrors of it, blind with patriotism and a misguided sense of romance. There's nothing romantic about war.'

'I'm afraid my Freddie is one of those young men.'

'I hope he has an angel watching over him, then.'

'So do I, Mr Heath.'

As she took up her bicycle once again her mind turned to Rufus and she wondered where he was. She thought of him going off to fight and her heart contracted with fear. It wasn't so very long ago that they had chatted on the lawn. He had called her Little Bee. She remembered now.

Later, when Grace returned in her protective clothing carrying a woven skep, she noticed Rufus's Alfa Romeo on the gravel at the front of the house and her stomach flipped over like a pancake. She hoped someone would tell him she was outside with the bees and perhaps he'd be inspired to come out and talk to her. With that thought, she almost skipped round to the back of the house.

No one had cleared away Lady Georgina's magazines or her tea, but they had stopped the music. It was dusk now. The air was balmy and heavily scented with all the sweet-smelling flowers in the garden. Mr Heath had taken it upon himself to bring round a ladder but there was no one ready to hold it for her. Until Rufus appeared like a phantom and then, suddenly, nothing else seemed important any more. Not the bees, not Lady Georgina's fear, not war.

'Well, you do look scary in that costume,' he said, chuckling softly as the end of his cigarette blazed scarlet in the half-light.

'It's my beekeeping costume,' she replied, heart pounding at the sight of him, so tall and elegant in a velvet dinner jacket and velvet slippers embroidered with the crest of the lion and dragon.

'Of course. You're the beekeeper.'

'There's a swarm.'

'So Georgie tells me.' He looked up at the roof. 'They seem to have gone to bed now.'

'Which is why I'm here to take them to their new home. I have a hive ready for them at the cottage.'

'You clever thing! How are you going to do that?'

'By putting on my hat, taking this skep here and literally wiping them off the wall. They'll come away in a ball.'

'And how are you proposing to take them back to their hive?'

'I was going to walk.'

'You were going to walk? In the dark?' He arched an eyebrow.

'It's not dark yet. I was hoping to get home before it's dark.'

He smiled and his teeth shone white against skin made brown by the impending night. 'But now you're talking to *me*.'

She laughed nervously. 'Yes, that might delay me a little.'

'So, if you're delayed because of me it'll be my duty to drive you home.'

'Really . . .' she began.

'I insist,' he interrupted crisply, then sighed wearily. 'Anything to avoid going into the drawing room. Mama and Georgie are having a heated discussion about what they're going to do when war is announced. It's very tiresome. Pigs or goats or sheep or cows? Neither of them knows one end of a cow from the other, so really it's a case of the blind leading the blind. Papa is in his study, building a model boat, and me: well, I can hardly stay listening to those two geese, can I? Not without losing my mind. So here I am, at the service of the beekeeper and very happy about it, too. Tell me how I can help? Perhaps I can delay you a little longer with my ineptitude.' His soliloquy had rendered her speechless. She stared at him, her face full of astonishment. 'You do need help, you know. If only to hold the ladder as you climb its dizzy heights.' He threw the remains of his cigarette into the hellebores.

'Yes, the ladder,' she replied at last. 'Goodness, you sound desperate.'

'I am, Grace. If Grandmama were still alive I'd have sought refuge with her. She would have understood.'

'I'm sorry about your grandmother.'

'So am I. Very sorry. I miss her every day. I imagine you miss your father, too.'

'Yes, I do. I visit him as often as I can.'

His face softened and he looked at her intently. 'Do you? Do you really?'

'Yes. He's only in the churchyard.'

'How sweet you are, Grace,' he said gently.

'Don't you visit your grandmother?'

'Not since her funeral.'

'Why not?'

'I've been busy in Bovington, I suppose.' He looked at his feet. 'I don't like churches or graveyards, Grace. That's the truth. I find death appalling.' He raised his eyes and smiled at her sadly. 'Am I a brute for not going to visit her?'

'Of course you aren't. She's not there anyway.'

'Really? Then where is she?'

'With *you*.'

'I admire your certainty. I do hope you're right, Grace.'

'I'm sure Dad is with me. I like to think of him in our garden or with the hives. I'm sure he's in all the places he loved the most.'

'You married,' he said suddenly.

'Yes. Thank you for the flowers. It was really very kind of you.'

'I'm glad you got them. Were they big enough?'

'They were enormous.'

He beamed, pleased. 'Good.'

'And for your letter when my father died. Really, you're much too attentive. I don't feel I can give anything back.'

'I don't want anything back, Grace.'

'Well, it's terribly kind of you, anyhow.' There was an awkward pause, but Grace was quick to fill it. 'You married, too. I forgot to congratulate you. Silly of me.'

'Yes, we're both married.'

Grace was sure she sensed a heaviness in those words. 'Yes, isn't it lovely,' she replied, ashamed that her voice sounded flat.

He looked at her with affection, as if her naïvety amused him. 'So, tell me what to do. I'm your assistant now. The ladder? I suppose there's no stopping you scaling it like a squirrel.'

'Yes, the ladder. I need to climb it to get to the bees.'

'Then I'll hold it for you so it doesn't wobble. Nothing worse than a wobbly ladder when one's at the top of it.' He chuckled and bent down to lift it off the grass. Once he had set it securely against the wall of the house, as near to the bees as possible without disturbing them, he turned to Grace triumphantly. 'How's this for service?'

'It's perfect.'

'Are you going to climb with that basket – or skep, as you call it? Shouldn't I hold it for you until you've reached the top?'

'I can manage, thank you.' With that she stepped closer and put her foot on the first rung. Rufus was right beside her now. She could smell the lime scent of his cologne and the tobacco on his breath.

'Do be careful up there,' he said.

She began to climb. Rufus held the bottom of the ladder and watched her as she ascended towards the ball of sleeping bees. 'Are you there yet?' he asked. 'Don't fall, I can't promise I'd catch you, though I'd try my damnedest.' When she reached the bees, she steadied herself, placed the basket beneath them, then swept them deftly off the wall with the other hand. Rufus watched her take both hands off the ladder and held onto the bottom of it with all his strength. 'Grace, you're making me very uneasy down here. What the devil is Mr Heath doing, leaving you to risk your life like this? Hurry up and come down. I insist. I won't have you up there a minute longer.'

When Grace reached the bottom she was laughing so much that her stomach was hurting.

'What are you laughing at?' he asked indignantly.

'You,' she replied. 'You were going on and on . . .' She laughed again.

'Well, you worried me, that's all.' He watched her put the lid on the basket. 'Did you get them all?'

'All of them.' She took off her hat. 'Thank you, Lord Melville.'

'Rufus. Dear God, we know each other well enough to use our first names. I told you to call me Rufus six years ago. Besides, I can't call you Mrs Valentine. That's absurd. I've just saved your life.' Now he smiled with her. 'You're mocking me, Grace.'

'You should hear yourself.'

'I'm showing you concern. You should be grateful.'

'I am, *very* grateful. You've made my day.' He couldn't know how true that was. They both laughed together.

'Come, I'll drive you home.'

'Hadn't you better tell someone where you're going?'

'Oh, they'll be drinking champagne and discussing cows for a good while yet. Besides, I told Johnson I was coming out to help with the bees.' He put his hand in the small of her back and guided her through the garden.

'There's something wonderfully alluring about the night, don't you think?' He inhaled the air enthusiastically. 'All those little animals scurrying about. One doesn't know how many pairs of eyes are watching from the bushes. Foxes, badgers, rabbits, pheasants, mice? I like the stars and the blue velvet sky. It excites me with its sense of danger and romance.'

'I like it too,' she agreed. 'Most people are frightened of the dark.'

'But not you and me, Grace. I bet you love the smells and sounds that only come out at night. Georgie has to sleep with the light on in the corridor. I find that very tiresome as I love to sleep with all the lights off and the curtains and windows wide open so I can experience the night in all its glory.' He chuckled softly. 'You and I are creatures of the night, perhaps. Unique in our delight and wonder.'

'It *is* very mysterious,' she agreed, intoxicated by the deep resonance of his voice. It was soft and granular, like fudge.

'If I didn't have to get back for dinner and you didn't have to get back to Freddie, I'd invite you to sit on a bench with me and listen to the rustlings of the garden.'

'I'd have liked that,' she said.

'I swear that one can hear the trees breathing. In the darkness our hearing is more acute because our eyes can't see and our ears have to work so much harder. One can hear the garden breathing, in and out, in and out, and it's the most intriguing sound in the world.'

'Truly? Can you really hear the garden breathing?'

'I tell you it's true, Grace. Perhaps one night, if we find ourselves alone in this little paradise, I'll show you.'

They reached the car at the front of the house and Rufus placed the basket carefully on the back seat. 'I hope they don't all wake up with the roar of the engine and swarm the car,' he said.

'They won't,' she replied. 'They're very dozy, and anyway, the lid is on firmly.' He opened the passenger door and she climbed in. Once again she savoured the smell of leather and polish, barely daring to believe that she was alone with Rufus and that he was promising to show her the gardens at night.

'So what will you do with the bees when you get them home?' he asked, climbing in beside her.

'I'll put them into a new hive.'

'Did you build it especially?'

'No, Dad had a few hives he wasn't using so I chose one of those. I'm hoping they'll like it and start producing honey.'

'And it'll arrive in jars on our breakfast table for our toast and tea.' He sighed and stared at the road ahead. 'I hope Freddie knows how lucky he is.'

'I'm sure he does,' she replied, then added hastily, 'And I'm very lucky, too.'

'Of course you are. I'm so pleased, because you're a treasure, Grace. I hope you don't mind me telling you that. It's rather forward of me, I know, but I've never been very good at keeping things to myself. You're a very special girl. I saw it when you were only a child and that quality hasn't gone; in fact, it's blossomed. You've grown into a very special *woman* and I hope Freddie sees it and appreciates it and cherishes it, because you deserve to be cherished.'

Grace had gone very hot. Her face burned and her chest was like a furnace inside her protective suit. 'Oh, Freddie's very loving,' she replied, wishing he'd talk about something else.

'I've embarrassed you. I'm sorry,' he said suddenly. 'It was wrong of me to assume that Freddie hasn't recognized your qualities. Of course he has. He'd be blind not to. Tell me, will he help you put the bees in their new hive or can you manage on your own?'

'I can manage on my own.'

'Do you just pour them in like gravel?'

'Yes.' She giggled at his simile. Rufus had a funny way of describing things.

'They'll be rather disorientated when they wake up in the morning.'

'I suspect they will. But they'll get used to it very quickly. As long as the queen is there, they'll know exactly what to do.'

Rufus drew up in front of her cottage. The lights were on but Freddie wasn't home, because his bicycle wasn't in its usual place. Grace suspected that he was still at the pub and was relieved, because she knew he'd feel jealous if he saw that Rufus had driven her home.

'I shall send Lemon with your bicycle tomorrow.'

'Don't worry, I can walk round and pick it up.'

'Why should you? If I was still going to be at home I'd insist you came to collect it, just so that I could talk to you again. But I'm leaving early in the morning for Bovington.'

Grace felt a sense of dread building in her chest. She thought of the impending war and his part in it. She wanted to tell him to be careful, but she wasn't his wife. She had no right to tell him anything at all. 'Thank you for driving me home,' she said instead.

'No, thank *you* for removing the bees. We shall all sleep better tonight knowing that Georgie is happy.' He smiled wistfully and climbed out of the motor car. He helped her carry the basket to the hives. 'I'd like to watch you do this, but I fear I shall be late for dinner.'

'Perhaps you can tell your mother and Lady Georgina that if they are at all worried about looking after animals, I'd be very happy to help.'

'I will tell them,' he said firmly. 'That should put an end to their quarrelling.'

He gazed at her for a long moment. Only the darkness filled the gap between them, and it was thrilling and mysterious. Grace forgot to breathe. The weight of his stare was almost unbearable. 'Goodnight, Little Bee,' he said at last.

'Goodnight, Rufus.'

Suddenly he was gone, and the garden seemed to shrink and cool until it was quiet and empty again. She took a deep breath and fought the longing that now crept over her with its sharp and ever-tightening grip. She was married. It was wrong to think of Rufus in this way; it was even worse to love him. But once she had emptied the bees into the hive and replaced the lid she stood very still and tried to hear the whispering breath of the garden at night.

Chapter 19

The bees took to their new home as Grace had hoped they would. She sat watching them, remembering her evening with Rufus, replaying their conversation over and over until she could hear the deep timbre of his voice as if he were sitting right beside her. She envisaged the endearing way he hunched his shoulders when he chuckled, a sheepish expression softening his finely chiselled face, and found a surprising vulnerability there that she hadn't noticed before. That moment by the ladder, when they had laughed together at his concern, had somehow brought him down to her level. He was no longer the lofty aristocrat on a pedestal, but a man who, for reasons she couldn't understand, cared about her.

In the evenings, while Freddie was at the pub with his father and friends, she began to make Rufus a blue silk lavender bag to help him sleep at night. She would have liked to embroider an *R* on the front, but she feared Freddie might find it. So she sewed a picture of a bee instead. She justified her project by telling herself that it was merely a way of thanking him for the very generous flowers he had sent her on her wedding day. There was no reason to feel guilty. She wasn't betraying Freddie; she was simply making a gift for a friend.

After the headiness of that evening Grace settled once more into married life and tried to focus on her husband and her duty as a wife. She took up Mr Heath's offer of gardening lessons, but every time she arrived at the Hall Rufus's motor car was absent. She couldn't help hoping he would appear around the corner as he had that evening with the bee swarm, but he never did. Instead, she occasionally saw Lady Georgina on the terrace with her mother-in-law, Lady Penselwood, and well-dressed women in pale sun hats who had come to stay. Their laughter resounded across the lawn as Johnson and the other servants brought them drinks and delicious-looking things to eat. Grace was invisible to those ladies as she trailed Mr Heath in a pair of brown dungarees with her hair tied up in a scarf. But once, when she happened to be helping him in the herbaceous border near the house, she looked up to see Lady Georgina staring at her, a cigarette smoking in its ebony holder a few inches from her crimson lips, a frown creasing the delicate white skin between her eyebrows. Grace dropped her eyes into the alchemilla mollis but she could feel the woman's gaze upon her back as if it were burning through her clothes. She wondered feverishly whether Lady Georgina had minded her husband driving her back with the bees, or had she perhaps overheard them talking as she scaled the ladder? As her mind swirled with possibilities she wasn't listening to a word Mr Heath was telling her. Eventually the old man turned to her and smiled. 'What's playing on your mind, Grace, because you're miles away?'

June slipped into July and Freddie's days stretched into long evenings in the fields as he brought in the wheat and barley, returning late covered with dust and smelling of sweat. He was never too tired to ask her about her day and to listen to her stories as she served him supper in the kitchen.

Sometimes, when it was very warm, they took their plates outside and ate in the garden, and Freddie would take her hand and reminisce. He loved more than anything to remember the first time he had kissed her down by the river.

The light grew mellow and Grace wondered whether this would be the last summer of life as she knew it. War was now certain. Freddie had joined the Dorset Yeomanry; Mrs Emerson told her that Rufus had followed in his father's footsteps and joined a tank regiment with the Blues & Royals. The men were no longer *playing* soldiers, they really *were* soldiers, and many would sacrifice their lives in a war which was only too real. She tried not to think about it, but when she went to check on the hives and all she could hear was the gentle knocking of a woodpecker, the light tweeting of finches and blue tits and the melodious song of the blackbird, her heart was filled with sadness for all that might be lost. From the serene beauty of her garden she looked to a horizon of darkness and death with a terrible dread. War was approaching, and like a mighty cyclone it would sweep away everything she loved.

On 3rd September Britain declared war on Germany. Grace huddled around the wireless with Freddie, May, Michael, Josephine and the locals in the Fox and Goose. It was better to hear it all together in the pub where they could seek comfort and support from each other. Grace ran her eyes over the rosy faces and feverish eyes of the young men, who were whipped into a state of patriotic fever and indignation at the audacity of Adolf Hitler. But she didn't see adventure and excitement as they did. All she could see was certain death and the misery of those, like her, who'd be left behind. She looked over to May and saw that she was crying.

When Grace said goodbye to Freddie she held him tightly, hoping that her fierce embrace would somehow make up for the lavender bag and her affection for Rufus. She closed her eyes and felt the tears squeezing through her eyelashes and onto his jacket, and silently asked God to forgive her and to preserve her darling Freddie, whose love she didn't deserve. Freddie kissed her passionately, but his eyes gleamed with excitement and her weeping only made him more determined to prove himself on the battlefield and return to her a hero – a hero who would think nothing of a bee sting.

With all the young men gone, old Mr Heath and Mr Swift were the only men left to manage the gardens and Mr Garner had been robbed of his farmworkers. It was up to Grace and the other women of Walbridge to take over, lest the place fall apart. The Marchioness of Penselwood, now without her husband and son to make all the decisions, rose to the occasion with the unflappable stoicism for which her class were famous, and galvanized the women as if she were a colonel rousing her troops. She summoned them all on the lawn, where Mrs Emerson served tea and cakes beneath the tree as she had done at Rufus and Lady Georgina's engagement party the previous summer, and encouraged them to rally together, for the war had to be fought on *all* fronts.

It was a warm September day, but a cool breeze swept over the grass to remind them that summer, and their carefree lives, were now over. Lady Penselwood was still a desirable woman in her early fifties with high cheekbones and a full, bow-shaped mouth. Her soft hair and pretty brown eyes did not disguise the strength in her jaw and chin, and if anyone doubted her ability, as a woman, to run the estate, her determined and businesslike demeanour were enough to convince them of her intention, at least. She stood tall and elegant in a light tweed skirt and jacket, a cream-coloured silk blouse buttoned at the neck and a pair of sensible brown lace-up shoes. She wore a simple brown hat with a striking fan of pheasant feathers pinned to one side. She looked dignified and dependable. She inspired them all with the belief that they were capable of anything, even beating back the Germans should they dare to set foot in Walbridge. So Grace swallowed her tears and decided to focus on Freddie's return. Surely the war would be over soon and everything would return to the way it was.

Christmas came and went and Grace anxiously awaited Freddie's letters. They didn't tell her much about life at war. They were full of reminiscences: about the lake, the farm, the woods in springtime and, above all, his love for her. The only insight he gave her was when he mentioned that her letters prevented him from 'descending into loneliness and home-sickness', and that he kept them close to his heart to read over and over. He dreamed of simple things, he wrote, and cherished their life together ever more fiercely.

Grace missed him. But she didn't have time to be lonely. She was part of a large and cheerful gang of women – the Women's Land Army, the government called them – who worked on the farm and in the vegetable gardens, increasing food production for the war effort. Women from London came down to help, and among them was a high-spirited girl from Bow called Ruby, who lodged with Grace. Initially Grace hadn't wanted anyone to occupy her father's old room, but Lady Penselwood had spoken to her personally and persuaded her that it was unhealthy to keep a shrine. 'We're at war now, dear, this is no time to be sentimental,' she had said, and Grace had seen Rufus in her rich brown eyes and chiselled features and relented at once.

Ruby was a good-time girl of nineteen, looking for adventure. With blonde curls, doll-blue eyes and porcelain skin she would have looked like Goldilocks were it not for her lips, which she painted scarlet, even for working in the fields, and the cigarette permanently stuck into the corner of her mouth like a barrow boy. Grace warmed to her immediately, especially as Ruby knew nothing about the countryside and roared with laughter every time she pulled out a weed to find a carrot or a radish on the end. They sat up late, listening to the wireless and gossiping – there was plenty of gossip to feed off at the Hall.

Walbridge Hall was suddenly full of children, sent down to safety from London in their Fair Isle knits and lace-up shoes. Grace, whose primary job was assisting Mr Heath in the vegetable gardens, carried the produce in crates to the kitchens, where Mrs Emerson would make her a cup of tea and chat a while. Mrs Emerson whispered to Grace that Lady Penselwood had always longed for more children, so she had deliberately taken three sets of siblings, bringing the number of evacuee children up to seven. 'Goodness, this house is big enough for twice that,' she told Grace with a sniff. She sipped her tea then continued in a low voice. 'Lady Melville was so horrified by the sudden invasion of little 'uns, she locked herself in her bedroom for two whole days. I don't think she likes children. Fancy that, eh? Not liking children. The trouble is, she's spoilt. Lady Penselwood, on the other hand, is quite ready to roll up her sleeves and get down to work with the rest of us. You know she came and helped with the children's tea yesterday? Imagine that! She sat with them and they were all laughing and chatting like one big, happy family. She's come into her own now. This war has given her a new lease of life. She's bought those cows for milk. She's asked Mr

Garner to show her how to milk them. Imagine that, eh? The Marchioness of Penselwood milking a cow. That would never have happened before the war. As for Lady Melville, she won't go near the animals. She says they give her itchy eyes. She won't even collect the eggs. We have enough to make omelettes for the entire county. Lady Penselwood has taken up riding again and goes off with Mr Swift. It's a good way to see the land and check on things. I do admire her. I'm not so admiring of Lady Melville, though I suppose she's doing her bit knitting socks for the WI.'

Freddie came home on leave in the spring in his belted brown uniform and cap. He didn't want to talk about the war. He wanted to make love to his wife, drink with his friends and family at the Fox and Goose and inspect the farm with Mr Garner. Grace was overjoyed to see him. The months on the Western Front had darkened his skin and taken the fat off his bones, but he was still the same Freddie, with his raffish charm and gentle teasing. He smoked a great deal and, together with Ruby, filled the kitchen with fog in minutes. Grace cooked him large meals from her mother's cookery book. Rationing affected country folk less than city folk, thanks to the vegetables and dairy products supplied by the Hall, and she used the honey she collected from the hives in place of sugar, so Freddie ate well. He devoured enormous quantities, and when he returned to his regiment at the end of his leave his face had filled out and the rosy colour was restored to his cheeks.

Grace had relished having her husband at home. Once he left she was engulfed by a deep loneliness that neither May nor Ruby could fill. Part of her longed for a child so that she'd have someone to love and look after, but the idea of bringing a baby into such a frightening and uncertain world terrified her, so it was with mixed feelings that a month after Freddie had left she discovered that she was not pregnant. She threw herself into her beekeeping and the vegetable gardens at the Hall, and wrote Freddie long letters on airmail paper in her smallest handwriting, and prayed for him before she went to bed.

She had long since finished the lavender bag for Rufus, but she didn't know how to get it to him. It sat on her dressing table with her hairbrushes and perfume, inducing memories and longings she'd have been better off discarding. But as the weeks went by she found herself delving with increasing regularity into the drawer to read the letter he had written after her father's death and the card that had come with the flowers on her wedding day. Silently, she sent words to the Lord for his safety, too, and in the same ardent prayers she asked for forgiveness for her wild and foolish heart.

And then one day in late summer Rufus came home.

Grace was pushing her bike back through the woods after a long day in the gardens at the Hall. The air was humid and little midges hovered in clouds, caught in the spotlight as the setting sun showered its beams through gaps in the leaves. She listened with pleasure to the rustling of animals in the undergrowth and reflected again on the nocturnal breathing that Rufus had claimed to detect when darkness sharpened one's sense of hearing. Just as she thought of him, he appeared before her, having walked down a narrow path adjacent to hers.

He caught her off guard and the surprise was so sudden and so immense that it whipped away her inhibitions. 'Rufus!' she cried happily. 'You're home!'

Her enthusiasm pleased him. He smiled broadly and took off his hat. 'I'm home,' he replied. 'And it's jolly nice to be here.'

She ran her eyes up and down his captain's uniform. He looked more striking than ever and she felt the adrenalin course through her veins. 'Are you on leave?'

'I've been reassigned to General Doncaster's headquarters at Bovington,' he replied.

'That's wonderful,' she exclaimed.

'Just a brief visit. I'll be off again soon. To Africa."

'Oh.' Her eyes betrayed her disappointment and he smiled affectionately, as if he saw plainly her burning love for him and was moved by it.

'But I'm here now,' he said quietly.

'When did you get back?'

'This afternoon.'

'You look well.'

'I feel well enough, although the food is dismal. I miss Mrs Emerson's steak and kidney pie. It's an adventure out there but it's going to be a long, hard slog, I'm afraid.'

'Don't say that,' she groaned. 'I don't think I can bear it.'

'Then let's not talk about the war. Isn't it lovely here?' He sighed with relish, sweeping his eyes over the ferns and bramble bushes as if seeing it all for the first time. 'Put down your bike, Grace. I want to show you something.'

She hesitated a moment, suddenly aware that she was alone with him and fearful of how it might look, were they to be seen. 'I'll only be a minute,' he said, and his face was so endearing that she let her bicycle fall onto the grass and followed him back up the path he had just come down, which led further into the wood.

The bracken was waist high and the path so narrow they had to walk in single file. He strode up an incline, taking her to a part of the woods she knew well, having accompanied Mr Swift from time to time to help him with the pheasants. But then he turned off the path and started to wade through the undergrowth. She followed without speaking until the trees opened into a small clearing. At one end of the clearing was a child's wooden playhouse. 'Papa built this for me when I was a boy,' he told her. 'I thought it was marvellous.'

'How clever of him.'

'He loves building things. Of course, he'd have been happier if it had been a boat.' He chuckled softly, hunching his shoulders. 'But come and see what I just discovered.' He took her hand, and the feeling of his skin against hers caused her cheeks to burn. She knew she should take her hand away, but it felt so comfortable in his that she left it there, trying to persuade herself that he was simply being friendly.

He turned and put a finger across his lips. Her curiosity was aroused and she forgot about her hand. Gently, he pushed open the door with his foot and signalled for her to look inside. She stepped forward, finally letting go of his hand. There in the top corner of the little house was a bird's nest full of little furry chicks, their yellow beaks opening in anticipation of food. She remained there a moment, watching them, and all her fear of being alone with Rufus dissolved in the touching scene before her.

'It's extraordinary to see a full nest of chicks in late summer!' she whispered, withdrawing. 'How lucky we are to get so close. But how does the mother bird fly in?'

'Through the window. She doesn't need much room. I came up to see the house, to step into my childhood for a moment. To rest among my memories. Life is rather too serious now for my taste.' He smiled sadly and Grace noticed something dark in his eyes that hadn't been there before.

'I came to escape and then I heard you humming down on the track.'

'I was humming?'

'Yes, you were.'

'I never noticed.'

'I thought you'd like to see the chicks. Of all the people I know, I said to myself, Grace Valentine is the only person who would truly appreciate them.'

'They're adorable,' she replied, flattered.

He gazed down at her, the tenderness in his eyes blatant and unashamed. 'No, *you're* adorable,' he said softly. Grace stared at him, startled by this unexpected declaration. 'God help me, Grace, but I love you. I can't deny it and I can't suppress it any longer. I love you with all my heart.'

Afraid, Grace let out a gasp. 'Don't!' she uttered, but even *she* heard the weakness in her voice and knew he could see that she returned his love, for it declared itself in the blushes that now set her cheeks aflame. Undeterred by her feeble protest, he bent down and pressed his lips to hers in a gentle kiss.

He pulled away. 'If you don't love me back, say, and I won't kiss you again. I promise. We can pretend this never happened.'

Grace shook her head slowly. 'I do love you, Rufus,' she replied slowly. The words, said out loud, were like doves set free from their cage and she knew then that she could never take them back. She knew, too, as he pulled her into his arms to kiss her again, that she'd never want to.

Chapter 20

As Rufus kissed her, Grace didn't think of Freddie. It was as if he belonged to another life, like a dream, and only this moment with Rufus was real. With his arms around her and nothing between them but the sound of their quickening hearts, they were as one. There was no difference in class or upbringing to set them apart. They were simply two people whose love for each other had grown steadily and irrevocably from the first moment they had met on the grass outside the church eight years before. Grace had imagined this moment a thousand times, and in her mind it had always felt right. Now she knew her imagination had not deceived her. They were two wandering souls who had found each other at last.

'Oh, Grace,' Rufus sighed, sweeping the stray wisps of hair off her face. 'I'm the luckiest man in the world to be loved by you. I should have carried you off into the sunset long ago and saved you for myself.'

'I loved you from the moment I put that bee on your arm. You remember?'

He laughed. 'My darling Grace, of course I remember. You were a young girl then. I knew you'd blossom into a beautiful woman. Look at you now, how lovely you are. I want to hear what you've been doing while I've been away.

I want to hear everything. Don't spare any details. I want to hear about the bees and the broccoli! I want to take it all with me when I return to this damned awful war.' He took her hands. 'Let's not talk about that. Come, walk with me. I know every inch of these woods and I want to enjoy them with you where no one can find us. This little house here, in this delightful clearing, will be our secret place. No one will ever discover us here. While we're here we can pretend there is no Georgie and no Freddie, just you and me.' He kissed her forehead. 'My Little Bee.'

Grace worked as usual during the day and then in the evenings, as she walked home through the woods, Rufus would appear like one of King Arthur's gallant knights to sweep her into his arms and away to the realm of fantasy. He had stored blankets in the playhouse which they would spread on the grass and lie entwined, savouring the brief time they had together. He'd play with the long strands of her hair, curling them behind her ear or twirling them through his fingers, and tell her how beautiful she was and how she had rescued him from a dull and pointless life. Grace told him about the bees and Ruby, the work she did in the vegetable garden and on the farm, and gossip divulged from the Hall. He loved to hear what Mrs Emerson had to say about them all, but she was careful not to repeat anything she was told about Lady Georgina. It was better that they didn't discuss their spouses at all.

Like his mother, the Marchioness, Rufus adored the young evacuees who had come to stay. Grace listened to him talking about them and felt a gentle tugging somewhere deep in her belly, for she, too, felt a growing desire to have children. How she wished she could have Rufus's, but that was impossible. Lady Georgina would give him an heir, and God willing Grace would bear Freddie's child, and nothing of their love would remain on earth. No one would ever know. It would remain forever hidden and one day die with them. How Grace wished that some small token could endure.

She gave Rufus the lavender bag the evening before he left for Africa. 'My darling, how thoughtful you are. I shall treasure it always,' he said, pressing it to his nose and sniffing it. 'You clever thing, you.' Then he buried his face in her neck and kissed her there. 'I wish you could put *this* smell into a little bag so I could carry a bit of *you* off to war.'

She wriggled on the blanket. 'You're tickling me.'

He made the growling noise of a bear. 'And here?' He swept his lips over her collarbone.

She laughed uncontrollably. 'Yes, stop!' But she didn't really want him to.

He unhooked her dungarees and opened her blouse, one pearly button at a time, until her chest and the white cotton of her brassiere were exposed. Slowly and deliberately he kissed the soft skin between her breasts. She stopped laughing. He had never touched her there before. Without saying a word he slid his hand round to unclip her brassiere. She didn't move to stop him. The air had stilled around them, the woods grown suddenly quiet, as if acknowledging the sacred nature of the moment. Now her breasts were exposed, she caught her breath. He brought his mouth to hers again and with his hand caressed the swell of her bosom until her breathing grew shallow and she let out a low moan. Then tongue replaced fingers and she lifted her chin and closed her eyes and felt the tension building in her core of her belly, like a fire raging out of control.

She knew this was the last time she would see him for months. It could even be the last time she would see him, ever. War made the future so uncertain and the present all-important; nothing else mattered but now, because it was everything she had. Presently, with her senses heightened and her longing acute, she allowed him to undress her. He pulled off her dungarees and she wriggled out of her blouse and brassiere. Then he hooked his fingers over her knickers and slid them down her legs, tossing them into the grass. As she lay naked in the dappled light that quivered through the leaves, she allowed Rufus's eyes to consume her. Her husband had been the only man ever to see her naked; now she lay vulnerable and bare for her lover, who wasted no time in exploring every curve and crevice with greedy delight, inducing sighs and moans the like of which had never left her throat before.

When they had made love, Rufus delved into his jacket pocket and pulled out a packet of Camel cigarettes. He lit one and inhaled. 'I shall take the memory of this day with me to blot out the horrors of war,' he told her. 'I feel closer to you now, Grace. I've taken you in my arms and made you mine.'

'When will you come back?'

'I don't know.'

'I'll think of you every day.'

'I like that. I like to think of you, thinking of me. And I have something for you to remember me by.' He put his hand into another pocket and pulled out a red velvet box. 'I was rather pleased when I found this. I bought it in London before the war and have kept it all this time. It wasn't appropriate to give it to you then.'

'Oh, Rufus, you shouldn't have.'

'Of course I *shouldn't* have, but that's never stopped one doing what one wants to, and I wanted to *very* much. It's been burning a hole in my pocket.'

She pressed the little gold knob and lifted the lid. There, glittering and sparkling, was a diamond bumblebee brooch. She gasped with pleasure. 'Oh, it's beautiful,' she exclaimed admiringly. 'It's perfect. I don't imagine there's anything in the world more appropriate for me than this. It must have been very dear, Rufus. I'm quite embarrassed . . .'

'How sweet you are, darling.'

'Well, they're diamonds, aren't they?'

'Of course they're diamonds. Yellow ones and white ones. You're worth more to me than cut glass. You see, I loved you then and you didn't know it.'

'And I loved *you* and *you* didn't know it,' she laughed.

'You must wear it always.'

'Oh, I will.'

'And if Freddie asks?'

'I'll make something up.'

'You can say my grandmother left it to you as a thank you for helping ease her arthritis.'

'That's a very good idea. Then that's what I shall say. He won't question that.'

'Every time I see a bee I shall buy it for you until your house is full of my tokens of love. I'll buy you a collection so enormous that you will never forget about me.'

'But I won't want to forget about you, ever,' she protested, feeling as light as confectioner's sugar.

'And I won't ever forget about you. You do know that, don't you, Grace? You do know that whatever happens, I'll never forget my Little Bee. You will always be my one and only true love.'

At that moment they heard voices deeper in the wood. They stared at each other in horror. 'Get dressed,' he whispered, tossing his cigarette into the bushes. Hastily, they scrambled into their clothes. Grace had gone white with fear. She put the red velvet box in her dungarees pocket and tied up her hair with a scarf. The voices didn't seem to be getting any closer. Now there was soft laughter, carried on the breeze with the low murmur of a man's voice. Rufus took her hand. 'Come,' he hissed. She shook her head. 'It's all right. I know where they are. They don't know where *we* are. Trust me.' He led her slowly towards the voices. Grace winced every time the ground crackled beneath her feet. She wanted to tell him he was being reckless. If they were discovered, what would they say? But he was holding her hand tightly, and with determined steps making his way softly through the undergrowth. At last he told her to crouch down. Together they peered through the trees.

What they saw alarmed Grace more than the idea of getting caught. But Rufus was highly entertained. 'Good Lord!' he exclaimed in amusement. 'Who'd have thought it? Mama and Mr Swift!'

'Let's go!' Grace hissed, mortified to have caught the Marchioness of Penselwood pressed up against a tree by the gamekeeper. She'd read *Lady Chatterley's Lover* on the sly after Josephine had lent it to her, but she never imagined that sort of thing could really happen, certainly not to Lady Penselwood.

'You see, everyone's at it. I bet there isn't a faithful wife in the entire country. I don't imagine Mama gets much excitement with Papa. Good old Mr Swift. I never knew he had it in him. *Lady Penselwood's Lover*,' he chortled, speaking Grace's thoughts aloud.

'We can't watch them. It's rude,' Grace murmured, wondering whether he included Lady Georgina in his sweeping statement about unfaithful wives.

'All right. Come on. Let's get out of here.' He stood up and walked normally back the way they'd come.

'You're making a lot of noise,' she whispered anxiously.

'Oh, they're far too busy to notice us.' He laughed again and shook his head. 'Mother's gone up in my estimation. What a girl!'

'You're not upset?'

'Why would I be upset? I'd be a terrible old humbug if my mother's infidelity upset me. Papa's never been a very attentive husband at the best of times. He spends every free moment building boats when he should be making love to his wife. I don't blame her at all for seeking affection elsewhere. I'm just surprised it's Mr Swift. I suppose all the men of her class have gone off to war.' He took Grace's hand and brought it to his lips. 'You have natural nobility, Grace. There are plenty of countesses who aren't ladies. Then there's you. A lady in everything but name and, by God, I wish it were in my power to make you one. I'd make you a countess and you'd have more poise and refinement than all the ladies of the aristocracy.' He kissed her tenderly. 'You're a lady to me, Grace.'

Suddenly the thought of parting overwhelmed her. She threw herself into his arms. 'If only we belonged to each other,' she said. 'If only it were possible. But we're doomed to live apart forever. And now you're leaving and I might never see you again.'

'Darling, you must have more faith in Old Blighty,' he said, squeezing her hard. 'When I come back I'm going to push you up against a tree like Mr Swift.'

She laughed in spite of her misery. 'You're wicked.'

'I think that's a case of the kettle calling the pot black.'

She looked up at him with glistening eyes. 'Oh, I do love you, Rufus.'

'I know you do, and that will sustain me through to the end of the war, when we'll be reunited, here in our secret place, where no one but Mr Swift and Mama can find us.' His eyes grew serious as he caressed the contours of her face. 'Whenever you miss me, put your fingers on the brooch I gave you and that will send a telepathic message straight to my heart.'

'Oh Rufus, don't. You'll make me cry.'

He bent down to kiss her again. 'If God spares me, Grace, I'll come back and marry you. I promise you that. I'll divorce Georgie. You'll divorce Freddie. There's nothing on earth that can keep us apart.'

The following day Rufus went back to war and Grace went back to work and on the outside nothing seemed to have changed at all. But on the inside, everything had changed. Grace discovered she had a surprising ability to live two separate lives. An external life where she wrote long letters to Freddie, moaned about how much she missed him to Ruby, Josephine and May, and an internal life where her heart pined for Rufus. She discovered to her shame that she also had a surprising ability to lie.

Rufus wrote her long letters from Africa, always addressed to Miss Bernadette Short, which was a name they'd made up in case Freddie was ever home on leave and chanced to come across one. She could always claim that Bernadette was a land girl from London who had briefly lodged with her, but had now gone. It was Rufus's idea and a good one. He wrote the letter itself to 'My darling little B' and signed 'your ever-faithful Broderick', in reference to the name of one of his ancestors which Grace had found particularly amusing. She treasured every letter, hiding them with the two she had previously kept in her dressing-table drawer beneath a loose floorboard under the bed. Unlike Freddie who never shared his experiences, Rufus was full of *his*, as much as the censors permitted. He seemed to want to offload, and Grace was flattered that he should write about his feelings in such detail, sharing his failures with her as well as his successes. He was a highly intelligent and witty young man and his letters were more like short stories, the men he described becoming characters she longed to read about, and, as the war raged on, characters she mourned when they were tragically killed. He wrote philosophically and wisely but there was one line which stayed with her for days, causing her to cry into her pillow.

The noise of war is so great it destroys all living things. Sometimes I feel that Earth herself has stopped breathing altogether, because when I sit under the stars and see nothing but my own fears, I try to hear her breathe, in and out, in and out, and hear nothing but a deathly silence and my own weak heart, beating still for my one and only true love.

She went and sat outside in the middle of the night, wrapped in a sheepskin coat, and closed her eyes. At first she heard only the fretful throbbing in her ears, but then, as her heart rate slowed and her hearing grew more acute, she began to hear the gentle scuffling of a small animal in the hedge. She didn't open her eyes but let her senses tune into the secret nocturnal life of her garden. She longed to hear the breathing that Rufus had spoken about, but she was reassured that war hadn't yet robbed *her* garden of its life.

Grace was pleased to discover that Mrs Emerson, the source of all gossip at the Hall, hadn't found out about Lady

Penselwood's affair with Mr Swift. The cook didn't treat *her* any differently, either, which reassured her that she suspected nothing of her own affair with Rufus. The only person Grace went to great lengths to avoid was Lady Georgina. Most of the time Rufus's wife kept herself to herself in the private part of the house. While the Marchioness strode around the farm and gardens, rallying the women, milking the cows, collecting eggs from the chickens, riding out with Mr Swift, her sulky daughter-in-law supposedly knitted socks for the WI in her little sitting room upstairs. Mrs Emerson was full of it, as were the land girls who were high on tales of grand ladies from all over the county who were donning overalls and getting their hands dirty with the common folk. But Lady Georgina had a strong character and an unbending will, according to Mrs Emerson, and not even Lady Penselwood could shame her into action.

Then, one spring day in 1942, Lady Georgina sought out Grace in the gardens. She seemed most determined to speak with her. By now, Grace's secret compartment beneath the floorboard in her bedroom contained not only Rufus's letters but a growing number of small ornamental bees which he had managed to send her. Among them was a porcelain box, a cigarette case, a silver bauble and a gold pendant. He had also taken to drawing bees in his letters, which made her smile.

'I need to talk to you,' said Lady Georgina in her habitual lofty manner.

Grace's heart leapt into her throat. 'Yes, m'lady?' she replied, trying to find traces of suspicion in her features. But Lady Georgina looked at her impassively, giving nothing away.

'I need to send a box of honey out to Lord Melville.'

'I delivered the honey to Mrs Emerson last September. There should be plenty left in the store cupboard.'

Lady Georgina appeared flustered. 'I want the labels written especially,' she said.

Grace knew that prisoners of war, billeted at a nearby farm, hand-painted labels for the Walbridge honey jars. 'I can organize that for you, if you like,' she said. 'I'll have to harvest early this year. I could certainly fill some jars for you, but not before May.'

'Aren't the bees making honey all the time?'

'Yes, but we only harvest it once or twice a year.'

Lady Georgina smiled cheerlessly. 'I thought one could simply pour the honey out whenever one wanted to.'

'The bees wouldn't like that very much,' said Grace. 'What would you like on the labels and I can organize it for you?'

'I want special ones for my husband. It'll be a gift. He's suddenly taken a great interest in bees.'

Grace knew she'd give herself away if she looked shifty, so she replied steadily, 'Probably because the Dowager Lady Penselwood used bees to cure her arthritis.'

Lady Georgina raised her eyebrows. 'Did it work?'

'It helped, I believe.' Grace noticed Lady Georgina's gaze settle on the bee brooch she always wore above her right breast.

She narrowed her eyes. 'That's a beautiful brooch you're wearing.'

'Thank you.'

'Who gave it to you?'

Grace knew she was right to assume she hadn't bought it for herself and her father would never have had the money to indulge in such an extravagant brooch. 'The Dowager Lady Penselwood gave it to me as a thank you for helping ease her arthritis. It was I who ministered the bee stings.' At least the old woman was dead and unable to refute her story.

Lady Georgina looked surprised. 'How generous of her. You must have made her very happy to inspire her to give you such a thoughtful and kind present.'

'I wear it all the time,' said Grace.

'I hope it doesn't fall off while you're working. It would be a shame to lose it. I would advise you to save it for your best dresses and jackets.'

'It's firmly fastened,' Grace replied, touching it with her fingers. She wanted to quip that nothing would cause it to fly away and almost smiled to herself because it was the sort of joke Rufus might have made.

'How is your Freddie?' Lady Georgina asked. 'Does he write often?'

'He writes as much as he can.'

'Lord Melville seems to have far too much time on his hands, for I get too many letters.' She gave a miserable little chuckle and Grace saw through her hollow boast.

She suddenly felt sorry for her. 'I pray for an end to this senseless war,' she said with feeling. 'I pray for the return of our husbands and a return to the way it was. I can't bear living in fear of the worst, of trying to keep my mind on other things, while all the time I'm worrying that Freddie might be hurt or afraid or homesick.' She laughed bitterly. 'I feel so useless here, and the not-knowing could drive me mad.'

Lady Georgina's eyes softened and for a moment they were two women scared for their men, and the distance imposed upon them by their unequal status was suddenly abridged. 'We're all in this together,' said Lady Georgina. 'You with your Freddie, me with my Rufus, Arabella with Aldrich, and so many others, like us, feeling cut off and anxious. It's beastly.'

'So, how many jars would you like?' Grace brought the subject back to honey. She didn't want to get too close to Rufus's wife. Lady Georgina's face hardened again and Grace knew it had little to do with *her* and a lot to do with her own unhappiness.

'Six, I think. I gather one can use honey to dress wounds.'

'It has antiseptic properties,' Grace told her.

'What a wonderful thing honey is. Aren't they clever, the bees? I envy you with your simple life.'

'Is yours so very complicated?' Grace asked.

'Oh yes, you have no idea. But it's all to do with expectation, you see, and I don't suppose you, with your bees and your little garden, have many expectations that aren't fulfilled.' Grace didn't know what she meant and frowned. 'I want the labels to be pretty. I want a picture of bluebells to remind him of our wedding at Thenfold, and I want our initials on them. *R* and *G*, intertwined. Do you think it can be done?'

'Most certainly,' Grace replied, suddenly feeling uncomfortable. However much Rufus loved *her*, his life would always be intertwined with Lady Georgina's, like the letters on the labels.

'Good. Bring them to me personally, won't you. I don't want them getting muddled with the ones for the house. Mrs Emerson can be quite batty, you know.'

'I will.'

'Well, I won't keep you any longer. I'm sure you've got something useful to do in the garden.' Grace watched her walk away. She wondered whether their conversation had been motivated by Lady Georgina's suspicions, or whether she really *did* only want honey jars sent out to the front. If she *did* have suspicions, Grace hoped she had allayed them.

Grace witnessed the devastating effects of war on those around her with a growing fear for her own fragile spirit. Mrs Emerson lost a grandson in France and Lady Penselwood lost a nephew in Africa. Alongside those two women were countless others who received letters informing them that their husbands and sons were killed, lost in action or dreadfully wounded. Walbridge mourned and the mourning dragged on for months. Grace spent evenings on her knees at her bedside, praying for Rufus and Freddie, bargaining with God, hoping that her infidelity wouldn't inspire Him to take Rufus from her out of spite. She knew that she should promise to end the affair, but it would be a promise she couldn't keep.

She wrote letters to both Freddie and Rufus at the kitchen table and posted them together. Sometimes she wondered how it was possible to love two men at the same time. But there are many ways of loving and the love between siblings, parents and children, friends, spouses and lovers are all different, just as the seven shades of the rainbow are all part of the same arc of colour. It seemed natural to tell *both* men that she loved them, and that was the truth.

And then in the autumn of 1942 Grace received a letter informing her that Freddie had been wounded in action in North Africa. She hadn't even been aware that he was *in* Africa. It gave her a strange feeling to think that the two men she loved had been fighting in the same place. Freddie was now at a military hospital in a stable condition and would be coming home at the earliest opportunity. Grace sought comfort in Freddie's family. None of them knew any details yet. Grace was grateful he was alive, but terrified of what his injuries might be. She knew of men who had returned without limbs, brutally disfigured, mentally damaged. She woke up in the middle of the night having dreamed that she didn't recognize him. As she searched his bloodied, monstrous features his indigo eyes turned into Rufus's brown ones and she cried out in horror.

Her prayers for Rufus grew more insistent. Her anxiety mounted as weeks went by without any word from him. If he had been killed, wounded or lost in action, how would she know? While she waited for Freddie's return, she waited, too, for news from her lover. None came. She went out of her way to bump into Lady Georgina or the Marchioness, inventing excuses to go into the house. There was nothing in the women's demeanour to give Grace reason to believe anything terrible had happened to Rufus. She wrote to him, begging for news, expressing her anguish in ever more convoluted sentences.

Then she wondered whether Lady Georgina had somehow discovered their affair. Feverishly, she went over their conversation in her head, trying to recall whether she had unwittingly given them away. Had Lady Georgina seen the bee brooch before he gave it to her? Had he left it lying about? Had she threatened to leave him if he ever contacted Grace again? These possibilities shuffled about in her mind like a pack of cards full of spades. He had said that nothing on earth could keep them apart, but in truth, there was a very great deal that could.

Freddie came home after Christmas. Besides the wound on the left side of his face and his eyepatch, he still looked like Freddie. But he wasn't the same on the inside. He was bitter, resentful and sad. It was as if his heart had been ripped out with his eye. Worst of all, he was silent.

He glared at Grace as if she were to blame. May reassured her that it was natural to take out one's hurt on those closest, but Grace wondered whether he could see into her soul and whether he saw Rufus there.

She longed to ask after Rufus but there was no one to ask. Months went by and still no letter. Presently, she stopped writing to him. It was more difficult now with Freddie at home. She never ceased believing that Rufus loved her, and when Freddie went to the pub to drown his sorrows, she opened the secret compartment beneath her bed and drowned her own sorrows in his letters. Perhaps he knew Freddie had come home and felt it was unsafe to send letters there, even if they *were* addressed to someone else. There was nothing she could do but wait for an end to the war and for Rufus's return. She touched her bee brooch so often it became like a nervous tic, and Freddie, if he noticed, never asked how she had come by it.

PART THREE

Chapter 21

New York, 1990

Trixie couldn't sleep. She felt a strange sense of dread in the pit of her stomach, as she used to at high school the night before an important exam. She looked across at the man sleeping peacefully beside her. He lay on his back, the covers carelessly swept aside, exposing his muscular torso and the glossy texture of his skin, which gleamed in the light from the street outside. His name was Leo and he was American of Italian descent. Attractive, athletic and funny, he had all the attributes most women would kill for. But Trixie didn't love him. She hadn't loved any of the men who had warmed her bed, and there had been many. But she was fond of him. He made her laugh and didn't annoy her, and it was nice to have someone to share her life with. He had lasted eight months. She knew it wouldn't be long before they parted company. Fourteen months had been the longest.

She got up and padded into the sitting room, wrapping her velour dressing gown around her body. She sat in front of the large glass window that glittered with the eternal lights of a city she had called home for the last seventeen years. She gazed at the forest of towering buildings and felt a sharp pang in her heart for the wide-open sea and star-studded sky of her youth.

In the beginning she had run away from her unhappiness. She thought if she lost herself in New York the pain wouldn't find her. The drugs, alcohol and heavy partying seemed to comply, and for a while masked the dead feeling inside and fooled her into believing she was happy and fulfilled. Big had pulled strings and got her a lowly position with a fashion magazine, making tea and filing, and she had slept with as many forgettable men as she could find in an attempt to erase Jasper from her consciousness. It had been Suzie Redford who had made her see sense, flushing the drugs down the lavatory and shouting at her to get a grip before she lost her job and her future. No man was worth her self-destruction.

Little by little her job had saved her. She loved fashion, and the girls in her department soon became firm friends. She wanted to succeed and gradually her ambition supplanted her hedonism. As long as she focused intently on something, she could avoid being dragged back into melancholy; as long as she was in New York, she could be someone else. She went home as little as possible because she didn't want to be that broken-hearted girl any more, wrestling memories on every sand dune.

Trixie was now thirty-six years old. Most of her friends had married and were having children, but Trixie was married to her job. She had worked hard to get to where she was. Fashion editor hadn't happened overnight. Everyone knew how dedicated she was; no one suspected why. To the outside world she had everything: beauty, a good job, a fine-looking boyfriend, a loyal circle of friends, a spacious loft apartment in Soho and a wardrobe full of designer clothes. To the outside world she had everything; to Trixie, she lacked the one thing that really mattered.

She was in her office when the telephone rang. She was surprised to hear her father's voice. He rarely called her. 'Hi, Dad. How are you?'

He hesitated a moment and the knot in her stomach grew tighter. 'I've got some bad news, I'm afraid,' he said. 'Your mother's got cancer.'

He might as well have announced her death sentence. 'Oh my God!' Trixie gasped, holding onto the desk as her office spun away from her. 'How bad is it?'

'It's not great. The tumour was detected late and being in the brain, it's inoperable. She's had chemotherapy but the tumour hasn't shrunk. There's nothing more they can do.'

'She's had chemotherapy? How long has this been going on for?'

'About six months.'

'Why didn't you tell me?'

'She didn't want me to. She didn't want to worry you.'

'Not worry me? Are you kidding?'

'We thought it best.'

'This is terrible. You should have told me. I should have been there. I'm coming home, right now,' she declared firmly. 'I'm on the next plane.'

Trixie flew up to Boston in a state of shock and took a connecting flight to the island. As she stared into the glittering ocean below she remembered her parting words to Jasper. *If you cry tears into the water of this harbour, it means you'll come back.* She had shed many tears when she had first left for New York. Now her tears were for her mother. She desperately regretted severing her ties with home. She had taken her parents for granted and the reality of their mortality hit her like a cold slap. It hadn't ever occurred to her that the safety net they provided would not always be there. She should have spent more time with them, she told herself crossly. Sobbing quietly into her scarf, she reflected on her mother's unconditional love, and, to her shame, realized how little she had given back. Besides being her mother, Grace was her best friend. It was inconceivable to think of life without her. She couldn't let it happen. Whatever it took, she wasn't going to let her mother die.

It was autumn and a cold wind swept over the water. Her father was at the airport to pick her up. She kissed him and noticed how gaunt he had become, as if it were *his* body being ravaged by cancer. She bitterly regretted not having come home more often. 'Your mother doesn't want any fuss,' he said. 'You know what she's like. The last thing she wants is everyone walking around with long faces.'

'Is there nothing that can be done?' she asked.

'Only a miracle will save her now.' He turned his eyes away. 'So, pray for one.'

They drove up the cobbled streets of pretty grey-shingled houses where trees had begun to shed their orange and yellow leaves like tears, and Trixie felt a rush of nostalgia for her childhood, when her heart was full of optimism. She watched the people wandering contentedly up the pavement, laughing in the soft evening sunshine, walking dogs on leads, holding the hands of small children, and she ached for what might have been. She gazed into the shop windows of the boutiques and imagined the serene, trouble-free lives of the shopkeepers. She'd spent so much time in New York she had forgotten how seductive Tekanasset was.

Her mother was in her cluttered sitting room lying beneath a blanket on the sofa. The fire was lit and classical music resounded from the CD player. Flowers adorned every surface and their perfume saturated the air with summer, long gone. Her dog lay at her feet, snoozing peacefully. When Grace saw her daughter, she reached out happily and smiled. 'Darling, what a lovely surprise!' Trixie bent down and gave her mother a kiss. She didn't look as bad as she had feared. In fact, her father looked much worse. Grace just looked older.

'You should have told me . . .'

Her mother cut her off. 'Really, it's not so bad.' But the weary resignation behind her smile betrayed the gravity of her illness.

'What wonderful flowers!' Trixie exclaimed, forcing back her tears.

Grace was happy to change the subject. 'Aren't they lovely? Of course, the biggest bouquet is from Big. She's been wonderful. Everyone's been very kind.' She smiled mischievously at Trixie. 'Evelyn has offered to lend me one of her cooks. Fancy that, eh? Of course I declined.'

'Silly woman. I imagine she wants to be chief mourner,' said Trixie.

'Well, she certainly wants to be in the know about everything.'

'So she can pass it on to everybody else.'

Grace suddenly looked a little tired. 'Darling, it's lovely to see you. How well you look. How long are you staying?'

'I've taken a week off. I've brought my laptop so I can work here.'

'That's good. I need help with the bees. We must put them to bed for the winter and I don't think I'm strong enough to do it on my own.'

Trixie's heart lifted at the thought of being useful. She had always loved helping her mother with the bees as a child and

Grace had made an extra-small beekeeper's suit especially. 'I'd love to,' she replied enthusiastically. 'We need to watch out for wax moths and check that they have sufficient stores.'

Grace smiled, pleased. 'Darling, you *were* listening!'

Trixie grinned sheepishly. 'A little. I only wish I had listened more.'

In the next few days Trixie helped her mother with the bees. In case Trixie had forgotten, Grace explained why it was important to check the hives regularly to see if the bees were storing pollen and nectar, whether the queen was healthy and laying eggs, whether the bees were crowded, or if they looked likely to swarm. She spoke in a patient, tender voice, as if she were talking about her children, and it brought a lump to Trixie's throat to see how much it mattered to her that the bees would be taken care of in the event of her death. 'You can't learn about beekeeping from books, Trixie,' said Grace. 'You have to watch an experienced beekeeper and learn that way, like I learned from my dad. It's all about keeping the bees happy. The way to do that is to disturb them as little as possible. You have to have a gentle touch. They're little characters, bees, and some of the older ones are very troublesome. You have to keep them especially happy.'

Trixie noticed that Grace was weak and tired easily. But she always smiled to mask any discomfort and her bees seemed to give her more pleasure than anything else. It was only when she took an insufferable amount of pills in the morning that Trixie realized how sick she was. Without them, she wondered whether Grace would be able to function at all.

She observed the gentle way her father looked after her mother. He had always been cold and aloof, but now, at seventy-three, he was thawing and a warm affection was growing between them, like blossom after a hard winter. She caught him gazing at her mother with a wistful expression on his face and his eyes were full of sorrow and regret. Having wondered what it was that had drawn her two very different parents together all those years ago, she now knew the answer. Love. Nothing else mattered.

'Mum, what is it about bees that fascinates you so much?' Trixie asked on the third evening, after they had lifted the lids on the hives and Grace had explained all the things a beekeeper has to look out for before putting them to bed until spring.

'Let's go and sit on the beach, shall we?' Grace suggested. 'I love sitting on the dunes and gazing out to sea. Come, we'll take a couple of blankets and we won't tell your father because he'll only worry.'

A cold wind swept up the beach and the sea was dark and agitated. Clouds raced across the sky, playing hide-and-seek with the stars. They positioned themselves on a grassy dune and wrapped the blankets around their shoulders. Trixie lit a cigarette. Grace gazed out to the end of the world and wondered what happened on the other side. What came after?

'You know what fascinates me about bees, Trixie? Life. That's what's astonishing about them. Their God-given creativity. Human beings can build cars and planes and fly to the moon. But it's an intelligence beyond our understanding that makes the body work. Scientists could probably create a body and a brain but they couldn't create intelligence, they couldn't bring the body to life. It's an intelligence beyond our understanding that governs the bees and their intricate way of life as well. We couldn't produce honey, but these tiny little creatures make enough for themselves and for us and don't complain. I find that extraordinary.' She turned to her daughter and smiled sadly. 'And it connects me to my youth and my father, who I loved so much.'

'Did he approve of Dad?'

'He loved Freddie. He knew Freddie was right for me long before I did.' She chuckled. 'He told me not to be so far-sighted that I'd miss what was under my nose. He was right, of course. I'd known Freddie all my life. We were very close, but I'd never thought of him in that way. He'd always been more like a brother.'

'You've been married about fifty-five years, Mom. That's quite an achievement.'

'Yes, it is,' she replied softly.

'Dad's always been remote, you know, hard to get close to. I think he's mellowing with age.'

'He's a sweet and kind man underneath.'

'That's what you always say.'

'Because I know him.'

'And because you love him?'

'Yes, I love him. We've been through tough times but I never contemplated leaving him. Your generation gives up the moment things get difficult. We have a sense of duty you don't have. Even when . . .' She hesitated, and her gaze was swallowed into the night. 'Even when things got very hard, I never, ever contemplated leaving him.' Her voice rose in a question, as if she couldn't quite believe it. As if she had only just realized what that meant.

Trixie watched her closely. She knew so little of their past because they never talked about it. But that sentence was heavy with suggestion, opening a crack in a door through which Trixie glimpsed the allusion to a secret life.

'I wish you would find someone to share your life with, Trixie,' said Grace. 'I'd feel happier going if I knew you were settled.'

'Mom, happiness isn't all about finding a man, you know. I don't need a husband and children to make me happy. I have my job and my friends. I'm very content.'

Grace looked at her daughter gravely. 'Listen to me, darling. Life is nothing if you don't love.'

'I love *you*,' she replied with a shrug, and tears stung behind her eyes.

'I know you do, darling, *and* you love Jasper.'

Trixie stubbed out her cigarette in the sand. 'That was a long time ago,' she answered quietly.

'Darling, love doesn't necessarily diminish over time and your first love is sometimes the strongest. But you have to let him go. You can't let a heartbreak in the past ruin your chances in the present.' She closed her eyes and laughed bitterly. It was a lesson her father might have tried to teach *her*, had he lived.

'No one comes close to Jasper, Mom. That's the truth. No one.' Trixie's eyes glittered in the flame as she cupped her hands around her lighter. 'There, I've said it out loud. No one can compare to him.' She looked defeated. Small, suddenly, and lost.

Grace put her arm around her daughter and drew her close. She pressed her cheek against her hair and sighed. 'I can't tell you who to love. The heart chooses for you and there's nothing anybody can do about that. I love you, Trixie. You'll always be my little girl even though you're grown-up now with a life that's independent of me. I'm proud of you.' She squeezed her eyes shut, unable to bear the thought of parting. 'I just want to be reassured that you're all right.'

* * *

That night Trixie couldn't sleep. She went downstairs and sat smoking on the swing chair, gazing out over the gardens and the sea beyond. She remembered love and what it had felt like. As much as she told herself she didn't care about marriage and a family, in truth she cared very much. She didn't yearn for children, but she yearned for someone to love. She longed to put her arms around a man and know that he loved her back. Her thoughts turned to Jasper, as they always did when she drank too much and grew morose. She wondered what he was doing now. Whether he had married and had children. Whether he was still playing the guitar, or whether he had lost it along with her and Tekanasset.

As she allowed her thoughts to wander she caught sight of a shadow by the bees. At first she thought it was her mother, but she was asleep upstairs and for some reason she sensed the presence was a man. She stood and walked around the side of the house. There was no one there, just the hives and the cold wind that blew in off the ocean. She remained a moment, listening to the waves and the slow rhythm of her breathing. She couldn't see anyone but she still felt as if she wasn't alone. A cold shiver rippled over her skin. She inhaled a final puff and threw her cigarette into the grass. As she did so her attention was drawn to the shed at the bottom of the garden. It was as if someone had tapped her shoulder and pointed. As if someone *wanted* her to look at the door, which was now ajar and rattling softly in the wind.

Slowly she wandered down the path. It was dark but for the silver light of the moon that caught the damp branches of leafless shrubs and glistened. She pushed open the door and stepped inside. In all the years she had lived in this house she had never set foot in her mother's garden shed. There had never been any reason to. Now she switched on the bulb that hung from a wire on the ceiling and looked about her. Her heart began to thump guiltily as she realized this was her mother's private place. Like Grace's sitting room, the shed was disorderly. There were gardening tools, packets of fertilizer and seed, boxes of dry bulbs, equipment for the hives, empty honey jars and old, disused crownboards and frames. It smelt sweet and musty. She glanced about, not sure what she was meant to be looking for.

Once again she felt the very strong presence of someone nearby. She glanced over her shoulder to find nothing but the draught blowing in through the door. She took a deep breath and silently asked, 'What do you want me to find?' She stood waiting a moment, expecting to be told. But no one answered. The door rattled, causing her to jump. Then her eyes lifted to a mahogany box on the shelf above the door frame. It was the last place she would have looked, being above her head and hidden beneath a pile of gardening books. Her heart rate accelerated as she reached up and brought it down. Hastily she lifted the lid. She gasped as she discovered within two thick piles of airmail letters tied up with string.

She lifted the first and saw that they were addressed to Miss Bernadette Short at the Beekeeper's Cottage in Walbridge. Her heart stumbled. Walbridge: *that* was where Jasper came from. Trembling, she looked at the address on the other bundle of letters. Captain Rufus Melville, written in her mother's distinctive hand, to the British Forces Post Office. She didn't recognize that name and had never heard her mother speak of him. At the bottom of the box were two other letters in the same handwriting as the ones to Bernadette, addressed simply to Miss Grace Hamblin. On the back of the envelopes was the family crest of lion and dragon that had been on the back of Jasper's envelopes. The blood pulsated in her temples. She couldn't ask her mother what it all meant because if she had wanted her to know, she would have told her.

She sank to the floor and read the two to Miss Grace Hamblin first. One was a letter written after her father's death, the other a note wishing her luck on her wedding day. Both were signed Rufus and had an embossed *R* at the top of the page, like the *J* on Jasper's. They must be related, but how? One was called Duncliffe, the other Melville.

Confused, she untied the bundle of letters addressed to Bernadette, which was loosely bound with garden string. She realized immediately that 'little B' was not Bernadette at all but Grace, and that they had devised the false name to avoid being discovered. By the dirty stains and creases on the paper, she presumed her mother must have read them many times over the years.

Rufus Melville's letters were romantic and sweet, with sketches of bees haphazardly placed among the words. He wrote profusely about the war and his experiences, and the ferocity of his love. He repeated his desire for a future together in every letter. The last one was dated September 1942.

Once she'd finished reading the letters from Rufus to her mother, she picked up the other pile and tried to untie the string. Unlike Rufus's letters, the string was tightly knotted and not of the gardening variety. The blood began to pulsate in her temples as she realized that these letters were the ones Grace had written to Rufus, which for some reason had been returned to her. From the spotless paper and unyielding knot it seemed that Grace had never opened them but simply placed them in the box for safekeeping. Now Trixie set about unpicking the tie. She wished she could just cut it.

It took her a long while, but she was determined to read the letters. Suddenly it seemed vitally important, as if her mother's survival depended on it. At last the string loosened and she carefully unthreaded the knot and began to read. It was apparent from the very first lines that her mother loved this man. Trixie's heart raced as she skimmed the words. They were poetic and charming and full of news as well as reminiscences about a bee swarm and the first time he had kissed her in the woods. Tears welled in her eyes. She didn't know whether she was crying for her mother's love or for her father's loss.

She didn't notice the hours passing, so engrossed was she in the large pile of her mother's love letters. The more she read, the more astonished she became as her mother's secret life unfolded before her. Then, one letter stood out amongst all the rest. The envelope, like all the others, was addressed to Captain Rufus Melville, but the letter inside was to Freddie. Trixie's face flushed as she realized to her horror that if her mother had sent Freddie's letter to Rufus, there was a good chance that she had sent Rufus's letter to Freddie. Trixie put her hand to her mouth and gasped at the implications. Did her mother know that she had done this? Why would she read her own letters to Rufus? Of course she wouldn't. She'd read *his* letters to *her*. What were the chances that she wasn't aware she had made such a terrible error? And what were the chances that Freddie did?

The last letter Grace had written to Rufus was in March 1943, seven months after Rufus had stopped writing to her. In those seven months Grace's letters had become increasingly frantic. Why had Rufus stopped writing? Why had her letters been returned? Had he died in action?

It was past four in the morning when she finally finished the last letter. She didn't feel tired at all. Her body quivered like a horse at the starting gate, much as it had done in her cocaine days. She was fired up and full of questions that needed to be answered.

Then her mind sprang back to the time her mother had sobbed quite uncontrollably at the thought of losing her to Jasper. They had been sitting on the swing chair. She remembered it very clearly because her mother's grief had been so acute that it had seemed out of all proportion. What if she hadn't been crying about Trixie, but about Jasper's father, *who was dead*? Trixie put her head in her hands and groaned. Suddenly everything shifted into sharp focus. It made sense now. Rufus must have been Jasper's father. That's why her parents knew he'd never marry her. They knew the family. They knew what they were like and they both knew that Grace had loved Rufus. As for the different names, there was bound to be a simple explanation. An English tradition of titles she wasn't aware of.

But that didn't answer the question of why Rufus had returned all Grace's letters. If he hadn't died in the war, what had ended the affair? She couldn't ask her mother – she sensed her mother didn't know anyway – or indeed her father.

There was only one person who might be able to help her get to the bottom of it and that was Rufus Melville's son, Jasper. It was a long shot: after all, she hadn't known about her mother's affair, so there was every chance that he hadn't a clue about his father's, but it was worth a try.

Chapter 22

Trixie had never been to England. She hadn't thought it odd before: after all, England was very far away and her parents had rarely spoken about it, but it *was* odd, considering that England was where they had both grown up and where they had married. If only she had taken the trouble to ask them about their lives, but she had been so engrossed in her own little dramas that she had never imagined her mother had lived a drama of her own. She hadn't imagined her mother had suffered a broken heart, either. She had believed her incapable of understanding when Jasper had ended their relationship. How wrong she had been.

Now that Trixie had discovered her mother's affair, she understood why she had never been taken to England: neither parent wanted to revisit the past. Moving to America had probably been a fresh start for both of them. It had put distance between Grace and Rufus and given Grace and Freddie a chance to rebuild. Or so it looked to Trixie, staring out of the window of the plane as it slowly descended into London.

She felt guilty sneaking to their home town without telling them. It was snooping and intrusive. Like snooping through her mother's old love letters, she thought uncomfortably. She wondered how much this visit had to do with Rufus Melville, and how much *more* it had to do with Jasper Duncliffe.

It had been easy to arrange the trip. The London-based designer Rifat Ozbek was popular in New York, and he had granted her an interview at Claridge's. After that she'd take the train down to Dorchester in Dorset. Her assistant had booked her into the Fox and Goose Inn in Walbridge. She'd explore from there. She didn't know what to expect and she hadn't dared ask anyone in the office, even though two of the girls were British.

From the window of the aeroplane her first impression of London was of a dull, grey city of toy-sized houses and tree-lined streets, whose autumn leaves broke the monotony with welcome splashes of orange and yellow. Heavy cloud hung low and persistent, as if always there, like the wet tarmac that glistened feebly in the lacklustre light.

She made her way through passport control and customs and outside to the taxi rank. Her spirits lifted at the sight of a London cab, and she enjoyed her drive into the city like a child enjoying her first ride on a merry-go-round. It didn't seem real. She gazed out of the taxi window in wonder, taking in the big red buses, the quaint townhouses and the pretty, narrow streets, cluttered with umbrellas. She had made the mistake of telling her cabbie that she was new to London, so he took it upon himself to be her guide, pointing out all the landmarks in such a strong cockney accent she could barely understand him.

They passed the Natural History Museum, Harrods, the Duke of Wellington's house at Hyde Park Corner and, in an expensive detour, the cabbie took her past Buckingham Palace and St James's Palace, finally reaching Claridge's from the south. London was thrilling. She wished she had more time to see the sights. She wished she had someone to share them with.

Claridge's did not disappoint. With its scarlet carpets and white mouldings it was like stepping back in time to an age of grandeur and elegance. Trixie was reminded of one of her mother's favourite television series, *The Pallisers*, which she had at home on video and occasionally watched. Set in the mid-nineteenth century, the series had supplied her first and lasting impression of England. Now, as she stepped through the revolving doors, she savoured the familiar sounds of English accents and silver spoons on china cups with a pleasant sense of nostalgia and déjà vu.

She gave her bag to the concierge to store and took a small case to the ladies' room to freshen up before her meeting. It had been a long flight and she felt like a crumpled dress in need of ironing. Staring at her face in the mirror, she wondered whether Jasper would find her much changed.

Rifat was a charming and engaging man who entertained her throughout lunch. It wasn't until she was on the train bound for Dorset that she turned her thoughts back to her mission. She'd start at the Beekeeper's Cottage. If Jasper lived in a big house on a grand estate she didn't imagine she'd have any trouble finding him. Judging by the fuss that was made over his return, she doubted he'd have gone anywhere. 'His sort', as his father liked to call them, put duty before anything else. Perhaps it was duty that had prompted Rufus to send all Grace's letters back? Had he, like his son, sacrificed his love for tradition? Had he done it with sorrow or with cold calculation? Had both men lived to regret their decisions?

As the train cut deep into the English countryside the suburbs melted into undulating green hills and forests. Even in the drizzle the vibrant autumn colours seemed to blaze like flames against the soggy grey sky. Townhouses were replaced by farms and picture-book cottages, and cars gave way to cows and sheep grazing peacefully on rolling hills. Fields were boxed in by hedges, and from a distance those squares looked like a patchwork quilt of varying tones of green. Trixie stared out of the window, uplifted by England's wistful beauty, wondering how often her parents had stared out onto the same scenery.

It was dark by the time she reached Dorchester. The rain had stopped but the air was cold and damp. It reminded her of winter on Tekanasset, when the cold penetrated right to the bone. She tucked her scarf into her coat and dragged her suitcase out to the taxi rank. A porcine man smelling of tobacco and takeaway food drove her down the narrow lanes into Walbridge, asking her a dozen questions when she'd have preferred to contemplate the place in silence. Had she been in America she would have told him to be quiet, but she felt less confident in this country where she was a stranger.

'This here is Walbridge,' the cabbie told her in his rich country drawl as they drove over a grey stone bridge into the town. The road swept between rows of shops and houses in a gentle curve and Trixie was reminded of Main Street on Tekanasset because Walbridge looked as if time had forgotten it too. The houses were built in a soft, weathered yellow stone, some were even thatched, and rickety old chimneys smoked like nightwatchmen pausing on their round. One or two cottages looked as if they were inhabited by hobbits because the front doors were so small and the windows only a few feet higher than the ground. Street lamps shone orange onto the pavements, where leaves had collected in clusters like playthings discarded by the wind. Trixie gazed at it all in wonder. This was Jasper's home town. This was where *she* might have lived had she married him. Unbelievably, this quaint Dorset town was what her parents had left behind.

The Fox and Goose Inn was an old-fashioned pub, painted white with black beams and a swinging sign showing a wily fox contemplating his dinner. The windows were medieval-looking with small diamond-shaped glass panes set deep into thick walls. She paid the cabbie then stood a moment staring up the narrow street. The houses on either side leaned in like old people no longer able to stand straight, and she wondered whether they had been built like that or whether they had subsided over the years.

There were two doors: one which was the entrance to the pub and another, farther left, which was painted with the letters B & B in white. The golden glow from the first one was more alluring, promising company and a stiff drink – she could hear the rumble of voices inside and smell wood smoke in the air. But it was late and she was tired after her journey. New York seemed far away now. So she opened the second door and walked into a lobby.

'You must be Miss Valentine?' said a comely lady from behind a desk.

'Yes, I am,' Trixie replied.

The lady smiled warmly. 'I thought so. Let me help you with your case, love. Where have you come from? You don't sound English.' She set off up the narrow stair.

'America.'

'Are you here on holiday?'

'Just for a few days.'

'Fancy choosing Walbridge. It's hardly a tourist destination. People come for the birds. We have lots of rare ones around the river. And the fishing, of course. We're not far from the sea if you like that sort of thing.'

'My parents grew up here.'

'Did they?'

'Yes, I'm hoping to find someone who might have known them.'

'What are their names, dear?'

'Freddie and Grace Valentine.' When the woman's face failed to register recognition, Trixie added, 'They left just after the war, but my father's family remained.'

'Well, I wouldn't know, then. I wasn't born here. We moved twelve years ago from Sussex to be near our daughter, who married a Walbridge man. You need to talk to some of the older people. You'll find them in the pub.' She chuckled. 'They're the ones propping up the bar. You can't miss 'em.'

'Thank you, I will.'

'You must be hungry.'

'A little.'

The woman unlocked a red door and showed Trixie into a small room with a double bed and a window. 'The bathroom is down the corridor. I've taken the liberty of closing your curtains, but in the morning you'll see the river. It's very pretty. Come down to the pub when you're ready and I'll cook you something. How about a nice cottage pie to warm you up? I don't imagine you're used to cold weather in America.'

Grace smiled. The woman had obviously never been there. 'Thank you. I'd love the cottage pie.' She didn't know what that was but the word 'warm' was promising.

She felt much better after a long bath and a change of clothes, and went downstairs to the pub. Groups of people sat at heavy wooden tables and others on stools at the bar. They looked up when she entered. She didn't imagine they got many newcomers in a small town like this. The room smelt strongly of smoke, from the fire that burned comfortingly in the grate and the cigarettes that smouldered in people's fingers. Trixie slid onto a stool and lit one of her own. The bartender eyed her up appreciatively and took her order. He was a man of about forty with thinning hair and a fresh, open face. She knew it wouldn't be long before he started chatting. He passed her a rum cocktail and the lady, who the man referred to as Maeve, brought the cottage pie, which was both hot and tasty.

'So, where are you from?' he asked eventually, unable to disguise the fact that he found her attractive.

'America,' she replied, and repeated the conversation she had had with Maeve.

He nodded, keen to be of help. 'Valentine,' he mumbled, narrowing his eyes, which were a bright forget-me-not blue. 'There used to be a shop on the high street called Red Valentine; it sold women's clothes, but that was years ago, when I was a boy. I'll ask my mother. She might know. I'm almost certain there's no one by that name here now. I know most people who live here. This pub's the heart of Walbridge, you see, and it's a small town. The family probably moved away.'

'I'll find the oldest person in the room and ask him,' she said with a smile, glancing around the pub.

'I'll introduce you,' he told her enthusiastically. 'The one thing old people have in common is that they all like talking about the past.' *Not my parents*, Trixie thought sadly. 'How long are you staying?' he asked.

'A few days.'

'Do you know anyone here?'

'No.'

He grinned happily. 'Well, you do now. My name's Robert Heath, by the way.' He extended his hand.

She shook it. 'Hello, Robert. My name's Trixie.' He frowned. 'Short for Beatrix,' she added helpfully.

'As in Potter?'

'Or Queen.' He frowned again. 'Of Holland?'

'The only queen I know is *our* Queen,' he said, picking up a wet glass and drying it with a cloth. 'So, what are you going to do when you find someone who knew your parents?'

'Ask a lot of questions.'

He raised his eyebrows. 'Mysterious.'

She grinned wryly. 'You have no idea!'

'Well, I hope you find the answers you're looking for.'

'I will,' she replied. 'I'm not leaving without them.'

She stubbed out her cigarette and lit another. 'Does the name Jasper Duncliffe ring a bell?' she asked.

Robert's face lit up with recognition. 'You mean Jasper *Penselwood*. They live at the Hall.'

Her heart began to pound. 'Walbridge Hall?'

'Yes. The very same.'

'But he was called Duncliffe, not Penselwood, right?'

'"Was" being the operative word. He's Penselwood now. The Marquess of Penselwood.'

It was her turn to be confused. 'I don't understand. Why the change of name?'

'English titles are very complicated,' he said, taking pleasure in her ignorance. 'If my family didn't have a history of working for aristocrats I wouldn't know them either. Let me explain. The Marquess of Penselwood's son is the Earl of Melville. Lord Melville's son is the Lord Duncliffe. Three names for one family. Absurd, really. Jasper Duncliffe used to come and drink in here with his mates when I started working behind the bar. Then he went off to America to play in a band. He used to play here, you know, before it all went belly up. He had a good voice. I thought he'd go far, we all did. But then his brother died.' Robert shook his head gravely. 'It was a tragedy. He wasn't the sort to be driving too fast. He wasn't reckless. It was an accident. He was a nice man. I remember the funeral . . .' He paused his drying a moment and frowned. 'A sad day for the whole town.'

'What happened when Jasper returned from America?'

He put down the glass and began to dry another. 'He became Marquess of Penselwood and married Charlotte Hanbury-Johnson.'

'What's she like, his wife?'

'Do you know Lord Penselwood?' He eyed her suspiciously and she realized she had to admit to knowing Jasper if she was going to get any more information out of him.

'I met him in America when he was trying to become a rock star.' She laughed wistfully. 'Many years ago now. We were friends. Does he still play guitar?'

'I doubt it. I remember him sitting where you're sitting now, leaning over a whiskey, lamenting the fact that his parents didn't understand him. They wanted him to go into the army.'

'He would have hated that.'

'That's why he went off to America. It was a shame he had to come back. He might have become famous.'

'Like the Beatles.'

He smiled reflectively. 'Yeah, like the Beatles. That would have been great. Free tickets to concerts.'

'Is the Hall nearby?'

'You can walk there. The gardens are open to the public in the summer, so there are brown signs everywhere. You can't miss them.'

'I don't suppose they're open now?'

He shook his head. 'No, they aren't. You should have come in May or June. Those gardens are spectacular.'

'Does he come into the pub these days?'

'No.' He grinned. 'His son comes in to buy cigarettes, though.'

'How old is he?'

'About fifteen. I turn a blind eye.'

'So, what's Jasper's wife like?'

He shrugged non-committally. 'She's all right. Busy, you know, as you'd expect. She's just like her mother-in-law, Lady Georgina. They're joined at the hip. Both very *busy*.' He said 'busy' with emphasis and Trixie deduced that they were both rather trying. He put down the glass. 'Do you fancy another drink?'

'Why not,' she replied. 'Make it weak.'

'As you wish.' He unscrewed the cap of the Bacardi bottle and poured a fresh glass. 'What did your father do?'

'He worked on the farm.'

'On the Walbridge estate?'

'Yes. My mother was the beekeeper.'

His face opened into a broad smile and he put his hands on his hips. 'Well, why didn't you say so? My grandfather was the head gardener during the war. I bet he knew your parents. What a shame he's no longer alive. My mother might know, though. She's worked for the family for years. She now works for old Lady Penselwood who has a house at the other end of town. She's in her nineties and still going strong.'

'That's Jasper's grandmother, right?' she asked.

'That's right. There's no love lost between her and the other women in her family. That's why she lives the other end of town. She's a tough old bird. Indestructible, like a Sherman tank.'

'Good for her, reaching such a great age.'

'Those sort of women live forever. I bet the Queen Mother will make it to a hundred.'

'Why's that, do you think?'

'Breeding. We common folk kick the bucket much younger.' He leaned across the bar and lowered his voice. 'Or it's simply because they're too damned stubborn to give up a moment before they're ready.'

As Trixie put her head on the pillow she thought about Jasper. How was she going to meet him? Could she simply turn up at the house and ring the bell? Would that be a terrible faux pas? She imagined life at the Hall would be formal, like Plantagenet Palliser's home in the television drama, and besides, what would his wife think of her showing up without an invitation? His wife . . . She hid her face in the pillow and muffled a groan. What was she thinking? She was crazy turning up here. It had been seventeen years since she and Jasper had declared their love. Seventeen years since he had told her he couldn't marry her. Seventeen years of drought for Trixie's parched heart. What was she hoping would happen? That he would lament his decision and leave his wife and children for her? That was never going to happen and as much as she missed him – and oh, how she missed him – she did not wish to tear his family apart.

Far from seeing her as the girl he had fallen in love with, he would look on her as a figure to be pitied. While he had married and had children she had remained in the same place like a stagnant pond, wallowing in self-pity and regret. The fact was that she hadn't moved on and he had. What was the use of seeing him again? Where would it lead? Nowhere, and that was the truth. It would be like peeling off a scab and exposing the sore, only to start the healing process all over again. She hadn't thought of that. She hadn't thought of anything except laying eyes on the man she loved. Now she realized how futile the whole idea was.

Her head told her to pack her bags in the morning and take the train back to London. But her heart insisted she stay. Here she was in the town where her parents had grown up and married. Where her mother had fallen in love with the Earl of Melville and where that affair had dramatically ended, without explanation. Her mother had left England for ever, broken-hearted. And what of her father? What of *him*?

As she drifted off to sleep the memory of her mother howling on the swing chair floated into her mind and strengthened her resolve to do whatever she could to find out the truth. She knew it was important. Someone was tugging at her conscience, driving her on, silently insisting that it was indeed *very* important. Before she sank into the cool darkness of slumber she saw in her mind's eye the silhouette of a man, standing by the beehives. She couldn't see him clearly and yet she recognized him. Yes, she knew him on some deep and unconscious level, and he was smiling at her with love.

Chapter 23

Dawn broke through the dark with an enthusiasm akin to summer. Sunshine set the trees aflame and seagulls cried mournfully as they glided over the river. Trixie opened the curtains and her heart inflated with joy as she took in the tranquil scene before her. A row of mallards floated on the surface like a convoy of little ships and a willow wept its delicate branches into the water. Orange leaves gathered near the bank where a young dog played excitedly until its owner summoned it back with a whistle. She looked up at the pale blue sky where wisps of white cloud wafted on a gentle breeze and sighed with pleasure. She could see now why people considered England beautiful. The drizzle was gone and the sunshine had transmuted the grey into a bright golden light.

She breakfasted downstairs in the pub and Robert told her proudly that he had arranged for her to meet his mother here at lunchtime. 'She knew your mother,' he said. 'Grace was her name, wasn't it? Not only that, but she worked for a Josephine Valentine for a while when she was in her twenties. Red Valentine, that was the name of the shop. I've got an exceedingly good memory.' He grinned playfully.

Trixie was impressed. 'Josephine is my father's sister. I remember her coming out to visit with my grandparents when I was little. She wore very red lipstick and a perfume that made my head ache. But I thought her incredibly glamorous. She looked like a film star. I wonder where she is now.'

'You can ask my mother. She loves to talk about the past. Once you get her going, there'll be no stopping her. So, what are you going to do this morning?'

'I'm going to go in search of the Beekeeper's Cottage.'

'Do you have any idea where it is?'

'No. I was hoping you were going to enlighten me.'

He laughed. 'Maeve will know. She's on the Parish Committee, so she's visited every house in Walbridge.'

Maeve stepped into the pub from the hall. 'Do I hear my name being taken in vain?'

'Trixie's looking for the Beekeeper's Cottage,' said Robert. 'I told her you'd know where it is.'

'And I do,' Maeve replied loftily. Then to Trixie: 'I distribute the parish magazine, you see. There's not a house in Walbridge I haven't been to.'

'My mother was a beekeeper,' said Trixie.

'Oh, I love bees. Such fascinating insects,' Maeve cooed. 'To think they make honey all by themselves. Such clever little things. There are still hives up there. Robin Arkwright is the beekeeper now. He's also the gamekeeper. There's nothing he doesn't know about birds. I sometimes send our guests up to see him, those that are interested in birds, because he's an encyclopaedia. Ask him about the Pied-billed Grebe or the Balearic Shearwater. Wonderful names, don't you think?'

'Wonderful,' Trixie humoured her. 'Where do I find the cottage?'

'It's a beautiful day to walk there. You can take the road, but it's the long way round. I'd take the footpath that cuts through the estate. That's the scenic route and the one I recommend to my paying guests. Here, let me draw you a map.' She began to write on the notepad beside the till. 'Past the church, take the farm entrance *here*. Past cottages and through the gate *there*. You'll see a sign that clearly marks the footpath. Apparently they went to court to try to stop the public walking through their land, but they lost. The judge said people had a right to admire such a historic and beautiful house. Fancy that, eh? So, you have a right, too, dear. Enjoy it.'

Trixie set off up the narrow lane that opened into the high street. The street was wide and picturesque with sandy-coloured shops and houses built haphazardly on either side, their roofs and chimneys jutting into the sky at differing heights and angles, giving the place a charming inconsistency. A few people wandered up the pavement and one or two cars motored past, but it was generally quiet.

She reached the church. The graveyard was still, the headstones bathed in the morning sunshine. Blackbirds scavenged amongst the fallen leaves on the grass and Trixie wondered whether her grandfather was buried there. She'd have a look later. At that moment the church door opened and the vicar came out with an elderly lady in a headscarf, tweed skirt and gumboots. She was leaning on a walking stick and gesticulating vigorously with the other hand. The vicar threw his head back and laughed heartily. Trixie was intrigued to know what was amusing them so much and paused to listen. As they wandered down the path towards her their voices could be heard. The old lady's tone was strident. She was clearly a woman accustomed to getting her way.

'So, the doctor bound my leg up and told me to rest it for a few days. Bloody fool! When I got home I pulled off the bandage, had a large sherry and took Magnus for a walk. I only went to the doctor to please Georgie, who insisted. Really, people nowadays make a fuss about everything. My generation just got on with it. We didn't have time to sit about in doctors' waiting rooms. Lottie takes those children to the doctor every time they sniff, which is quite often. I have to keep my mouth shut; after all, I'm only their great-grandmother, what do I know?' She chortled. 'So, it's settled, then?'

'Yes, it is, Lady Penselwood.'

'Good.'

'I do hope it's not anytime soon.'

'*Que sera, sera*, as the old saying goes. Forewarned is forearmed is another one. And don't let Georgie change anything. I might be ten feet under but I won't like it if she overrules me. Do you understand?'

'Of course, Lady Penselwood.'

'She has horrible taste in music, always did.' Lady Penselwood sniffed. 'If only Rufus . . .' Her voice trailed off and Trixie went pink at the mention of Rufus's name, as if she were guilty of having the affair and not her mother. They reached the road and Lady Penselwood turned her formidable gaze on Trixie, who recoiled. 'Hello,' she said. 'Beautiful morning, isn't it?'

'It certainly is,' Trixie agreed. Lady Penselwood narrowed her eyes, probably wondering who the stranger with the American accent was, then walked on to the waiting car, leaving behind a faint smell of lilac.

Trixie watched the car drive off. So, that was Rufus's mother, she mused. Lady Penselwood. How confusing that there were *three* Lady Penselwoods. Lottie, Jasper's wife; Georgie, who must be his mother; and this great lady,

Georgie's mother-in-law. She longed to pick up the telephone and ask her mother all about them. But she couldn't reveal where she was. She would then have to admit to reading the letters. No, she had to find it all out on her own without any help from the two people who knew the most.

She followed Maeve's map and set off along the footpath that cut through the fields towards the woods. Sheep grazed and birds twittered, and Trixie took pleasure in the tranquillity of the countryside. It was unlike anything she had seen in America. Everything was on a smaller scale and it all seemed so old-fashioned and charming to her foreign eye.

She climbed a hill, stopping every now and then to catch her breath and admire the surroundings. She imagined her mother had taken this route through the farm many times. Did she ever return in her imagination? Did she miss it? At length Trixie walked along the edge of a field, recently ploughed. On her left was a tall hedge that ran all the way to the woods. When she reached the end she glimpsed, through the thinning branches, chimneys rising out of the valley below. Curiosity drew her through a gap in the hedge. When she emerged the other side she caught her breath. There below her, surrounded by endless gardens, was a magnificent old mansion.

She walked along the field beneath the line of the woods, then stood and allowed her eyes to take in the beauty of the Penselwood family estate, Walbridge Hall. She had never seen a house of such splendour except on the television and in books. Hands on hips, she laughed out loud at her ignorance. So *this* was the house Jasper gave up his career for. *This* was his heritage, the estate that demanded his total commitment. The family seat that obliged its heirs to sacrifice their own personal happiness so it could survive from generation to generation, like a minotaur of brick and stone. Jasper had sacrificed *her*. Had Rufus sacrificed her mother?

She stopped laughing and gazed with bitterness upon the house that had stolen her one true love. She now saw beyond its beauty to its cold and heartless core. Was Jasper happy? Did he ever think of her? Did he ever pick up his guitar and play the song he wrote for her? Did he sing at all?

She dragged herself away, fearing that if she remained she might see him and be unable to restrain herself. She continued along the footpath, down the hill to the bottom of the wood where a path led her through thick bracken, ferns and gnarled old oak trees that scrutinized her loftily like ancient dukes questioning her business there. The forest rustled with creatures she couldn't see, and she began to feel afraid.

At last she could make out the end of the wood and a tantalizing glimpse of open fields, bathed in sunshine. As she walked into the light she saw a cottage, not too far away, partly obscured by a cluster of trees. The Beekeeper's Cottage; she had no doubt. She made her way slowly towards it, and the knowledge that she was retracing her mother's footsteps made her feel unexpectedly emotional. The cottage was thatched with white walls and sleepy windows. She wished she could know what those windows had seen.

She knocked on the door and waited. No one answered. She remained there, wondering what to do. She didn't fancy getting caught spying, but the desire to look at the hives made her reckless. She wandered round to the back. 'Hello,' she called. 'Is anyone at home?'

A woolly head appeared above a shrub like a scarecrow. 'Who's asking?'

'Oh hello,' she replied, surprised. 'Maeve said I'd find you here.'

'You're one of her guests, are you?'

'Yes. She said she sends people up to talk to you about birds.'

'Ah, you're interested in birds, are you?' he said in a more friendly tone, stepping out of the border onto the lawn.

'Bees, actually.'

His face lit up. 'Even better. I have lots of bees.' He brushed his hand on his trousers. 'Robin Arkwright.'

She gave it a firm shake. 'Trixie Valentine.'

'Valentine, that's a romantic name.'

'Thank you. My parents used to live here.'

'Ah, *that* Valentine?'

'My mother was the beekeeper during the war.'

'Grace Valentine,' he said with a nod.

Trixie's heart gave a little skip. 'Did you know her?'

'No, I arrived in 1962, but Tom Garner was my mother's brother and he used to speak very highly of Grace and Freddie.'

'That's nice to hear. Who was Tom Garner?'

'He was estate manager here right into his seventies. They had to force him into retirement. As soon as he retired, he keeled over and pegged it. He employed your father, Freddie Valentine.' He scratched his greying curls and grinned. 'Funny to hear that name after all these years.'

'They moved to America.'

'That's right. They just disappeared from one day to the next. He was wounded in the war, wasn't he?'

'Yes, he only has one eye.'

Robin shook his head. 'Poor devil. Uncle Tom used to refer to him as a hero.'

'Really? Dad?'

'That's right. He was a hero in the war. Didn't he tell you?'

'He never speaks about the war.'

'No, I don't suppose he does. My uncle never spoke about Ypres where he lost his leg. I suppose they wanted to come back and forget all about it.'

'Have you lived here since '62?'

'No, I lived with my uncle to start with. I was a young lad with no experience of gamekeeping or beekeeping, but I worked with Mr Swift, who was the gamekeeper at the time, and old Benedict Latimer, who was the beekeeper, taught me about bees. When he retired I took over. My uncle couldn't find anyone who knew about beekeeping, or he didn't have the energy to look, so I found myself in the enviable position of moving in here.'

'It's a very pretty cottage.'

'My wife thought it was too small, so we built a conservatory. Apart from that, it probably hasn't changed much since your parents lived here.'

'I'd love to see the hives.'

'Of course. I'll show you.' He led her down the garden. 'You do a bit of beekeeping yourself, do you?'

'Yes, my mother has hives and I help her look after them.'

'It's an addictive hobby, beekeeping. Once you start you can't stop. Fascinating creatures, aren't they?'

'They certainly are.'

Robin proudly showed her a row of eight hives, standing against a hedge that ran along the bottom of the garden. 'I would bet half these hives were here when your mother kept bees. Besides the odd repairs and replacements they're the very same ones. I've added a few and I'm sure Mr Latimer added some new ones too, but look at those three over there, they look like they've been here for centuries!' He chuckled. 'You here visiting, then?'

'I came to see where my parents grew up and married.'

'Are they . . . ?'

'No, they're very much alive. I was in London on business and decided to take a detour.'

'Ah, very nice. You can tell your mother that the bees are still thriving in Walbridge. She'd like to know that, I bet.'

'She would.'

They chatted about the bees, the recent harvest and the trouble with pesticides and moths. Trixie wondered what her mother would make of her visit. She so wished she could share it with her. It was mid-morning by the time she made her way back through the wood. She reflected on what Robin had told her about her father being a hero. He had never mentioned it and neither had her mother, which was odd, because it was the sort of thing a man should be proud of. So far her questions hadn't been answered, only added to.

As she wandered through the wood she heard a panting noise in the bracken. The green stalks began to part as the creature came bounding through the undergrowth towards her. At first she feared it might be a wild boar or a fox, but then a black nose, followed by large black paws and sleek black fur, tumbled onto the track in the shape of a Labrador. Relieved, she bent down to pat him. He didn't seem as surprised to see her as she was to see him. He wagged his tail and thrust his nose between her knees in the friendliest manner. She looked about for the owner, but the woods remained still and silent.

After a while she realized the dog was alone. She saw a tag dangling at his neck. *Ralph, The White House, Walbridge Hall.* It gave a telephone number. 'Well, Ralph, I'd better take you home, hadn't I?' she said, striding off down the track. She didn't know where the White House was, but she knew

Walbridge Hall. She had no option but to go there. Perhaps it was her destiny to see Jasper again after all.

With her stomach tying itself into knots, she walked down the hill towards the Hall with the dog at her heels. Now she had a legitimate reason to be there. Gone was the fear of making a faux pas. She'd ring the bell and ask for the White House. She envisaged Jasper at the door and the look on his face when he saw her standing there with the dog. He was going to be knocked for six, she mused. She ran her hands through her hair, smoothing it down self-consciously.

The house was much more formidable close up. The sand-coloured walls were high and austere, the windows gazing out at the world imperiously. Her heart quickened with nervousness. Just as she was about to ring the bell that hung in a thick rope to the right of the great door, a voice spoke to her from behind. 'Can I help you?' She spun round, disappointed to find she was being addressed by a gardener.

'I've found this dog in the woods. I've come to return it,' she explained.

'That's Ralph. Hello, Ralph.' He patted his knees and the dog leapt up at him excitedly. 'Silly boy, he's always wandering off. That's dogs for you; bitches are less trouble. He's Lady Georgina's. Do you know where the White House is?'

Trixie didn't welcome the idea of having to meet the woman who had persuaded Jasper not to marry her. 'No, I'm not from here,' she replied, backing away. 'Perhaps I can leave him with you?'

'Come, I'll show you. It's through the garden. The other side of the vegetable garden.'

Reluctantly she followed him round to the side of the house. An immaculately mown lawn stretched into the distance where a statue of a rearing horse on a pedestal was silhouetted against the deep crimson of a maple tree. The borders were ablaze with purple, red and yellow flowers, and towering trees shed their golden leaves to be picked up by the wind and playfully tossed about. The effect was so dramatic that it looked as if the gardens were on fire. Trixie slowed her pace to take it all in. She didn't think she had ever seen a more beautiful place. She realized then that every garden her mother had designed on Tekanasset was a poor imitation of this; every flower and shrub and tree was planted with nostalgia and longing. Her mother might have left England for ever, but the gardens she created kept bringing her back.

Trixie could see a tennis court through a gap in a yew hedge and hear the faint putt-putting of balls on rackets. She hoped the gardener would lead her past the court in case Jasper was playing, but he took her through a walled vegetable garden to the other side where a large white house was nestled in a glorious crimson-and-gold garden of its own. In a hurry to return to his duties, the gardener left her there. 'I'm sure Lady G. would like to thank you personally,' he told her, before disappearing back into the walled garden.

Trixie wondered whether Jasper's mother was a terrifying character: otherwise why hadn't he offered to take the dog back himself? She huffed irritably and rang the bell, cursing the gardener for being such a coward. A moment later the door opened and a tall, willowy woman with ash-blonde hair cut into a severe bob stared down at her with ice-blue eyes. 'And you are?' she asked without even a hint of a smile.

Trixie took in the sharp cheekbones, the full mouth, the neat nose and thought her beauty well preserved, albeit frosty. 'I found your dog in the woods,' said Trixie, staring back at her boldly.

Lady Georgina dropped her eyes to her dog. 'Ralph, not again?' she sighed impatiently. 'Where was he?'

'I don't know, somewhere in the middle?'

'Of course you wouldn't know, you're American. Are you a tourist?'

'I suppose I am,' she replied. Lady Georgina gave a little sniff. She narrowed her eyes and looked at Trixie more closely. She seemed suddenly disarmed by what she saw. 'The gardens are incredibly beautiful,' said Trixie. 'Really, I've never seen such magnificent colours.'

'Yes, it is a rather special place, isn't it?' The dog wandered past her into the house. 'Well, thank you for bringing him back.'

'Is that Ralph?' came a voice from inside.

'Yes, he ran off again.'

A man appeared behind Lady Georgina. 'And you brought him back?' He smiled at Trixie warmly. 'Aren't you an angel!'

'Well, not really. I was just visiting the Beekeeper's Cottage. My mother used to live there.' She noticed Lady Georgina's face twitch with recognition.

'Grace Valentine?' she said slowly. 'Good Lord, you're the image of her.'

'Really? I don't know.'

'Yes, you are! Come in. Would you like a cup of tea? We really must thank you for bringing Rufus back. It's terribly kind of you.' Trixie was overwhelmed by the sudden change in her manner. 'Grace and Freddie Valentine, well, those are names from the past. Tell me, how are they?'

Trixie was ushered into a pretty pale-blue sitting room. 'Darling, take her coat for her. What did you say your name was?'

'Beatrix,' she replied, sensing her proper name would be more appropriate in the formal surroundings of Lady's Georgina's house.

'I'm Georgina Stapleton and this is my husband Teddy. Do sit down. Darling, we'd like tea.'

'I'll pass it on,' he replied, wandering out into the hall.

Lady Georgina smiled at Trixie. 'Oh, you're most welcome here,' she gushed, and Trixie was surprised to find her face had suddenly defrosted. 'Tell me, how are your parents?'

'They're very well, thank you,' she replied, not wanting to share her mother's illness with a stranger.

'I'm so pleased. What did your father do when he moved to America?'

'He worked on a cranberry farm. Of course, he's retired now. He mainly plays golf.'

'And your mother? She was a terrific beekeeper and a keen gardener, too. She followed Mr Heath around like a loyal Labrador.'

'She's still a gardener. Well, she's sort of retired now, although she can't stop herself because she loves it. But most of the gardens on Tekanasset have been designed by her.'

'How lovely. I'm so pleased it worked out for them. Tell me, do you have brothers and sisters?'

'No, I'm an only child.'

'You're married?'

'No.'

Lady Georgina raised her eyebrows in surprise. 'Not married? And you're so pretty.'

'I've yet to find Mr Right.'

'Ah, well, don't waste too much time looking or you'll be too old to have children.'

'I don't think it's my destiny to have children, Lady Georgina.'

'Nonsense, all women are destined to have children. I had three and I'm now a grandmother of seven. A woman without children is hardly relevant.'

Trixie bristled. 'I disagree. I don't think having children is the only avenue to fulfilment. I have a successful career . . .'

'A career is all very well, my dear, but trust me, there will come a time when you will regret not having bred. After all, it's what we're here for, isn't it?'

Before Trixie had time to reply, a young woman appeared with a tray of tea, followed by Teddy carrying the teapot. 'So, Beatrix, is this the first time you've been to Walbridge?' he asked.

'Yes, it is.'

'Surely your parents have been back?'

'No, they haven't.'

'How surprising,' Teddy mused.

'America's a long way away,' Lady Georgina interjected. 'And besides, plane tickets don't come cheap.'

'Your father is legendary here at Walbridge,' said Teddy cheerfully. 'I married Georgie fifteen years ago. But before me she was married to a man called Rufus. It's thanks to your father that Rufus survived the war.'

'What did my father do?' Trixie asked.

Lady Georgina gasped. 'My dear, you don't know?'

'Know what?'

'He saved my husband's life.' Trixie stared at Lady Georgina in disbelief. 'He was a hero. If it hadn't been for him Rufus would have been shot dead.'

Teddy interrupted. 'He took a bullet for him in North Africa.'

'He took a bullet for Rufus?'

'Absolutely,' said Lady Georgina. 'Rufus's tank was hit. They took shelter in a settlement somewhere near El Alamein. The Germans counter-attacked. Your father arrived with his battalion to reinforce the position. He saw a German sniper aiming at Rufus and dived at him.' She had clearly told the story many times before.

'He literally threw himself onto Rufus,' added Teddy, gesticulating vigorously. 'Bang! The sniper fired and got Freddie in the side of his face.'

'Poor Freddie lost his eye, but he saved my husband's life,' said Lady Georgina softly. 'We are enormously grateful.'

'Dad's never mentioned it,' said Trixie, trying to make sense of it. 'Why would he keep something like that secret?'

'Well, now you know, you'll have to ask him. Perhaps he's just very modest and doesn't want any fuss. Will you tell him that we still remember him with gratitude even though Lord Penselwood is no longer with us?'

'I'm sorry for your loss,' said Trixie. *I'm sorry for my mother's loss*, she thought quietly.

'Thank you, my dear. His heart simply gave out. He wasn't old.' She frowned. 'It was as if it just decided it had had enough.' Her eyes wandered to the window and she sighed wistfully. 'He died on a bench in the garden. He liked to sit out in the middle of the night, under the stars, listening to the rustling of animals. When he came back from the war he used to sit there all the time. I think, after the ugliness of it all, he wanted to be surrounded by beauty. He adored the garden.'

Trixie followed her gaze. She knew now why Rufus had ended the affair: not because he had stopped loving Grace, but because he had had to, out of loyalty and respect for the man who had saved his life. And from Lady Georgina's baffled expression Trixie was able to deduce *why* Rufus had died. She knew she was right. He had died of a broken heart.

Chapter 24

Trixie left, not the way she had come, but by Lady Georgina's own front drive, which led back into the lane. As she walked she reflected on the extraordinary revelation of her father's bravery. She couldn't imagine why he had never told her. She couldn't imagine why her *mother* had never told her. Surely his courage was something to be celebrated, not hidden away like a crime? She consoled herself that he couldn't possibly have known about the affair, because then he would not have leapt so swiftly to Rufus's aid. She smiled sadly at the irony. Her father had saved Lord Melville's life; instinctively perhaps, given that he was in the employ of the Penselwood family, and in so doing saved the life of his wife's lover. Because of his heroism Earl Melville was left with no option but to end the affair; how bitter must his gratitude have been. Considered from another angle, Earl Melville stole not only her father's wife, but his eye as well. Trixie felt a growing resentment for the man her mother had loved and a deep sympathy for her father. She hoped with all her heart that he had never known about her mother's infidelity.

She arrived at the Fox and Goose a little before half past twelve, feeling depleted. So engrossed was she in her parents' past that she had forgotten all about Jasper. When she entered,

Robert was behind the bar, serving customers. He waved and pointed to a fair-haired woman sitting at a corner table by the window. 'Mother's waiting for you. I'll send Maeve over to take your orders for lunch,' he told her. Trixie ignored the stares from curious locals and made her way across the room.

'Hello,' she said, pulling out a spindle-back chair and sitting down. 'You must be Robert's mother.'

The woman smiled sweetly, revealing a set of small, crooked teeth. She had the same bright-blue eyes as her son. 'And you must be Trixie Valentine.'

'It's very nice to meet you, Mrs Heath.'

'Call me Joan.' She patted Trixie's hand. 'So, you're Grace Hamblin's daughter. You are the image of her. She was a beautiful girl.'

'I'm so pleased to meet someone who knew her,' said Trixie, cheering up in the warmth of Joan's enthusiasm. Maeve came and took the orders, returning a moment later with drinks.

Joan was keen to share her stories with someone who was eager to hear them. 'I was about ten when she married your father. But I remember the wedding at the church because Freddie and Grace were very popular and everyone turned out to watch. It was just before the war. Like a perfect summer's day before the storm.'

'Mom told me she bought the dress off the peg at a department store.'

'In Dorchester, most likely,' she said, crinkling up her nose. 'Not a glamorous town.'

'The dress was pretty, though.'

'Oh, it was, Trixie, very pretty,' Joan repeated with emphasis. 'Then war came and Freddie went off to fight with all the other young men, my older brothers included, although

Charlie was only just seventeen and as fresh-faced as a schoolboy. My mother cried for a week then threw all her energy into the war effort, working on the farm with your mother, although Grace was soon taken under my grandfather's wing in the gardens. He was the head gardener at the Hall, you see, and he chose Grace to work with him. He had a soft spot for her. I think everyone did.' She laughed wistfully. 'They had the most marvellous vegetable gardens and orchards at the Hall. You should have seen the quantity of produce they got out of the land. My grandfather used to say Grace had a magic touch but I think it was simply love. If you love living things they grow, don't they? Lady Penselwood was a shrewd woman. She bought cows and sheep and pigs before the war. I tell you, the only rationing that affected us here in Walbridge was petrol. We ate like kings. Eggs, milk, cheese, and honey in the place of sugar. We had lots of honey, thanks to your mother. Those bees were very industrious.'

Joan's eyes were shiny and alert and the apples of her cheeks flushed pink with pleasure as she travelled back into the past. The war years had clearly been exciting for her. 'Oh, they were, Trixie, very exciting,' she said. 'I was lucky, my brothers came home in one piece. Others weren't so fortunate. Like your father, God bless him.'

Maeve brought over their food and set the steaming dishes on the table, but Trixie was almost too engrossed in their conversation to eat.

'I bumped into Lady Georgina this morning who told me that Dad had been a hero,' she said.

'A hero?' Joan raised her eyebrows.

'Yes, apparently he saved Lord Melville's life.'

'Did he indeed?'

'Don't you think it odd that he never told me?'

Joan patted Trixie's hand again. 'The men who returned from the war never spoke of it to anyone. They wanted to forget it and rebuild their lives. I suspect your father was a modest man and considered his act of bravery simply the actions of a good soldier. He might have been a little embarrassed by the fuss, don't you think?'

'He lost his eye because of it.'

'But Lord Penselwood – I mean Rufus, he was Rufus Melville then – lived because of your father's sacrifice. What an incredible thing to give someone, the gift of life.'

'What was he like?'

'Rufus? He was like a handsome prince in a fairy tale. Tall with dark-brown eyes, deeply set, and lots of thick brown hair. Long face with a mouth that seemed to find everything amusing.' She gesticulated energetically with her hands. 'He had good bones, Rufus did, high cheekbones and a strong, straight nose. He was dashing. As a little girl I'd glimpse him from time to time and be so overtaken by shyness as to lose my tongue altogether. Then when I was working in Red Valentine for your aunt Josie, he came in with Lady Georgina. Now *she* was so beautiful she took your breath away. Not soft, like your mother, but icy like the Snow Queen.' She laughed, pleased with her comparison. 'They made a gorgeous couple, the two of them, although I'd say the war rubbed the gloss off him. He had always had a cheerful nature and a certain sheen, but after the war he didn't smile any more, not with his eyes, anyhow. You can always tell a person is truly happy if he smiles with his eyes. Rufus didn't.'

'That's so sad.'

'I'm afraid there were many like him. They'd seen too much, I suspect. Lady P. used to complain that he'd grown grumpy and short-tempered. She complained with affection, though. She adored her son. He used to lunch with her twice a week, just the two of them. He smiled when he was with her, mind you. In those days she lived in the White House on the estate, but when Jasper married she moved to the other side of town. She and Lady Georgina are not friends.'

'Is that because they're both very strong characters?'

If Joan knew, she wasn't going to elaborate. She smiled her sweet smile and patted Trixie's hand. 'You should go and pay her a visit. She'd love to see you. She was very fond of Grace. The war did a lot to break the barriers down between people. My grandfather said that Lady P. rolled up her sleeves and got her hands dirty with the rest of them. Lady Georgina remained in her ivory tower, of course. The war did nothing to change *her*. But Lady P. has no airs and graces.'

'What do you do for her?'

'Everything. I'm her Girl Friday.' She laughed. 'Although I'm not a girl any more. I'm nearly sixty!'

'You're a girl to her.'

'I suppose I am. She's well into her nineties now but there's no slowing her down.' She shook her head. 'God broke the mould after He made her. There's no one else like her. I'll be sorry when she goes.'

'Whatever happened to my aunt, Josephine?'

'Ah, the glamorous Josephine!' Joan sighed with pleasure. 'She was a lovely-looking girl, but much too ambitious for a small town like Walbridge. She sold her shop and moved to London where she married some rich businessman, I think. I heard she was treading the boards in the West End but I never got up to London to see her. I don't think her career amounted to much. I don't think she was ever the famous star she hoped she'd be. When her father died her mother moved up there to be close to her. I didn't hear about her after that. Her mother was a good woman. May Valentine. She used to bake cakes and sell them at the summer fair. I remember her because she had such warmth in her eyes.'

At that moment the door opened and Trixie looked up. There, standing in the wind that swept in off the lane, was Jasper.

Trixie's heart stalled at the sight of the man she had once loved. She stared at him in disbelief. He was older, weathered, with receding hair and a touch of grey about the temples, but handsome still, and her heart was jolted back to life.

Jasper's eyes stopped when they settled on her and his face expanded into a wide, surprised smile. He hurried across the pub until he reached their table. 'Excuse me, Joan,' he said politely. Then to Trixie: 'So it's true. You really *are* here!'

Trixie wondered whether Joan noticed, as she did, the ill-disguised longing in his eyes. 'How did you know?'

'Mother told me.'

Trixie felt Joan deserved an explanation. 'I met Jasper in America seventeen years ago,' she said, her cheeks reddening beneath Jasper's gaze.

'And you haven't changed at all,' he said. 'Not at all.'

Joan put her hands on the table to push herself up. 'I'll leave you two old friends together,' she said.

'I don't want to interrupt your lunch,' Jasper began.

'You haven't. I was just rattling on. Really, we could have sat here all afternoon, couldn't we, Trixie?'

'Lunch is on me,' said Jasper courteously.

'That's very kind of you, Lord Penselwood. Thank you.' Joan got to her feet. 'It's been a pleasure talking to you, Trixie. How long are you staying?'

'A couple of days.'

'Well, I hope you enjoy them. The weather's nice for you. Perhaps I'll see you again.'

When she had gone, Jasper lowered his voice. 'My God, Trixie. I can't believe you're here.' It was then that she noticed a shadow of unhappiness behind his smile. 'Why didn't you tell me you were coming?'

'I didn't know how.'

'You could have written.' His eyes searched hers for the girl he'd left on the beach. 'You could have knocked.'

'Jasper . . .' She glanced about the room self-consciously.

He immediately understood her reticence. 'Let's go somewhere quiet,' he suggested. Trixie watched him go to the bar to pay. He was wearing a pair of corduroy trousers and a pale-blue cashmere sweater beneath an old, moth-eaten tweed jacket. He looked every inch the country squire, she thought, and her heart buckled for the boy with the big dreams of being a rock star, sacrificed to duty and tradition. 'Come,' he said and she almost gave him her hand as she had done all those years ago on the beach in Tekanasset.

She followed him out into the sunshine. The lane was empty. They were alone. Without a word he wrapped his arms around her and pressed her to his chest. She was sure he released a groan as he held her there for a long moment. She closed her eyes and swallowed back tears that suddenly surged in a tide of longing. 'Oh, Trixie, I don't know where to begin.' He pulled away and smiled bitterly. 'I have visualized this moment for years, but now it's here I don't know what to say.'

'You don't have to say anything. It's enough just to see you,' she replied.

'No, it isn't,' he said gravely. 'I owe you an explanation. Come, let's go for a drive.'

His dusty Volvo estate was parked in the shade by the river. He opened the passenger door and she climbed in. She immediately smelt dog and on closer inspection saw white hairs all over the upholstery. 'Where's your dog?' she asked as he climbed in beside her.

He grinned. 'Bendico's at home. I'm sorry his fur's all over the seats.'

'I don't mind. Mum's always had big dogs, remember?'

'I remember everything,' he said, and Trixie detected the wistfulness in his voice. He drove into the street. 'I couldn't believe my ears when Mother said Beatrix Valentine found Ralph in the woods and brought him back. I thought, "That can't be *my* Beatrix Valentine, can it?" Were you going to leave without seeing me?'

'I came to find out about my parents. I didn't think you'd *want* to see me.'

He shook his head. 'You have no idea, Trixie. Look at you. You're the same. *Exactly* the same. It's as if we're young again. I wish to God we were. I wish we could turn the clock back. I'd do things so differently.' He glanced at her and his grey-green eyes had darkened with sorrow. 'Letting you go was the most foolish thing I've ever done in my life.' Trixie was astonished that he should make that confession within five minutes of meeting, but he was right. It *did* feel like they were back on Tekanasset. He was as familiar to her now as he had been then and she almost reached out and put her hand on his arm to reassure him that she felt the same.

He seemed to regret his outburst. 'I'm sorry, Trixie. I shouldn't be burdening you with my troubles. I suppose you're married . . . why ever did I assume you weren't?'

'I'm not married, Jasper,' she replied softly.

'Do you still live on Tekanasset?'

'My parents do, but I moved to New York.'

He grinned. 'Did you get to work for *Vogue*?'

'Not quite *Vogue*, but I'm fashion editor for one of the big glossies.'

'I knew you could be anything you wanted to be.'

'Do you still play guitar?'

He shook his head. 'I haven't played since I left Tekanasset.'

Trixie was appalled. 'You were so talented!'

'I gave up all the things I loved.' His face crumpled with guilt. 'I gave *you* up, too.'

'It's OK. It was a long time ago.' She turned her gaze to the window. 'Where are we going?'

'To the beach. I need a walk. I want to be alone with you where we can talk and catch up. I have so many questions.'

She knitted her fingers and kept her eyes on the road ahead, fighting the impulse to reach out and touch him.

Jasper drove down the narrow lanes until they reached a farm entrance. He turned off the road and motored up a muddy track. At the end he parked on the crest of the hill and switched off the engine. Before them the sparkling ocean spread out vast and wide as far as the eye could see. 'What a beautiful view,' Trixie sighed. 'I didn't know we were so close to the sea.'

'Come, there's a path down to the beach.' He looked at her leather jacket and thin scarf. 'Are you going to be warm enough?'

'I'm fine,' she replied. But he went round and opened the boot. 'Here, put this on. It'll be too big for you and it's not very fashionable for a fashion editor, but it'll stop you getting cold in the wind.'

She took the green coat he offered her. 'What about you?'

He smiled playfully. 'I'm a man,' he said, putting on a gruff voice.

She laughed. 'Even men get cold, Jasper.'

'Not real ones!'

They walked down a narrow footpath that wound its way through rocks and long grass to the beach below. Only gulls flew in and out of that secluded stretch of sand. The tide had gone out, leaving small crustaceans for the birds to fight over, and the air was pierced every now and then by their indignant cries. 'I'm sorry I hurt you, Trixie,' Jasper said suddenly. He took a deep breath and thrust his hands into his jacket pockets. 'I never wanted to lead you on like that. I hoped . . .'

She cut him off. 'It's OK, Jasper. It's water under the bridge. Really.'

'Not for me, it isn't. Regret isn't something one can throw off so easily. It ate me up on the inside.'

'It wasn't meant to be,' she told him, trying to be philosophical when she really wanted to throw herself against him and tell him how he had ruined love for her, because she hadn't been able to love anyone else since.

'I don't believe in fate. We make our own lives,' he argued. 'We make mistakes and we live to regret them. If I'd married you, Trixie, I wouldn't be standing here wishing I had done things differently. I wouldn't be unhappy.'

She reached out and touched his arm. 'Let's walk,' she suggested, turning away and allowing the wind to sweep away her tears.

They began to walk slowly, side by side, with the bracing wind at their backs. Jasper collected himself by standing tall with his shoulders back. The effort he made to control his feelings made Trixie want to cry all the more. 'So tell me,' he began. 'What's this about your parents living in Walbridge?'

'They both grew up here,' Trixie began. 'They married in your little church and my dad worked on the farm and Mom was the beekeeper. She worked with your gardener, Mr Heath, during the war. Then they left for America.'

'And you never knew?'

'They never told me. They never spoke of their past. I've only just found out.'

'How *did* you find out?'

She took a deep breath. 'I found a box of love letters in my mother's garden shed, addressed to her in Walbridge. They weren't from Dad,' she added gravely.

'Oh, God. They were from another man.'

'Yes. She had an affair at the beginning of the war.'

'Do you know who with?'

She braced herself, not sure whether she was doing the right thing in telling him. 'Your father,' she replied.

Jasper stopped walking. 'My father?' He looked horror-struck.

'Yes,' she replied, hunching her shoulders defensively. 'I'm afraid so.'

'Are you sure?'

'There was only one Earl of Melville, right?'

He nodded. 'Good God. Papa and your mother? What a twist of fate.'

'I know, it was a shock for me, too.'

'It's extraordinary.' He shook his head, trying to make sense of it all. 'I suppose one never really knows one's parents.'

'I've learned that the hard way,' said Trixie.

'How long did it go on for?'

'About two years, I think. The letters are very sweet. If they weren't to my mother from her lover I'd find them really romantic.'

'When did it end?'

'It's unclear. But he stops writing to her at the end of 1942. Her last letter is dated March 1943. I know that because he returned all her letters after the war.'

'Why did he do that?'

'My father saved your father's life in Africa, according to your mother. I assume he realized he couldn't cuckold a man who had taken a bullet for him, so he did the right thing. He ended it. To be honest, I don't think my mother's ever got over it.'

'Did she tell you?'

'No, I'm not even sure my father knows. Mom certainly doesn't know that I know. I read her letters by chance. She doesn't even know I'm here.'

'So, you came to Walbridge in search of your parents' past?'

'Yes,' she replied. But as the word came out she realized that, in truth, she had come here in search of Jasper.

They walked on in silence, Jasper absorbing the revelation of his father's affair, Trixie recognizing at last that the Jasper-shaped hole in her heart could only ever be filled by him, and no one else. The wind slipped between them and the distance could have been as wide as a canyon for the sudden loneliness that engulfed her, and the realization that she would always be alone.

'Jasper, Mom's got cancer,' she said, giving in to the need to share. Yielding to the need to be comforted.

'Oh, Trixie, I'm so sorry.'

The sympathy in his voice brought tears to her eyes again. 'I don't think she's got long. That's why I wanted to find out why your father returned her letters and what happened to him. Her final letters to him, begging for reassurance that he was still alive and still loving her, are desperate.'

He took her hand in his large rough one as if it belonged there. 'You're not OK, are you?'

'Not really.' She felt immediately soothed by the warmth of his hand. 'But I'll be fine. I'll get through this.' She took a deep breath. 'The thing is, I've only recently discovered my mother again after years of living in New York. She's my best friend. We share so much. Until I discovered the letters, I didn't realize just *how* much.'

'Do you think your parents knew who I was?' Jasper asked.

'Yes, and they weren't happy about it. I remember they said people like you always marry your own sort and that you wouldn't honour your promise. Mom knew more than I realized.'

'Papa gave nothing away, but that's no surprise. An affair isn't something one shouts about, is it? I doubt Mother knew. They had a good marriage, as far as I recall.'

'I'm certain your mother never knew. She'd hardly have been so welcoming to me had she known. She told me how grateful she was that Dad took that bullet and saved Rufus's life. I don't think she'd have been so thankful had she known about those letters.'

Jasper chuckled. 'How did you introduce yourself?'

'Beatrix. Would Trixie have given me away?'

'Absolutely. She was adamant that I shouldn't marry you. She wouldn't have recognized the name Beatrix, but she would have jumped at the name Trixie.'

'How lucky, then, that I chose to be formal. She's a formal-looking woman, isn't she?'

'She's made of steel.' He sighed bitterly. 'In the end I caved. I thought she was probably right. You'd have hated this life. You're a free spirit, not a lady of the manor labouring under good works and duty.'

Trixie stopped walking and gazed up at him in frustration. 'Then what are you, if not a free spirit? You should be wandering the globe with your voice and your guitar, not stuck here in corduroy and tweed, running a grand estate.'

'It was my duty.'

'What is this word "duty"? Duty to what? To a pile of old bricks? You're a man of flesh and blood, Jasper, and one day you're not going to be around any more. You have to live for yourself, too.'

He groaned, as if he laboured under the impossible burden of family and responsibility. 'I have three children and a wife. I have tied myself to Walbridge. I am committed and for the life of me I can't imagine how I can ever leave.'

A spark of hope ignited in Trixie's heart. 'You want to leave?'

'I'm miserable, Trixie. I was in a dark place before you arrived to shine a beacon of hope. You're like a lighthouse I can see in the distance but can't get to. You've always been there, far away, shining through the gloom, and as hard as I paddle I just can't reach you.'

With that he bent down and kissed her ardently, as he had done in Tekanasset when they were young and free and bursting with ambition. Trixie responded urgently, and the years that had dragged by in loneliness and longing evaporated like a dream. She wound her arms around his neck, inhaled the familiar scent of him and knew then what her mother had also known, that love isn't something that wears out or disintegrates with the passing of the years, but something that glows forever like an eternal sun.

Chapter 25

Jasper pulled away. He cupped Trixie's face in his hands and gazed lovingly at her features, as if he were slowly remembering the kisses and caresses shared on those windy Tekanasset beaches. His expression had softened. Gone was the tension in his jaw and the strain on his forehead, and his eyes were no longer dark with unhappiness but bright, reflecting the light in hers – the lighthouse he had reached at last.

'What a fool I was to let you go,' he murmured, smiling with joy now that they were miraculously reunited.

She placed her hands on top of his and returned his smile. 'I never stopped loving you, Jasper.'

'Really? Do you mean that?'

'I do.' She shrugged. 'I tried to move on, but no one compared to you.'

'Oh, Trixie,' he groaned. 'If I'd known then what I know now I would never have listened to my mother. I'd have believed my own heart.'

'I never imagined you'd be unhappy.'

'Lottie is not a bad person. We're just ill suited. On paper we were well matched because we had grown up together. Our parents were great friends and she was bred to run a big estate. But in reality she would have been better off marrying my brother. Like Edward, she hasn't an artistic bone in her body and loves horses more than people. The truth is, Mama persuaded me that I needed her – and I did need her, in the beginning. She took over the running of the place, and as Marchioness of Penselwood she was without fault, but as my wife she was desperately lacking. We never loved each other, you see. I didn't think it mattered. I thought we would be a team. I believed we'd be great friends. But we're not even friends any more.' He squeezed her hands. 'I've lost myself over the years, Trixie. I've become someone else entirely. I look into your eyes and see the reflection of the boy I once was. I see the man I thought I'd become. But instead I've become this conventional old bore.' He withdrew his hands and turned to face the sea. The wind swept his hair off his forehead, revealing the disenchantment in his profile. 'I've become my father. He became his. There's no way of breaking the pattern destiny imposes on us all.'

Trixie laughed softly at his self-indulgence. 'Of course you can break the pattern. You can be whoever you want to be, Jasper.'

'No, I can't. I have duties and responsibilities as Marquess of Penselwood.'

'It's a name and a position, but it doesn't prevent you from being the person you want to be. You could start playing the guitar again.'

He shrugged. 'I don't know.'

'Jasper,' she exclaimed, 'you're not a puppet on a string. You are your own person. Get your guitar out and write a song. If you're miserable it'll be the best song you've ever written!'

He smiled at her efforts to cajole him out of his melancholy and took her hand. 'You're right. I've allowed myself to wallow in self-pity.' He led her back down the beach towards the path that snaked up the cliff. 'I wanted to fulfil my duty, Trixie. I wanted to make my mother proud. I was aware I was less qualified than Edward, who had studied at agricultural college, worked here with Papa and consequently knew how to manage a big estate. No one thought I could do it. I was the wild card. I wanted to prove everyone wrong. I wanted to do it right.' He glanced at her, and his eyes smouldered with regret. 'Pride,' he stated resentfully. 'It was pride that motivated me. Pride that inspired me to marry Lottie. Pride that made me give up the one person I really loved.'

'Lottie has given you children. Don't regret your marriage. You have a family. That counts for a lot.'

'But *you*!' He gripped her hand. 'I've denied *you* a family. God, how I wish it were you in Lottie's place . . .'

'I'm not bitter, Jasper. I've had a fascinating working life. I've had opportunities, too, to settle down. If I really wanted children, I could have married and raised a family. I chose not to. *My* choice, not yours. No one forced me to live like this. I've actually enjoyed my life. I didn't want to settle for second best. If I couldn't have you, I didn't want anybody else. That's the truth, but it doesn't mean I've been living a life of denial. I haven't. I've had good times.'

'I wish I had been part of those good times.'

'I wish you had been, too. I think my mother has pined for your father for years; that's why she kept the letters in a secret box in the garden shed. That's why she collapsed in tears when I told her he had died. I realize that now. The past is beginning to make sense. I think her longing for Rufus has damaged her marriage,' she reflected wistfully. 'I used to think Dad was unfairly remote and unaffectionate.

Now I wonder whether he didn't feel remoteness and coldness from *her.* It's not healthy to pine, Jasper. If Mom has taught me anything, she's taught me that. We have to let the past go and live in the moment, otherwise we don't live, we just dream.'

'I can let the past go now you're here,' he said with a grin.

'That's cheating.'

'I don't care.' He swung her round to kiss her again. 'I'm living in the moment now and it's good enough for me.'

A while later they drove back towards Walbridge. The light was fading, with dark clouds gathering above them, greedily eating the last remains of pale blue sky. 'I want to see you tomorrow,' Jasper said seriously.

'I don't know . . .' Trixie hesitated.

'You can't go back to New York now!' he exclaimed. She knew he was right. Everything had changed. She couldn't leave and pretend that things were as before.

'I don't know what to do.' She gazed helplessly at the darkening sky.

'I'll take you to meet my grandmother,' he suggested. 'She might be able to shed some light on Papa's affair with your mother. Although we'll have to tread carefully; she's a different generation. I'll pick you up in the morning.'

She looked at him anxiously. 'Is this wise, Jasper?'

'You said you wanted to know why Papa returned her letters.'

'I *know* why. It was a matter of honour. Soldier to soldier. That makes sense.'

'I still think you should talk to Grandma. She might know something more.' He glanced back at her and she noticed the panic in his eyes. 'I want to see you again, Trixie. You can't leave . . .'

She took his hand across the gearbox. 'OK. I'll come and meet your grandmother.'

His shoulders dropped. 'Good. I'll pick you up at nine. Is that OK for you?'

'That's OK. What will you tell Lottie?'

'I'll tell her the truth. That I met an old friend and am taking her to see Grandma. She'll think nothing of it.'

'I'm leaving the day after tomorrow.'

'That means we have a day all to ourselves.'

Trixie felt her throat constrict. 'One day,' she said.

'One day? Two days? You don't have to leave.'

She shook her head. 'I have a life to get back to, Jasper.'

He gripped the steering wheel. 'I'll pick you up at nine.'

Trixie couldn't face dinner in the pub, talking to Robert, so she found a small Italian restaurant on the high street and ate there at a table by the window. It had started to drizzle. She watched the raindrops slide down the glass in wiggly trails. Occasionally the bright lights of a car turned them to gold. She ate her pizza half-heartedly. Seeing Jasper had given her a high, like a sniff of the drugs she used to take, and now she felt the pain of withdrawal. Was the thrill of his kiss worth the agony of knowing it couldn't last? She had got used to being on her own, but Jasper had reminded her of what it felt like to be in the arms of the man she loved. The comparison only emphasized the hollowness of the many relationships she had had over the years. The life she had lived was reduced to a sham and she wasn't sure she wanted to go back to it. A small part of her wished she had never come, because what had been acceptable before was now intolerable in the light of their reunion. Nothing would ever be the same again, because the same wasn't good enough.

She drained her glass of Pinot Grigio and paid the bill. Hugging her coat around her, she walked back up the high street towards the lane that led to the inn and the river beyond. She should leave, she thought, before she got in too deep. Before it became too hard to extricate herself. She didn't want to break up his family. However miserable he was with his wife, she didn't want that on her conscience. In which case, there was no point in staying. She couldn't have Jasper. They could never be together. Seeing him had only reminded her of what she lacked. She'd return to her life in New York and try to get over him, just as she had done nearly two decades before. Having climbed to the summit of an emotional mountain, she had slid right back to the bottom. How would she even manage the first few steps?

She returned to the Fox and Goose and crept up the stairs to her room without being seen. She didn't feel like talking to Maeve or Robert. She didn't feel like talking at all. As she climbed into bed and switched out the light she thought of Grace, and her heart flooded with compassion. If her mother had pined for Rufus as she was now pining for Jasper she must have suffered indeed.

Loneliness engulfed her and she gave in to the longing and the unbearable sense of defeat. Hugging her pillow, she cried for herself and for her mother, realizing that, because she had been so fixated on herself, she didn't really know Grace, the woman, at all.

The following morning she awoke with a nervous feeling in her stomach. She knew she should leave before Jasper arrived at nine, but as much as she knew what was right, she was unable to comply. Her heart eclipsed her head and she was powerless. Instead of packing her suitcase, she applied some make-up and allowed the anticipation to smother her doubt.

She took her breakfast in the little dining room, where Maeve brought her coffee and toast. She was almost too anxious to eat. 'So, are you having a nice stay, dear?' Maeve asked. 'Shame about the weather. Yesterday was lovely but we're paying for it today.'

'Yes, thank you. I'm having a very nice time,' Trixie replied blandly, not wanting to engage the woman in conversation.

'I hope Joan was able to enlighten you on your relations. She's a lovely woman, Joan.'

'Yes, she was very interesting.'

Maeve leaned on the back of the chair as if she intended to be there a while. 'She's worked for Lady P. for years. They're more like mother and daughter than employer and employee. She's having a terrible time at the moment, though, poor dear. Lady P. is intent on arranging her own funeral. Well, I suppose at her age it could come at any time, couldn't it? Joan doesn't want to think about that. She's very fond of the old lady.'

'It does sound rather morbid arranging her own funeral. I don't really want to think about death.'

'That's what Lady Georgina says. The poor vicar is caught between Lady P. bombarding him with ideas for music and readings and Lady Georgina insisting that he ignore her because she's clearly going mad! Yes, Lady Georgina thinks her mother-in-law is a few sandwiches short of a picnic!' Maeve laughed heartily. 'Do you know what I think?'

'What do you think?' Trixie sipped her coffee, not in the least interested in Maeve's opinion.

'I think Lady P. is preparing her final attack.'

'What do you mean?'

'Well, from what I gather, she's choosing a rather unconventional funeral, which would certainly rile Lady Georgina, who is very traditional. It would be a final insult from beyond the grave for Lady Georgina to have to suffer a gospel choir . . .'

'A gospel choir?' *That* had caught Trixie's interest.

'Oh yes, Lady P. wants a black gospel choir.'

'That's quite radical.'

'It certainly is. I'm not sure she'll get her way. Once she's dead Lady Georgina will do as she wishes. She's a strong woman. I can't imagine the poor vicar will be able to stand up to her.'

'What a drama.'

'Oh yes, indeed. There's always a drama of some sort going on here in Walbridge. It's never dull, otherwise I would have left years ago. Who wants to live in a small place if there's no entertainment?' She chuckled. 'There's plenty of entertainment here.'

Robert poked his head round the door. 'Morning, Trixie,' he said, smiling broadly. Trixie smiled back and stifled an irritable sigh. It didn't look as if she was going to get any peace. 'Lord Penselwood is in the pub.'

'Oh,' she replied, perking up. 'I'll come right away. Thank you.' She put her napkin on the table and stood up.

'Mother enjoyed meeting you yesterday,' he said.

'I might see her today. Jasper is going to introduce me to his grandmother.' She regretted the need to explain and hoped it hadn't exposed her guilty conscience.

'Did you have a good day yesterday?'

'Yes, thank you.'

'You found the Beekeeper's Cottage?'

'Yes.'

'And Robin?'

'Yes, we had a long chat.'

'Good.' He hesitated a moment. 'If you'd like a guided tour, I'm free this afternoon.'

'Thank you, Robert. That's sweet of you to offer. I'll let you know.'

'I get off at two,' he informed her eagerly.

She nodded and slipped past him into the corridor. 'I'll bear it in mind,' she replied and immediately forgot all about it.

Jasper greeted her cordially and showed her out to the car. She noticed his guitar on the back seat. 'Ah, your music!' she said, climbing into the passenger seat.

'I've taken your advice,' he replied. She noticed how raffish he looked with his hair swept off his face. He wore jeans and a thick green sweater which emphasized the grey-green colour of his eyes. Once in the car he leaned over and slid his hand behind her neck and pressed his lips to hers. She smelt his lime aftershave and the familiar scent of his skin; that alone had the power to peel back the years. As he kissed her all her doubts melted away and the golden light of endless possibilities shone bright and alluring, lifting her high above the ground. Suddenly nothing mattered but today.

He drove through the town. 'I've told Grandma we're coming. She sounded very excited when I told her you're Grace Valentine's daughter. She says she remembers Grace with fondness.'

'That's so sweet,' Trixie replied. 'I'm sure they didn't have a great deal to do with one another, my mother being an employee and all.'

'I think you'll be surprised. My grandmother is famous for treating everyone as an equal. Not like my mother!'

'Your mother is quite formidable.'

'She's a terrible snob, I'm afraid. I hate to say it . . .'

'. . . but you're going to anyway,' she laughed.

He smiled. 'Yes, I'm going to say it anyway. She's insecure, frightened of anything that's not familiar, so she clings to the way things were without realizing that times have changed. She's stuck in another world and digging her heels in, determined not to change. To her, the aristocracy still rule the world.'

'If it makes her happy, what harm can it do?'

'A lot of harm, when it makes other people unhappy. I broke away when I went to America, but when I came back I gave in and conformed. That hasn't made me happy.'

'Do you have a son?'

'Yes, Fergus, he's fifteen.'

'Then you can use your wisdom to allow him to be who he wants to be.'

'Not so easy with a mother like Lottie.'

'I hadn't accounted for Lottie.'

'No, she and my mother are very much alike, which is probably why they get along so well. They use the same words: duty, responsibility, community, tradition, heritage, inheritance . . .' He sighed. 'There's a special dictionary for people like them!'

'Then you must encourage Fergus to go his own way.'

'Fortunately, I think times have changed and with them the demands. He's a strong boy. He will do just as he pleases.'

He grinned at her. 'I will never put pressure on him to do anything against his own wishes. I'm afraid his mother might not be so agreeable.'

'Does Fergus have brothers or sisters?' Trixie asked, curious about Jasper's family.

'Two younger sisters. Eliza and Cassandra.'

'How lucky they are to have a father like you.'

'I adore them,' he said with feeling, and Trixie realized that his love for his children just made it more impossible for him ever to leave Lottie.

Jasper turned into a driveway where a large sandy-coloured stone house peeped shyly out from behind a thick feather boa of yellow wisteria. The wheels crunched on the gravel, alerting a dog to their arrival, who began to bark excitedly. 'That's Winston, Grandma's boxer. He looks alarming, but is as gentle as a Labrador.' The front door opened and the old woman Trixie had seen with the vicar stood in the door frame with a wide and welcoming smile. Winston pushed past her and set about sniffing the car importantly. He pressed his nose to Trixie's window and lifted his ears curiously. Jasper walked round and moved him away. He opened Trixie's door. 'Give him a pat, then he'll leave you alone.'

'He's adorable!' she gushed, scratching the dog behind his ears.

'If you do that he'll *never* leave you alone! Hello, Grandma.'

'Darling, do come in. It's about to rain,' said Lady Penselwood.

'Hello, Lady Penselwood,' Trixie said, extending her hand.

Lady Penselwood took it and gave it a firm shake. In the other hand she held a walking stick. 'Now, you look familiar,' she said, narrowing her eyes.

'We met briefly outside the church . . .' Trixie volunteered.

'Ah yes, I remember now. You see, I might have one foot in the grave, but my mind is still all there. Come inside, dear. Don't mind Winston, he'll leave his calling card on Jasper's wheels, then he'll come inside through the garden.' She closed the door behind them. 'Joan has lit a fire in the sitting room so it's nice and warm. What a damp day. Frightful.'

'You have a beautiful home,' said Trixie, looking around at the Persian rugs and antique furniture that gave the house a stately feel.

'I took a few things with me when I moved out of the Hall,' Lady Penselwood told her. 'I was rather pleased when I found this place. It has charm, don't you think?'

'Oh, it really does,' Trixie agreed, following Jasper into the sitting room.

She was immediately struck by the pictures on the walls. They were all Tekanasset scenes that she recognized at once. 'Jasper, did you buy these for your grandmother?' she asked in surprise.

'No, they were my grandfather's.'

Trixie gasped at the emergence of a vague memory. 'Of course, I remember you told me your grandparents once had a house on Tekanasset.'

'Aldrich loved sailing,' Lady Penselwood explained, settling into an armchair beside the fire. She placed her walking stick on the floor beside her. 'Jasper, be a dear and go and tell Joan to bring in some tea. I bought some delicious ginger biscuits at the delicatessen.' She turned to Trixie, who was gazing at the paintings. 'My husband was obsessed with boats. I have all his models in the dining room. He used to make them. It was his hobby. A hobby that drove me close to madness.' She gave an impatient sniff. 'I think he preferred building boats to being with people.'

'How did he know the island?'

'Have you ever come across the Wilson family? Randall Wilson Junior was a friend of my husband. We used to summer there regularly.'

'Big is a great friend of my mother's,' Trixie said, encouraged by the connection.

Lady Penselwood smiled in surprise. 'How extraordinary! What a small world it is. She's really called Henrietta, you know.'

'I know, but everyone calls her Big.'

'Tell me, did she ever marry?' Lady Penselwood asked as Jasper wandered back into the room.

'No. I don't think there's anyone brave enough to take her on,' Trixie replied.

Lady Penselwood laughed. 'She was a very spirited, outspoken young woman when I knew her.'

'She's exactly the same now.'

'Do sit down, dear. Joan will bring in the tea. I suspect you want to warm up. It's getting chilly, isn't it? I remember wintering once on Tekanasset and the sea froze. It was jolly cold there, too. Jasper tells me this is your first time in Walbridge,' she said as Joan entered with a tray of tea and biscuits. 'Ah, Joan, you're an angel. Put them on the coffee table and we'll help ourselves. Where's the dreaded Winston?'

'Asleep in front of the Aga,' Joan replied. She smiled at Trixie. 'Hello, dear, lovely to see you again.'

'I gather you're interested in your family history,' Lady Penselwood continued. 'I find it most peculiar that your father didn't ever tell you of his heroism.'

'No, he's never mentioned it.'

'Pour us tea, Jasper. Do try a biscuit, Trixie, they're awfully good. The thing is, my dear, the war changed us all. I thrived.' Her brown eyes sparkled as she remembered her past. 'It was an exciting time. I rallied the women and we all mucked in. Well, *nearly* all of us.' She gave her grandson a disapproving look and Trixie guessed she was referring to his mother, Lady Georgina. 'We opened our doors to children from London and we had a very jolly time. Your mother was a wonder in the gardens. She and Mr Heath worked tirelessly. She was brilliant with the animals, brilliant with the bees, brilliant in the gardens. She was a great enthusiast and I was extremely fond of her. Then Freddie saved Rufus's life and we were all so terribly grateful.'

'Did you suggest they move to Tekanasset?' Trixie asked, sipping her tea.

'Well, it's a funny story.' She sat back in her chair and sighed. 'A peculiar story, I think. Pass me a biscuit, will you, Jasper?'

Lady Penselwood took a bite and her whole face confirmed her satisfaction. 'Well, we all wanted to thank Freddie for what he had done. The war was over and Rufus was alive, thanks to him. Poor Freddie had lost his eye, we were all desperately sorry for that but eternally grateful to him for his act of courage. But he would hear none of it. He came up to the house. I remember it well. Myself, Aldrich and Rufus in the library. Freddie looked desperate, as if he were coming to be punished, not rewarded. Aldrich gave him a whiskey, which calmed him down a bit, but he was frightfully nervous. Then I saw a look pass between Freddie and Rufus and I understood. Freddie *resented* Rufus. Well, I was not surprised, given that he had lost his eye. I suppose he rather regretted his impulsiveness. But one often acts instinctively, without giving it much thought, and I think Freddie felt a certain deference towards Rufus and our family. Anyway, Aldrich told Freddie how much we were in his debt, and that we would relish the opportunity to show our gratitude. Then he came out with it. This extraordinary request to leave the country. To go as far away from England as possible. We were stunned. I mean, Freddie and Grace had lived in Walbridge all their lives. They were part of the fabric of the community, not to mention that Mr Garner had high hopes for Freddie taking over when he retired. So, Aldrich suggested Tekanasset, bearing in mind that Randall was such a dear friend and would think nothing of helping him find a job and a house. It all turned out very well. Randall was a man who got things done. We bought the house within a few weeks and Randall had organized a job for Freddie at the cranberry farm. We were terribly sad to see them go, but it was what Freddie wanted. We never saw them again.'

'It's sad that they never came back, not even to visit,' said Trixie quietly.

'It was a long way in those days. It still is,' said Lady Penselwood, putting down her teacup. 'And I think they didn't want to remember the past.'

Lady Penselwood looked deeply into Trixie's eyes. Her expression darkened and her brown eyes brimmed with sorrow. 'The war changed Rufus, too,' she said softly. 'Or rather, the *end* of the war changed him.' She gave the word 'end' a heavy emphasis and Trixie realized that she didn't just mean the war, but the era. 'You see, we lived in an unrealistic time. Everything was so intense, so immediate. We all thought we'd die in the morning. Life had to be grabbed and savoured for its frail and fleeting sweetness. But at the end, when it was over, we had to return to our lives, and in a funny way normality was dreary by comparison. The excitement was gone. The surreal quality that enabled us to live dangerously was gone, too. People had indulged in affairs. They had loved fiercely because they realized that life was short and they wanted to cling to it. Rufus suffered terribly.' She tilted her head and smiled sadly at Trixie. 'I hope your mother found happiness on Tekanasset.'

'She did, thank you. Although—' Trixie hesitated, holding Lady Penselwood's stare in her own. 'I think she left something precious behind. Something she could never get back.'

At that moment Lady Penselwood was inspired by an idea. Her face grew alive again and her brown eyes twinkled with intent. 'Jasper, be a dear and go upstairs. In the right-hand drawer of my dressing table is a blue velvet bag. Bring it, will you?' Jasper disappeared into the hall and up the stairs. 'There's something I want you to give your mother. It's a silly trifle. But it will mean something to her. When are you leaving?'

'Tomorrow.'

'How lovely to have met you, Trixie. Tell me, how is your mother?'

'She's not well, I'm afraid. She has cancer.'

'What poor luck.'

'It is, but she doesn't want any fuss. She's determined to carry on as if she's well.'

'I will pray for her recovery.'

'Thank you, Lady Penselwood.'

Jasper appeared with the velvet bag. Trixie was curious. He handed it to his grandmother. The old lady looked at it fondly, as if it had a special sentimental value and it cost her to part with it. 'Give this to Grace with my love,' she said, holding it out.

Trixie took it. 'May I open it?' she asked.

'You may,' Lady Penselwood replied. Trixie put her hand inside and pulled out a lavender bag. It was worn, like a much-beloved child's toy. On the front was a large, embroidered bee.

Chapter 26

Trixie and Jasper wandered around the churchyard, searching the gravestones for the name Arthur Henry Hamblin. A brisk wind tossed brown and yellow leaves across the grass, sweeping them up against the headstones and the bright flowers recently left in remembrance of the deceased. Trixie didn't like to think too much about the bodies lying beneath the ground. She preferred the more spiritual idea of souls released from their earthly bodies to wander at peace. She recalled the feeling of having been directed to her mother's garden shed by an invisible but perceptible presence, and wondered now in the clear light of day whether she had simply imagined it. Was it possible to cheat death and live on, or were human beings conditioned to believe because the alternative was simply too horrible to contemplate?

She shivered in the cold and thrust her hands into her coat pockets. Jasper was walking up and down the rows of graves, reading out the very old ones whose engraved letters had worn away over time. 'This one was born in 1556,' he said. 'Incredible.'

'Where are your relations buried?'

'There's a family crypt beneath the church.'

'Spooky,' she said with another shiver.

'I can't say I go down there very often.'

'Is there a space for you?'

'I suppose there is, but I don't really want to think about it.'

'Apparently your grandmother is planning her funeral,' she said.

'I know. She's loving it. It's keeping her very busy and entertained, and irritating my mother, of course, which I suppose is her main objective.'

'Ah, here it is,' Trixie announced, crouching down to read the headstone. 'Arthur Henry Hamblin. 1889–1938. He was only forty-eight when he died. That's so young,' she said, wiping away the long grass so that she could read more. '"In memory of a loving father and dear friend. May he rest in peace in God's keeping."'

'He's buried next to his wife,' said Jasper, looking at the headstone beside Arthur's.

'Mom never knew her mother. Her father was all she had. It must have been a terrible loss when he died. She was left on her own.' Trixie did a quick calculation. 'You know, she was only eighteen or nineteen. She married Dad at that age. Thank goodness she had him.' She wondered whether Grace had married him because she was afraid of being on her own again. That was just before the war. Just before her letters to Rufus. Her affair began around that time, too.

'I've been thinking, Trixie. Dad was a grumpy sod. He worked much too hard, spent hours outside on the estate and in the gardens on his own, as if he wanted to lose himself. He was embittered, his humour sarcastic, caustic even, when he was in company. He could be cruel and intolerant. He was quick to anger, and as children we were afraid of him. I ask myself whether ending the affair with Grace killed something inside him that could never be revived. Grandma says he was a carefree and witty young man. The person she describes is nothing like the father I knew.' He looked at her and frowned. 'Am I just like him? Have I become a grumpy, intolerant man because I, too, lost the woman I love? Am I simply repeating the pattern? Lottie complains that I'm scathing and unbearable, but I wasn't always like that. Has my nature been altered by disappointment?' He searched Trixie's face for the answer, but she said nothing. She just looked at him with compassion, her eyes sad and enquiring. 'Let's get out of here,' he said.

'Where shall we go?'

'I want to be alone with you. I can't bear to be this close and not able to touch you.'

She noticed a couple on the street below, casting a glance in their direction. 'All right. Let's go somewhere. Anywhere but here.'

They drove down the winding lanes to the coast. But this time he parked the car at sea level and led her along a grassy path to an old boathouse, snuggled like a nesting partridge among overgrown shrubbery and sheltered by trees. A pier jutted out over the water and a fishing boat was tethered to a bollard, looking forlorn in its desolation. 'This was my grandfather's. He was obsessed with boats. I used to take it out with the children, but in the last few years I've neglected it.'

'The first time we made love was in Joe Hornby's boathouse,' she said.

He pulled her into his arms and smiled wistfully. 'How appropriate, then, that we find ourselves here. Alone at last.' He kissed her urgently, and although she knew this was wrong her conscience was clear because it *felt* so right. There was nothing new about their intimacy. They had made love many times before. They were simply continuing from where they had left off, seventeen years before, on the quay in Tekanasset. They were just older, he a little greyer, she a little plumper, and their battered hearts hungrier for the years they had spent hankering after the lost half of themselves.

They made love in the belly of the boat, beneath picnic rugs for warmth. In their fevered actions they relived the past, rediscovering each other, delighting in the familiar taste and feel of their bodies, each determined to find the people they had once been in the eyes of the other.

Trixie lay back against the blankets smoking, as Jasper played his guitar and sang the song he had written for her on the beach in Tekanasset. She watched him through the smoke, her eyes lazy and full of affection, her head dizzy, drunk on love. She smiled, a small, satisfied smile, as he sang. His voice was grittier now that he was older. It possessed a raw quality owing to not having practised. She was moved by his lack of polish. As a young man he had been glossy, insouciant, golden; now his face was lined, the crow's feet deep and wide, the grey in his stubble and hair betraying his age as well as his unhappiness. Her heart buckled and she wanted time to stand still so that she didn't ever have to leave. She felt needed and his need pulled at her, somewhere deep in the pit of her pain.

'I feel myself when I'm with you,' he said, strumming softly. 'I know you see me as I was. In your eyes I'm talented. I'm a free spirit. I'm unconventional . . .' He grinned bashfully. 'I'm a little wild.' He laughed at himself.

'You still are all those things, Jasper. We don't really change, not deep down. I suppose layers have built up around you, but underneath you're no different.'

'Then with you I can peel back the layers. It feels so good. I feel alive again.' He raised his eyes to the ceiling and sighed heavily. 'I've felt trapped, Trixie. It's been suffocating. I know now how my father felt.' He turned his gaze to her and his eyes darkened. 'I don't want to die young like he did.'

'Do you think he died of a broken heart?'

He shrugged. 'It's a romantic thought, isn't it? Is it possible to die of such a thing?'

'Is Mom's cancer a physical manifestation of her emotional pain? I think it's perfectly possible.'

'I need you, Trixie.'

'I need you, too.'

They lay entwined as the sun began to sink in the sky, signalling the end of the day. 'The sand is running out of the hourglass,' he said at length, holding her tightly. Outside the clouds were thickening and turning a deep purple. The wind began to whistle about the side of the boat, causing it to rock gently on the water.

'I feel like we're in Tekanasset.'

'I wish we were.'

'Those days were fun, weren't they? Kind of ideal.'

'I knew I had it good but I never realized *how* good. That summer has grown out of all proportion in my mind. It stands alone and dazzling. The beaches, the music, the sunshine, the girl.' He squeezed her. 'Especially the girl. I never expected to live the life I'm living. I thought I'd be singing to stadiums full of people.' He chuckled bitterly. 'You've reminded me of what it felt like to be Jasper Duncliffe.'

'You might not be Jasper Duncliffe any more, but you must play your guitar and compose music, if only to keep in touch with him. Music is part of who you are. You stop playing and you cut yourself off from your core.'

'It feels good to play again,' he agreed. 'And what of you, darling Trixie? Are you yourself?'

'I'm doing what I've always wanted to do. I'm happy at the magazine. I love fashion. I'm good at writing about it. I've made a name for myself in the industry. I earn well. I have lots of friends. I feel I'm myself.'

He kissed her temple. 'I want you to say you're incomplete without me.'

She laughed again at his self-indulgence. 'You *know* I'm incomplete without you.'

'Then stay.'

They remained in the boat until late. Their stomachs began to growl with hunger. Reluctantly, they made their way back down the path to the car. There was a tear in the cloud where the stars twinkled through and the light of the moon shone down to illuminate their way. All was silent except for the water lapping against the rocks. Jasper took her hand and they stopped to gaze out over the ebony sea. With the cold wind blowing against their faces and raking icy fingers through their hair, they searched for their future in the black, empty horizon and found nothing.

'What time do you leave tomorrow?' he asked.

'Early. Please don't come to say goodbye. I've said goodbye to you once before and I've never gotten over it,' she said.

'I have to see you again.'

She turned to him sadly. 'You're married, Jasper. You have a family. We cannot build our happiness on the unhappiness of those around you. I'm not going to allow it. I'd rather spend the rest of my life pining for you than regretting the devastation our relationship would cause.'

'You're much too wise, Trixie. I wish you were as selfish as me.'

She laughed and let go of his hand. 'You're not as selfish as you think. You've asked me to stay. You haven't asked me to marry you and you haven't suggested you'll leave your family. You know as well as I do that you're too honourable to do that. So, take me back to the hotel and leave me to treasure today as it is – beautiful, sad and perfect.'

He drove her back to the inn and kissed her one final time. 'If I want to write to you, where shall I send my letters?'

'Jasper . . .'

'Letters, that's all. Please, let me keep in touch. I can't shut you out of my life. If you never open them, I'll never know. You don't have to write back.'

She swallowed but the tears broke through her resistance and spilled down her cheeks. 'Tekanasset.'

'Sunset Slip.'

'You know it.'

'Trixie . . .'

'Don't . . . please.'

'I love you.'

She gripped him hard and pressed her lips to his, leaving salt and sorrow there. 'And I love you. I always will.'

She didn't watch him drive away, but slipped into the inn, head down, afraid of bumping into Maeve or Robert. It didn't matter that she hadn't eaten since Lady Penselwood's biscuits. She didn't think she could get any food past her throat anyway. She ran a hot bath and submerged herself beneath the water, wishing the world would be a different place when she came up to breathe.

* * *

The following morning the taxi arrived to take her to the station. It was early. The dawn light shone weakly through the dark, streaking the eastern sky with pale yellow, like broken egg yolk. Rain fell softly onto the pavement as she jumped a puddle to the waiting car. Maeve had made her a cup of coffee and toast, but it was too early for Robert, so Trixie left a message, knowing that he might perhaps have been disappointed that she hadn't taken up his offer of a tour the previous afternoon. 'You have a safe flight back to New York,' said Maeve. 'If you ever want to come back, you know where you'll receive the warmest welcome.' But she didn't think she ever would come back. As it did for her mother, Walbridge now held painful memories.

When she arrived at Heathrow, she found herself searching the faces for Jasper. She was sure he'd followed her. She hoped he had. But the faces were those of strangers and it wasn't until she was on the plane that she realized her life was not like a movie; he wasn't coming with her.

She sat sobbing in her seat, gazing forlornly out of the window at the glistening tarmac and grey skies. An air stewardess with a kind face and red lipstick took pity on her and upgraded her to Business Class, but the bigger seat and superior menu did little to lift her spirits. She thought of Jasper, reliving the afternoon in the boat as if it were a tape she could rewind and replay at will. She doubted she had done the right thing. She began to wish she had agreed to stay. Right now, as the plane soared over the Atlantic, she ceased to care about her life in New York and would happily have given up everything just to spend another day with Jasper.

At last she slept a little, aided by the wine and a sleeping pill. She felt dizzy and disconnected. Thoughts swam about in her head like a chaotic shoal of fish with nowhere to go.

What did her future hold? If she couldn't have Jasper, would anybody else do? Was she destined always to be alone? She knew she should let him go. But she also knew she couldn't.

The morning after touching down in New York, Trixie was on a plane bound for Boston. She would request leave on compassionate grounds and spend some time with her mother. Nothing else was as important as that. Right now, she needed her – and she sensed her mother needed her, too. She could do most of her work from home, anyhow. Her assistant would sail the ship while she was away. She was more than capable. The editor would understand. Her own mother had died of breast cancer and Trixie had helped raise money for research by running in the New York Marathon.

Trixie flew into Tekanasset airport on a small aircraft that bounced about, buffeted by the slightest gust of wind. The landing made her feel nauseous, but she was crying again when the plane touched down, not because she felt sick, but because she was so relieved to be home. She inhaled the familiar sea air, infused with the sweet, damp scent of fall, and wondered why she had ever left.

In the cab on her way to her parents' house, she gazed out of the window with new eyes. The island gleamed in the early afternoon sunshine. The pinky-red leaves of the maple trees seemed to catch fire in the golden light as the sun began to descend in the west, dragging the day with it. Trixie's heart ached for the familiar. She longed to be in her mother's arms. She wanted to curl up in the security of the past and lose the agony of knowing she could never have the man she loved.

The taxi dropped her off on Sunset Slip. She contemplated her home with a new understanding. This was the house her parents had fled to when their world back in England had fallen apart. Her mother had lost her lover, her father his eye, and this was compensation for their loss. She ran down the path, pulling her suitcase behind her. She pushed open the screen door, then the heavier door behind it. A gust of wind caught it and slammed it shut with a bang. Her mother's dog began to bark. 'Mom!' she shouted. Her throat constricted. The thought that her mother might have died sprang into her head like an unwanted demon. 'Mom!' she shouted again. 'I'm home!' She left her bag in the hall and hurried into her mother's sitting room. The fire was lit. Papers were strewn about the surfaces as usual. The cushions on the sofa were reassuringly dented. She went into the kitchen. A draught swept through the room. She shivered. Then she noticed the door was open. She looked outside. She noticed the door to the shed was open, too.

She stepped onto the veranda. 'Mom!'

Grace appeared, looking smaller, Trixie thought, than when she had last seen her. 'Darling, how lovely, you're here.'

'Oh, Mom!' Trixie wailed, striding down the garden to meet her. She threw her arms around her mother, who patted her back in bewilderment.

'Are you all right, darling? What's the matter? Why are you upset?'

Trixie pulled away and gazed at her, knowing that she would now have to be honest about everything. 'I couldn't find you.'

Grace nodded in understanding. 'You thought I had popped off.'

'Well . . .'

'I'm not going anywhere,' she said briskly. 'Come on, let's go inside. Do you want a drink? I can make a pot of tea.'

Trixie looked over her mother's shoulder. 'What were you doing in there?' she asked. But she knew now. Her mother's hands were clean. She hadn't been gardening. There was only one reason why she was in the garden shed.

They went into the kitchen. Grace began to make the tea. 'So, how's New York?' she asked.

Trixie took a deep breath. 'I haven't been in New York.'

'Oh?'

'I've been in England.'

Her mother looked surprised. 'England? What were you doing there?'

'I went to Walbridge.'

Grace blanched. 'Walbridge?' Then she collected herself. 'You went to find Jasper?'

Trixie shook her head slowly. 'Not exactly. I went to find *you*.'

'Me?'

'Yes . . . I . . .' She paused, not knowing where to start. She didn't want to admit she'd found the letters. She wasn't sure how her mother would feel if she knew her daughter had snooped. 'I have something for you,' she said. She hurried into the hall and withdrew the velvet bag from her suitcase.

She gave it to her mother, who looked at it in confusion. 'What is it?'

'Lady Penselwood gave it to me to give to you. She said you'd know what it means.'

Grace's face had now turned as white as clay. 'You met Lady Penselwood?'

'Yes, and Lady Georgina.'

Grace's eyes began to glisten. 'Why?' When Trixie didn't answer, Grace pulled open the drawstring bag and put her hand inside. She felt the squidgy texture of the lavender bag and knew instantly what it was.

When she saw the silk bag, embroidered with the bee, she didn't know where to look or what to say. Her lips trembled and her eyes filled with tears. She swallowed with effort. Then she pressed the bag to her nose and closed her eyes for a moment. 'I think we need a glass of wine,' she said at last.

'I'll get it,' Trixie offered.

'We should go and sit outside. It's still sunny.'

'OK, good idea,' said Trixie. There was an urgency to her mother's voice. Her expression had changed. She had a look of intent. 'Where's Dad?' Trixie asked.

'Playing golf. He won't be back until late, which is a very good thing.'

Trixie poured two glasses of wine from the fridge and followed her mother onto the veranda. 'How much do you know?' Grace asked.

'Everything,' Trixie replied. 'And more.'

Chapter 27

Grace and Trixie settled onto the swing chair as they had done so often in the past. Grace took a large swig of wine. 'OK, darling. Start from the beginning. Why did you go to Walbridge?'

Trixie lifted her handbag onto her lap. 'Do you mind if I smoke?' she asked.

'Of course not, though you should really try to quit. It's a horrible habit, not to mention bad for your health.'

'I know. I will. I promise.' She delved into the bag for her packet and lighter. She lit one and blew the smoke out of the side of her mouth, away from her mother. Grace noticed her hand was trembling. 'I found your box of letters in the shed,' Trixie confessed.

Grace inhaled slowly. 'I see.'

'I wasn't looking for them. The door was open and I went to close it.' She couldn't tell her mother about the strange presence she had felt. She was certain she'd think her crazy. 'They're beautiful, Mom. Really romantic.' Grace drew her lips into a thin line and turned her eyes to the sea. Trixie continued. 'I wondered why Rufus returned your letters.'

'It was his way of ending the affair, I suppose.'

'But why did he end it?'

Grace shrugged. 'I don't know why. He gave no explanation. He simply returned my letters. I was devastated. Perhaps his wife found out. I don't know. It was a long time ago . . .'

Trixie looked at her mother with such compassion, Grace's eyes overflowed. 'Mom, he returned your letters because he *had* to end the affair. He had to end the affair because Dad saved his life in the war. The bullet that took Dad's eye was meant for Rufus, but Dad leapt in front of him. He was heroic. Didn't he ever tell you?'

Grace frowned and shook her head. 'No! He never told me. How do *you* know?'

'Lady Georgina told me. She thanked me. She said Dad was a hero and they were eternally grateful to him.'

'Why wouldn't he have told me?'

'I don't know. But then I had tea with old Lady Penselwood.'

'Is she still alive?'

'She certainly is, Mom. She told me that Dad didn't want any fuss. They wanted to thank him and offered him anything he desired as a reward. He asked for a new life in America. Do you know who found this house and set him up on the farm?' Grace shook her head. By her contorted features Trixie knew this was all coming as a terrible shock. 'Randall Wilson Jr.'

'I don't understand . . . How?'

'Because Aldrich Penselwood was a good friend of Randall Wilson.'

'I knew that,' said Grace in a quiet voice, remembering her conversation with Big. 'Go on.'

'Aldrich Penselwood bought this house for you to thank Dad for saving his son's life.'

'Freddie never told me. He just said we were moving to America. He was so strange. So distant. Not the Freddie I knew. The war had changed him so much, I barely recognized him. He was hostile and cold.' Her shoulders began to shake. 'It was awful. I not only lost Rufus but I lost Freddie, too. I lost both of them and I lost my home. The only things I had left were my letters and my memories.'

Trixie put her arms around her mother and pulled her close. She felt small and fragile. 'It was a callous way to end the relationship with the woman he loved,' said Trixie. 'He could have told you why. Did you ever read them?'

'My own letters? No, I couldn't bear to. I put them in the bottom of the box. Why? Did you?'

'Yes, I did . . .' Trixie was about to tell her that she'd also found a letter that was meant for Freddie, but something held her back. She didn't want to compound her mother's distress. 'They were beautiful,' she said instead.

'Rufus must have been furious that it was Freddie who leapt in front of him. Because due to that act of courage Rufus had to give me up. How ironic that fate should throw them both together in that way.'

'Returning your letters seems like an act of defeat.'

'I suppose it was. There were many obvious obstacles in the way of our happiness together, but Rufus would never have foreseen that one.'

'And none would have been as decisive,' Trixie added. She squeezed her mother gently. 'I never thought I'd say poor Rufus. But I mean it. Poor, poor man.'

Grace chuckled softly. 'That's because you have been hurt by love.'

'Perhaps. I love Jasper with all my heart but I had to leave him.'

'Darling, I'm so sorry.'

'I always thought you couldn't understand, but I now realize you're the only person who really does understand, because you have loved and lost too.'

'When you lost Jasper all those years ago, I wanted to confess that I had loved his father. But I couldn't. I didn't want to betray your father. I love him too, Trixie. It might sound strange, but I love your father. I love the man beneath the coldness. He wasn't always like that. He's not like that really. I love him in spite of it.'

Trixie rested her head on her mother's shoulder. 'I know I can get through it with your help. If I can talk to you about it, I know I will eventually move on.'

'A problem shared is a problem halved.' Grace gently pushed her daughter away. She looked into her eyes and recognized the sorrow there. 'I never wanted you to suffer like I have.'

'It's worth it, though, isn't it? You'd do it all again, wouldn't you?'

Grace smiled. 'I think I would.'

'Well, so would I.'

'Tell me. How did Rufus die? I've often wondered.'

'He went into the garden in the middle of the night, sat on a bench, gazed at the stars and died.'

Grace's eyes spilled over again. 'Listening to the sounds of the garden at night.'

She nodded and laughed through her tears. 'He told me that if I listened carefully enough I'd hear the very breath of the garden, going in and out, in and out.'

'I think he died of a broken heart, Mom. I bet he never stopped loving you. His mother said the end of the war changed him. I think she meant the end of his *affair*.'

'Lady Penselwood,' said Grace slowly. 'The war changed her, too. She had a wild affair with the gamekeeper.'

'Really? Like *Lady Chatterley's Lover*?' Trixie exclaimed gleefully. 'Who'd have thought she had it in her?'

'She was very beautiful in her day. She came alive during the war. Rufus and I were in the woods and we saw her and Mr Swift, up against a tree. It was frightfully shocking.'

'What did Rufus say?'

'He thought nothing of it. I think he rather admired her for her zest!'

They both laughed. Grace gazed at her daughter with affection. She took her hand. 'I'm glad you know, Trixie. I'm glad we can share it.'

'You look better now you know the truth.'

'I feel better. It's as if a weight has been lifted off my shoulders. I feel light.' She kissed her daughter's cheek. 'Thank you, darling. But what of you?'

'That's what Jasper asked.'

'And how did you respond?'

Trixie took another drag. 'I told him I'd be fine. He has a wife, children, duties and responsibilities that come with his position.' She laughed at herself. 'To think it never occurred to me that he was a lord. I never worked it out. No wonder it amused him when I called him Mr Duncliffe.'

'Darling, how could you have known?'

'I don't know. It seems so obvious now. Anyway, he asked me to stay, but he knew it was impossible. He never suggested he leave Lottie. I don't think I'd hold him in such high esteem if he was capable of turning his back on his family like that. So I'm the loser. But I'll bounce back.'

'You will, darling. *I* did. We had you. We found happiness of sorts. I threw myself into the gardens I created. I discovered that the human spirit has a great capacity to heal and adapt. I haven't been unhappy, Trixie. Yes, I have my memories and even though they make me a little sad, they bring me joy, too. I remember the good times with Freddie, before the war. He was adorable and very romantic. You can't imagine, but he was playful and sweet. I hold onto those.'

'So what's with the lavender bag?' Trixie asked.

'I made it for Rufus, to help him sleep.'

'It looks like he slept with it for years. It's totally worn out.'

Grace smiled softly. 'I think he did.'

'And how are *you*, Mom? I know you don't like to talk about it, but I need to know. I can't bear to lose you too.'

Grace pulled her daughter close and ran a hand down her hair. 'I'm a fighter, Trixie.' She kissed her forehead. 'After all, I have so much to fight for.'

As the day finally surrendered to the darkness, Grace and Trixie filled their glasses with more wine and Grace listened, transfixed, as Trixie told her about her brief vacation. She wanted to hear every detail. She wanted to know what Walbridge was like now. She wanted to hear about the Beekeeper's Cottage, the Hall, the Fox and Goose, Lady Georgina and Lady Penselwood. And when she had heard all the stories, she wanted to hear them all over again.

By the time Freddie returned home, Grace was in bed. The excitement had exhausted her. 'Hello, Trixie,' he said, surprised to find his youngest daughter in Grace's sitting room. 'How are things in the Big Apple?'

'Great, Dad, thanks. I thought I'd spend some time with Mom.'

'I bet she was happy to see you.'

She grinned. 'Very.'

Freddie hovered in the doorway, looking awkward. 'Well, I'll help myself to something from the fridge.'

'Dad,' said Trixie, getting up and walking across the room towards him.

'Yes?'

'I love you.' She laughed at the astonished look on his face. 'I know I sound like I'm going crazy. But I just wanted to tell you. I love you and appreciate everything you've done for me over the years. I often thought you too controlling, but now I know you had my best interests at heart. I wish I had known that then.' She put her arms around him and felt him stiffen. Undeterred, she held him firmly. Slowly and barely perceptibly, he softened and patted her hard on the back. Harder than he had ever patted her before, and her throat contracted and her heart seemed to fold in on itself. She remained there for a long moment, her tears staining a dark patch on his shirt.

Trixie made her father pasta while he disappeared into his office to help himself to a drink. He returned with a glass of whiskey on the rocks. He asked her about New York, so she told him about her interview with Rifat Ozbek, omitting the fact that it had taken place in London. She couldn't bring herself to tell him about her trip. She wasn't sure he'd be as understanding as her mother. She remembered Lady Penselwood telling her that Freddie resented Rufus for having come out of the battle unscathed. He probably regretted having saved him. Bringing up his heroism now might undermine their moment in the sitting room. She hadn't felt this close to him, ever. She wasn't about to go and ruin it by bringing up his past.

* * *

Freddie felt a little lightheaded when he climbed the stairs to his bedroom. He had drunk two whiskies and a glass of wine. Trixie had joined him at the dining-room table and they had both eaten the pasta she had made. She had asked him about his golf and questioned him about his first days on the farm just after the war. She had looked at him intensely and listened without interrupting. He was surprised she was interested. She had never been interested before.

He crept into the darkened room. He could see his wife in bed, peacefully sleeping. She had left the light on in the bathroom and he went in there to undress so as not to wake her. He showered and changed into his pyjamas. Then he switched off the light and climbed into bed, doing his best to slip in quietly, disturbing the mattress as little as possible. He lay there a moment, staring at the ceiling.

'Freddie.' It was Grace. Her voice was a sleepy whisper.

'I thought you were asleep,' he replied.

'I was, but I'm awake now. Have you seen Trixie?'

'Yes, a nice surprise to see her.'

'Freddie?' Her voice sounded heavy.

'Yes?'

'I need to talk to you and I need you to be honest with me.'

'All right.'

'Did you save Rufus's life in the war?'

There was a long silence. A laboured, uncomfortable silence, as if the room were holding its breath and struggling with the effort. Grace waited. While she waited for his reply she felt the blood pulsate in her temples. She expected him to shut her out. She expected the air to turn cold with him. But it didn't. 'I took a bullet for him,' Freddie said quietly. Grace was stunned by his openness. Perhaps the darkness, the whiskey or the fact that he knew she was dying gave him the courage to speak about it.

'You were a hero. Why didn't you tell me?'

'I wasn't a hero.'

'But you were. I mocked you when you cried about the bee sting, and your mother said that boys are courageous when it matters. She was right and I was wrong. You gave your eye in exchange for Rufus's life. If that's not heroic, nothing is.'

She felt him stiffen beside her. There was another long pause. The bed grew hot but she dared not move. 'I loathed him,' he said, and the tone of his voice sent a cold shiver rippling across her skin. 'I knew you loved him, Grace. I received a letter from you that was meant for him.' She let out a gasp. The bed seemed to be falling away beneath her. She spread her fingers over the sheets to steady it. 'I didn't jump to save him, Grace,' he said. 'I jumped to punch his lights out.'

They lay still beneath the weight of his confession. Grace didn't know how to respond. She blinked into the darkness, sick to her stomach, not at the thought of his violent intent, but at the thought of his having suffered in silence all these years, knowing that she had loved another. She had assumed his coldness was due to the horror of war. She never imagined it was because of her. Now she understood and her heart swelled with compassion. War hadn't changed him; *she* had. She moved her hand beneath the covers and found his. He gripped it hard, and the ferocity of it moved her to tears.

'It was a moment of madness, Grace,' he continued, his eyes fixed on the ceiling above them. 'A moment of jealousy. As I lunged towards him I saw the pistol pointing right at him. It happened so quickly, but at the time it felt as if it was all in slow motion, as if I was under water. I looked at Fritz with his finger on the trigger and his face twisted with hatred, and I didn't draw back. Something urged me on. I honestly don't know whether in that moment I threw myself at Lord Melville to save him or kill him.' He stifled a sob. 'I wanted him dead, but I saved his life. When Lord Penselwood invited me to the Hall to reward me for my bravery, I was so disgusted with myself I could barely look him in the eye. As for Rufus, I loathed him. He lived to love you still and I had lost my eye.' His voice thinned. 'Losing you hurt more than losing my eye. I would have given both eyes for your love, Grace.'

'He returned all my letters, Freddie,' said Grace, trying to console him but finding there was little she could say to absolve herself. Warm tears trailed down her neck and grew cold on the pillow beneath her head.

'But you still loved him,' he groaned. 'You always had. But I knew he'd never leave his wife for you. He was selfish and self-indulgent. You were like a helpless fish on a hook and you thought I didn't notice.' He heaved a sigh. 'I noticed every time I looked into your eyes. Because you gazed at me with longing and I knew you wished I was him.' She struggled against the force of regret that threatened to carry her away like a strong undercurrent. She held his hand tightly and focused on a strip of moonlight that painted a slice of silver on the far wall. 'So, I asked to start a new life in America and Lord Penselwood arranged it. Big's father was a friend of his and he organized everything. I thought if I took you to the other side of the world, you'd forget Rufus.' He chuckled bitterly. 'But I was wrong. You never forgot him and I felt invisible. You cared for your bees, for the children, for your gardens, but you never cared for me.'

Grace could bear it no longer. She rolled over and placed her head on his shoulder, wrapping her arms around him. 'You're wrong. I thought the war had changed you. I thought you resented me for not understanding what you'd been through. I weathered your resentment because I remembered the Freddie I had grown up with and fallen in love with. I knew you were still there and I waited patiently for you to emerge. I thought time would heal.' She nuzzled her face into his neck. 'I love you, Freddie. I don't think I would have pined for Rufus if I had believed *you* loved me. Rufus was a brief infatuation. I wish I could erase it. I wish it had never happened. It was an illusion. I was flattered. I don't know. I was a fool. My father was right. You were always the man for me. But after the war I needed to feel loved and I believed he loved me. Can't you see? There was a void. He filled it. But all the time I longed for you to look at me like you used to.'

Freddie placed his hand on her back and slowly stroked her. 'I wanted to go back to the river. To our secret clearing where Rufus couldn't reach us. I wanted you to admire me like you did when I dived off the bridge. Do you remember how cross you got when I hid underwater?'

'You frightened me. I thought you were dead.'

'I wanted to frighten you. I wanted proof that you cared.'

'And you got it.'

'And I kissed you for the first time.'

'That was the most beautiful kiss I have ever had.' She buried her face against his cheek and closed her eyes. 'I want you back. I might not have much time to live, but I want to spend the time I do have with my old friend and lover. My old Freddie Valentine.'

She felt his arms envelop her as they had done on their wedding night in the Beekeeper's Cottage, and as his hands wandered over the forgotten contours of her body she felt the same sensations of being loved for the very first time. His lips searched for hers in the darkness and his kiss was as tender and ardent as it had been then, before betrayal and mistrust had turned them into strangers. With each gentle caress the desolate landscape of her being slowly thawed like winter soil that begins to flower with the warm caress of spring.

When Grace eventually fell asleep, a contented smile hovered over her lips. The tears had dried on her pillow. Her hand, still holding Freddie's, relaxed and opened slightly. She slipped into unconsciousness, but unlike other nights, she was aware of where she was. As if she dwelt above herself and was looking down at her own sleeping body. She remained like that, at peace, observant, strangely comfortable, as if she had been outside herself many times, only forgotten.

Then she heard a familiar voice and saw a bright light in the distance, far, far away. She turned her attention from the bed and the sight of herself and Freddie lying hand in hand, and flew towards it, propelled by longing and the ever-expanding love in her heart. *So this is what it feels like to die,* she thought, and she wasn't in the least afraid, so strong was her desire to reach the other side. To return home.

The light grew bigger and brighter and more intense. In the middle of it stood the familiar figure of her father in his overalls and tweed cap, and she realized then that the presence by the bees had been him all along. That he had never left her, just as he had promised. 'Dad!' she exclaimed. 'You're here.'

'I've always been with you, Gracey,' he said and he looked young, vibrant and full of joy.

'And Mother?'

He smiled. 'She's here too. She never left. Love connects us, Gracey. It's a bond that never dies. You have to trust what you sense.'

'Am I dead?'

He shook his head. 'I'm here to tell you that it is not your time. Trixie needs you now more than ever, and so does Freddie.'

'Can't I stay?'

'You have to go back. You have more to do.' The light began to fade, her father with it.

'But I have cancer. I'm dying.'

His voice grew faint. 'You're going to get better, Gracey.'

'You're going to get better . . .' Grace opened her eyes to see Freddie's anxious face gazing down at her. 'You're going to get better, Grace,' he repeated.

She frowned up at him. The dawn light was already sliding through the gaps in the shutters. 'What happened?'

'You had a bad dream, darling,' said Freddie, wiping her damp hair off her forehead.

'No, I've had a *good* dream.'

He smiled. 'You're awake now.' When she continued to look confused, he added: 'You were saying you're dying. But you're going to get well. I'm not going to let you die, now that I've found you again.'

She returned his smile and placed her hand on his stubbly cheek. 'Darling Freddie. I'm glad *that* wasn't a dream.'

He bent down and kissed her forehead. 'So am I.' He swept his eyes over her face and Grace felt her stomach lurch, as it used to when he really *looked* at her. 'I forgot how beautiful you are in the morning,' he said softly.

'Then stay.' She held his upper arms to detain him. 'It's early. There's no rush. Come back to bed.' She saw the old Freddie in the mischievous grin that now spread across his face, and she smiled back as she had done that day by the river, when Freddie was all she saw.

Chapter 28

Three months later Trixie stood on the snow-covered gravel in front of Big's front door, and rang the bell. She heard the scuffling of dogs on the other side. She peered through the glass panel to see Big's pack of mongrels wagging their tails and panting, and tapped it, which excited them all the more. A moment later Big herself appeared in a bright yellow cardigan and tartan trousers, and opened the door.

'Well, this is a nice surprise,' she said, smiling cheerfully. 'Goodness, Trixie, you look in rude health. What have you been up to? New York shouldn't make you glow like that.'

'I've given up smoking,' Trixie replied proudly.

'About time, too. Come on in. It's bitter out there.'

'Oh, it's beautiful,' Trixie exclaimed. 'The sun is out, the sky is bright blue and the snow is twinkling like diamonds. I don't think I've ever seen the island look so lovely.'

'I suppose it does look pretty when it's fresh. It won't be long before it looks a little tired, though. Would you like a hot drink? Hot chocolate?'

'I'd love a hot chocolate.'

'Fancy something stronger to give it an edge?' Big asked with a wink.

'No, just plain milk and chocolate for me, thank you.'

'I'll go and tell Hudson, he'll be delighted to have something to do. It's been a very dull day so far. You're my first visitor. I don't suppose anyone wants to go out in the snow but the very brave. Go into the sitting room and warm up.'

Trixie took off her coat and wandered over to the fire in Big's airy sitting room. Big's home was unpretentious, with shiny wicker sofas and pale-blue cushions a person could sink into and never want to leave. A large display of winter berries was placed in the middle of the glass coffee table, surrounded by glossy hardback books on art and Island living. Big liked to support local craftsmen and her house was full of baskets, scrimshaw and painted antique furniture. Trixie flopped onto the sofa where she had sat so many times in her life and gave a satisfied sigh. It was good to be on Tekanasset, surrounded by the people she really cared about. She noticed Mr Doorwood curled up on the other end and reached out to give him a gentle stroke. He purred in his sleep, his fat body rising and falling contentedly. A moment later Big returned and sat regally in the armchair by the fire.

'How's your mother?' she asked.

'She's getting better,' Trixie said happily. 'It's miraculous, really. The doctors had written her off, but I really think she's going to beat it, Big.'

'She's looking well, that's for sure,' Big agreed. 'I put it down to the power of prayer. Miracles happen in our modern world to remind us that in spite of our technological advances, God is still mighty and all-powerful.'

'The most surprising part of her recovery is that she and Dad are getting along so well. It's like he's a different person.'

'I think he's just grateful to have her back. He thought he was going to lose her.' Big inhaled through dilated nostrils. 'We *all* thought we were going to lose her.'

'It's early days, but she's certainly feeling stronger, which is such a relief. I need her now more than ever.'

'So how long are you here this time?' Big asked.

Trixie looked as if she were about to burst with happiness. 'I'm staying,' she announced, dropping both hands onto her knees with a decisive pat. 'I've quit New York and the magazine. I need a total life change. I've decided to come home for good.'

'Well, that *is* a surprise and I'm not often surprised.' Hudson appeared with hot chocolate and cake, and Big watched Trixie take a mug off the tray. 'Have a slice of cake. You look like you could do with some feeding up. You young girls survive on nothing but air these days and it's not attractive. People look a lot better with a little flesh on their bones, especially pretty girls like you.' Hudson put the cake on the coffee table and Trixie took a small slice. Hudson handed Big the largest slice on a china plate. 'Thank you, Hudson,' she said, biting off the end and giving a moan of pleasure. 'I think chocolate cake is your secret weapon.'

The old man smiled with gratitude. 'Thank you, Miss Wilson.'

Big chewed happily. 'And I think you know it, too,' she chuckled. 'So what's your plan, Trixie?' She narrowed her eyes. 'I assume you have a plan and you'd like my help.'

'As I was saying, I want to come and live here. I'm going to learn how to be a beekeeper and help Mom with her gardens. She's not very strong but she loves horticulture so much she doesn't want to stop. So I'm going to be her assistant,' she announced gleefully. 'I'm very excited about it.'

'But you don't want to live at home?' Big guessed.

'No, I think I should be independent.'

'You're right. So I imagine you want my guest house?'

Trixie smiled sheepishly. 'I hope I'm not being presumptuous, but I was hoping you might rent it out to me for a while.'

'My dear child, you can have it for as long as you want it. I'll charge you a peppercorn rent to cover the costs.' Big smiled mischievously. 'It'll be lovely having you close by, and you can walk to your mother's along the beach.'

'I know, that's what I thought, and I love to be by the sea. It's so romantic.'

'It is. Which brings me to the question, why have you suddenly decided to move back home? I thought New York was a great success?'

'It was.' She grinned secretively. 'Something has, well, changed my perception of the world. It's made me realize what's important. I love this place. It's where I've always been happiest. I'm not ambitious any more. There are more important things than making lots of money and being a success. Quality of life is my priority now.'

'You're right about that. It'll make your parents very happy to have you here. So when would you like to move in?'

'As soon as you'll have me. I haven't told Mom of my plan yet. I thought I'd sort out my accommodation first.'

'Well, you can tell her now. The guest house is yours. The heating is on to stop the pipes freezing, so it's perfectly habitable. Are you sure you won't have something stronger to celebrate?'

Trixie shook her head. 'Hot chocolate is fine, thank you. And you're right. That cake is delicious. May I have another slice?'

* * *

Trixie hurried down the snowy path through the trees to the beach. The snow sparkled defiantly in the weak winter sunlight but the wind had blown it into thick drifts against the dunes and it would be weeks before it melted. Big's guest house stood facing the sea, nestled against the grassy bluff, sheltered by large shrubs and small trees. It was built in the same grey-shingled style as most of the houses on the island, with a sturdy veranda now laden with snow. It looked forlorn there, gazing out across the ocean with dark, empty eyes, but to Trixie it was romantic in its solitude, and she couldn't wait to claim it as her own and fill those eyes with life.

She put the key in the lock and pushed open the door. As she stepped over the threshold she was struck immediately by the familiar damp smell of the sea, which filled her heart with a warm sense of nostalgia. She looked around at the cosy hall with its polished wooden floorboards and the staircase that swept up to the first floor in a graceful curve, and sighed with satisfaction. This was where she belonged. She inhaled deeply: home at last.

She wandered through the rooms. Big had hired a decorator for her guest house and the woman, well known on the island, had stuck to her trademark nautical theme, using blues and whites and a lot of wicker furniture. Trixie decided she'd add some crimson here and there to make it her own, and to see her through to spring with its vibrant warmth. She wandered into the sitting room, which was arranged around a fireplace, and sat on one of the sofas. Sunshine shone feebly through the glass, illuminating the blue-and-white rug that softened the floor and dominated the room. The silence of the empty house filled her with peace. Outside the waves lapped the snowy beach with weary regularity, as if the cold had robbed their strength.

So what did her future hold? Ever since she had left Jasper in Walbridge she had known for certain that she would never love another as she loved him. At that time she had believed she might find someone to share her life with; after all, she was young and perhaps second best was better than nothing at all. She had many years ahead of her and life was lonely on one's own. But in the last few days it had become blissfully clear that she didn't need a man after all, not even Jasper. She had discovered that she had returned to America with a stowaway: a tiny part of Jasper hiding out in her belly and slowly growing. The love she already felt for her child would be enough to sustain her for the rest of her life. They'd be fine, just the two of them. They'd be perfectly happy. Nothing mattered now but this beautiful little soul. She put her hand on her stomach and silently thanked God for His compassion.

Chapter 29

Three years later

The autumn sun cast long shadows over Sunset Slip and set the purple clouds aflame in a dramatic display of crimson and red. Trixie walked up the beach with her son, Arthur, and cast her eyes out to sea, where the splendour of sunset was reflected on the water. The beauty of it strained her heart-strings and she gave in to a wave of melancholy, stopping a moment to savour the splendour of another sunset on Tekanasset, the magnificence of which never lost the power to disarm her. Arthur ran across the sand in pursuit of a piping plover. The child's gurgling laughter was carried on the breeze with the lone cry of a gull.

It was the end of summer. Soon the plovers and terns would fly off to warmer shores and the winds would grow strong and cold, and moan at night outside her bedroom window. She loved Big's guest house. She loved the beach. She had never been happier.

Jasper's letters, so ardent at the beginning, had now dwindled as she thought they might, given that she had never encouraged him by writing back. Perhaps he believed that she no longer loved him. That thought gave her pain and she had often put pen to paper to bare her soul, only to regret her impulsiveness and toss the unfinished letter into the fire. No good could come of it. There was nothing she could do. She was powerless to change the past and unwilling to alter the present. At least she didn't have the destruction of his family on her conscience.

She watched Arthur and recalled her parents' surprising reaction on learning that she was carrying Jasper's child. The old prejudices upheld by their generation seemed so trivial in the wake of Grace's illness. They had learned that life was a gift and that love was the only important thing in it. Ultimately they simply wanted their daughter's happiness. When the baby arrived they embraced him with joy. Grace said he looked like her father, Freddie claimed a resemblance to his mother. But later, as her son grew, Trixie saw Jasper in his smile and in the grey-green colour of his eyes. And they all appreciated the gift of love he had brought into the world and the enormous pleasure he gave to every one of them.

Trixie had made many new friends on Tekanasset since she had moved back three years before. Lucy Durlacher, recently divorced from Ben (who had exchanged his drumsticks for a suit and now worked for an investment bank in Washington), had returned to the island with her three children, and surprisingly the two women had grown close. It seemed that Tekanasset was the place to settle when life got too hectic, or when the soul was in need of its healing waters. Its beaches were balm to battered hearts and the vast skies of shifting colours and shades lifted the spirit and gave the lost an invaluable sense of belonging. When Trixie gazed out at that immense horizon she was reminded of what was important: friends, family and home. Boiled down they all meant the same thing: love.

She wrapped her cardigan about her body and folded her arms. The sun was setting and it was chilly in the shadows. She saw a figure in the distance walking towards her. Probably a man with his dog, she thought, shifting her eyes to her son who now crouched on the sand, playing with a piece of bright-blue sea glass. She decided to turn back to the house. 'Arthur,' she called. 'Come on, darling. Time for tea.' The little boy stood up and ran towards her. As he put out his arms, she lifted her gaze to see the man, closer now, walking faster and with intent. She bent down and lifted the child into her arms. She hugged him close, relishing the solid feeling of his body against hers.

She was about to turn around when she noticed something familiar about the man's gait. He moved with long strides and, as he got closer, he seemed to pick up his pace. She froze. It couldn't be. How could it? It was just her eyes, playing tricks on her. Hadn't she thought she had seen him countless times before? Hadn't she been crippled by disappointment every time she realized she was wrong? Surely this was simply one of those times. She swallowed back tears, cursing the red sky and golden sea for making her emotional. She was perfectly happy. Perfectly fine. She had Arthur. What more could she wish for?

But the man began to run. His long legs raced over the sand and his voice was carried on the wind. She was sure he was calling her name. 'Trixie . . .' She blinked to focus, but the tears blurred her vision and she saw nothing, just her own longing, now falling in streams down her cheeks.

'Mummy cry,' said Arthur, concerned. She kissed his cold face. But she couldn't reply. Her voice was lost, squeezed to death by her constricting throat.

And then he was before her. Panting, red in the face, desperate. They stared at one another for a moment, neither knowing what to say.

'She's left me,' Jasper said at last. His eyes took in the child and his shoulders dropped in defeat. He was too late.

Trixie read his mind and she smiled through her tears. 'Jasper, this is Arthur,' she whispered, moving her shoulder so he could see the child's face. The little boy turned around and stared at the strange man shyly, his grey-green eyes large and enquiring. Jasper looked at his son, then back at Trixie. Words were now inadequate. He shook his head in astonishment, strode forward and wrapped his arms around the two of them, drawing them close.

Trixie rested her head on his shoulder and sighed. 'You came back,' she said softly.

'Because I cried tears into the harbour waters,' he replied. He squeezed her hard. 'But more truthfully, because I love you,' he added, squeezing her harder. 'I love you, Trixie, and always will.'

Acknowledgements

My most frequently asked question is: how do I come up with stories for my books? Well, in this particular case, it all began one summer's evening in 2012 when I was pulling out weeds in my cottage garden in Hampshire. I noticed a ball of bees clinging to the bricks beside my daughter's bedroom window. I had never seen anything like it and was naturally quite alarmed. It was enormous. I called my father, who lives next door, to come and have a look, and soon the whole family stood beneath, staring up in bewilderment at the seething ball. My father suggested they might move away the following morning, so I thought nothing more about it until I woke up at dawn to loud buzzing outside my window. The air was thick with thousands of bees who clearly had no intention of leaving. My father called the local beekeeper who keeps hives on his farm, and his daughter arrived to explain the situation, that basically they were trying to find a new place to build a hive. 'Not in *my* brickwork!' I announced defiantly. As much as I like bees, I didn't want them settling inside my wall. She told me that if they formed a ball again she would come that evening and literally scoop them into a basket and take them home with her, to try to introduce them to one of her father's vacant hives. As it happened they did eventually leave on their own. But I reflected on how good the title 'The Beekeeper's Cottage' sounded and an idea began to form. Later we changed the title, but that 'evening of the bees' was the catalyst for this book.

While I was in the process of researching I happened to talk to a very nice grandmother at a match tea at my son's school. She told me that she enjoyed my novels and asked what I was currently working on. I told her: a beekeeper's daughter during the Second World War. Her eyes lit up and she declared that her father had been a beekeeper during the war. I was less astonished than she, because every time I embark on a novel, I send out a request for help and it's amazing how everything I need just happens to fall into my lap. Elizabeth Kennerley, *you* fell into my lap and I thank the angels for organizing the meeting! Before we met I knew very little about bees. Now I know a great deal. Much more than I was able to put into the book. Thank you for all your advice and for lending me a beautiful old book that was so informative I really didn't have to look anywhere else.

I based Tekanasset Island on Nantucket. I always like to invent my own locations because that way I have the freedom to design it just as I want it, as well as knowing it better than anyone else. I spent a heavenly week on Nantucket with Peter and Flora Soros many years ago but I remember thinking, even then, that one day I would base a novel there. So, thank you, Peter and Flora, for a fabulous holiday and for sowing the seed that eventually flowered into this book.

I always write to music. I make a different playlist for every novel and spend a great deal of time searching for the right tunes to inspire me. I love John Barry, Howard Shore and Ennio Morricone, but for *The Beekeeper's Daughter* I discovered a very talented composer I hadn't heard before; Guy

Farley writes music for movies, I can't imagine he ever thought he would be the constant soundtrack to the conception of a novel. I downloaded every one of his tracks and played them on a loop. I know them all by heart and love them passionately. Thank you, Guy, for transporting me to the windy beaches of Tekanasset Island and the lush green hills of Dorset. The moment I switched on my iPod nothing could distract me from the beauty of your music and the splendour of the scenes it inspired.

I have dedicated this book to my uncle Jeremy Palmer-Tomkinson. Along with his wife, Clare, Jeremy has always been an enthusiastic supporter of my books. So, when I needed advice on a particular scene that takes place during the war, I invited him out to lunch, knowing what an expert he is on World War II. Clare came as well and I told them the plot over a hearty meal. Jeremy duly told me what I needed to know in order to write the scene, but more importantly he gave me a word of advice about the general plot. Now you have read the novel you may know what I am referring to, but all I can say is that the entire novel depends on that small but important thing. I hadn't planned for the plot to go that way at all, but Jeremy's idea was a very good one, therefore, I felt it right and proper to dedicate the book to him, and to him alone. When I told him he was very embarrassed, because he didn't think he deserved it. But he hasn't read the book yet, so how could he know? Well, I can tell you, Jeremy, that you really *do* deserve it. Sometimes angels don't have wings, they have lunch with me and share a bottle of wine!

I would like to thank my mother, Patty Palmer-Tomkinson, who is always the first person to read my manuscripts. She read *The Beekeeper's Daughter* with a sharp eye for detail and saved my editor a lot of work on correcting bad grammar and ill-chosen words! Thank you, Mummy, for taking the time and trouble to save me from myself.

I'd also like to thank my mother-in-law, April Sebag-Montefiore (what would we do without generous-spirited mothers!) who read through the sections of the book that related to the 1940s. She was crucial. Without her help I would not have captured a sense of time. I can't thank you enough, April, for giving me so much of your time and energy, and for your constant support and enthusiasm.

My old friend Harry Legge-Bourke was also helpful in answering questions about the army, having been in the Welsh Guards (*not* during the war!) – really, research can be very pleasant when it's done in the sunshine outside Colbert over a cocktail or two! Thank you, Harry, for your help.

I'd also like to thank Bob and Nancy Phifer, my friends from Boston, who have been incredibly helpful in answering questions and recommending books to read in order to bring my Tekanasset scenes to life, and their local book shop, The Brewster Bookstore, who have been so supportive and kind.

My father is evident in the book as the wind is evident in the rustling of the leaves in the woods. I have absorbed his philosophies and wisdom over the years like an eager sponge and it all goes into my characters as they learn lessons from the cards life deals them and the choices they make. That is the part of writing I enjoy so much, because it is the part of life that interests me most. Thank you, Daddy, for arousing my curiosity.

My darling children teach me more about life than anything else. Love is why we're all here and it's what we take with us when our lives are done. They are a constant inspiration and I'm so grateful for them. My husband, Sebag, is my dearest friend, my most fervent ally and my greatest champion. I extend my deepest gratitude to him for giving me the time and space to be creative.

I wouldn't even be published if it wasn't for my wonderful and dynamic agent, Sheila Crowley at Curtis Brown. Sheila, you are a brilliant agent and I couldn't do without you! I really do believe you are there for me and *only* me, because every time I need you, you appear like my fairy godmother and wave your magic wand and tell me I *can* go to the ball if I want to!

I'd also like to thank Katie McGowan and Rebecca Ritchie at Curtis Brown for all their hard work.

An enormous and big-hearted thank you to my fabulously effective team at Simon & Schuster. My commander-in-chief, Ian Chapman, my editor, Suzanne Baboneau, and their colleagues Clare Hey, James Horobin, Dawn Burnett, Hannah Corbett, Sara-Jade Virtue, Melissa Four, Ally Grant, Gill Richardson, Rumana Haider and Dominic Brendon. You are all talented, energetic and passionate about what you do and I can't thank you enough for being the wind in my sails and pushing me so far!